W. H Higgins

The Life and Times of Joseph Gould

Ex-Member of the Canadian Parliament

W. H Higgins

The Life and Times of Joseph Gould
Ex-Member of the Canadian Parliament

ISBN/EAN: 9783337163334

Printed in Europe, USA, Canada, Australia, Japan

Cover: Foto ©Raphael Reischuk / pixelio.de

More available books at **www.hansebooks.com**

THE LIFE AND TIMES

OF

JOSEPH GOULD,

EX-MEMBER OF THE CANADIAN PARLIAMENT.

STRUGGLES OF THE EARLY CANADIAN SETTLERS—SETTLEMENT OF UXBRIDGE—
SKETCH OF THE HISTORY OF THE COUNTY OF ONTARIO—
THE REBELLION OF 1837—PARLIAMENTARY
CAREER, ETC., ETC.

REMINISCENCES OF SIXTY YEARS OF ACTIVE POLITICAL AND MUNICIPAL LIFE.

BY W. H. HIGGINS.

TORONTO:
C. BLACKETT ROBINSON, 5 JORDAN STREET.
1887.

CONTENTS.

viii.   CONTENTS.

CHAPTER VII.

CHAPTER VIII.

CHAPTER IX.

CHAPTER X.

CHAPTER XI.

CONTENTS.   ix.

CHAPTER XVI.

CHAPTER XVII.

CHAPTER XVIII.

CHAPTER XIX.

INTRODUCTORY.

THE Life and Times of Joseph Gould—extending from the opening to almost the closing decade of the present century—embrace an important and exciting period of Canadian history. It is a period full of stirring events, and in which he played no unimportant part. The history of the trials and struggles of the pioneers of early settlement—of those first Canadian settlers who courageously entered "the forest primeval," and manfully hewed out homes for themselves—must always form a subject of deep interest and reflection, more especially to the Canadian reader. It has already been told, and well told, and no doubt read with profit, in various publications. Taken from the lips of one born in the midst of the hardships and privations incident to the position, the story can scarcely fail to awaken fresh interest. The story of Mr. Gould's life not only tells of unremitting toil, and of difficulties overcome in the early condition of the country, but it also exhibits the reward which awaits honourable industry, self-denial and heroic perseverance. Born in a log cabin in the woods, Joseph Gould endured all the vicissitudes, and experienced in his own person almost all the varying fortunes of Canadian life. From a barefooted boy, assisting his parents to pile up and burn a heap of "brush" in a "clearing," he advanced, as he grew to manhood, through all the gradations of pathmaster, municipal councillor, school trustee, and warden, to the honour of a seat in Parliament as representative of his native county.

Mr. Gould was self-taught, and considering his early educational opportunities, or rather the want of them, his proficiency was wonderful. He was an insatiable reader and fairly devoured all the books and newspapers that came in his way. His first real political lessons were learned from Mackenzie's *Colonial Advocate,* although long before that he had taken part in election contests against "The Family Compact," and was looked up to as something of an active local leader. The most prominent feature of his character was, however, a stern conscientiousness, and an intense love of liberty, combined with a determination to assert his own rights, and never, come what may, fail in meeting his business engagements. Before he ever read Shakespeare he had adopted Hamlet's grand precept—

> This above all—To thine own self be true;
> And it must follow as the night the day,
> Thou canst not then be false to any man.

The following pages disclose these characteristics, and also, while glancing at the manners and customs of the early days of settlement, exhibit the growth and progress of the country, from an unimportant Crown colony, to its present grandeur as the Dominion of Canada.

———

The printing of his memoirs had been for some years contemplated by Mr. Gould. A few months before his death he expressed a strong desire to avail himself of the author's services for that purpose. Invitations had been given to visit him and "talk matters over." But—

> Life's latest hour is nimble in approach—

Death, all too swiftly, stepped in and prevented the conference that from various causes had been from time to time deferred.

The family of Mr. Gould, desiring to carry out what they believe to be his wishes, have now undertaken the publication of his memoirs as a filial duty. To further that object, they have placed an accumulation of miscellaneous papers and memoranda—the greater portion of them in the deceased gentleman's own hand-writing—at my disposal. Amongst these papers I find what was intended as an autobiography, continued up to the year 1837, and which is here made available as far as possible in the task I have undertaken. In these prefatory remarks, I also deem it entirely proper to give the reasons supplied by Mr. Gould (and which must have weighed with his family), for wishing to print the account of his life. They must enlist the sympathies of the reader for the yearnings of the man, who, with nothing to back him but his native energy and extraordinary industry, fought his way to a front place in his own little world, and who longed to be remembered in the story of his successful life-battle. Here is how he expresses his sentiments on this head:—

"It has been stated by the author of the history of one of the early settlements of Ontario that there exists, as one characteristic of the nineteenth century, an earnest desire on the part of many to recall, and in mind to live over the days and years that are past. And I, too, most frankly confess that I have great pleasure in pondering over and musing upon the scenes of bygone days, and in thinking over again the hardships and struggles of pioneer life. And whilst this feeling is pretty general amongst the early settlers of Canada, it has for its justification the fact that those men lived longer and saw more in the same space of time than most other men in any other age or country. The man of seventy, who has lived either in Canada or the United States all his lifetime, will have witnessed greater changes and more material improvement than has probably taken place in Europe for a thousand years anterior to his time. He will have more to talk about and more to leave to posterity than the men who have preceded him of any former time. Take for instance the social, political and commercial condition of this country at the present time, and contrast it with what it was sixty or seventy years ago. Is not the mind bewildered and amazed at the progress that has been made? And as a son of one of the earliest pioneers of Upper Canada—born in one of the first shanties built in the backwoods—and having taken some part in the political and material progress and development of the Province, and assisted in my humble way in bringing about those great changes, I may be excused if I acknowledge the gratification afforded me in reviewing the past; in contemplating the scenes of my youth, and pointing out what the country was then, and what it is now, and in narrating some of the trials and privations and early struggles in which I have been engaged, and in describing the humble part I have taken in assisting the men of progress of my day in bringing about the happy and prosperous state of things which now obtains in the country of my birth. It is the great pleasure which I feel in all this that prompts the desire to write a short history of what my memory still retains of my own life and times, having reference to Canadian progress in general, and of the town and township of Uxbridge in particular."

Although acquiescing in the rule universally respected—*De mortuis nil nisi bonum*—I have felt throughout the preparation of this work that nothing could justify any departure from the strict historical record; and whatever its deficiencies in other respects, I trust that I may be able to claim for it at least the merit of truthfulness and impartiality.

W. H. Higgins.

16 Clarence Square, Toronto,
July 2nd, 1887.

CHAPTER I.

JOSEPH GOULD was born on the old Gould Farm, lot 32 in the 6th concession of Uxbridge, on the 29th of December, 1808. According to the received traditions of the locality, he was the second male child (of white parents), born in the township. His father obtained a deed of this lot—then part of the primeval forest —from a Mr. Cornell, of Scarborough, and settled upon it in the early spring of the same year.

Like so many other instances in which the future of man's life is determined by unexpected, and what are sometimes considered trivial events, the settlement of the Goulds in Uxbridge was brought about by an accidental circumstance of the kind. Mr. Gould's father had saved some $200 to enable him to remove to Ohio. This money he left in the hands of his employer, a Mr. Beaman. The employer failed in business and Gould, the father's, savings were lost. Beaman being an honourable man, and anxious to discharge his obligation to his employé, did the next best thing he could, by procuring for him the deed of the lot. The alternative of having to accept 200 acres of wild land in Uxbridge, instead of his $200 cash, was regarded at the time by old Mr. Gould as a serious setting back to his future prospects. He wished to go to Ohio; he was compelled to remain in Canada; and this he regarded as a calamity. In after years, when speaking of this incident, and of man's blindness touching the ways of Providence,

Mr. Gould liked to quote the familiar lines from Pope's "Essay on Man"—

> O blindness to the future! kindly given,
> That each may fill the circle marked by heaven.

as *apropos* to the position.

Joseph Gould was of Irish extraction. He gives the following account of his ancestry, which is authenticated by family records, and an old, well-preserved family Bible, of the date of 1714, and now amongst the most valued heirlooms that have descended to his children.

"My great-grandfather, Michael Gold, emigrated from the north of Ireland to Philadelphia about the year 1720. My grandfather, Joseph Gold, was born in 1740; and my father, Jonathan Gold, was born in Germantown, Pennsylvania, on the 5th day of October, 1774. My great-grandfather settled and married amongst the Dutch, and lived and died in Germantown. He went by the nickname of 'Michael Killbuck,' from the circumstance of his having killed a buck by breaking his back with a blow of a cudgel which he constantly carried, as the deer rushed past him. My grandfather also married into a Dutch family of the name of Carr, at the same place, and where my father was born. My grandfather and his family afterwards moved from Germantown to Western Pennsylvania, and settled near a village called Catawissa, in the iron region. Of the date of removal thence, my authority, an old family Bible, does not inform me. There my father married his first wife, Anna Hilborn. She was the oldest daughter of Thomas Hilborn, who afterwards came to Canada, in 1804, and settled on lot No. 35 in the 6th concession of Uxbridge. Anna died in giving birth to her third child, leaving surviving her a son and daughter, Isaiah and Hannah. About a year after her death, my father married again. His second wife, Rachel Lee, was my mother. She was daughter of Daniel Lee, who belonged to the State of Maryland, and was of Irish descent. She was a near relative—a cousin in the second degree, it has been traced—of Robert E. Lee, the celebrated Confederate General. Her mother's maiden name was Buckman, from Buck's County, where many branches of the family still reside."

From this, it will be seen that, although the father, Jonathan, had a dash of Dutch blood in him, on the female side, Joseph Gould was of Irish extraction through both parents.

Speaking of the family name, he tells us:—"Our name should be GOLD, as the family records show, for 170 years back. It has been corrupted by the introduction of the letter 'u' since my time; and the change is chargeable to myself, I am very sorry to say, through a whim in boyhood while attending school." And then he very *naively* gives the following account, which from some may perhaps provoke a smile, at the "whim" that caused him to make the change in the spelling of his name: "I may say that the only book I ever learned spelling from was the old Webster spelling-book. It had a page or two of words with the meanings attached, and I noticed the words—G-o-l-d—a metal; G-o-u-l-d—*a man's name.* In the evening after going home, I asked my father why he wrote his name *Gold*, which was a metal, when *Gould* was a man's name. He said that the family had always written it so, as far back as he had any record. 'Well,' I replied, 'I think I shall write my name G-o-u-l-d, Gould, as I want a man's name and not the name of a metal.' And so I commenced writing the name GOULD,* and in a few years the whole family did the same."

---

* In the record, carefully kept in the Bible, and inspected by the author, the name is invariably spelt GOLD.

CHAPTER II.

AFTER his father and mother had been married a year or so, and
had one child, they were induced to migrate to Canada. This
was in the year 1805. Several families from the same neighbourhood moved in together at the same time. Between the years 1800
and 1810 a very considerable migration took place from the State
of Pennsylvania, to Upper Canada, of German families. They were
commonly called "Pennsylvania-Dutch;" most of them were members of the Society of Friends, or Quakers, and all were an excellent
class of settlers. From that element, principally, the townships of
Markham and Vaughan received their first contribution of early
settlers. The townships of King, Whitchurch, East Gwillimbury
and Uxbridge also received a chief portion of their first settlers
from the same source. And it was with a batch of neighbours and
friends of this class that the parents of the subject of these memoirs
arrived in this country.

The long journey from Pennsylvania was, we are told, accomplished in large covered waggons, of the most primitive style, with
four-horse teams. One of such teams was driven by the father,
Jonathan. Over the ample waggon-boxes there were raised large
bent hoops, and these were securely covered over with strong
canvas. In these receptacles were stowed away the beds and

bedding, the provisions, the feed for the horses, all the necessary cooking and other household utensils, the family clothing, and all the other useful household belongings for which space could be found. In journeying along, they stopped wherever night overtook them, gave the horses a small feed of oats, and turned them loose to pick up whatever grass they could by the wayside. Some of the party were able to bring with them a cow, to provide their little child with milk on the way, and this was the means of supplying most needful wants to the young. They travelled slowly, making no more than twenty miles a day, and taking three weeks to make the journey. They crossed over the Niagara River above the Falls, and so around by Hamilton and down to Little York, and thence north, up Yonge Street to Newmarket.

On arriving in Canada, continues Mr. Gould's narrative, my father made his first halting place on Yonge Street, in the township of King, a mile or so west of Newmarket. He had the right to a free grant of 400 acres of land for himself, and 200 acres for his eldest son, Isaiah Gold. But he was disappointed with what he saw and did not like the country. He therefore determined to return to the States and settle in Ohio, where he and his wife had relatives. Having no money to help him make the return journey, and the season being far advanced, he was obliged to stay over the winter. He rented a small farm of forty acres, which he worked; and he also got work at teaming goods from old Mr. Beaman—his regular trips being between Newmarket and York (now Toronto). At this work he continued for nearly two years, hoping to save money enough to enable him to remove to Ohio. But just then, Beaman failed, owing the father $200. The intention of going to Ohio had to be abandoned for want of means. And so the patent of the lot of wild land was accepted by Jonathan in lieu of his carefully hoarded earnings, as has been already stated. Indeed he had no other alternative. And so we find him settling down on the 200 acres, composing lot 32 in the 6th concession of Uxbridge, in the spring of 1808. It was a lonely location in the depth of the woods. The place was over thirty miles distant from the settlement on Yonge Street. There was no road, only a track, for the greater part of the way, through a dense forest. The few settlers were scattered miles apart. There were only about a dozen of them altogether—all from the State of Pennsylvania. Mr. Gould gives the names. They were, Elijah Collins, James Hughes, George Webb, Charles Chapman, Samuel Siddens, Samuel Hains, Job Webb, Ezekiel Roberts, Robert Wilson, Amos Hilborn, Joseph Collins, William Gold, Ezekiel James, Thomas Hilborn, and Jonathan Gold. Those families for several years constituted the only settlers of Uxbridge. And there was not a solitary white settler further north at this time, none, it is asserted, north of Uxbridge range of townships to the north pole.

The Indians were then numerous, and they were friendly and sociable. Sparse and scattered as the settlers were—some of them living at as great a distance as six or seven miles apart—they assisted one another in "blazing" and "brushing" roads and cutting pathways through the woods and swamps, and over and around the hills, and at "logging-bees," and otherwise in exchanging work from one clearing to another. Their helpful sympathies were awakened towards each other, and Quakers, or Friends, as they mostly all were, composing one little community, their offices of good neighbourhood were extended to each other in constant acts of ready brotherly kindness.

CHAPTER III.

NATURALLY, the providing of a place of shelter for his family was the first thought of Jonathan Gold. The building of anything approaching what would be considered a dwelling-house in modern days was out of the question. The log shanty was the all-prevailing habitation of the early settler. In fact it was the only kind of dwelling that could be provided, with the means and material at hand. And so the log cabin, the first residence of the Goulds in Uxbridge, was put up. In after years, when Joseph Gould was occupying his splendid mansion, when he had reached a position of affluence and was surrounded with all the comforts and refinements of civilized life, his thoughts often turned with fondness to the humble home in which he was born. Those who only knew him as the practical, industrious, money-making, self-made business man and astute politician, would never have guessed that beneath that calculating exterior there was a highly imaginative and sentimental nature. But it is a fact that Joseph Gould indulged his fancy in courting the Muses, and that he was "guilty" of making rhymes and verses. Amongst his papers there are several pages, headed "Early Poetry," and scattered throughout an old memorandum book are to be found many fragments in rhyme, and some seemingly most industrious attempts at verse-making. The following, descriptive of the first log cabin, is here introduced. It is prefaced :—

"On my birthplace; composed for my wife, while musing over the past."

MY FATHER'S LOG CABIN.

There was a man in early time—
  When Canada in childhood stood—
Came from a southern, warmer clime,
  And sheltered in her shady wood.

His wealth was in his head and hands;
  His team; a wife and children three;
He wanted house, and home, and lands;
  But how to get them could not see.

With two years' toil of self and team,
  He bought a lot whereon to rest;
The price he paid, too dear did seem—
  The land was good, but not the best.

This lot lay twenty miles away
  From settlement, in forest lone;
Where tall green pines, and large oaks, gray,
  Showed worlds of wealth, to him unknown.

On this my father built a hut—
  A preface to Canadian life—
In which, when finished, he could put
  His children, self and faithful wife.

With small, straight logs the walls were made—
  The gables same; all well notched down—
With basswood troughs the roof was laid,
  Alternately, turn'd upside down.

With split bass logs, he laid the floor—
  Hewed smooth and jointed with his axe—
With two rough boards he made the door—
  With moss and mud he stopped the cracks.

Beside the door, a window placed—
  A six-light sash, just seven by nine—
Th' opposite wall another graced
  Of the same size, and square in line.

A chimney built with straight split sticks,
   And plastered well with clay and straw;
No jambs were built; there were no bricks,
   Nor cash to buy, nor roads to draw.

The floor above, with rough boards tight,
   Had made a loft, the chamber over,
In which we, children, slept at night,
   On ticks of chaff with feather cover.

In winter time, the snow would sift,
   And sprinkle well the chamber over;
But it without might blow and drift,
   We slept secure beneath our cover.

Of good flat stones, the hearth was laid—
   Full eight feet long at least, and longer—
The logs cut out, the back wall made—
   Built up substantially, and stronger.

To reach the loft, a ladder stands
   Perpendicular in the corner—

Secure from winter's frost and snow—
   From bears and wolves, then prowling round—
A Home, that wealth could not bestow—
   Content and Happiness we found.

                          JOSEPH GOULD.

In such a log shanty Joseph Gould was born; and in such his father and mother and brothers and sisters dwelt for a quarter of a century, until its place was supplied by Joseph with a new frame house, the work of his own hands, built for their better accommodation.

Jonathan Gold, the father, and Rachel, the mother, lived the remainder of their days in the house built by their dutiful son, on the old homestead. The building is still standing (in part), rebuilt; very much added to, and the old homestead and farm owned by Mr. Joseph Gould's youngest son, Mr. Harvey J. Gould. Jonathan died

27th October, 1850, and his aged wife, Rachel, on the 5th of the same month, eight years afterwards. The remains of both are interred, side by side, in the lonely little Friends' burial-ground, on the top of Quaker Hill—

> Where heaves the turf in many a mouldering heap.
> Each in his narrow cell for ever laid,
> The rude forefathers of the hamlet sleep.

There were ten children issue of the marriage of Jonathan and Rachel; the names of the latter, according to priority of birth, were :—

Annie, born 30th August, 1806. She married Mark Shell, and died some thirty years ago, leaving a numerous family.

Ruth, born 1807, married Joseph Collins, of the township of Whitchurch. Both died several years ago, leaving one son surviving them, J. J. Collins, of St. Catharines.

Joseph, born 29th December, 1808, died 29th June, 1886.

Margaret, born September 19th, 1810, died December 15th, 1812.

Joel, born March 3rd, 1812, died April 4th, 1859; left two children, a son and daughter; the latter only survives. The widow is still living.

Daniel Lee, born 26th November, 1813, died 27th June, 1851. He was twice married. First to Amy and afterwards to Jane, her sister, daughters of William Hilborn. He leaves issue, by the first wife five children, and the second wife, one child. All are residing in the States.

Jessie, born October 9th, 1815; still living, and resides near Thornbury, county of Grey.

Sarah, born 27th November, 1817; married George Hilborn; still living, and resides at St. Thomas, county of Elgin.

John (who died an infant), born 1820.

John Lee, born October 19th, 1822; still living, and residing in Dakota, U. S.

Of the three children of the first marriage of Jonathan with

Anna Hilborn, the youngest, Abigail, died an infant. Hannah, the second, died in 1817, aged sixteen years. The eldest boy, Isaiah Gold, born 7th June, 1800, left the parental roof about the time of the death of his sister Hannah, to seek his fortune amongst his relatives in Ohio. Correspondence was kept up with him until 1850, when all letters from him ceased, and since which time nothing has been heard of him by his Canadian relatives.

The log cabin verses have been taken out of their proper order, as to the date of their production. But they seemed to fit in more appropriately where they are placed than anywhere else in these pages. And what more accurate or interesting description could there be given of the mode of building the old Canadian log cabin of the early settlers ? Snug and comfortable, withal, were those old-time shanties ; and the first years of hard probation over, after smiling plenty had blessed the toil of the pioneer, the wayfarer might easily find worse halting-places. There was always an abundant table, and hospitable welcome was everywhere the rule in the good old time of the log shanties. And what roaring fires warmed and cheered them of a winter's night ! Here is how they made them :—

" To get the firewood into the house, we would take a horse, hitch on to, and draw the logs into the house. Then we would pile a tier of them one on top of the other, with three huge back logs ; and by such fires, on winter evenings, I listened attentively and with the most exciting interest to many thrilling stories of the past. It was by the light of such a fire that, as a boy, I was taught my letters by my dear mother, and it was she who also, thus early, first instilled into my youthful mind that profound reverence for the Holy Scriptures which through all my life I humbly hope I have retained."

CHAPTER IV.

THE Pennsylvanian people coming into Canada had been in the habit of grubbing their land with a mattock. This implement had an axe at one end and a hoe at the other. They would cut the underbrush down and pile it up in small heaps; then they would cut down the oak and other large trees. They next cut the bodies of the trees into logs; took the tops and chopped them up fine, and piled them up in separate heaps. Next they set fire to the brush and burned up the heaps. In this way, it would take a good hand from eight to ten days to chop an acre. Then it would take five men and a yoke of oxen a day to clear up from one-half to an acre, logging; and it would take a man a day or two to pick up the chunks of wood and do the burning of the logs. "I once saw a fallow cut so that in felling the trees they would be felled in windrows, and about the length of a tree between them. But it did not work well. I undertook to improve on this mode, just so that the tops of one would fall over the tops of the other; then I would lop them down and, if there were any trees standing at the side that would fall with their tops into the first ones, I would fell them also, and finally I would roll all the old logs into those, and in this way, on our first trial, with four of us, we could chop one acre every day"—says Mr. Gould.

In clearing the land little regard appears to have been paid to the value of the magnificent timber, which everywhere grew so abundantly. Vast forests of the finest pine and oak were ruthlessly felled and given to the flames, without a thought of the value of the sacrifice. The splendid trees were looked upon as an incumbrance upon the face of the earth, and a hindrance to the cultivation of the soil. The one grand object appeared to be to get rid of the growth of the forest anyhow, no matter by what destructive means, in order to speedily secure clearings for crops. And good crops they got in those days from the virgin soil.

About the 10th of September was the time selected for sowing wheat. It was harrowed over with a "three-cornered drag" and oxen. Good crops were the invariable result.

The mode of harvesting, we are informed, was to cut down the grain with an American sickle. This was part of women's as well as men's work. All, male and female, young and old, turned out to help at haying and through harvest-time. In old cleared fallows the wheat was sown in "lands" or ridges. The best reaper was selected to take the lead; the others started about a stroke of the sickle, each, behind and followed each other in rotation. It was part of the duty of the foreman to go back after the reapers, and see that each had laid his or her sheaf down evenly, so that there would be no trouble in binding. Oats were mostly cut with a hand-cradle; in lodged places the sickle was used. The threshing was done either by hand-flails, or on the barn floor by driving oxen or horses over the grain until threshed. The meadows were all cut with a scythe, and raked up by hand, and pitched on with a hand-fork. No steam, nor yet horse-power threshing machines, nor self-loaders or unloaders in those days. But, in time, the flail was driven out by the horse-power, and that in turn gave way to the steam thresher, while the reaper and mower, and the self-binder have taken the place of the scythe and sickle, and of the "leader" and the rows of men and women reapers who followed after him in the grain field.

It was the custom of the early settlers to come together and help one another at all "raisings" and "logging-bees." They also "exchanged work," one neighbour with another in a friendly way during haying and harvest-time. Those living at a distance, and who would be returning home late, carried horns. These horns they blew, in case they got lost in the woods (which was frequently the case), to arouse attention to their position. The horns were generally made of tin, and could be heard a distance of three or four miles. Mr. Gould tells us that his mother had a sea-shell, which was used as a substitute for the horn, and it could be heard at a distance of five miles, on a calm night. Guns were also fired off for the same purpose, and a regular code of signals had been established and well understood. Those who heard the first alarm fired an answering signal, or tooted on the horn, and others responsively followed as soon as the nearest answering sound reached them. When safety was reached by the lost one, a general "tattoo" was sounded which made known the fact, and the search and the "music of the woods" discontinued at the same time. Failure of a member of the family to reach home after nightfall caused the alarm to be sounded. Nor were the precautions and pre-concerted signals for search unnecessary. Bears and wolves, and wolverines, were then plentiful in the new settlements, and, in severe seasons, were bold as well as numerous. To have to remain a night in the woods was a dangerous experience for the belated traveller who had lost his way. Stories almost innumerable are told of persons who were safely directed homeward by the tooting of the horn, and of the hair-breadth escapes of others, who were obliged to spend a cold night in the woods, and take up their lodging in the branch of a tree out of harm's way. Mr. Gould heard many instances in his childhood of women and children having been devoured by wolves, and of solitary settlers escaping from the ferocious animals by taking refuge in a tree, while a pack of twenty kept howling and snapping at him until daylight brought relief. He remembers that when quite a lad one of his father's hogs was killed by a bear, and that it was in the daytime and close by the house. That season, he tells us, the bears were so thick that not a day passed over without some neighbour having a cow, or a calf, or sheep, or hogs killed by the bears. So serious were the depredations of those animals that the whole settlement turned out, with dogs and guns, to hunt them; traps were also set, and deadfalls, and other devices resorted to to destroy them, and very great was the slaughter amongst the family of bruin. Other fur-bearing animals were also plentiful at that time in Uxbridge, and mink, foxes, marten, otter and musk-rat, and some beaver are mentioned as having been shot and trapped by him during his boyhood. Of the stories told at the cabin fireside of a winter's night of the depredations of the wolves, the following is amongst the saddest and most thrilling :—

On the removal of the seat of Government from Niagara to York, in 1796, amongst those who followed in its wake were Corporal Crawford, his wife and two children. He was a discharged soldier, having left the British army a short time previously, on account of the loss of an eye, through an accident. He was a very fine-looking man, athletic and well proportioned, and standing over six feet in height. His wife, Mary, whom Crawford had married six months before, was the widow of a deceased soldier, and her two children, a girl and a boy, four and six years of age, respectively, were by the first husband. She was a tidy, clever, hearty young Irishwoman of five-and-twenty; Crawford, who was about ten years her senior, was a Scotchman. He was much given to hunting and fishing, spent a good deal of his time in the woods, and was a most successful sportsman. Although he was privileged to take up 400 acres of land, and might have done so almost anywhere in the front along the Lake shore at the time, he was careless about selecting his location. In company with a friendly young Indian of the Mississagua tribe, for whom he had done some friendly office, and who was very much attached to him, Crawford spent days and weeks camping in the woods, and trapping fur-bearing animals, which were then so numerous in the unbroken forest. In one of those excursions, the soldier was taken to a " beaver meadow," on the borders of a little stream flowing into Lake Simcoe (supposed to be somewhere near the site of the present village of Beaverton), where the game was very abundant. There were many delightful spots on the margin of the lake, look-ing out over the tranquil waters, and to one of these Crawford was specially attracted, and had determined upon making it his home. He managed to build a hut, and made a little clearing, and to this spot, with the help of the friendly Indian, the wife and children were removed in the early spring. The wife was charmed with the beauty of the place and its surroundings; and if the hut was small it was well provided. Venison was plentiful and could be had almost anywhere in the woods with little trouble, and the most delicious fish might be taken at pleasure from the stream and lake. Wild strawberries and raspberries also grew in great abundance about the place. The wife was soon able to manage a canoe and paddle over the waters of the lake with the delighted children. Summer and fall passed over joyously for the contented little family in the woods. There was an early snow-fall, and with this intimation of the coming winter, the wife wished to be nearer the settlement at York. She had an additional reason for this, being near her confinement. The Indians were, however, very friendly, and the Indian trail from their village (now Orillia), to Lake Ontario, led by the hut. Their departure was delayed; the wife was suddenly overtaken in her confinement; her illness brought her to death's door, and her life would be endangered by any attempt at removal. Winter in all its severity came on apace, and this year, much earlier than usual. The husband exhausted all his ingenuity and resources in providing for the wants of his family. Indeed from the ample means at command, he had no difficulty in laying in stores of food and procuring firewood—bread, and flour to make it with, was the one great deficiency, and the little stock on hand was supplemented by large gatherings of nuts. The mother and infant grew stronger. But by this time the snow was so deep that a journey through the forest, for the woman and young children, was out of the question.

That winter was one of unusual severity. Towards its close, the howling of the starving wolves was incessant throughout the night, and filled the poor woman and children with terror. Crawford had his gun, but only a scant supply of ammunition. He was in the habit of making short excursions, in order to get supplies of fresh venison, which he was always able to fetch to the hut before night to the expectant family. From one of these—the last in this tragic story—he did not return as usual. Night came on, and the uneasiness of the wife grew to alarm at the husband's absence. She "tooted the horn" again and again, but there was no answering response. Solitary wolves were seen prowling about the hut when the affrighted wife looked out at the door and "tooted" in the blinding snow storm which came on. This it became unsafe for her to do any longer, so the door of the hut was kept shut and barred. Far into the night, the howling of the pack, at first distant, came nearer and nearer to the hut; the watching woman heard a rush past, and believing that her husband was pursued, in her fond eagerness to give him succour opened the door. Fatal step! The ferocious brutes rushed in, tumbling over each other in their bloody eagerness; the woman, with her infant in her arms, was knocked down, and the savage animals fought and tore each other in glutting on their defenceless prey. A child's crib, clumsily made of heavy timber, was overturned in the dreadful onslaught, and covered up in it was the little girl, the oldest of the children. She was completely hidden by the overturned crib, and, rendered unconscious by fright, never moved. Daylight broke in upon this horrible scene in the woods when Crawford arrived, to see the wolves, some of them with bloody jaws, slinking away from his wretched cabin. He had followed too far after a buck which he had wounded, and on his return home night had fallen, the snow-storm had come on, and pursued by a hungry pack which had got on the trail of the wounded deer, he had taken refuge in a tree. This was scarcely a mile distant from his home. While in this place of safety, the wolves, which were howling and jumping at the foot of the tree, suddenly followed in pursuit of the buck, which unluckily had taken a course that led towards the hut. Crawford could tell from the savage howling which arose above the storm that something terrible was going on in that direction. With the first streak of daylight he made his way for home, where, frantic and heartbroken in his agony, he encountered the tragic scene described.

Turning up the crib, the little girl was found, unhurt. Some bloody tresses of his poor wife's hair, some fragments of clothing and the half-devoured carcass of a wolf were all that was left to shew the dreadful havoc that had taken place over the bodies of the defenceless woman and two younger children. Immediately outside the door of the hut were found the antlers of the deer, from which it was conjectured that the hunted animal ran towards the light when the door was opened by Mrs. Crawford.

Corporal Crawford never again returned to civilized life. The events of that dreadful night completely unhinged his mind. Through his friendly Indian companion, he was adopted by the Mississaguas, who regarded his infirmity of mind as an additional reason for their protection. The little girl, whose life was so miraculously preserved from the ravening jaws of the wolves, was returned to relatives of her mother on the American side, and was afterwards lost sight of in the march of events and settlement.

Joseph Gould lived to see a thriving village grow up on the spot to which the foregoing story relates, and to see a populous, well settled county, with railways and telegraphs, and all the adjuncts of advanced civilization take the place of the dense forest which sheltered the wolves.

CHAPTER V.

OF the educational facilities of those days, or rather the want of them, we have the following interesting details:—

"Until I was about ten years old, there was no school in the township; nor was there any nigher than the Quaker schoolhouse on Yonge Street, about twenty miles west of our place. In 1817 or '18, a log schoolhouse was built on the north-west corner of lot 31, in the 6th concession. A little Irishman [he does not give his name] was employed to teach the school. But the teacher was like the house, a very poor one. I had been taught the alphabet by my mother, before I went to this school, and was able to spell and read a little. I shall never forget the delight it gave me to be able to spell and comprehend a short reading lesson—an interesting little anecdote. The people were all poor, and poor as was the school, they could only keep it open for three or four months during the winter season. I got a smattering of the three R's there, and such was the extent of my schooling."

Young Gould, however, studied all he could at home and—

Read his book by chimney nook

in the evenings, by the light of the cheerful blaze of the heaped-up log fire, and was further encouraged and helped on by his kindly, good Quaker mother, Rachel Lee. But his father was working hard on the clearing, in trying to convert it into a farm, and the boy's help, young as he was, was needed. Young Joseph was strong and hardy; he was fond of chopping, and became quite handy in the use of the axe. "I took great delight," he says, "in a good axe and in keeping it in good order." And further on— "I was the oldest son that was at home, my elder brother Isaiah having gone away to the west. That was another reason for my being anxious to make myself useful, and I was soon able to do a man's work. Before I was seventeen, I was able to chop acres after acres—in four days to the acre—fit for the logging. I have known many of our old jobbers clearing land, to chop and clear large fallows, at an average of ten days to the acre. Ten dollars an acre used to be the average ruling price for chopping, clearing and fencing an acre of land fit for the harrow."

He tells us that he paid for his first pair of boots by cutting seven cords of wood, and laughs over his disappointment that on taking them home, and tugging and pulling at them for an hour to get them on, he found that one was a number seven and the other a number nine!

The Gould connection with the Hilborn family, their near neighbours, stood in this relation:—Jonathan married Anna, the daughter of Thomas Hilborn, his first wife, as already related. William Gold, Jonathan's brother, married Rachel Hilborn, another daughter, and Sarah Gold, their sister, married John Hilborn, a son of Thomas Hilborn. So that Joseph Gould's father and uncle and aunt all married Hilborns. In the next generation, Joseph Gould's sister, Sarah, married a Hilborn, and his brother Daniel L., married two Hilborns for his first and second wives. Through the Hilborns the Gould family connection extends to the Hambleton family. Mr. Eli H. Hilborn, who occupies such a leading position in Grange matters, is now the most prominent member of the Hilborn family in Uxbridge.

CHAPTER VI.

THE War of 1812-14 completely checked all emigration from the United States; there was very little from Great Britain and Ireland, or from European countries, and settlement appeared to be at a stand-still. Worse than that, instead of Canadian progress through immigration, the movement appeared to be in the other direction. On the breaking out of the war, many American settlers, who refused to take the oath of allegiance or bear arms against the United States, were at this stormy time imprisoned, and numbers of others went back to the States rather than renounce their citizenship, leaving large farms of excellent land behind them. Much of this land was confiscated, and sold under what is known as the Alien Act, creating widespread discontent and causing much fierce agitation for many years afterwards.

The outlook was a gloomy one for the hardy pioneers from Pennsylvania. They were disappointed in the country; they were dissatisfied with their position; they were despondent, and they believed there were grounds for alarm and apprehension as to their future prospects. Still they held on. They worked and toiled bravely, and although discouraged, they were not disheartened. Much progress had been made notwithstanding all drawbacks. The dense woods were year by year giving place to enlarged clearings;

roads were being made through the "bush," and better facilities for travelling to mill and market provided. The pioneers saw their children growing up around them, and becoming a help instead of being an incumbrance. There were wooings and marryings and merrymakings amongst themselves, and social relations and interests established which, in a way, rooted them to the soil, and after a while these influences had their share in removing from their minds all inclination for change. During this period of toil and trial and uncertainty, Joseph Gould found himself rapidly advancing to man's estate. His was a well knit, well developed frame, about five feet ten inches in height; he had a clear strong gray eye, fair complexion, and was considered a rather good-looking young fellow. With the fair sex he was a decided favourite, and we have more than family tradition in support of the statement of his youthful conquests and susceptibilities. His character was ardent and impulsive, and he was of a generous and adventurous nature. Amongst the books which then came in his way—and he tells us that he read everything he could lay his hands on in the shape of a book—were, The American History of the Early Settlement of each State; History of the Revolutionary War; History of England, and Blackstone's Commentaries. Those books, he says, "I read and re-read carefully, for I had none other for a long time afterwards." And there is little doubt but that such reading must have largely aided in enlightening his understanding and in enlarging his views of men and things, and in prompting the inward stirrings of his nature to the achievement of something better in life than the daily drudgery of a backwoodsman.

Meanwhile, although immigration was almost at a stand-still, and the growth of population was but slowly advancing, the old log shanties and cob-roofed barns were beginning to give place to a better class of farm buildings. Frame buildings were erected wherever the settlers were able to do so, and young Joseph did not fail to observe that there was a brisk demand for carpenters. He had made up his mind to learn the trade of a carpenter—he was then in his nineteenth year—and here is his account of how he went about it :—

"The necessity for new buildings was everywhere visible. My father's house and barn, like most of his neighbours, were about done, and required to be replaced by new ones. I, therefore, proposed to him to let me go for two years to learn the carpenter trade—promising to build him a new frame house and barn for the two years of time I had yet to serve him before I was of age. This he consented to. Accordingly, I engaged myself to Jared Irwin, a carpenter of Yonge Street, in the township of King. I spent one summer with him, for which he paid me three and one-third dollars per month. Small though the amount of wages was, I have always considered that the insight which I got that summer into the carpenter trade was worth more to me than any other thing I could have done, as it gave a different bent to my mind, and a new stimulus to my ambition. Hitherto I had lived in the woods exclusively, with little education, and no current reading matter. There was not a post-office within twenty miles of me; and as to newspapers, up to that time I had never seen one; so that I was perfectly oblivious of what was going on in the world. During the four months that I worked for Jared Irwin, four of us framed and finished a number of large barns and two houses. With Irwin I also got a knowledge of the sawmill business, as my master had a sawmill, and I had to assist in repairing and working it occasionally. This knowledge did me good service afterwards, when I bought the Uxbridge sawmill property. The season that I was with Irwin learning the trade was very unhealthy. A great deal of low fever prevailed. Irwin was taken down with typhoid fever, and I had to wait upon him part of the time. Having gone to assist my father in the harvest field, I was also taken down with the same kind of fever, and was very ill. Ezekiel James, our near neighbour, was also taken very ill at the same time. He sent to

Newmarket for Dr. Thompson.   The doctor also visited me, and by his treatment we both got well."   It was during this illness that a startling and cruel murder took place, which excited not only the indignation of the people of the new settlement, but of the whole Province, and of those beyond its boundaries who read the particulars, which are detailed in the next chapter.   The Provincial Government offered a reward of $400 for the apprehension of the murderer.

CHAPTER VII.

THE sad story of the cruel murder of young Isaac James, which occurred at this time, is narrated as follows by Mr. Gould:—

It so turned out that Ezekiel James had hired a man by the name of Christie, who called himself an Irishman, to help him through with the harvest. This was in 1828. Mr. James had agreed, as part of the compensation, to move Christie and his wife and two children to York, now in the city of Toronto, at the end of the season. . Mr. James was very fond of good horses, and had a very fine span of dappled-grey mares. They had black manes and tales, and were the admiration of the whole country round about. He was very proud of them, and always drove them himself. Just at the time that he was to take Christie to York, Ezekiel James was taken down with the sickness, and his eldest son, Isaac, had to take his place, and drive the team. His father had not hitherto allowed him to drive the young mares, but there was no alternative, and he had to let them go. Young Isaac James was a fine young fellow of eighteen, of a most amiable disposition, and much beloved by all who knew him. The mares were hitched to a light double-waggon, with hoops bent over the box, and a canvas cover over all. Into this Christie, his wife and children, bed and traps were taken. Young James, who had never made the journey alone before, received from his mother and sick father all proper advice and direction, and started upon what was then looked upon as a very long journey, going to and returning from York. It took four days'

travel. The only way to get from Uxbridge to York in those days
was by way of Newmarket and Yonge Street. Between Uxbridge
and Newmarket there were twelve miles of solid "bush," with the
road merely brushed out around the trees. It was the lonesomest
part of the way.

As young James's return was not looked for until after the
fourth day, his absence up to that time would have caused no
uneasiness, were it not for a dream which greatly troubled his
mother. The night of the day on which he left home, she dreamt
that she saw her son wounded, and bruised, and bloody, and groan-
ing in pain and agony. She awoke, greatly excited and alarmed.
She was by no means a superstitious woman, nor were any of the
staid James, Quaker-family that way disposed. She slept again,
and the dream was so vividly repeated that she was terribly troubled.
She got out of bed, being unable to rest any longer, and alarmed
the whole household, telling them the dream that came to her, and
of its vivid repetition. She wanted to set out at once and follow
her son. This, however, she was prevented doing, as her husband
was very sick. The next day, and the next, she was anxious to follow and make enquiries on the road, but Mr. James would not
consent until after the fourth night, when the son was expected
home. He did not arrive as expected. The alarm was given to the
neighbours, who had meanwhile been told the story of the anxious
mother's dreams and fears. Early on the fifth day, she took with
her her son John, a lad of fifteen; two horses were procured and
saddled, and Mrs. James, who was noted for her good riding,
impatiently led the way through the bush, taking the road to Newmarket. They looked carefully into every thicket and swamp at
both sides of the road as they passed along, without, however,
finding any traces to excite suspicion. At one point, when within
about a mile of being through the twelve miles of woods, the horses
became frightened. They sniffed and snorted, and shied off as
they passed a log-heap beside the road track. This was not much

minded at the moment, as it was thought that some small animal might be in hiding in the log-heap. They pressed forward until they reached her brother, Isaac Lundy's, at Whitchurch, where she expected to find some tidings of her son and the team. There was none; the team had not been seen passing. Mr. Lundy, taking the alarm, immediately went along Yonge Street to a blacksmith's shop where the horses had been frequently shod, to make enquiries. The blacksmith told him that he had seen the team pass his shop on the day they had left home; that a strange man was driving, and a woman and a child or two with him, but that he had seen nothing of Isaac. This information being circulated alarmed the whole neighbourhood. It was then late, and nothing could be done before next day. Mrs. James stayed that night at her brother's. Her mind was very much agitated, and she could not sleep, and it was while lying down in this condition, trying to compose herself to rest, that she heard a voice in her room saying very distinctly three times—"In the woods!"—"In the woods!"—"In the woods!" She was so startled that she immediately got up and called her brother. She told him what she had heard, and she persisted in the statement that her son was murdered in the woods. Mr. Lundy tried to pacify her, but finally yielded to her entreaties to search the woods. He accordingly went himself, and sent men on horseback to alarm the settlers in Whitchurch and East Gwillimbury to turn out and search the woods, on both sides of the road, for a distance of forty rods; and a man was sent to Uxbridge to warn the settlers there to turn out and search in the same way, from the Uxbridge side, until both parties met. Next day the search began—Mrs. James still remaining at her brother's. She led the Whitchurch party. They had proceeded only a little beyond a mile in the woods, when Mrs. James, pointing to a log-heap on the right-hand side of the road, told the party to "Search there." This was the spot where the horses had shied on her journey forward. The search had not proceeded far when the body of the missing Isaac was discovered. He had been shot through the head, and pounded with the gun in the hands of the murderer. The pieces of the broken gun had been found as evidence of this. It was also plain that the shot had not been fatal, and that the poor victim must have lived for some days after being left for dead, for he had scratched up the leaves and dirt for some distance from where he lay, and he had evidently dragged himself some distance from where he had been shot. The scene presented was heart-rending in the extreme—of the fond mother lamenting over the disfigured body of her foully-murdered boy.

An inquest was held, and a verdict of wilful murder returned against Christie. And the Government of Upper Canada issued a proclamation offering a reward of $400 for his arrest. Meanwhile, the murderer got away with the horses and waggon. He avoided the town of York and the public roads, and succeeded in getting around the head of Lake Ontario, and crossing into the State of New York, stopping at Troy. In those days, before the era of railways and telegraphs, it was not very difficult for criminals to get away by crossing into the States, where it would be afterwards very hard to trace them.

The shocking circumstances attending the commission of the crime and the reward offered by the Government in this case, stimulated many to action, who rushed in every direction in pursuit of the murderer. William Reid, of Sharon, a high-spirited young fellow, was amongst the foremost. Enquiries at Hamilton first placed him on the track, which he had no difficulty in following up, on account of the remarkable appearance of the team of dappled-greys. He travelled rapidly on horseback until he reached Troy, distributing along the route taken by him printed copies of the proclamation offering the reward and containing a description of the murderer and of the team. He posted up a copy in a bar-room at Troy, and there related the circumstances of the murder to an eager crowd present. Amongst those present, he noticed particularly one

young man, carefully reading the document, and who asked him for
" a copy of the hand-bill," saying, " he was going into the country,
and would stick it up." He got one, and started for a farm, about
three miles outside the city, where he had seen a team and a man
answering the description, at work in a cornfield earlier in the day.
On the strength of this, he arrested Christie, without resistance,
and brought him into Troy. This man's name was Brown, a 'cute
Yankee. He refused to give up the prisoner to the Canadian, who
had the warrant, stating that he would deliver him to the Canadian
authorities himself, which he did, and got the reward. In less than
a week from his arrest, Christie was lodged in the gaol of York, and
as the court was sitting at the time, he was immediately placed on
trial. He made a full confession of his guilt, and was hanged.

From the confession, it would appear that the murder of Isaac
James must have taken place within four or five hours after he had
left home. Christie, who had carried a shot-gun, was going on
before the team, on foot. When they had got within nearly the last
mile of being through the woods, between Uxbridge and Newmarket,
Christie stopped, and told Isaac that he had got a ground-hog under
a log-heap. He asked Isaac to punch it out with a stick, while he
(Christie) shot it. And as poor Isaac, all unconscious of harm,
stooped to look under the log, Christie raised the gun and shot him
in the head. As the shot did not kill his victim outright, the
murdering villain beat the poor youth over the head with the stock
of the gun, destroying the breach and breaking the weapon to
pieces, as was seen afterwards when the body was found. It was to
a sister of this young man that Joseph Gould was subsequently
married. As might be expected, the sad story of the murder is a
prominent one amongst the family records, and has been handed
down to their children and children's children.

CHAPTER VIII.

MR. GOULD did not recover readily from the fever ; the typhoid gave way to fever and ague, and that in turn to fever and dumb ague. He was so prostrated that he had to remain home at his father's that winter and all the next summer. He did not return to Irwin. In the fall following he worked for a short time with a Mr. Lewis, of Yonge Street, at the joiner trade. The ensuing spring he took up the trade of carpenter on his own account. And although, as he tells us, he had only devoted one regular season to acquiring a knowledge of the handicraft, he had already gained the reputation of being a skilful artisan. One of his first jobs was the building of the promised house and barn for his father. The building of other houses and barns followed in quick succession, and plenty of orders awaited his acceptance. But in the midst of his career as a thriving young tradesman—or rather at the outset of it—he was again overtaken by sickness. This time the trouble was a "fungus" growing out of the left nostril. Speaking of this as the "great misfortune of his life," he has left the following interesting particulars :—

About this time (1830), I had the misfortune to have a fungus grow out of the left nostril. It was judged at first that it was a polypus, and was treated as such by a Doctor Beswick. He first tried to cut it out, and that failing, he next tried to burn it out with caustic. But as it still continued to grow, he pronounced it a cancer. Now this was very alarming to me, as a cancer was considered as good [bad] as a death-warrant. We had no doctor in Uxbridge, and there was none in any of the adjoining townships that made any pretence to cure cancer. I therefore, with the assistance of my father, made arrangements to go to New York, to an eminent doctor there, to see what could be done. I was also advised to call upon Dr. Widmer, at York, before going farther. This I did. When my father and I called the doctor happened to be out. The housemaid ushered us into a consulting room, which she had kept darkened to keep out the flies, it being sultry weather. She set my father a chair and me another. After sitting down I leant back in my seat, and something that felt bony and uncanny touched my head and made a rattling noise. As I turned to see what damage I had done, the girl raised the blind to let in the light, and behold there, to my horror, was a human skeleton ! It was hanging right over my head, with the bony fingers dangling in my hair ! With a bound, I sprang out of the chair, but I knocked down a pile of skulls near by, which served to increase the horror of my situation. Just at this moment the doctor came in, and whilst calming my fears, laughed heartily, as indeed did my father, at my fright and consternation. The doctor, turning to me, said, "You should not be afraid of your neighbour ; he will not hurt you ; he has done all the harm he will ever do again in your neighbourhood." Turning to my father, he said, pointing to the skeleton : " That is Christie who murdered young James ; he was the strongest, the best proportioned, and most perfect man I ever dissected in my life." [The body of the murderer had been given for dissection.]

After examining my nose carefully, and swearing a good deal at

the "quacks" and "fools" who had been "butchering" me, he
stated his opinion that there were no cancerous symptoms, but that
no one could tell what it was, in such an inflamed state as it was
then in.   He advised me to go home, bathe it in cold water, and
sniff some up the nostril, four or five times a day for three weeks,
and then come to him again. . . .   When I went to the doctor's
again, Dr. Widmer and his partner, Dr. Givins, examined the nose
and pronounced it a fungus growth at the inside of the bridge of
the nose, and that it had resulted from a wound which must have
been at some time inflicted upon that organ, and that the bridge of
the nose must have been broken. . . .   I told them that the
only time that I could remember of my nose getting hurt was when
I was ten or eleven years old, at a "logging-bee."   In helping to
roll a log on the heap, I ran my handspike too far, and the log
falling on one end, the other end flew up, striking me in the face,
knocking me senseless, and completely flattening the nose.   I bled
profusely, and my father had to take me home.   The doctor said
that that was the origin of all my trouble.   I had to stay in York
some three months for treatment, when I was declared to be cured
and allowed to go home.   I was to follow certain treatment, which
I did faithfully, but the wound did not harden and shrink down, as
I was told it would do.   On the contrary the substance grew, and
filled up the cavity of the nostril so tightly that from that day to
this I have never been able to draw a natural breath through it.
And through this very impediment, of not being able to breath
through the nostril, I may truthfully say that I owe more of my
troubles in life than to all other first causes combined.   In fact, I
think it has brought the principal part of my troubles on me—
being always obliged to talk, read, speak, and breathe through the
mouth at the same time.

In the manuscript left behind him Mr. Gould complains at
considerably further length of the trouble caused him by his

affliction.   He mentions further visits to Dr. Widmer, all resulting
in the assurance that the swelling of the substance in the nostril
would go down, and that a complete cure would be effected in time.
But no complete cure was ever effected.   The trouble in the nostril
continued to the end of his days, and he went down to his grave
still calling it " the great calamity of his life."

CHAPTER IX.

IT was in the summer of 1830 that Mr. Gould first placed himself under Dr. Widmer's treatment. He was then just twenty-one years old. Giving his impressions of this, his first visit to York, or indeed to a town of any size, he says :—

Having lived all my lifetime in the woods, except the four months that I had been learning the trade with Irwin, and the short time that I was with Lewis the joiner, my sojourn at York (then a town of three or four thousand inhabitants), was to me a most wonderful and bewildering experience. A new world seemed opening out before me, the contemplation of which brought me some strange impressions. The inhabitants were mostly well dressed, and, as appeared to me, had very little, if anything, to do. Yet they bought liberally at the market, and lived sumptuously. But how they got the means to live I could not understand. A large number seemed to employ their time in talking politics and walking the streets. I boarded and lodged with Monice Lawrence, who kept a hotel on the east side of the Market square, and my room overlooked the market. At first, for a few weeks, I was obliged to keep my room, and keep out of the air and sun. And here it was that I may say I learned my A B C's in politics—this being the first time that I had ever had free access to a newspaper. I made the most of my time reading the newspapers that came to the house—the principal one being the *Colonial Advocate*, published by William Lyon Mackenzie. It was chock-full of politics and of the grievances of the time. From that paper I got my first lesson in politics. I was a young man, entirely unbiassed, and profoundly ignorant of the world, and of governments, and laws, and politics. Here was a new field opened to my view like a panorama—all the public characters of the day standing out in bold relief. Here, first to be seen, was the Lieutenant-Governor, a mere figurehead, surrounded by six placemen, called Executive Councillors, who held the Governor as a mere puppet in their hands to do their will. These were appointed by the Crown during pleasure, and were not responsible to any other body. They received large pay and salaries for their services, and had sinecures that made them quite independent of the popular will. Their duty was to advise the Governor on all matters pertaining to the Government, and to recommend candidates to office. Below them sat an assembly—mostly of old men—some lame, some halt, some nearly blind, and some quite deaf. Those men had a chairman, or speaker, to preside over them—mounted upon a high chair, called a throne, with a table in front of him. A clerk sat at the table to record the proceedings, and before him on the table was laid the mace, representing a brass crown ; and at the other end of the room stood a little black-haired, black-eyed man in black coat and black knee-breeches, and black silk stockings and pumps. The duty of the latter was to carry the brass crown before the speaker when he left the chair, and to summon the chamber below when required by the Governor. On these latter occasions, he carried a little black rod in his hand to rap at the door of the other chamber with, and from this was called "Black Rod." The men composing this chamber were called the Legislative Council. They were appointed by the Crown for life, and were not responsible to any man or set of men for anything they should do, and could only be impeached for cause. They had the power of supervision over all legislation.

Immediately below them again sat a much larger assembly of men, much younger, and much more active and earnest, and zealous in the discharge of their duties. These men were from the country, and country towns, elected by the free franchise of the people ; and their duty was to make and amend the laws, in accordance with the well understood wishes of the people.

Such is the record left by Mr. Gould of the first impressions made upon his mind as an untutored young backwoodsman, on his first visit to the seat of Government. His first political lessons from the *Advocate*, it is apparent, were not calculated to inspire him with much reverence for the men who had the control of Government without any responsibility to the people.

Later on, he continues his reflections :—

In the background, we had presented one of the finest countries in the world. The largest lakes, the largest rivers, the best land and the finest timber were all ours. But with one-seventh part of this land already given away to support a Protestant clergy, and claimed and held by the then Established Church—the Church of England—whose members in this country did not represent one-twentieth part of the population—small wonder there were complaints of injustice. Yet this was but one of the grievances in the picture drawn by the *Advocate*.

Farther on, drawing his inspiration from the *Advocate*, no doubt, he adds :—

The following are a portion of those questions termed "grievances," that the country was labouring under at the time, and which Mackenzie was demanding that the House and the country should settle at once :—The first and principal demand, and which, if granted, would have settled all the rest, was that the Executive Council should be swept clean of priests, bishops and placemen, and made directly responsible to a majority of the people's representatives in the Lower House of Parliament. Next, that the Legislative Council should be purged of all members receiving contracts, allowances, or perquisites from the Government. Then, that the Crown and Clergy Reserves be abolished. That laws be enacted for the better management and sale of the public lands. That means be provided for the support of a good system of education. That laws be passed for the abolition of banking monopolies ; for the reduction of law fees, and the simplification of law practice ; for the equitable distribution of intestate estates ; for establishing a mode for trying impeachments ; for assuring the control of the whole public revenue ; for a revision of the corrupt jury-packing system ; for the repeal of the everlasting Salary Bill ; for disqualifying priests and bishops from holding seats in the councils of the country ; for taking the freeholders' votes at convenient places, and for giving the people the control of their local taxes.

These, he tells us, were some of the questions which Mackenzie had pressed upon Parliament the previous session. And he adds :—The people's representatives in Parliament then were some of the best men that ever represented Canadian constituencies. Amongst them were Mackenzie, Baldwin, Rolph, Bidwell, Perry and Randal. But so little was known of the principles of Responsible Government at the time, and so little was that principle favoured, that an address containing a vote of censure on the advisers of the Governor, although supported by every vote in the House (except one), produced no effect. A large number of most necessary measures of reform had passed the House last session—not one of which was allowed to become law. Amongst those was the Bill for the Secularization of the Clergy Reserves.

The Legislative Council, the Executive Council and the Governor, Sir John Colborne, were all hostile to reform, and opposed to the will of the people as expressed through their representatives in the House of Assembly. They would allow no measure to pass that would be likely to weaken their own power and influence. Nor would they allow of any reform that would weaken the Church of England, of which most of them were adherents. They showed their hostility to the Lower House in every possible way.

Members of Parliament were then elected only for two years, and as the term of the late Parliament had expired an election was to come off in the fall. Mackenzie was busy with his *Advocate*, firing up for the occasion. Every number was filled with charges of corruption and tyranny against the Government, and the people were called upon to stand by their friends in the late Parliament. The people of York were all politicians, or appeared so to me, some taking one side and some the other, and excitement ran so high that quarrels between neighbours were of frequent occurrence. This was the state of affairs in the town of York in 1830, when I arrived there from the backwoods of Uxbridge. I had never had the opportunity to read or study anything political. I knew little or nothing of the constitution of the country, or how the Government was, or should be carried on, and hence did not know one party from the other. But now, having access to the newspapers of the day, I read both sides, and being a little forward and inquisitive, I talked with both sides, in order to form my own conclusions as to which of the two parties had the best interests of the country at heart, and which was the safest and best to entrust with the government of the country. And I came to the deliberate conclusion that the Reformers were the party who were in the right, and the party whose principles would secure the largest amount of liberty and happiness to the people of the country. And from that time forth I was a Reformer. Thus, having selected the party to which I was pleased to belong, I was ever after ready and willing, to the best of my ability, to assist in working out the reforms so much required by the country.

CHAPTER X.

THE doctor having decided that he might safely go home, he
followed his advice and remained at home that winter. Next
spring he engaged himself to run a sawmill for James Taylor in the
township of Pickering. The mill was a new one, and the dam was
new and had not settled properly. The consequence was that, after
running the mill some five or six weeks, the spring freshets came
and carried the dam away. That put an end to his job with Mr.
Taylor. His next venture was to hire a young carpenter, and a
good journeyman carpenter. With this help, he took and completed
contracts for buildings of various kinds, in Uxbridge and the surrounding townships, and put up "a large barn for old Reuben
Crandell in Reach."

The prospects of the trade, however, do not appear to have been
so encouraging in his own immediate neighbourhood as he could
have desired. Or, perhaps, influenced by his experience of town-
life in York, and the insight obtained by him into the better opportunities which centres of population offered to a man of push and
energy for making his way upward, he wished to try a wider field.
At all events, he was becoming restless in his circumscribed position
and longed to make a change. What he says himself is : "Having

seen an account that there was a great demand for carpenters in
Cleveland, in Ohio, I determined to strike out and try my fortune
amongst my cousins in the States.   I therefore made me a good
strong tool-chest, and a chest for my clothes, and arranged to start."

The Sunday following this determination, he went "with the
family to our little Quaker meeting," as he fully expected for the last
time.   On the road home, while walking along with his father and
their old friend and neighbour Ezekiel James, the latter enquired
if it were true that Joseph was about to leave home and go to the
States.   On being answered that such was the intention, Mr. James
began to "reason the case" with father and son.   He pointed out
the large field that would soon be opened at home to Joseph, if he
choose to continue at his trade.   Meantime he made a suggestion.
He suggested (says Mr. Gould in his narrative) that I had better
lease "that Clergy Reserve lot beside him, and go to work on it,
and that father should help me."   My father said he was "owing
me for building the house, and had no means of paying me, but
that if I would take up that lot and go to work on it, or let the job
of clearing, he would board me and my men until I got a good start
on it."   Mr. James said: "There's a good chance; better than
going to the States."   I said: "Evans Jones had leased the lot,
and although he wants to sell, I have no money to buy him out."
To this Mr. James replied: "I will lend thee the money to buy him
out and wait until thee can pay me conveniently."   And being hard
pressed by his father and mother, and by Mr. and Mrs. James, he
took a little time to look the lot over, and finally concluded to lease
it, and abandoned his intention of going to the States.

Having made this decision, he immediately let a job to Samuel
Widdifield to chop, clear and fence twenty acres the next summer.
He also set to work himself with his wonted energy, and the same
summer chopped and cleared ten acres.   He successfully sowed
both "fallows" in fall wheat the same season.   And, with par-
donable pride, he mentions the fact that all the work done, and

all the seeding was paid for; and that his putting in thirty acres
of a crop was regarded as an "extraordinary feat" by his neighbours at that time—"for none of our ablest farmers could clear
over ten acres and sow the land to wheat in one year; that even
that breadth was considered a large fallow, and most of them would
be more or less in debt for chopping or logging."

The spirit of self-laudation in which he mentions this event is
quite excusable, when we bear in mind the means and resources at
his command. He was, as he says himself, "a mere boy," and to
have cleared and sown thirty acres of land in one summer, and all
paid for, could not fail to be regarded, as it was, "a wonderful big
affair." Nor can our admiration be withheld, when, speaking in
the same connection, he says: "This work thoroughly established
my credit as a business man, and gave me an advantage which I
determined never to lose." And he never from that time forward
did lose it in after life. But the next question was what to do with
the wheat when it was harvested. He must have a barn to put it
in. He could build one, to be sure. But where was he to get the
lumber? "There was only one sawmill within twenty miles of
me," he writes, "that belonged to John P. Plank. But the dam
was destroyed, and the mill undermined and all wrecked to pieces.
I must go and have him repair it, and have him saw me some
lumber, and so build a barn in the spring." He interviewed Mr.
Plank and made known his wishes, but did not succeed. Mr.
Plank would not put the mill in repair. "I urged him and tried
to induce him all I could," says the persevering young farmer;
"offering to assist him with my oxen; but this was the third
time that the dam had broken with him, and he was perfectly
disheartened and did not feel like touching it." After further
unsuccessful parleying, Mr. Plank made an offer to sell him the
sawmill and farm. "I laughed at the idea of his offering to sell
me a sawmill," says Mr. Gould. "I assured him that I had put
every dollar that I had or could get into the new land and wheat-

fields, and therefore could not think of buying. I again renewed my proposal to assist him with my team in building the dam and repairing the mill; that I should work for him myself in every possible way, and take my pay in his sawing lumber for a barn." All was useless. Plank would not accede to the proposition, and young Gould withdrew from all further attempts at negotiation. A few days afterwards, Plank called upon him, and pressed upon him the following proposition : To sell the mill, with a good stock of saw-logs, then in the yard, and the farm; all for $1,200 ; and "to give me five years to pay for it without interest, and agreed to repair the mill and dam, and put the whole in good order that fall for me, and to allow me to superintend the work, and have it done to my own satisfaction." After some days' reflection and consultation with his father and friend, Ezekiel James, the terms were accepted.

Of this, the turning point in his life, and the foundation of his large fortune, Mr. Gould says :—"I concluded to accept, and commenced work at once, which was my first stake stuck down in the future town of Uxbridge." The building of the dam was, however, a more troublesome and expensive job than he had anticipated. He was inexperienced in such work, and after spending some six weeks in its repair, it broke away again, and matters were worse than ever. It was then too late in the fall to rebuild; he lost the value of all his work and materials, and lost besides the use of the mill for six months. This unforeseen difficulty interfered with his plans and put back his prospects, and he regrets his temerity in taking upon himself the superintendence of the building of the dam. He also mentions another " misfortune " which he met with during the winter, which came near causing him the loss of his life, and which is related in the next chapter.

CHAPTER XI.

ON Christmas Day he started to go to York "with old Mr. Flewell" in a cutter. The horse was "a great overgrown brute, hard in the mouth, and bad to hold, very skittish, ugly going down hill, and inclined to run away whenever he got the chance, and had made several attempts to run down hill with us that morning." When they got to within about two miles of Joseph Wixson's, of Pickering, here is his account of what happened to them with the undesirable brute whose qualities as a driving horse are so graphically enumerated :—" While going down the hill, he made a dash and threw us both out of the cutter; but I held on to the lines. He slid me down the hill at a rapid pace, and a hemlock knot, frozen fast in the ground and sticking up an inch or two, caught me in the fleshy part of the hip and held me fast, and I held the horse fast at the same time! Mr. Flewell, having got up after his fall, without being hurt, came down the hill, and seeing my situation, sprang to my aid, and lifted me loose from the knot. Next he fastened the horse to a tree, took hold of me and helped me into the cutter, and after gathering up what had been thrown out of the cutter, took the horse by the head and led him gently forward to Joseph Wixson's. They had all gone to meeting, but the hired girl, who with Mr. Flewell, took me out of the cutter and into the house, and placing my buffalo robe on the floor in front of the fire, placed me on it with my feet to the fire." The character of the wound was alarming; it did not bleed a great deal; but the leg, hip and side became numb and lifeless. His companion remained with him until the Wixson family returned from meeting, and then pursued his way alone on foot to York. A doctor was sent for to Stouffville, ten miles away, and did not arrive until late in the evening. He was greatly astonished, as he well might be, at the tremendous size of the wound, and took out of the gaping cavity in the torn flesh a large piece of the hemlock knot, which was tightly embedded in it to the hip bone. After dressing the wound, the doctor's opinion was favourable to recovery, and he cheered up his patient with the assurance that he would not be a cripple. After remaining at Wixson's two weeks (of the kindness of whose family he speaks in the most grateful terms), and several visits from the doctor, the latter assented to his removal. "My people," says Mr. Gould, "came down with a bed swung up in a sleigh, and took me home, where I remained most of the winter confined to the house." He bemoans this accident and its results as "a fearful loss"; but he was very thankful for his escape, and at being able to go to work again, "not much the worse for the wound." In the course of time it became perfectly healed.

He had arranged to put in a large stock of saw-logs and to prepare material for building the dam, but of course the accident disarranged all his plans. The sawmill frame and machinery had been badly wrecked by former breaks, but this last one had about made everything useless, and he was "left without a shilling to help himself." But he was soon again up and doing, and in his emergency, he adopted the wise course of calling the experience of his old master, Mr. Irwin, to his aid. Mr. Irwin helped him to overhaul the mill; put in a new wheel, the machinery was fixed, and everything put into proper trim. And while this was being done, the dam was efficiently repaired, and the mill started at work in the "fore part of June." A good job had been made this time, and the mill "ran splendidly." He "soon cut a large quantity of lumber, for which there was a ready sale, but mostly on credit; for nobody ever thought of paying money in summer time. Farmers could only move their produce to market in winter time, and consequently could only pay their accounts in winter. The custom of the country was regulated by the state of the roads and the time of the market for selling grain. And, at this time, all men in business trusted their goods from one winter to the next." Of course he had to do the same with his lumber, and this made it difficult for him, he says, "to make ends meet." But where there is a will there is a way. He did make ends meet; and not only that, but also met the heavy expenses of repairing the mill and the dam (an item of some $300), which was not coming badly out of such a struggle with untoward circumstances. He was also able to provide money enough to pay the board of himself and his "hands," which, he adds, was no small item; and also the following: "I was fortunate in getting a good boarding-house near the mill on the farm. Mr. Plank, who sold me the mill, and who kept a hotel, had rented the hotel and moved his family into the house that he sold me on the farm, and his wife boarded me and all my hands that summer, while he set up a store of goods in the township of Brock and tended that himself."

CHAPTER XII.

THIS brings us to the summer of 1833.

The village of Uxbridge consisted at that time of J. P. Plank's
little old frame tavern; Carleton Lynde's little frame store; a little
old gristmill with a small pair of native-rock stones; an old log house,
on the present site of the Mansion House, and a small unoccupied
blacksmith's shop. These little old buildings were all that constituted the village of Uxbridge at that time. What a mighty change
has half a century brought about! We turn again to Mr. Gould's
interesting narrative.

The farm and sawmill that I had then bought from J. P. Plank
were not then considered part of the village. They were a quarter
of a mile south of it, up stream. And since I have begun to
describe the village, it might make it more interesting if I should
state when and by whom the first break was made in the forest
where the town now stands. Lot 30 in the 6th concession was
patented in 1806 to Dr. Beswick. This gentleman made a start to
build a gristmill and sawmill, on the present mill site, in the same
year. After getting out the timber for the mill and probably building the dam, he became discouraged with his prospects, and the next

year sold out to Joseph Collins. The latter continued the work and
finished the building of the mills in 1809. In 1807 Robert Wilson
patented lot 29 in the 6th concession, settling thereon the same year,
and making a considerable clearing. He continued his improvements,
bringing into cultivation quite a farm, upon which he resided for
about twenty years. Wilson sold out to J. P. Plank, who, after
building a sawmill, and holding the property for about five years,
sold out to Mr. Gould in 1832. Joseph Collins, who was also from
Pennsylvania, was, we are told, a man of enterprise, and that "had
he lived he would have made quite a stirring place of Uxbridge
much sooner than it was possible for any one else to do." Unfortunately for the progress of the new settlement, Collins met with a
sudden death through an accident at the mill, in December, 1815.
This accident and its cause are described at length by Mr. Gould.
The death caused quite a sensation at the time. The account is
here condensed.

   The mill was of the old-fashioned sawmill pattern, with a flutter-
wheel and a crank attached to the end of it, to which a pitman
was fastened extending to the saw-gate, or saw-frame which held
the saw. When the wheel moved the crank shoved the saw up
and down, and thus ran the mill. The crank in turning dipped
into the water and splashed it in every direction. The water so
splashed would, in cold weather, freeze on the pitman, and the
ice so accumulated would frequently have to be knocked off in
order to give the mill freedom to run. On the morning of his
death, Collins went to start the mill, and it is thought that, finding
the pitman loaded with ice, he took his axe, and lying down on his
breast on the fender under the saw-frame and striking the pitman,
started the wheel half around, bringing down the saw-frame on his
back, pressing with all its weight on the beam and killing him
instantly. There was not a man about the place at the time.
Collins's wife, a young woman, with three little children, after waiting a long time for the husband to come to breakfast, and he not

answering to her call, she went to the mill to look for him. She found him in the position mentioned—the body wedged under the saw-frame, as has been stated, and life quite extinct. With the strength and nerve of a woman in despair, she managed to raise the heavy frame. In doing so, the body slipped off, falling beneath, and rolling outward before the eyes of the agonized wife.

The death of Collins was regarded as a great calamity to the whole neighbourhood. It must have been a severe blow to the progress of the place, the sudden taking off of such a man, just as his enterprise and resources were being actively employed for its development. Certainly it resulted in the utter ruin almost of the property which he left behind him, and which, for nearly thirty years afterwards, we are told, remained in a state of "utter stagnation and ruination."

Joseph Collins had leased lot 31 in the 6th concession, and that lot, together with lot 30 held by him at his death, contained the principal village plot that now forms the populous and prosperous town of Uxbridge. Collins died intestate, leaving one daughter and two sons—the eldest son being then only about two years of age. As the law of primogeniture then prevailed, this little boy was the heir-at-law and the property could not be sold until he came of age. The renting of the premises, the constant removal of tenants, and the need of proper repairs and due attention, led to the total dilapidation of the sawmill, so that in time it rotted down altogether. The gristmill was but a poor thing at best, and it was allowed to get so much out of repair that it did not run half the time, and it sometimes remained altogether idle for more than a year at a stretch. For nearly twenty years the people of the settlement were obliged to go to Newmarket to mill to get their gristing done. And when the heir, John Collins, arrived at his majority, the property was in such a wretched state of dilapidation, and the general stagnation and backwardness of the settlement so disheartened him, that he determined to sell out. This he did in 1833, selling the east half of lot 30, and the whole of lot 31 for $1,300. Mr. J. P. Plank was the purchaser of one acre of the north-east corner of lot 30, and Joel Bardwell bought the whole of lot 31.

About the year 1825 Mr. J. P. Plank bought the west half of lot 30 in the 7th concession and built a small hotel thereon. Two years afterwards he built a small store house. This latter he rented to Carleton Lynde from Whitby, who filled it with goods, and was the first merchant that located in Uxbridge. When Mr. Gould settled down as a young man in the village, in the fall of 1832, the whole of the buildings standing within the present limits of the town of Uxbridge were the little old gristmill and barn built by Joseph Collins, a small log house and blacksmith shop, built by John Lyons; a little frame tavern and driving house, occupied by J. P. Plank, a small cooper shop, built by Thomas Arnold, the store of Carleton Lynde, and the sawmill, house and barn purchased by Mr. Gould from Mr. Plank, and situated a quarter of a mile south of the other buildings.

CHAPTER XIII.

AFTER the last good job made of the sawmill, it was now running smoothly. Thomas Hilborn, a good sawyer, was hired to run it, and he did his work well. That summer a large quantity of lumber was cut, which sold very readily amongst the farmers of the vicinity. Indeed the demand of the neighbourhood was greater than the supply. "This enabled me," says Mr. Gould, "to redeem myself considerably. My wheat turned out a heavy crop of straw, and upon the whole was a pretty fair crop of wheat. It cost a large sum to harvest it, although men then worked for seventy-five cents a day. But it took three very good men to cut, bind and stock an acre a day. I had, however, the good fortune to get my friend, Ezekiel James, to harvest and thresh ten acres of it." Mr. Gould drew the produce of about sixteen acres down to the village and put it in the barn belonging to the mill property, where he threshed it out in the winter. With his harvest safely housed and his sawmill in successful operation, everything was going on prosperously until one day in September, of which he says:—
"I happened to notice some 'muddy' water running out behind the dam, and, on examination, found a small hole in front of the

dam. I ran and got a bundle of straw and attempted to stop it
by treading the straw into the hole.   Whilst on the straw, trying
to squeeze it into the hole, the bank, which was undermined, completely gave way under me, and it required all the effort I was
able to make to keep me from being carried under.   Had I once
gone down, nothing could have saved me.   My escape was most
providential, and made a deep impression upon my mind for
many years afterwards."

This break in the dam turned out to be a very serious affair.
The water poured in over it in a large and rapid stream, cutting
a hole twelve feet deep behind the dam, through which it rushed
down to the bottom of the creek, carrying away and destroying
everything in its course.   Disheartened at this, the mill property
was regarded by him with disfavour, and he felt as if he had made
a bad bargain with Mr. Plank.   On the other hand, he felt elated
over the success of his farming operations, and he believed that if he
could now confine himself to the latter he would be more successful.
In this frame of mind, when Mr. Abraham Bagshaw came that
way and expressed a desire to "trade" a good farming lot for the
mill property, Mr. Gould was not indisposed to come to his terms;
and so the mill and farm were "traded" for lot No. 5 in the 6th
concession of Scott, subject, of course, to the lien to Plank.
Bagshaw at once set about rebuilding the dam; but before the
water was raised to the top it all broke away again, and the
concern was left on Bagshaw's hands in as bad a plight as ever.
The latter in turn became disheartened at his failure, and
insisted upon Mr. Gould taking the mill property back again.
But Gould had now made up his mind to be a farmer.   He
was well pleased with the 200 acres in Scott, and refused to
"trade back" with Bagshaw.   Bagshaw believed himself to be in
a quandary; he regarded the mill as an elephant upon his hands,
and actually ran away from it and left the place altogether.   After
he had left, he wrote Mr. Gould a letter giving all up to him, and

declaring he would never touch the mill again. Mr. Gould was not altogether satisfied at this state of things. A suspicion was aroused in his mind in some way about the bond for the lot that had been traded him by Bagshaw for the mill. He went to York, and there, to his infinite disappointment, learned that Bagshaw did not own the land mentioned in the bond. Mr. Bagshaw's whole claim to lot 5 in the 6th concession of Scott appeared to be founded upon an offer to buy it from Mr. Billings; but he had never paid anything on it, and Mr. Billings had determined not to let him have it. Mr. Gould was now in a "fix." He, however, as was his wont, acted promptly. He took out a capias for the arrest of Bagshaw for fraud, and, acting upon the advice of his lawyer, repossessed himself of the mill. As Mr. Bagshaw was not to be found, the sheriff made a return of *non est*. Mr. Gould being in possession, which he claimed never to have fully given up, and being further strengthened in that possession by Bagshaw's letter of disclaimer, went on stocking the mill and repairing the dam, at the same time advertising Bagshaw through the newspapers. A thorough job was made of the dam this time, and so securely was it rebuilt that it has never since given way. Meanwhile nothing had been heard from Mr. Bagshaw. About six months afterwards, however, he suddenly put in an appearance one fine morning, and entering the mill laid claim to the property! Of course Mr. Gould was surprised, but he did not allow himself to be taken at a disadvantage. Here is his account of the scene: "He [Bagshaw], began to abuse me and threaten me with the law and all its terrors for trespassing upon *his* property. His voice was loud and threatening, and his language was quite offensive. But I was in no humour to put up with his abuse, as I was the sufferer at his hands. He went on threatening and provoking me so that I could stand it no longer. I had a long ox-gad in my hand, and so I dashed up to him, and raising the gad, said I would soon give him something to take the

law for, if it was law he wanted.   As I drew to put it about
his legs, he quickly got out of my way and made off—his legs
saving him from the danger of another ' mill.' "

Next day the landlord of the tavern came on behalf of Mr. Bagshaw with a message of peace.   He had, he said, come back to give
up the property.   There was an amicable meeting of the belligerents;
writings were drawn up, and Mr. Gould was left in the enjoyment
of quiet possession.   Everything was now satisfactory, and the
mill and dam in good order; a large stock of saw-logs was laid in,
and Mr. Gould's whole attention was turned to the work of the mill.
He tried to get rid of his good fortune, but it stuck to him almost in
spite of himself.

Of his arrangements at this time he informs us—"I got Mark
Shell, my brother-in-law, to run the mill, and my sister, his wife,
to keep house for me.   He was a good sawyer, and she was a careful housekeeper, and all went on well and I soon seemed to be
getting on my feet."

Pausing in his narrative, he takes occasion to present the following result of his reflections:—

I have no doubt but that some will think that I have gone too
much into *minutiæ* in detailing more circumstances in the early
history of Uxbridge than was warranted.   But many small efforts
bring about great events.   Great success is often preceded by great
disappointments.   Many great cities are now found resting on the
ashes of old dilapidated villages.   Such seems to be a law of nature.
May I not say that it is the law of God?   The Mountain of Prosperity is only reached through the Valley of Adversity.   Let no
man think that he can jump all at once from poverty to opulence
and *stand*, without the knowledge gained in the Valley of Adversity.
The truth of this is verified every day.   We see opulent and wealthy
persons who began life at the lowest round of the ladder, and who
by prudence and industry accumulated large estates, leaving at
death large fortunes to their inexperienced sons and daughters, who

in the course of a few years have wasted the life-long savings of the parent. The prudence and economy of the parent is outraged by the worthless extravagance of the child. My own observation has been that our sons are not willing to begin the world where their fathers did; but they must begin where their fathers left off, and end in almost every instance by leaving off where their fathers began. And this law seems to apply to villages and towns as well as to individuals.

CHAPTER XIV.

The Collins family—What became of the widow and children—Poetic epistle to Joseph Collins, enclosing a $10 bill—John Bogart—Further particulars of early settlement—"A wide-awake Dutchman"—Tribute to Mrs. Plank—Renewed immigration—Further additions—1834—Joel and Rufus Bardwell—Two "smart" Yankees—Rufus "wanted" at the American side—How the deputy sheriff and constable were tricked—Epistle to a brother poet—Still rhyming and romantic.

RESUMING the thread of his story, Mr. Gould nforms us, in respect to the widow and young children of Joseph Collins, whose early death took place in the sad way already mentioned, that Mrs. Anna Collins, the widow, removed with her three children to her father's near Newmarket. "She married again, and raised another family by her second husband, and at her death left them well off. John Collins, the heir-at-law, raised one family, lost one wife and got another, and is now 1875 living in North Gwillimbury. Joseph Collins, his brother, is now and has been Town Clerk of Whitchurch for over thirty years." It was to this Joseph Collins, with whom Mr. Gould had some intimate business dealings, that we find him addressing the following poetic epistle, on one occasion, when enclosing him a ten-dollar bill.

EPISTLE

TO

JOSEPH COLLINS,

WHITCHURCH.

———

How do you do? my noble friend—
And how are all around you?
Has wealth, with health and peace to mend
Your pleasures, ever found you?

If all is well—then all is right—
  For we're fat, tough and lazy—
Yet lack the dust that shines so bright,
  And makes the world so crazy !

For other things we're rather scant,
  But yet we're not repining—
Our only need and greatest want—
  The yellow gold so shining.

If man had all his eyes could see,
  But gold—his heart would crave it—
Nor would he e'er contented be—
  Unless allowed to have it !

Nor then contented would be long—
  But schemes would be contriving—
To scrape the world, all in a throng,
  To keep his store a thriving.

Thus man for self is made a slave—
  He never is contented —
When got what most his heart would crave—
  Then something else is wanted !

I've tried in vain to break this bill—
  To get what change is due you—
And thought, for fear you'd take it ill,
  I'd better send it to you.

So, friend, if you can make it crack—
  And get what change is wanting—
Then by the bearer send it back—
  For money I am panting !

I owe Jake Laing about two pounds—
  If you can plan to pay it,
In work, or trade, or turn it round—
  From your account I'll stay it.

Long may you live in wealth, I pray—
  Still by the plough to thrive, sir ;
So fare you woll—this second May,
  Of eighteen thirty-five, sir.

Uxbridge.   J. GOULD.

John Bogart, the uncle of John Collins, took out letters of administration to the deceased Joseph, and managed the property during the minority of John, "the heir," renting the mill from time to time, as has been already stated, to different parties. At the time of Collins's death there had been no further additions to the village or settlement, nor was there, we are told, a solitary settler in Reach, Brock or Scott. Mr. Bogart put Stephen Hilborn in possession of the mill for a short time; then it was rented to a Dutchman, named Abram Mericle, who ran it for two or three years. Next, Robert Widdifield rented it for a year or two, and after him Amos Hilborn, who remained in occupation up to 1831.

In the spring of 1826 a permanent acquisition was added to the village by the arrival of John P. Plank, "a wide-awake Dutchman," whose name has been already so often mentioned. He came from York State. He located on the west-half of lot 30 in the 7th concession, built the tavern, and being a "jolly good fellow," and assisted by his "clean, tidy Dutch wife—one of the best housewives that ever cooked a turkey or broiled a beef-steak—they soon established for themselves a reputation that has served the family as a passport up to the present time."

By this time a strong current of immigration had set in from the Old Country. The townships of Brock, Thorah and Mariposa began to be settled. The only road by which the immigrants to those townships could reach their destination was through Uxbridge. Mr. Plank's tavern became their resting place, and in this way he began to pick up money very fast. It was at this period that Mr. Plank, who saw the great advantage of a grist and sawmill to the locality, bought out Robert Wilson, the owner of lot 29, and became possessed of the sawmill privilege. Plank built the sawmill, which afterwards became the property of Mr. Gould. Chapman failed to complete his contract, sold out, and removed to Pickering. The changes already noted went on up to 1834. In the spring of that year, a young man named Joel

Bardwell, an American, and his cousin Rufus Bardwell (who had in the previous fall rented Plank's hotel), bought out the Collins property for $1,200—paying $200 down. They made some repairs in the gristmill. Shortly afterwards, continues Mr. Gould, Rufus, who supplied the funds, appeared to be very much "wanted" in the States by some acquaintances across the line who had an interest in him. And in order that he might not miss his way in going back, one of those acquaintances called upon him one evening with the deputy sheriff and constable and offered him a safe conduct, pledging themselves to take good care of him by the way. For this polite invitation, Mr. Bardwell (not being destitute of the characteristics of his countrymen) expressed his most grateful thanks. He expressed himself profoundly sensible of their love and affection, and of the interest manifested for his safe return. He told them that he had anticipated their anxiety in this respect, and that he had fully made up his mind to go back and visit them in a week or so, but that now as they had arrived, it would be the greatest pleasure to him to return in such company. And he added that he was quite well aware, when obliged to leave them somewhat hurriedly, that he omitted calling upon some friends who had pressing claims upon his attention, and that the fact of his having in his possession plenty of money, which he felt under an obligation to distribute amongst those same friends, would not be the means of making his welcome on their return the less cordial. • "But," he added, "you shall not pass from under my roof without resting and refreshing yourselves." Turning to his son, he said, "Put up these gentlemen's horses, and tell the ostler to groom them well, and have them and my two best horses well fed and ready by to-morrow morning, as you will have to come with me to accompany these gentlemen as far as Toronto." "Now, gentlemen," said the hospitable host, "have something to drink; don't spare good liquor; we will also soon have supper, and when you are refreshed, we will make an early start betimes in the morning." Mrs. Bardwell did not know what to make of all this fuss, and coming on the scene, asked in an uneasy way—"What's all this hurry about, Rufus?" "It's all right," he replied, "these gentlemen want me to go with them to the States, and I'm going in the morning; it's a little sooner, you know, than I had intended to go; but I want *that* matter settled; and having the money, I may as well go now and settle it as a few days later." The constables accepted this as confirmatory of the already expressed intention of mine host to revisit the States, without their pressing invitation, and his offhand manner completely lulled their suspicions. Their entertainment was of the most bounteous and liberal character—more especially in the liquor line—they drank freely, went to bed in a most glorious condition and slept soundly.

But while the emissaries of the law slept soundly, Mr. Rufus Bardwell was wide awake, and kept his weather-eye open too. In the quiet of the midnight hour, guided by the calm moonlight, he was "making tracks" from Uxbridge, out of the reach of the slumbering "minions of the law." Rufus and his son, Silas, were well mounted on the "two best horses" that were to take them to Toronto with the constables, and they were accompanied by an American who had two racehorses in training at the place. They did not wish to disturb the peaceful rest of the constables, even to bid them good-bye, and merely left word that they had taken advantage of the fine weather to ride out early, and would likely reach Toronto before their friends.

It was rather late in the morning when the constables arose, after sleeping off the effects of the night's carousal. Breakfast was ready for them, and after making a leisurely meal, they enquired for mine host. The message left by Rufus was delivered to them, and further inquiries satisfied them that the father and son and their "best horses" had fled at midnight in the company of the American and his racers.

It is not related how the visitors returned to Toronto, or what account they gave of their expedition to Uxbridge. But it is mentioned that they had to groom and saddle their own horses on leaving that morning; there is something added about "sadder and wiser men."

Mr. Gould still mounted his Pegasus upon occasions, and gave the steed of the Muses a free course, whenever moved thereto by the poetic fancy. About this time, judging from the date, he must have written the following :—

AN EPISTLE

TO J. B. PEARSON, OF MARIPOSA, A BROTHER POET.

Written in extremely cold weather, March 3rd, 1855.

Dearest friend, I got your letter ;
   Kindly thank you for the same ;
Humbly own I am your debtor
   For your well composed strain.

Pleased I was, beyond expression,
   When I read the subject through ;
Found your heart had made confession
   Of that friendship that is true.

Yet more joyed by far to know it,
   That the plan that had been laid
Had inspired a brother poet
   To join in the pleasing trade.

Early for to hail that season,
   When the Muses love to sing ;
And though March is sharp and freezing,
   Yet it is a month of Spring.

One more Winter 's gone and left us,
   His record Above to give ;
And to tell how he's bereft us
   Of one winter less to live.

The old vet'ran when he started
   For his upper destined sphere—
At that moment when he parted—
   Sent us Spring, our hearts to cheer.

"Virgin Spring !" said he, "you're welcome,
  My inheritance to share ;
All my subjects—you can tell them,—
  You are my right, lawful heir."

Then he clasped the smiling infant
  To his death-cold frozen heart ;
Breathed farewell—on the instant—
  Chilled her through in every part !

Yet, my friend, the season 's near us
  When the flowery fields appear ,
When all nature, smiling, cheers us,
  Then expect from me to hear.

Then my Muse shall soar with pleasure ;
  Range her thoughts in pleasing rhyme ;
Sing again—when I'm at leisure—
  Now, no more, I'm scant of time.

May passing seasons ever find us
  Both engaged in virtue's cause ;
Wrapt in peace, with love to bind us
  Closer still in friendship's laws.

                    I remain, yours truly,
                         JOSEPH GOULD.

Nor were his strains confined to the sentimental. He made
love ditties and humorous ballads, and his productions of this
character were in great demand by the neighbouring youths of both
sexes. Those who knew Mr. Gould only during the last twenty
years of his life would not credit him with the authorship of such
verses as the following—made at the age of twenty-five.

SONG.

Come all ye jolly young men
  Who glory in your youth ;
Come ! listen to my story,
  While I relate the truth.
The tale that I shall tell you—
  You may believe is so—
      For I love to kiss a charming lass
      That will not say me, No !

Such verses in abundance were the veritable productions of his pen. They are here given as written, with some slight corrections in the spelling. His love letters to handsome Mary James (afterwards his wife)—some of them written while he was in prison—are models of that class of literature, and invest both with a romantic character that, after the lapse of fifty years, is still interesting. But here we draw the veil, and continue those matter-of-fact details and events more intimately connected with our subject.

CHAPTER XV.

Abraham Anderson settles—1835—Buys from the Bardwells—Joel Bardwell buys the Gould gristmill and farm—Joel "wanted "—His escape from the constable—The constable turns up as the owner of the farm !—Suspicions about the transfer—Robert Taylor builds and does a "smashing" business—Joseph Bascom starts a tannery, etc. —First mail route—First postmaster of Uxbridge—Weekly mails—Mr. Bascom's improvements—Other improvements—Joseph Marsland—His improvements—Mr. Anderson's improvements—1836—Unsuccessful merchants—The mills—Price of lumber—Other old settlers.

WHEN "the coast was clear" Rufus Bardwell and his son returned, but their stay in Uxbridge was short after this little performance with the constables. They soon left, it was supposed for Michigan. Before leaving, Rufus gave Joel instructions to sell the Collins property. This was accomplished after a short time. Abraham Anderson was the purchaser. He came in, in the spring of 1835, and repaired the gristmill and rebuilt the sawmill. Joel Bardwell then purchased Mr. Gould's gristmill privilege, together with the farm of 107 acres. He made very few improvements beyond the putting up of a little log house, and after occupying it for a couple of years he, too, was "wanted," and a special messenger was despatched for him with a missive commanding him to visit his cousins in Uncle Sam's dominions. The story was long afterwards current that, on the way to Toronto, Joel gave the bailiff the slip in the thick woods near the Rouge Hill, and shortly afterwards joined his cousin, Rufus. And when the bailiff appeared a short time afterwards as the owner of the 107 acres belonging to his prisoner, there was a second story told. And here is how Mr. Gould tells it :—

The bailiff called upon Joel to accompany him to Toronto ; and this time was determined that his bird should not slip out of his hands—at any rate, not until he had picked his feathers. The 107 acres were transferred (on the way) from Bardwell to the bailiff, for a consideration, the amount of which was never made known, further than the bailiff's admission that he gave his prisoner a new suit of clothes, and otherwise fitted him out "in good *running trim*"; that Joel slipped off the horse (they were both riding), and ran into the woods, and that he (the bailiff) could not catch him, and that he never tried to do so afterwards.

Shortly before Bardwell bought the Collins property, Mr. Robert Taylor had purchased one acre of the north-east corner upon which he built a store, and where for a time he did a considerable business. A "smashing" business it was called, perhaps because he shortly afterwards failed. The property then fell into the hands of Mr. Plank, and is the site of the present Plank House, and of some of the best business stores in Uxbridge.

In 1835 Abram Anderson having, as already mentioned, purchased the Collins property, came in that spring; he repaired the gristmill and built a new sawmill. He induced Joseph Bascom to settle. Mr. Bascom started a tannery and shoe shop, built a house, and acquired property which has since grown valuable. He was a thrifty, honest, industrious man, and a great acquisition to the village. He was mainly instrumental in securing a mail route through from Duffin's Creek into Brock, and was the first postmaster of Uxbridge. The mails were only delivered once a week. At that time, and for seven or eight years afterwards, there was no road connecting the east side of the creek with the west—a passage over the milldam serving for a thoroughfare. Mr. Bascom built the tannery fronting the milldam. The first post office was kept in the tannery. Mr. Bascom first built a little log house to live in, but he afterwards built the frame dwelling on the west end of Dr. Bascom's lot. About the same time Joseph Marsland settled, and built a little tavern and blacksmith's shop on the spot where the late Joseph Finch's tavern and shed stood.

By 1836, Anderson had got three or four little frame houses built on the west side of Toronto Street, and had also got a small schoolhouse built upon the old schoolhouse grounds. These houses were occupied by Anderson's labouring men. At the commencement of 1837 the houses upon Anderson's property, on the west side of the creek, were seven or eight in number, and certainly did not exceed the latter figure. On the east side, there were only those already enumerated. This was all the progress that had been made in the five years, from 1832 to 1836. The few merchants who had tried to start business in Uxbridge, up to that time, were unsuccessful, and had either failed or moved away. The gristmill was of the poorest possible description. Anderson's sawmill was not kept regularly running and cut very little lumber. Mr. Gould's sawmill was kept constantly running at its full capacity, cutting on an average about 9,000 feet a week, and supplying the country round about. He sold clear lumber of the very best quality, at the mill, for six dollars per thousand feet.

CHAPTER XVI.

FROM the time that Mr. Gould engaged his brother-in-law, Mr. Shell, to run the sawmill, everything seemed to go on well. The mill was run steadily, and large quantities of lumber were cut and sold. The name of Gould's Mill had grown into high repute and popularity. Mr. Gould had a firmly established business, and his prosperity was daily on the increase. He had to pay Mr. Plank $200 a year on the mill and farm, and the heavy expense, which he was put to of repairing the dam, during the first two years, came hard upon him ; but by struggling bravely, by industry and self-denial, he was able to meet all his engagements. Of the efforts then made by him as a young man, he says :—" This struggle was to me a most beneficial lesson ; it compelled me to be industrious and prudent, and to practise the most rigid economy in order to be punctual in my payments—which I determined to meet when due, no matter what the consequence. And I soon found that punctuality was a most profitable principle to act upon, as it soon gave me a reputation. My word became as valuable as my money, and more convenient, for I had it always by me, and just the right change, and could pass it as currently as money for anything I wanted to buy. But it took a great deal of care in protecting it, for it is a thing that if once broken, it takes a long time to patch it up again. And I knew very well that if once there was a flaw found in it, it would never be considered so good again."

He had by this time made for himself a reputation for industry and good management, and was reputed to be growing wealthy. He was twenty-seven years of age; he was "pretty comfortably fixed," as he says, and his careful sister, Mrs. Shell, was keeping house for him. He thought it was time for him to be looking about for a helpmate for life. He confesses that he was becoming "a little wild," and was fond of "balls, dancing and wild company." He had his love affairs of "callow youth," like other young men, and he does not conceal from us the fact that he had been "gallanting, first with one girl and then with another." He gives us the assurance, however, that latterly, since the noticeable improvement in his worldly circumstances, he had been "trying to find one whose social position, habits of industry, and feelings and sympathies, and religious sentiments should harmonize" with his own—"believing that conjugal happiness greatly depended upon these qualities, and upon similarity of temperament."

He gave up the "balls and dances and wild company," and the "gallanting," and like the sensible young man that he was—"determined, if possible, to retrace his steps" and "go back to his friends the Quakers, in whose society he had been brought up," and there seek himself out a wife. It was a wise determination—such an eminently proper step in every way as to almost come up to the moral conveyed in Cowper's fable—"Pairing Time Anticipated":—

> Misses ! the tale that I relate
> This lesson seems to carry—
> Choose not alone a proper mate,
> But proper time to marry.

At twenty-seven, and in Mr. Gould's position, the "time to marry" seemed all that was "proper." And where could he have

gone to make a better choice of a " proper mate " than amongst
the friends " in whose society he was brought up "—the Quakers ?
No wonder that he " soon felt himself at home with them," for he
tells us :—" Our neighbour, Ezekiel James, the leading man in the
community, had three fine daughters, whom his excellent wife,
Ruth, had carefully brought up, and well trained both as to religion
and the practical duties of housewifery. Mary, the oldest of them,
was nearly eight years younger than myself ; and the whole three,
at this time, were blooming into womanhood. They dressed
strictly in the old Quaker style—rich, plain, clean and tidy.   And
to my mind, no dress in the world sets off a young woman so well
as the Quaker dress.   No trail to sweep the streets, sidewalks and
barnyard ; no flounces, frills or tuckbacks to catch the dust, rain
and snow, and shackle the agility of a girl's movements. They
take less material, less making, less time in washing and ironing,
and are warmer, and far more durable, and in every way the most
sensible kind of dress. Now those girls were perfect models of what
a good Christian girl should be ; so innocently pure, unassuming
and modest that, after my wild career, I despised myself in their
presence, and frequently wished that I could obliterate the history
of the last five years of my life."

It would be an unpardonable omission to have excluded from
this work Mr. Gould's admiration of the ladies, and the excellent
qualities for which he gives them credit ; and it would be a
thousand pities to have left out his description and estimate of the
style of dress which he admired as most becoming to the fair sex.
The fair ladies who condescend to read these pages may now be
able to take a " pointer " as to the style of dress which is considered
most becoming and likely to capture the· heart of a prosperous
young man in his wooing. As was very natural, Mr. James invited
his young friend—to whom indeed, as we have seen, he had always
proved a friend and counsellor—to his house. And what more
natural than that Joseph Gould, who did not find himself an un-

welcome visitor, notwithstanding his self-depreciation, should have renewed his visits.   And having obtained that friendly footing, we can readily believe him that he "went home with the girls from meeting."   And who shall blame him—indeed how could he help himself—when finding, as he soon did, that Mary, the oldest, "had quite an attraction for him, that he became fondly attached to her, and doubly so, if possible, when he found out that she reciprocated his attachment ?"

Mr. James received his proposal with favour, and gave him some further good advice.   To Mrs. James he was also quite acceptable as a son-in-law ; both his own parents were satisfied with his choice, and Mary told him, one never-to-be-forgotten night, with all the demureness and candour of the young Quakeress, that " she should have great pleasure in joining fortunes with him" and becoming his wife, and "fixed the day."   "I went home," he says, " with a light heart, and bright hopes of the future, for the day was fixed, and in four months we were to be married."   But in his case, as in so many others, the old saw of—

Many a slip 'twixt the cup and the lip

held good.   The dark shadow of the " rising " of 1837 was looming up in the horizon, and Joseph Gould, in spite of himself, became involved in the struggle.

CHAPTER XVII.

FROM what has been already observed as to his political leanings, it need scarcely be added that Joseph Gould was a Reformer. As soon as they got a post-office and a mail to Uxbridge, he took the *Advocate*, Mackenzie's paper, from which his first lessons in politics had been gleaned. He was soon found discussing the political questions of the day, and upholding the Reform side. He was very active at election times; had all Mackenzie's political grievances, and their bearings and remedies by heart, and could denounce Tory wrong-doing, and the political sins of the "Family Compact," in as vituperative language as Mackenzie himself. He was frequently called upon to speak at public meetings, and was always chosen to lead in the canvass, in his own and neighbouring townships. Meanwhile York had been changed to Toronto, and Mackenzie elected first Mayor, in 1834. In those times the Government selected the places of nomination in the constituencies to suit themselves. The places thus selected became the places of polling; and as there was only one polling place allowed for each riding, the poll was kept open for a week at a time, and frequently longer. The law was that the poll should be kept open as long as votes offered, provided an interval of an hour did not elapse without a vote being polled. It was only necessary to poll a single vote each hour in order to prolong an election contest. It was the season in which the tavern-keepers reaped a rich harvest, and it was a common practice with this class of gentry to hold a number of votes in reserve, bringing up one at a time within the hour when necessary to keep the contest going on. It was also the practice of the candidates, who expected voters from the distant townships, to keep a "reserve." And, if they were behind, this reserve was drawn upon and the battle kept up, so as to allow time for the arrival of their reinforcements. It was the practice then for candidates to keep open houses, providing refreshments and accommodation for their supporters. There was no restriction to the sale of liquors, or to treating. And as might be expected, those open public houses were fertile spots for securing plentiful crops of violence and bloodshed. Broken-heads and black-eyes were ordinary events. And sometimes men were maimed for life, or were killed outright, at those scenes of strife during an election contest. The constituencies were very large—some of them of as large an area as two of our present counties. The settlements were new and very much scattered, and the roads execrable. The amount of travelling and pulling and hauling required to get out the "free and independent" voters entailed an enormous amount of hard work. The franchise was then confined to freeholders exclusively, and as not many of them had their deeds, a freeholder who had was a very important person—at election time. A canvasser would drive a great many miles to secure even one vote. "I have myself," says Mr. Gould, "driven ten miles to get a voter, and found when I got to his house that my opponent had been there before me, and had secured the prize." That was no uncommon experience. In the struggle to get votes, he who could outwit his opponents was regarded not only as the "smartest" man, but he was considered the ablest man, and deserving of all honour. Mr. Gould remembered some amusing incidents in this connection.

At the general election of 1828, he first took a prominent part, and worked hard for Mackenzie, who came out "on his own hook" as a candidate for the county of York. The election managers did all in their power to keep Mackenzie out of the field. At a meeting of the committee held at Newmarket, Mackenzie only got three votes on the ballot for candidates. Mr. Small received nine votes, the other candidates, Roe and Ketchum, received, respectively, fifty-seven and forty-one. Mr. Gould distributed large numbers of Mackenzie's election address, one of which is preserved amongst his papers, and is here given:—

To the Electors of the County of York:

GENTLEMEN,—I have the honour to inform you that it is my intention to come forward as a candidate at the next election of members to serve for our County in the Provincial Parliament, and I most respectfully solicit your votes and support.

I have no end in view but the well-being of the people at large—no ambition to serve but that of contributing to the happiness and prosperity of our common country. The influence and authority with which you may invest me shall always be directed according to the best of my judgment for the general good, and it will be my care to uphold your rights to the utmost of my power, with that firmness, moderation and perseverance which become the representative of a free people.

If honoured with your suffrages it will be alike my duty and my pleasure to watch over the local interests of this great county, and to promote every public improvement and useful undertaking which shall be found conducive to your prosperity and the general welfare.

I have ever been opposed to ecclesiastical domination; it is at enmity with the free spirit of Christianity, and nations which have bowed to its yoke are become the dark abodes of ignorance and superstition, oppression and misery.

That corrupt, powerful and long-endured influence which has hitherto interfered with your rights and liberties can only be overthrown by your unanimity and zeal. An independent House of Assembly to Upper Canada would be inestimable.

I have been a careful observer of the conduct of the people's representatives in the Colonial Assemblies; I have seen men in whom was placed the utmost confidence fall from their integrity and betray their sacred trust; men, too, who had entered upon their legislative duties with the best intentions towards the people, and who evinced for a time a firm determination to support their rights. But there are others who continue to maintain and uphold the interests of their country unshaken and undismayed, who consider it their highest honour to persevere in a faithful discharge of their public duties, and eagerly strive to deserve the good-will, the affection and the confidence of their fellow subjects.

Among this latter class I am desirous of being numbered, and unless I shall be found deserting the cause of the people, I trust that the people will never desert me.

Accept my sincere thanks for the abundant proofs of kindness and confidence and for the liberal assurance of support with which you have honoured me, and believe me, gentlemen,

Your faithful and humble servant,

W. L. MACKENZIE.

York, December 17, 1827.

Mackenzie was elected, and his return was secured mainly through the activity and hard work of young Reformers like Mr. Gould.

At the general election in 1830, Mackenzie was again a candidate, and on the same side with him in the Reform interest was Mr. Jesse Ketchum. The candidates of the official party were Messrs. Washburn and Thorne. Again Mr. Gould worked heartily for his favourite, and with such good effect that both the Reform candidates were elected by large majorities.

Mackenzie having been expelled the Assembly for an alleged libel, his seat was declared vacant, and another election ordered. In January, 1832, Mackenzie was again returned by an overwhelming majority—his opponent, Mr. Street, receiving a very inconsiderable number of votes. Mackenzie was expelled a second time, and was also declared disqualified. Notwithstanding the disqualification he again appealed to the electors of York at the new election that had been ordered. The other candidates in this contest were Small and Washburn. Mr. Gould took his usual active part at the side of Mackenzie, and the latter was again returned by an overwhelming vote of the electorate. In the struggle that followed, between Mackenzie and the electors of York on the one hand, and the ruling faction and Family Compact on the other, who desired to exclude Mackenzie from a seat in the House, Mr. Gould was an active partisan on the Liberal side. Mackenzie might be dragged from his seat in the House, and resolutions of disqualification might be passed to prevent his election; but again and again was his cause taken up by Mr. Gould and his friends and Mackenzie sent back to the House. Even during Mackenzie's absence in England, with the petitions for the redress of grievances (1883–4), the men of York stood by him and secured his re-election. Mackenzie was expelled the House five times in all, and five times did Mr. Gould do successful battle for him in the county of York. After the division of the county into four ridings, when Mackenzie was defeated by E. W. Thomson, in the general election of 1836, none felt the defeat more keenly than Joseph Gould. The scenes which he witnessed, and the work which he went through in all these contests were ever afterwards remembered, and some of them frequently described in a most entertaining manner. One incident he was fond of recalling, which took place during the contest between Lafontaine and Roe for one of the ridings of York. Peter Tyler, an old bachelor, son of old Major Tyler, a great Tory, was working hard for Roe. The polling took place at Newmarket. Peter was sent to Uxbridge to assist in the campaign and get out all the votes he could. "But," says Mr. Gould, "I had forestalled him and had most of the votes forwarded for the Reform candidate before his arrival. Peter was told that there was one freeholder who had a deed of a lot beside my farm, that had not been brought out, but that the voter lived in Brock, some eight miles away, that the name was Mary Doble, an Irishwoman, and that she had a good deed. In speaking of Mrs. Doble, I do so with every respect, for she was a respectable woman and the mother of a respectable family. Well, away went Peter in search of the old lady. He found her out and managed to get her into the waggon, with five or six Orangemen, and started for Newmarket late in the after-noon. Before they had got half way through the twelve miles of unbroken forest, between Uxbridge and Newmarket, the axle of the

waggon broke, and they were all dumped down on the road. There
they were obliged to camp all night. It so happened that three of
our young men—wide-awake young Radicals from Sharon—who
had been out canvassing in Reach and Brock, came by that way
on horseback with several voters, and they overtook Peter with his
carload, just as the waggon had broken down. They asked them
if they were going to the election and who they intended to vote
for, and where the woman was going. She said she had as good a
deed as any of them, and that she was going to vote for Roe. Of
course they had a good laugh over the woman-voter that Peter was
taking to the poll, escorted by the Orangemen, and they rode off to
Newmarket, without attempting to give aid or comfort to the
enemy with the broken-down waggon. Mrs. Doble was met by one
of her neighbours before being taken to the poll, and upon his
assurance that women were not qualified to vote, she was induced
to turn back without exposing herself to further humiliation. But
Peter's predicament was long afterwards the subject of jokes and
fun at his expense, and from that out he was never seen at an
election contest." The Orangemen had long been a terror to the
peaceably disposed at elections, and, armed with bludgeons, and
sometimes with fire-arms, used to take possession of the polls, and
they subjected those who differed from them in opinion to all kinds
of ill-treatment.

Mr. Gould was upon one of those occasions attacked by four
red-hot Tories, who had previously threatened him with personal
violence; but he was prepared for them. He knocked down the
leader and the others fled. A warrant for his arrest was obtained
from Squire Bagshaw (his old enemy), and three constables were
sent to execute it. Mr. Gould heard of their coming towards his
house, and being dubious of the kind of justice that would be meted
out to him, and acting on the advice of friends, he resolved upon
having a second magistrate to try the case. With this intention

he mounted a spirited horse that he kept ready saddled. The constables tried to intercept him, and being armed, threatened to fire. But he made a sudden dash; rode the party down, and got safely away. He rode to Pickering and told his story to Squire Leys, who agreed to "sit on the case" with Bagshaw and prevent injustice being done. The result was the discharge of Mr. Gould, on payment of a nominal fine.

CHAPTER XVIII.

THE history of the misgovernment of Canada, which led up to the rebellion of 1837, is so well known to the average Canadian reader as to be now regarded as an old story. It has been already glanced at in these pages. Authors have printed their opinions respecting it, from various points of view. Viewed from Mr. Gould's standpoint the subject cannot be devoid of some further interest. He has, besides, a right to be heard in his own defence. In what follows his personal narrative is given, and in his own way as much as possible, and as far as is deemed consistent with the scope of this work, without too much repetition. The events recorded are taken altogether from the account which he has left behind him. And only in this way—by letting him tell his own story—can the motives by which he was actuated be fairly judged, for the part taken by him in the events described.

From 1830 to 1837-8, both the Canadian Provinces were in a state of ferment and continuous political excitement. Lower Canada had her old Feudal Tenure system of holding land, imported from despotic France; and her British constitution, imposed upon her after the Conquest by General Wolfe. The latter was only a cross between British freedom and French despotism, the former arranged expressly to protect the latter. And whilst her population was fully four-fifths of French origin, who had their French laws, their French language, their Catholic religion, and their nationality secured to them by the Treaty stipulations of 1763,— yet they were governed by a Governor and an Executive Council, appointed by the King during pleasure, and who were responsible to him alone. Their legislation was controlled by a House of Assembly, elected by the people, and a Legislative Council, appointed by the Crown for life, and responsible to no one. One cannot help wondering that the authors of such a system should not have foreseen the dangers of constant clashing between such discordant elements. With the power of the Crown so largely preponderating over the popular branch, it was impossible that any harmony could long subsist between legislative bodies so constituted. Crude and absurd as it was, however, it seems to have lasted without much modification for a period of nearly seventy years, culminating at length in open rebellion.

In Upper Canada political differences ran very high for the ten years prior to 1837. Petitions upon petitions were sent to England asking for the secularization of the Clergy Reserves, and for local self-government, but without effect. Delegates were sent to England to plead the cause of Canada, but without avail; the way to the throne was blocked by the Governor and by the Family Compact, who kept their agents in England. My reading informed me of all that was going on, and of what should have been the relative positions of the governed and the governor under the British constitution. I was firmly convinced that the demand of the people of Canada for responsible government was only what was fair, just and reasonable and should have been acceded to. And I never failed to speak out my sentiments in this respect when occasion called for it. I also took my stand against Orangeism. When Ogle R. Gowan was establishing Orange lodges and became Grand Master, and was getting up hostile demonstrations, not only against the Catholics, but against the Reformers, I opposed the views of such oath-bound secret societies. But the Orangemen were patronized by the Tory party, and have ever since been used as their tools.

When the petition signed by thirty thousand Canadians was sent to England laying our grievances at the foot of the throne, I did not shrink from saying that, just as was the demand, Mackenzie was not the most likely man to succeed in getting what was asked for. I admired the man and his noble advocacy of the cause of the people ; but he was blunt and outspoken and had a stand-and-deliver kind of a way that caused him to be an unsuitable negotiator. Mackenzie was a great agitator and an honest opponent of all jobbery and corruption, but he was very unyielding in his opinion. He found opposed to him in England such men as Bishop Strachan, Chief Justice Robinson, and Chief Justice Draper, who lobbied against him and obtained the ear of the British Government. They represented the French and Upper Canadians as being all disloyal, and as wishing to shake off their allegiance to Great Britain and become annexed to the United States. The result was that our petitions were thrown under the table, and were only unearthed after Lord Durham had made his report.

The irritation of the people by this neglect and injustice, the apparent indifference of the Home Government to all complaints and representations, the outrageous exclusiveness and nepotism of the governing faction, the powerless position of the Legislative Assembly, and the irresponsible form of government, all combined, must be a standing excuse for the unfortunate rebellion.

For myself, let me say that I was from my earliest recollection driven into antagonism against the ruling powers in Canada. First, by the action of the Government on the Alien Act. I saw my father deprived of his franchise under that infamous Act. He could neither vote nor receive votes, although he had the necessary property qualification and had worked hard for it. I saw the entire government in the hands of a lot of political sharks, known as the Family Compact. I saw an Executive Council ruling without responsibility. Judges, and confidential salaried officers of the Crown holding office, and expending the taxes raised from the people without any accountability for their acts, and generally controlling the legislation of the country. I saw, and could not fail to be influenced by the despotic tyranny, and the open corruption and bribery everywhere prevailing ; and I saw, with grief, the just remedy which the people demanded, of responsible government, refused them. Yet I did not believe in the extreme means resorted to, of open revolt. I thought and believed that we might still be able to convince the Home Government of the justice of our complaints without the last resort of taking up arms. And I certainly believe now that a remedy would have been applied, and all the trouble would have been avoided, had not the statesmen of England been misled by the Tory Family Compact of Canada. Had England sent out to us a statesman, such as Lord Durham, or Lord Elgin, at that time, when they sent Sir Francis Bond Head, I do not believe there would have been any rebellion. But instead of sending to Canada statesmen of ability and capacity, who would have seen through the monstrous working of the system imposed upon us, and who would have assisted in imposing restraints upon, or getting rid of a grasping oligarchy, they were constantly sending as our governors superannuated old military officers, or tenth-rate Poor Law Commissioners, who knew nothing about the principles of popular government, and had no sympathy with the people over whom they were sent to rule.

Of this last class, and the man who brought on the crisis, was Sir Francis Bond Head. He was an English Poor Law Commissioner, a weak wrong-headed man, whose government was even worse than that of any of his predecessors. He was appointed by the Whigs, then in power, and came out as a Reformer, with a flourish of trumpets, as the answer to the petitions carried home by Mackenzie, and pledged to remedy all our grievances. He commenced his administration by dismissing one half of the Executive Council, and appointing in their stead three leading Reformers, namely: Messrs. Baldwin, Rolph and Dunn. It was also known that he had instructions to appoint Mackenzie Postmaster-General, and to elevate Bidwell to a Superior Court Judgeship; and to initiate and bring about many of the reforms asked for. This change of policy, and the fact that Sir Francis was known to belong to the Liberal side of politics, was received with great rejoicing by Canadian Reformers. Public meetings were held and complimentary and loyal addresses to the Governor passed, and promises of cordial support given to assist him in his efforts to redress the grievances of the people, and he was everywhere received with acclaim as a tried and true Reformer and constitutional Governor. But those rejoicings were doomed to be of short duration. The Tories were at first quite shy of Sir Francis, and they petitioned the King against the first act of his administration. They also made an attempt at some public demonstrations against him. But the shrewd Family Compact leaders soon found out his weak side. They flattered him; and, being a weak man, he soon succumbed to their cajolery and blandishments. He turned his back upon his Reform friends and went over to the Tories completely. He acted with the latter quite privately at first. It was however, soon seen by his acts, and the character of the appointments which he made, what party was controlling the Administration. He made appointments to office without consulting his responsible advisers, and his selections were, with very few exceptions, taken from the Tory party. Sheriffs, magistrates, clerks of the peace, constables, etc., were appointed, not because of any qualifications they possessed for their offices, but because they were noisy Tory shouters and election canvassers. I have known magistrates to have been appointed at that time who could not sign their names. And young men, and even boys were appointed to office, and placed in the Commission of the Peace, simply because they happened to be sons of the ruling faction.

At first, Mr. Baldwin and his colleagues in the Government remonstrated, and claimed the right to be consulted upon all questions affecting the administration of the affairs of the country. They used strong and conclusive arguments to show that the claim was based upon the foundation of the Provincial Charter, and complained that they had incurred the odium of being held responsible for measures which they had never advised, and for appointments upon which they were not even consulted. And so far was popular opinion in favour of ministerial responsibility, even then, that the three Tory members of the Executive Council joined in the resignation of the Reform Ministers ; and all six united in an address to the Governor insisting upon their constitutional right of being consulted upon the affairs of the Province generally.

The Governor, upon the other hand, contended that he alone was responsible, being liable to removal and impeachment for misconduct, and that he was at liberty to have recourse to their advice only when he required it. As to consulting them upon all questions that he was called upon to decide he deemed it utterly impossible, and out of the question. He attempted to sustain his position by a reference to the charter and other instruments. The House of Assembly charged him directly with misquoting and garbling, and here ensued a hot, wordy war of windy paper-bulletins, in which the Governor got the worst of it. His correspondence with the House was mainly conspicuous for a total ignorance of the working of the British Constitution, and how it should be applied in our circumstances. It was also tinged with a haughty insolence that was sure to irritate, where sound policy required that he should have used all his influence to conciliate.

The author of the Life of "William Lyon Mackenzie" supplies a remarkable sample of Sir Francis Bond Head's style in this way, which is well worth reproducing :—

Sir Francis Bond Head having received an address, adopted at a public meeting of the citizens of Toronto, assured them that "he should feel it his duty to reply to them with as much attention as if it had proceeded from either branch of the Legislature; but that he should express himself *in plainer and more homely language*."

This was regarded as a slight by the "many-headed monster," and was resented with a bitterness that twenty years was too short to eradicate. The manner of the Governor gave as much offence as his words. He met the deputation, surrounded by a crowd of military officers, and the members fancied that he pried impudently into their faces as if he regarded them with a sort of curiosity that one would have looked upon a collection of ourang-outangs. The deputation left the presence of the Governor inspired with an intense feeling of indignation at the insolent slight that he had intentionally cast upon them, and determined to give him "a Roland for an Oliver," in the shape of a rejoinder. This was prepared by Dr. Rolph and Dr. O'Grady, and for biting, cutting, incisive sarcasm was a masterpiece. It was at the same time poorly calculated to narrow the breach that was fast growing wider between the Governor and the people's representatives in Parliament. And as this rejoinder is described by Mr. Mackenzie as the first low muttering of insurrection, and therefore is intended to include one of the excuses for the Rebellion, I think I cannot do better than copy Mr. Lindsey's version of it, which is as follows :—

" We thank Your Excellency," said the opening sentence, " for replying to our address—principally from the industrious classes of the city—with as much attention as if it had proceeded from either branch of the Legislature ; and we are duly sensible in receiving Your Excellency's reply of your great condescension in endeavouring to express yourself in plainer and more homely language ; presumed by Your Excellency to be thereby brought down to the lower level of our plainer and more homely understandings."

They then proceeded to explain the deplorable neglect of education, by the maladministration of former governments, of the endowment of King's College University, and the many attempts of the representative chamber, baffled by the Crown-nominated members of the Legislative Council, to apply three million acres of Clergy Reserve lands to the purposes of general education. " It is," they added, " because we have been thus maltreated, neglected and despised in our Educational and other interests, under the system of government that has hitherto prevailed, that we are now driven to insist upon a change, that cannot be for the worse."

The change which they wanted to bring about was—cheap, honest and responsible government.

The responsibility of the Governor to a Government four thousand miles off, and guarded by a system of secret despatches, like a system of espionage, which kept in utter darkness the very guilt, the disclosure of which could only consummate real and practical responsibility, had never, they said, saved a single martyr to the executive displeasure.

All peaceful means appearing to be exhausted, Mackenzie went on organizing his plan of political union of Reformers, regarding revolution as the only means of relief.

CHAPTER XIX.

MR. GOULD was not a willing participant in the active measures taken by Mackenzie which immediately followed. He repeats, with some emphasis, that he had confidence that the grievances complained of would be peacefully redressed by the Home Government, and he tells us that he personally tried to impress this conviction upon Mr. Mackenzie. "I told Mackenzie so," he says, "at Stouffville, one of his last secret meetings, only a week before the attack on Toronto, but was unable to dissuade him from his plans, and I was taunted with cowardice, because I refused to give encouragement or approval to violent measures."

Again, he says:—"On the same day that the attack was to be made, I found myself surrounded by about fifty of my friends from Brock, Scott and Uxbridge, who insisted upon my going with them. They refused to give heed to my remonstrances. They claimed that I should be manifesting a great deal of cowardice if I did not go with them after all I had said about the abuses we had complained of and from which the country was suffering. I therefore went with them. They were determined to go, and there was nothing else left for me, but to take my place amongst them. We arrived that evening at Montgomery's hotel, which was Mackenzie's headquarters, two miles north of the city. Mackenzie was then in the act of opening mail-bags and exhibiting their contents. I found that there was no order or discipline; that there had been no picket-guards put out, and that the whole party were liable to be surprised at any moment, and that probably before morning they would be surrounded and cut off. Tired as I was, after our long march, I determined to set pickets at once. This I did, and had the guard relieved until morning."

"Next morning they sent Captain Matthews with a few men (my brother Joel was one), to make a feint attack on Toronto, by the way of the Don Bridge, on the east side, while the main body was to make the attack on the north. But we had not got fairly organized when a messenger was sent to us from Toronto to say that the troops were marching up Yonge Street to attack us at Montgomery's. We soon got under arms and started down Yonge Street to meet them. The troops, however, turned to the west, and made as though they wanted to get round the west side to our rear. We hastened through the woods, climbing over dead hemlock trees and through the underbrush, and rushed to head them off. We had no arms but our rifles, and some had only rude pikes and pitchforks. The troops, besides their muskets and plenty of ammunition, had two small field pieces—one controlled by a friend of ours, and the other by an enemy. The friend fired grape shot, and fired over us into the tops of the trees, cutting off the dead and dry limbs of the hemlocks, which falling thickly amongst us scared the boys as much as if cannon balls had been rattling around us. The other gun was fired low, and so *careless* that I did not like it. One of the balls struck a sandbank by my feet and filled my eyes with sand, nearly blinding me. Another struck one of those dry hemlocks, scattering the bark and splinters about, and

into my face. Captain Wideman was killed on my left side, and
F. Shell was shot through the shoulder, to the left of the fallen
captain.   But we got to the west of the troops. They then turned
and crossed to Yonge Street behind us. It was soon known that
Montgomery's hotel was on fire and that the day was lost."

Such is the account left by Mr. Gould of his participation in
the rebellion of '37, and of the causes which influenced his action
in joining the ranks of the discontented.

Finding that "the day was," indeed, "lost," Mackenzie's undis-
ciplined host speedily dispersed in every direction, on the shortest
and quickest route to regain their homes. Mr. Gould and his
companions found themselves, he says, " on the wrong side of
Yonge Street to get home," without being intercepted by the
troops.   So he "and some six or seven more took to the woods,
thinking to go into the woods and camp out, or go to the States, by
Hamilton, or cross home by the woody ridge, by way of Stouffville,
and hide until we could go to the States." But they were surrounded and captured in the woods. They had supposed themselves safe, and had built a camp-fire in a swamp, where the
whole party was discovered and captured. They were escorted to
Toronto with other prisoners.

Prisoners were made right and left and brought into the city.
The gaol was crammed with them ; the courthouse was crowded ;
so were the Parliament Buildings.   Mr. Gould and his companions
were lodged in the Legislative Council chamber, the only quarters
that could be made available for their incarceration. And long
afterwards, it was one of his quiet jokes, when speaking of this
period of trouble, to refer to it, as the time when he first took his
seat in the Legislative Council ; or that his first seat in Parliament
was in the Legislative Council.

The principal land proprietors of Uxbridge were implicated in
the uprising. Amongst Mr. Gould's fellow-prisoners were Abram
Anderson, J. P. Plank, Bartholemew Plank and others.

After four or five weeks' confinement in the council chamber, the prisoners were brought up for examination before Messrs. Jamieson, Jones, Gurnett, Sullivan and W. B. Robinson. Mr. Gould was the first placed at the bar. He was questioned by Mr. Jamieson. Mr. Gould gives the following account of his examination :—

Jamieson asked me where I lived. I told him I lived at Uxbridge. "What do you do for a living?" he asked. I told him I had a sawmill. "A sawmill!" he exclaimed, as if that was a strong reason why I should not be there. "Yes, and a small farm, too," I added. "What! a farm and a sawmill! What more do you want?"—was his next remark. "What more do you want that you should rebel?" he continued. "I want my political rights," I answered. "Why," said he, "you have got them now—quite enough for so young a man as you are." I then had all our political grievances at the tip of my tongue, and began a rehearsal of the most prominent of them, when he stopped me.

After a pause he asked, "Do you believe all these complaints?"

I answered that the evidence was plain enough, and that the way the government of the country was administered was quite enough to show that, and that the people were denied their rights.

He then turned on his heel, and told me—"You are a dangerous fellow and you ought to be hung for believing and for spreading your treason."

I could only reply—"I am in your power, you can act your pleasure. I am neither afraid nor ashamed to express my sentiments."

He was then returned to prison.

Mr. Gould remained in custody until October, 1838, and having petitioned under 1 Vic. cap. 10 (passed 6th March, 1838), he was pardoned on giving security to keep the peace and be of good behaviour for three years. He had a narrow escape from transportation to Van Diemen's Land, as he was one of those unhappy prisoners singled out for penal servitude. The timely arrival of

Lord Durham in Canada fortunately saved him from that fate. His lordship arrived at Quebec on the 27th May, 1838, clothed with extraordinary powers. One of his first acts was a proclamation of amnesty to the political prisoners. Taking advantage of an auspicious season—the day fixed for the coronation of the Queen—he suddenly proclaimed a general amnesty of all political offences committed during the recent troubles: making exception, however of the cases of eighty persons; but even in their regard an intimation was made in the proclamation, that, after undergoing an exile for unspecified periods, they might hope to be restored to their country and homes as soon as the public safety would permit. There were further excepted from final pardon the murderers of a British subaltern officer, who was intercepted and slain while carrying despatches to his superiors at the outbreak of the late revolt. Of the eighty persons designated for banishment, some were in prison and the rest had fled abroad. The former were to be sent to Van Diemen's Land or Bermuda, and retained as convicts usually are. The Government having but a speculative power over the latter class of accused parties, could only forbid their return to the colony—unless by special permission—under severe penalties. This seemed to be a sage and humane as well as an easy way of surmounting a great difficulty. But unhappily, by ordaining the transportation of accused persons to penal colonies without the accustomed forms of law, Lord Durham became himself a violator of his country's laws; and as he had many enemies in the British legislature, the occasion was eagerly seized by the latter to denounce him personally, and damage the credit of the Cabinet under whose instructions he acted. By Canadians, and of course by those more immediately interested, charged with sedition and rebellion, his lordship's act of grace was most favourably regarded. It resulted in Lord Durham's resignation, but it served to tranquillize the country, and it gave peaceful security to the "disaffected" or those to whom suspicion was directed as such, by their "loyalist" neighbours.

Mr. Gould was not long in the enjoyment of freedom from his prison bonds until he surrendered himself (a willing captive) to the bonds of matrimony. Trusting, handsome Mary James remained faithful to her plighted troth, and welcomed his release from prison with open arms. Their marriage was duly solemnized on the first day of January, 1839. They were married by special license by the Revd. Mr. Stewart, Baptist minister, at the house of their mutual friend, Mr. Reid, corner of Queen and Yonge streets, Toronto. His fond hopes were at last realized. Throughout all his struggles and vicissitudes of fortune, he tells us, the hope of such a realization was his guiding star, and the affectionate assurances of his future wife his great support and comfort in all his troubles.

> And say, without our hopes, without our fears;
> Without the home that plighted love endears;
> Without the smile from partial beauty won,
> O! what were man?—a world without a sun!

Mrs. Gould survives her husband. She was born 14th October, 1816. For close on half a century of married life she was his devoted helpmate and true friend and companion. And in making ample provision for her future worldly comfort, Mr. Gould acknowledged how much both he and their children were indebted to the careful and economical habits, excellent management, and tender training of the good and loving wife and mother.

CHAPTER XX.

THE name of the county of Ontario is derived from the smallest of the great lakes, whose waters wash its shores on the south, and form the three harbours of Whitby, Pickering and Oshawa within the county on the south. While the extreme breadth of the county is only the width of two townships, or about eighteen miles, the length extends northward a distance of about sixty-six miles. The county of Ontario is bounded on the north by the township of Morrison in the county of Simcoe, on the south by Lake Ontario, on the east by the counties of Victoria and Durham, and on the west by the county of York, Lakes Simcoe and Couchiching, and the River Severn, which also separates it from the county of Simcoe.

The encroachments of the waters of Lake Simcoe on the west and north-west reduce the width of the county to a single township north of Brock—the average width thence being about eight miles, and the narrowest point (about the 9th concession of Thorah) extending but five miles across, from Lake Simcoe to the boundary line of Victoria.

The general face of the county, in the south, is rolling, the soil mostly a rich loamy clay. In the north, beyond the Ridges, which cross the county about eleven miles from Lake Ontario, the land is more of a level character, the soil fertile, and with plenty of limestone northward. The county is divided into two ridings, North and South Ontario, each riding sending one member to the House of Commons, and one each to the Local Legislature. The North Riding is in the electoral division of Queen's and the South Riding in King's Division. The limits of both ridings have been altered for the purposes of Parliamentary representation, both by the Dominion and Local Parliaments. And under what is commonly known as the "Gerrymander Act" of Sir John Macdonald, a portion of the western part of the county has been detached for the purpose of forming a new constituency, known as West Ontario. An Uxbridge man, Mr. George Wheler, was the first representative of this new constituency; it is now represented by Mr. J. D. Edgar, the well-known Toronto barrister, in the House of Commons.

The county proper, for municipal and judicial purposes, is composed of the following municipalities: Rama, Mara, Thorah, Brock, Scott, Uxbridge, Reach, Scugog, the town of Uxbridge, and villages of Port Perry, Cannington and Beaverton in the north; Whitby, East Whitby and Pickering, and the towns of Whitby and Oshawa in the south. These municipalities send thirty-five representatives, composed of the reeves and deputies of each municipalities, to the County Council. The North Riding has now an aggregate of twenty representatives, and the municipalities of the South Riding fifteen representatives.

Up to 1852, the county of Ontario was included in and formed part of the county of York. Ontario did not obtain its separate municipal existence as a county until the first of January, 1854. By an Act of the Canadian Parliament, passed in 1851 (14th and 15th Victoria, cap. v.), which came into force on the first day of January, 1852, the old county of York was divided into three counties, viz.: Ontario, York and Peel—the union of the three counties, for municipal purposes, continuing until the first of

January, 1854, when Ontario left the union, and commenced house-keeping on her own account.

The following is the proclamation made under the Act, and by which the then village of Whitby is erected into the County Town of the new county:—

PROCLAMATION.

Province of Canada. } Elgin and Kincardine.

VICTORIA, by the Grace of God, of the United Kingdom of Great Britain and Ireland, Queen, Defender of the Faith, etc., etc., etc.

To all to whom these presents shall come—Greeting :

W. B. Richards, { WHEREAS, under and by virtue of the power and authority Attorney Genl. { contained in an Act of Parliament of Our Province of Canada, passed in the Session thereof, held in the fifteenth year of Our Reign, intituled "An Act to make certain alterations in the Territorial Divisions of Upper Canada," Our Governor in Council of Our said Province hath resolved that a Proclamation under the Great Seal of Our said Province should be prepared, naming the Village of Whitby as a place within the County of Ontario, in Our said Province, for a County Town, and erecting the Town Reeves and Deputy Town Reeves of the said County of Ontario into a Provisional Municipal Council for the said County, as provided by the fourth section of the Act, and directing that the first meeting of such Provisional Municipal Council should be held in the said Village of Whitby, on Monday the third day of May next after the teste of this Our Procla-mation. And whereas Our said Governor in Council hath ordered that such Proclamation should issue and bear teste on the eleventh day of this present month of March : Now know ye that having taken into Our Royal consideration the Resolution so come to by Our said Governor in Council and fully approving of the same, we do this by Our Royal Proclamation, and in the exercise of the powers in us vested in this behalf by the said Act, or otherwise however, declare, ordain, proclaim and appoint the said Village of Whitby as the place within the said County of Ontario for County Town, and we do hereby in further pursuance of the said powers erect the Town Reeves and Deputy Town Reeves of the said County of Ontario, at the teste of this Our Proclamation elected, or thereafter to be elected for the same, into a Provisional Municipal Council for such

County, and declare such Municipal Council a Provisional Municipal Council under the authority of the Act passed in the twelfth year of Our Reign, intituled "An Act for abolishing the Territorial Division of Upper Canada, into Districts and for providing for temporary unions of counties for judicial and other purposes, and for the future dissolution of such unions as the increase of wealth and population may require," until the dissolution of the said County of Ontario with the Counties of York and Peel in Our said Province. And we do hereby further order, proclaim, ordain and direct, that the first meeting of the said Provisional Municipal Council for the said County of Ontario shall be held in the said Village of Whitby on Monday, the third day of May following the date of this Our Proclamation ; of all which premises all Our loving subjects, and all others whom it doth or may in anywise concern, are hereby required to take notice and govern themselves accordingly.

In TESTIMONY WHEREOF, we have caused these Our Letters to be made Patent, and the Great Seal of Our said Province of Canada to be hereunto affixed : Witness, Our Right Trusty and Right Well-beloved Cousin, James Earl of Elgin and Kincardine, Knight of the Most Ancient and Most Noble Order of the Thistle, Governor General of British North America, and Captain General and Governor in Chief in and over Our Provinces of Canada, Nova Scotia, New Brunswick and the Island of Prince Edward, and Vice-Admiral of the same, etc., etc., at Quebec, in Our said Province, this eleventh day of March, in the year of Our Lord one thousand eight hundred and fifty-two, and the fifteenth year of Our Reign.

By Command,

A. N. MORIN, *Secretary.*

CHAPTER XXI.

AFTER the Conquest in 1760, when Canada passed under
British rule, the Province was divided into districts. These
district-divisions were extended in 1788 under the following
proclamation :—

PROCLAMATION.

GEORGE III., by the Grace of God, of Great Britain, France and
Ireland, King, Defender of the Faith, and so forth.

To all Our Loving Subjects, whom these presents may concern, greeting :

WHEREAS Our Province of Quebec stands at present divided only into two
Districts, and by virtue of two certain Acts or Ordinances, the one passed
by Our Governor and Legislative Council in the twenty-seventh year of Our
Reign, and the other in the present year, provision is made for forming and
organizing one or more new Districts : Now, therefore, know ye, that Our
Governor of Our said Provinces, and in pursuances of the Acts and Ordinances, hath formed, and doth hereby form the several new Districts herein-
after described and named, to wit : The District of Lunenburg bounded on
the east by the eastern limit of a tract lately called or known by the name
of Lancaster, protracted northerly and southerly as far as Our said Province
extends, and bounded westerly by a north and south line, intersecting the

mouth of the River Gananoque, now called the River Thames, about the rifts of the Saint Lawrence, and extending southerly and northerly to the limits of Our said Province, therein comprehending the several towns or tracts called or known by the names of Lancaster, Charlottenburg, Cornwall, Osnabruck, Williamsburg, Matilda, Edwardsburg, Augusta and Elizabethtown; and also one other District to be called Trent, discharging itself from the west into the head of the Bay of Quinty, and therein comprehending the several Towns or Tracts called or known by the names of Pittsburg, Kingstown, Ernestown, Fredericksburg, Adolphustown, Marysburg, Sophiasburg, Ameliasburg, Sydney, Thurlow, Richmond and Camden; and also one of the Districts to be called the District of Nassau, extending from the north and south bounds of Our said Province, from the western limit of the last mentioned District, so far westerly as to the north and south line, intersecting the extreme projection of Long Point into the Lake Erie on the northerly side of the said Lake Erie; and also one other District to be called the District of Hesse, which is to comprehend all the residue of Our said Province in the western or inland parts thereof, of the entire breadth thereof from the southerly to the northerly boundary of the same; and also one other District to be called the District of Gaspe, and to comprehend all that part of Our said Province on the southerly side of Saint Lawrence to the eastward of a north and south line, intersecting the north-easterly side of Cape Cat, which is on the southerly side of the said river; of which all Our Loving Subjects are to take due notice and govern themselves accordingly.

In Testimony Whereof, we have caused these Our letters to be made patent, and the Great Seal of Our said Province to be hereunto affixed. Witness Our Trusty and Well-beloved Guy Lord Dorchester, Captain General and Governor in Chief of Our said Province, at Our Castle of Saint Lewis, in Our City of Quebec, the twenty-fourth day of July, in the year of Our Lord one thousand seven hundred and eighty-eight, and of Our Reign the twenty-eighth.   GEORGE POWNALL,
                                                            Secretary.

At the end of the Revolutionary War many families who had settled in the States, and remained true to British connection, were persecuted by the triumphant insurgents for their loyalty. There was a general confiscation of their possessions and they were driven to seek a home elsewhere. Numbers of the refugees settled in Canada after undergoing terrible hardships. Other Americans sought a home under the British flag from less patriotic motives. They discovered the "sunny spots" along the north shore of Lake Ontario, found that the soil was good, drew their 200 or 400 acres of land, and the three-years' rations, (then supplied pioneer settlers), from the nearest fort or garrison. And this class of settlers had no objection whatever to be classed as U. E. L.'s, notwithstanding that their sympathies were altogether with the "patriots." They became excellent settlers, and they throve on the virgin soil of Canada. Not a few of this class entered and took up their abode in the county of Ontario during the years of calm which succeeded, and have been erroneously claimed as persecuted U. E. L.'s. They, however, in the course of time, and their families became good British subjects, and at this distance of time, it would be a difficult, as well as an unnecessary and ungracious task to point out who were the real and who the pretended "loyalists," who had found out that they were likely to fare better under the proclamation of Governor Simcoe, with the disbanded soldiers and loyalists, than in the struggle for a home in Uncle Sam's dominions.

The first settlers took possession of the most tempting and accessible spots along the Lake shore. In this way, Whitby and Pickering, the two front townships of the county of Ontario, were first entered. The family of Benjamin Wilson (claiming to be a U. E. L.), the first known settlers in the county, entered the township of Whitby in 1794. Wilson was a Vermonter, and was born in the town of Putney, in the "Green Mountain State." For a couple of years they had no other near neighbour than the Indians—and the latter appear to have been somewhat troublesome at first. The first year a band of Chippaways swooped down upon the lone white settlement, and carried off the whole year's provisions which had been supplied the family by the Government. The frightened family fled in terror from their little settlement, stopping at a point further down the Lake, afterwards called Barber's Creek, in Darlington. The chief of the tribe, named Wabokishees, had been absent when the settler's shanty was looted, and on his return was very angry at what had happened. He compelled the Indians to give back all the provisions that were left, and to make ample payment, in furs, to the Wilsons for such portion as had been consumed. This chief also gave Wilson a belt of wampum as a "peace belt," to hang up in his shanty, telling the white settler that thereafter, as long as the belt was kept in sight, there need be no apprehension of trouble from the Indians. After that the Indians became most friendly, and brought the white family plentiful supplies of fish and venison.

The settlement of the Farewells is another of the earliest traceable, and there is somewhat of a little spice of romance about it. A. Moody Farewell and his brother, William, were the sons of a widow who came with her two boys from Oswego to Niagara, where she settled down in the time of Governor Simcoe. There she contracted a second marriage with Sergeant Cranford, of the Queen's Rangers, and at the time of the removal from Niagara to York, in 1796, came with her husband to the latter place. Cranford got 400 acres of land and the ferry at the Humber. But it appears that, with a soldier's want of thrift, characteristic of the time, he permitted what would have been a splendid competence to slip through his hands without realizing any substantial benefit from his good fortune.

About the beginning of the century, the two Farewell boys started in a canoe from York down along the lake shore—literally "paddling their own canoe"—in order to spy out a place of settlement for themselves. They landed at the mouth of the Oshawa Creek. And there they took up and settled upon the land, where they made a home and afterwards lived for so many years, and on which their descendants still reside. A. Moody Farewell was the father of Mr. Abraham Farewell, ex-M.PP., who is still living, and the ancestor of the numerous family of the

Farewells of Harmony. The frame house, built by Mr. Abraham
Farewell, still standing at the latter place, was raised on the day
of the declaration of war between England and the United States
in 1812. Old Mr. Moody Farewell used to relate how he was
frequently chased by wolves along the front road, and especially at
the Cedar Swamp near Bartlett's, between Whitby and Oshawa,
in those early days. Up to 1804, there was no house between
Farewell's, east of Oshawa, and Lynd's, at Lynd's Creek, west of
the present town of Whitby.

The Farewell brothers, in addition to their farming operations,
engaged, as most settlers did at the time, in hunting and trapping,
disposing of the furs secured by them at York. About two years
after their settlement, the brothers went out to Lake Scugog to
trade with the Indians for furs. They left a man named John
Sharp in charge of the camp while they proceeded up the Scugog.
On their return they found the unfortunate Sharp murdered, his
skull having been smashed in with a club. They quickly left the
spot, and hastened back to their settlement. They told the story
of the murder to Eleazir Lockwood, then just settled on the lake
shore, and who afterwards (in 1802) became collector for the
townships of Whitby and Pickering, as portions of the Home
District. Lockwood stated that he had noticed the Indians
camped on the shore, on their way to Toronto, a day or two previously; some of them, he said, were intoxicated, and it was
dangerous venturing near them. One of them, whom he knew, a
desperate " brave," named O-go-ton-og-cut, was very demonstra-
tive, and went through all the motions, showing how he had killed
poor Sharp. This performance was watched by Lockwood from a
distance. Having got hold of the story of the murder and a clue
to the murderer in this way, Lockwood started for York after the
Indians. He gave information to Col. Givins, the Indian Superintendent. The band of Indians were found encamped on the island
outside York. A warrant was issued, a sergeant and guard pro-

cured and the murderer arrested, having been quietly given up by the same chief who compelled the restoration of Wilson's goods.

Counsel was assigned to the Indian, and on the trial at York he successfully raised the question of jurisdiction. The question was as to whether the crime had been committed within the Home District or the Newcastle District. The formation of the new districts had only a short time previously taken place. It was decided that the locality of the murder was within the Newcastle District, and that the prisoner should be tried at Newcastle. This Newcastle was at Presqu' Isle, near the Carrying Place, in the present county of Northumberland, at which a courthouse had been located. A schooner, *The Speedy*, had been provided, on which were embarked the judge, Judge Cochran, Mr. A. Mac-Donell, Sheriff, the Indian prisoner, constables, witnesses, Crown prosecutor, and others connected with the trial, or having business before the court. The schooner left York in fine calm weather with all on board well. Sad to say, she never arrived at her destination! The ill-fated vessel is supposed to have foundered, and all on board were lost!

The court was kept adjourning from day to day in the vain hope of the appearance of the prisoner and those on board with him, until all hope of the safety of the vessel was abandoned. Moody Farewell and Eleazir Lockwood went down to the beach to board the schooner, but they missed the passing boat—their tardiness in this instance saving them from a watery grave. Amongst those on board was the Solicitor-General for Upper Canada, Robert Isaac De Grey.

By the will of Solicitor-General De Grey, dated 1808, he devises 200 acres, lot No. 11, 1st concession of Whitby, to "his slave servant, Simon, and his heirs for ever; and to his 'other black servant, John, 200 acres, lot 17 in the 2nd concession, Whitby.'" Another provision of the will runs as follows: "I feel it a duty incumbent on me, in consequence of the long and faithful services of Dorinda, my black woman-servant, rendered to my family, to release, manumit and discharge her and all her children from the state of slavery in which she now is, and to give her and all her children their freedom. My will therefore is that she be released; and I hereby accordingly release, manumit and discharge the said Dorinda, and all and every one of her said children, both male and female, from slavery, and declare them and every of them to be free. And in order that provision may be made for the support of the said Dorinda and her children, and that she may not want after my decease, my will is, and I hereby empower my executors, out of my real estate to raise the sum of twelve hundred pounds currency, and place the same in some solvent and secure fund, and the interest accruing from the same, I give and bequeath to the said Dorinda, her heirs and assigns for ever, to be paid annually."

The black servant-men are also freed by the testator. According to this, it would appear that slavery existed in Canada as late as 1803, and that the two lots of land in the township of Whitby, mentioned in the will, were originally devised to manumitted slaves. Slavery was abolished by law in Upper Canada in 1793—a fact which of course must have been well known to the Solicitor-General. But it may be conjectured that he wished to place the right of his former slaves to hold real property beyond all doubt, by the terms of his will.

CHAPTER XXII.

THE names of the earliest recorded settlers along the lake shore are those of Wilson, Farewell, Lockwood, McGahen, Ransom, Majors, Wilson, Knight, Shales, Stiles, Cranford, Rummerfeld, Munger, Lloyd, Marvin. These occur in fragmentary records of the townships of Whitby and Pickering from 1801 to 1808. The Burks, Trulls and Conats had previously, in 1794, settled on Barber's Creek, now Darlington. Mr. Lovekin, an Irishman, settled in the adjoining township of Clarke, in 1795.

Whitby and Pickering, the two front townships of the county, were first surveyed part in 1791, and the remainder surveyed and laid out in 1795. The earliest record of township matters begins with 1801. There is an old municipal book extant, the first date in which is 4th June, 1801, giving the marks of cattle, sheep and hogs, "belonging to the inhabitants of Pickering and Whitby." The following extracts are given from the recorded minutes—the original orthography being retained:—

"*A record of a meeting for chusing the Town Officers and other Regula-*

tors for the towns of Pickering and Whitby, held at the house of Samuel Munger in Pickering—March 7th day, 1803."

EBENEZER RANSOM, *Town Clerk.*

JOHN MAJORS,
ELEAZIR LOCKWOOD, } *Assessors.*

ANTHONY RUMMERFIELD,
ADAM STEPHENS, } *Town Wardens.*

DAVID STEPHENS, *Collector.*

SAMUEL MUNGER,
MATTHEW DEWILLGER,
JOHN McGAHEN,
WM. PECK,
DAVID CRAWFORD, } *Pathmasters.*

DAVID LLOYD,
ABRAHAM TOWNSEND, } *Fenceviewers.*

SILAS MARVIN, *Poundkeeper.*

"A voted cal'd and passed that no Hogg shall be free comener Except they will wey more than Forty w't."

"Voted that no fence be Lawful except it mea sure 4½ Feet high and two feet at the bottom the Rails not to be more than 4 inches a part. Meeting closed until warned again." ·

"Received of Mr. E. Lockwood, Collector of the townships of Pickering and Whitby for the year 1802, Five pounds 19s. Halifax Currency being in full Accruing to the Assessment Roal for that year Returned."

"WM. ALLAN,
     Treasurer. } H. D.

"£5, 19sh.
"*York, 18th April, 1803."*

Whitby and Pickering would appear to have been united in the Home District at this date.

The names of Woodruff, Carr, Brisbin, Smith, Lynde are names of old settlers which occur in the old township records previous to 1812.

Jabez Lynde settled on the Creek, still known by his name, immediately west of the town of Whitby, in 1804. Splendid salmon were caught in the same creek in those early days. It was a usual method to kill the fish with a pitchfork from a log stretched across the creek. Deer were plentiful, and were frequently chased by wolves up to the door of the dwelling. Instances were mentioned by the old settlers of the hunted animals running into the little shanty dwellings along the creek for safety. Mr. Lynde was employed by the Government to forward despatches between York and Kingston; he also made purchases for the Government Commissariat. When his house—the present residence of Miss Lynde at the creek was built—it was considered the best dwelling between Kingston and Toronto. It was a stopping place for the troops on their marches, and appears to have been used as an hostelry. Dan Smith and a man named Quick lived on the lake shore of Whitby in 1803. A Miss Cross kept the first school in a little log hut opposite Nightingale's, now Mr. William Blair's farm. In 1811 Mr. Samuel Cochrane settled on the old Cochrane homestead; he was out in the War of 1812, and enjoyed a pension up to the time of his decease a few years ago. Mr. Cochrane came from Vermont, but was of Irish descent. John Hyland, John B. Warren and William Warren, Lawrence Hayden and O'Callaghan Holmes were all Irishmen who settled in the township of Whitby between 1812 and 1820. "Squire" Armstrong and "Dr." Still were their neighbours. The only post office on the front road next to Toronto was then at Hamer's Corners, then called Crawford's Corners, where Mr. John Spurrill now lives. The nearest doctor lived at Toronto. The Warrens commenced storekeeping in 1823 at Hamer's Corners, and kept the first post office. Theirs was the only store between Port Hope and Toronto at that time. The Warrens were called 'The Irishmen," two Scotchmen, brothers named McGregor, were called "the Scotchmen," and the two Huggins brothers, "the Englishmen." Land of the best quality in the township and along the front road could then be bought at $4 and $5 an acre. There were no settlers farther back than the 3rd concession. Mr. Lawrence Hayden kept a store for ten or a dozen years on the front road before moving to Toronto. The Warrens built the gristmills at Oshawa. William Warren held the office of Collector of Customs at Whitby for many years; he died a few months ago at a very advanced age. The Deharts and Mackies were early settlers, as were also the families of Hodge, Colley, Stevens, Pickell, Hall, McGregor, McGill, Hull, Trull, Henry, Dullea, Annes, Howard, Corneille, Ross, Bartlett, Skae, Wood, Nicols, Taylor, Crawford, Griffin, Losie and Farquharson.

James Hall settled on the lake shore in 1820. Ezra Annes was an earlier arrival, and was at first a clerk for Losie who kept a small store. Losie became embarrassed, and his estate was purchased by Ezra Annes. The latter became an active magistrate and raised a large family. Mr. Fred. Howard Annes, his grandson, now owns the old family homestead. George McGill, who settled in 1822, was a native of Wigton, but came from Paisley, Scotland, to Canada, and penetrated the woods as far back as the 3rd concession to make a homestead. He was the father of Dr. William McGill, ex-M.PP., of Oshawa, and of Col. John McGill. The old gentleman lived to see his ninety-seventh year.

Joseph Goreham built a fulling and carding mill south of the present town of Oshawa; and previous to that Moody Farewell built a mill and small distillery on the Little Creek.

John Gibbs settled in what is now South Oshawa, in 1829, and in conjunction with his brother Thomas bought the mills known as the South Oshawa Mills. The latter was the father of Hon. T. N. Gibbs and of William H. Gibbs, who for a number of years were extensively engaged in business in Oshawa, and both of whom represented the two ridings of North and South Ontario in the Dominion Parliament—T. N. Gibbs becoming a cabinet minister in the Government of Sir John Macdonald. Old Mr. Gibbs was an Englishman from Devonshire.

Dr. Lowe became a resident of Whitby in 1828. Dr. Hunter was cotemporary with him. Both gentlemen were subsequently prominent, at opposite sides, in the rebellion of 1837. Dr. Lowe commanded a company of the volunteer militia, and was " hot " after the " rebels." Dr. Hunter was arrested and kept a prisoner for some time, and was afterwards discharged after examination before the commissioners.

William Dow settled on the farm known as " Glendhu " (still owned by his grandson W. H. Dow), in the 3rd concession, in 1833. He came from Banffshire, Scotland, landing in Quebec with his family in August, 1832. From Quebec they went to the Eastern Townships, remaining at Stanstead until the February following. Thence, with three teams of six horses, they came up through the State of New York, crossing the ice at Ogdensburg, and arrived at Whitby in the beginning of March, 1833. Mr. Dow was one of the foremost agriculturists of his day, and led the way in agricultural improvements in the county. He joined with Francis Leys, of Pickering (mentioned elsewhere), in importing the first bull. Mr. Dow had a large family of sons and daughters, whose numerous descendants occupy respectable positions. The only surviving son is Mr. Thomas Dow, manager of the Western Bank at Whitby, now well up in years, and justly well esteemed by his friends and neighbours, amongst whom he has lived from his boyhood. The late Dr. Foote was married to one of the daughters. Mr. Hugh Miller, J.P., of Toronto, married another. John Ball Dow, barrister, of Whitby, also represents the family as a grandson of the first settler.

William Gordon, of Bayside, who died a few years ago, was another highly respected old settler on the lake shore of the old township of Whitby. He was father of Adam Gordon, late M.P. for North Ontario, of William Gordon, merchant, Toronto, J. K. Gordon, barrister, Whitby, and has left numerous descendants.

George McGillivray, of Inverlynn, west of the town of Whitby, is another very old settler. He came from Fergus, Scotland, some fifty-five years ago, and engaged in farming in Whitby. He married a daughter of Mr. Charles Fothergill, editor of the *Weekly Register*. Mr. Fothergill sat in the Provincial Parliament in 1832 as member for Northumberland, and took an active part in the politics of the day. He was deprived of the office of King's printer for giving expression to his liberal and independent opinions. It was he who first originated the law establishing agricultural societies. He published the " York Calendar " and " Royal Almanac " for several years. He was also an eminent naturalist. Mr. John Fothergill, of Whitby, his grandson, now represents the family name. Mr. and Mrs. McGillivray have a numerous family of sons and daughters, and are still hale and hearty though advanced in years. Mr. John A. McGillivray, barrister, of Uxbridge, and the opponent of Mr. Isaac Gould in the late Provincial elections contest, is one of the sons.

The Tweedies, Farquharsons, Howards, Campbells, of Brooklin, Drydens, the families of Betts, Delong, Fisher, Lamon, Heron, Blair, Burns, Michael, Spencer, Anderson, Calder, Ogston, Jeffrey, Thomson, Martin, Starr, were all early settlers of the township of Whitby long before the agitation for the setting off of the new county. John Dryden, the member for South Ontario in the Legislative Assembly, worthily represents the family name. He lives on the old homestead first settled by his father in 1826, on the 7th concession. His splendid property, known as Maple Shade Farm, comprising some six hundred acres, is one of the finest and best cultivated farms in the Province.

In those early days the kirk, built on Starr's Hill, between Whitby and Oshawa, accommodated all the residents of the old township, including the villages of Whitby and Oshawa, as a place of worship. Previous to that a little frame building, known as the Baptist Church, was the place in which all township meetings and public gatherings were held. An old resident says that after these meetings, and at all raisings and logging-bees, there was much drinking indulged in. Whiskey was the liquor invariably produced

ipon such occasions, and was consumed in large quantities. It was
sold at from twenty to twenty-five cents a gallon, and was often
indulged in to a deplorable extent.

The old township was divided into two separate municipalities
in 1857—the eastern division being since known as the township
of East Whitby, while the western part retained the old appellation
of the township of Whitby. The area of the present township is
31,660 acres, all good farming land. Valuation, $1,781,992.

The principal villages are Brooklin, Ashburn and Myrtle.

CHAPTER XXIII.

THE township of East Whitby embraces an area of 34,700 acres;
population about 8,400. According to last returns the assessed
value was $1,809,000; number of ratepayers on assessment roll
over 800. The first early settlers selected the land along the Reach
Road, or Simcoe Street. They were the families of Dearborn,
Ratcliffe, Widdifield, Kerr, Masson, Jameyson. Farther north, in
the vicinity of Columbus, or English's Corners, as the village was
formerly called, were the families of Wilcockson, Harper, Ashton,
Adams, Webster, Carey; and still further back the Smiths,
Hodgson, Fisher and Harnden. The latter built the first gristmill
on the stream near the Ridges. It was a curiosity in its way—the
bed-stone being an upright concave, and the moving-stone in the
form of a grindstone working in the cavity. The same stream was
utilized in several places to operate sawmills—there being, at that
time, quite a sprinkling of white pine on the Ridges.

On the extreme east of the township the Government cut out
one of the road allowances, two rods wide, as far back as the rear
of the 6th concession, in 1831, and nearly all that section of the
township was settled in that and the following year or two. The
ancestors of the families of Wright, Gould, Pickle, Beggs, Gilford,
Pascoe, Luke, Ormiston, Gregg, Hutchinson, Graham, Stephens,
Millar, Ratcliff, Campbell, Maltman, Hyland, Howden were all first

settlers in the bush in this neighbourhood. Most of those named were successful farmers, and the land reclaimed by them from the forest continues in great part in the hands of their descendants.

John Harper was the first settler to erect a sawmill on the east branch of the Oshawa Creek. Luke and Pascoe, Ray, Campbell and others afterwards used the same stream—Ray being the first to erect a gristmill on the spot now occupied by J. Goodman. This and the gristmill, put up some time later by W. H. Gibbs, half a mile east of Columbus, on the other branch of the Oshawa Creek—and where the first local market for wheat was established—were a a great boon to the young settlement, which quickly grew and expanded on the first-class land with which the whole locality is favoured. Few of the old pioneers could afford to keep a horse during the first years of occupation. Mr. Wright was an exception ; and to him many of the early settlers were obliged to have recourse for the use of his mare to carry a grist to the mill on a pinch. Indeed, we are told, that the mare was always at the service of a neighbour whenever required upon an emergency. An ox-cart belonging to the same neighbourly old gentleman was for a long time the only vehicle in the settlement. It was never refused to a neighbour. If a neighbour wanted to borrow it, and it had not then been returned by the previous borrower, Mr. Wright would say :—" I have an ox-cart somewhere ; if you can find it take it ; but for long spells I only see it when passing on the road behind somebody's oxen." The old gentleman, very far advanced in years, was still living, at Harriston, up to a few years ago.

The principal villages in the township are Columbus, Raglan, Cedar Dale, Foley and Harmony.

CHAPTER XXIV.

PART of the record of the old township of Whitby also belongs to Pickering. Like Whitby it is a fine, fruitful, well-tilled, well-farmed and well-settled township ; the character of the soil a loamy clay, and the face of the country well watered. It embraces an area of 74,660 acres ; Population, 7,375 ; number of ratepayers, nearly 2,000. Total value of real and personal property, $3,918,429. The principal villages are Pickering, Brougham, Greenwood, Claremont, Whitevale, Balsam, Kinsale, Green River, Dunbarton and Audley.

The name of Peak, of Duffin's Creek, occurs in old records previous to the year 1800, and is the oldest ascertained in connection with the settlement of the township. The names of the earliest settlers have been already given in the lists of the township of Whitby. In subsequent records, having reference to Pickering alone, the following are found. Under date of 1811, this is the entry in the first township book in which any records were regularly kept :—

"*Agreeable to an Act of the Legislature of this Province, made and passed in the thirty-third year of His Majesty's reign, for the purpose of choosing and nominating certain fit and proper persons to serve as Parish and Town officers, we, the inhabitants of this Town, met the first Monday of March for the purpose of choosing the following officers :*

THOMAS HUBBARD, *Town Clerk.*

DAVID CRAWFORD,
JOHN HAIGHT, } *Assessors.*

ABRAHAM TOWNSEND, *Collector.*

NOADIAH WOODRUFF,
THOMAS MATTHEWS, } *Pathmasters.*
JOHN LAWRENCE,

JOSEPH WIXSON, } *Poundkeepers.*
TIMOTHY ROGERS,

JOHN RICHARD, } *Town Wardens.*
JAMES POWELL,

"By-law.—Voted that fences be four and a half feet high, and not more than five inches between rails."

In the next year, under date of March 2, 1812, the name of Nicholas Brown is to be found as one of the "Sessors." James "Lamoru" occurs as pathmaster. And there is the following brief and very explicit memorandum at foot :—

"Our Town offisors war Put in By the Qarter Sesons for the year, A.D., 1813, By Reason of the Wor that was Declearede against us By the States in the year 1812."

"By the Same Reason our townd metin war omited in the year, A.D., 1814 and our Town officors war Put in the same manner.

Timothy Rogers, who built a small mill at Duffin's Creek, was one of the earliest settlers. Nicholas Brown came in from Vermont in 1810, and after him came the Quaker settlement of the same numerous family in Pickering. The family of the Haights were of the same period.

In 1815 the names of McCauslin (McCausland), Stott, Clark and Smith occur amongst the town officers.

In 1816 Vanceleek (Vankleek), Post, Flowerfield, Powell, Crawford, Ray are new names occurring amongst the elected officers. And there is a by-law passed, as follows :—

"Hogs is not to run as free commoners nor horses."

If the grammar be not the best, there is a brevity in this early law-making phraseology that might well commend itself to the law-makers of the present day.

The names of James Sharrard, Peter Matthews, Joseph Brown and Samuel Doolittle appear in the list of township officers for 1817.

And in 1818 the names of Spenser, Udell and Andrew Losson. In this year the following by-law was passed, which is given *verbatim* from the original.

" By-law.—Hogs is not allowed to run on the commons without a yoak that is six inches above the Neck and four Below."

There are added to the list of township officers for 1820 the names of Zephania Jones, James Wood and Daniel Yeak. The entries made are :—

" Voted—That our fences is to be Nabourly and Law full."
" Voted—That Horses shal not be commoners."

In 1821 the names of Joseph Winters, George Caster, Asher Wilson and Joseph Webster are found amongst the list of officers.

Similar by-laws to the specimens already given were passed restraining horses, hogs and cattle from running at large; and also a resolution appointing " the next meeting to be holden at John Major's in 1822."

In this latter year James Brown, Samuel Eves, Solomon Sly, George Anderson, John Albright and Cornelius Churchill appear as township officers. By-laws as to fences and cattle are again passed at the annual meeting.

Next year (1823), John Sharrard becomes " town clerk," and Thomas Hubbard, collector; Joshua Richardson, John Blair and David Wood, pathmasters.

The family of the Richardsons came from the Queen's County, Ireland, and have numerous representatives of the old stock in Pickering and Whitby.

In 1824 Silas Orvis, Reuben Steel, John Henry, Daniel Betts,

William Smith and William Losie appear on the list; and the following are placed under the head of by-laws:—

"Firstly—Voted that the fences shall be five feet high, and not more than four inches between rails two feet from the ground."

"2nd—That hogs are to run at large till they do damage, and then the owner of the hogs is to pay the same, and yoke them with a croch yoke, six inches above the neck and four inches below the neck, and let them run."

"3rd.—That any unruly Creature of any description, either horse, cow, bull, mully, or young creature of any sort or size shall not be a free commoner, but shall be liable to be taken up and put in the pound by any person, either man or woman, or boy, and the owner shall pay all damages, poundage and costs, whether said Creature was found doing damage or not."

These samples of early by-laws are worth preserving, although they are unlikely to be followed as precedents by the Pickering Councils of to-day.

William Sleigh appears as township clerk in 1825. Elijah Foster and George Clark are new names amongst the township officers of this year. And in the next few years up to 1835, we find, year after year, the addition of well-known names long connected with the township, such as Francis Leys, Joseph Morel, John Cair, Anos Griswold, George Barclay, George Caster, Robert Gager, William Carling, William Peck, Alexander Dunlop, Benjamin Cool, Ezekiel McWain, Eli Leavens, John Davis, Lawrence Smith, Geo. Berry, Abraham Stoner, James Monger, Thos. Thompson, Parnell Webb, John Laur, William Crothers (Carruthers), William Hattrick, Nicholas Austin, John Palmer, Joel Hughes, Timothy Gates, Benjamin Locke, Robert Richardson, James Richardson, William Wright, John Tool, Job Burton, David Richmond, Michael B. Judge, James McKay, Abm. Knowles, Landon Wurts, Ashael Scott, B. Blanchard, Christian Stoffer, Joseph Chapman, John Terry, Israel Gibbs, Benjamin Holmes, Chas. Ward, John Laman, Jno. Van Horne, Platt Betts, Alex. Horsburg, Richard Lankern, Danl. O'Brien, Thomas Reazin, Isaac Campbell, Chas. Hadley,

Josh. Thornton, Martin Niswander, Allan Granger, Saml. Plumb, Jas. Rowe, Peter Rushnell, David Crider, Robt. Knox, Roland Brown, Ambrose Boon, Richard Dale, Urick Burkholder, John Jackson, Joseph Gormley, William Wilkie, Ebenezer Birrell, Wm. Bice, Wm. Tracey, A. K. Stevens, Wm. Dunbar, Thos. Annan, Jacob Waltenberger and others, amongst the Wixsons, Woodruffs, Rogers, Sharrards, Browns, Haights, Posts, Mathews, Dales, Reazins, and Churchills of earlier years.

When Mr. Birrell settled in 1834, there were few settlers back of the 6th concession, and even that concession line was but partially opened. The leading roads were the front, or Kingston Road, and the Brock Road, running through the centre of the township north into Brock. The leading men on the front road then were Squire Galbraith, a P.L.S., and Squire Leys, who kept the only store and post office in Pickering for years. Mr. Leys was a very prominent man in the township; he was a commissioner of the Court of Requests, and his house was a great place of resort. The court sat in what was known as Squire Leys's schoolhouse. The other members of the court at that time were Mr. Smith, J.P., who lived at the "Creek," Donald McKay, Squire Fothergill and Dr. Boyes. Mr. Francis Leys was father of John Leys, M.PP. for Toronto. He died in 1853, much esteemed and deservedly regretted.

Caleb Powell and Henry Powell came into Pickering as early as 1810. Caleb was the father of Mr. J. B. Powell, merchant, Whitby.

Along the old Brock Road, Elder Barclay, James Sharrard and Joshua Wixson lived on the 9th concession, and had cleared farms. Mr. Wixson's was then the only gristmill in the neighbourhood; it was built a mile east of where Claremont now stands.

Shortly afterwards Mr. Fothergill commenced building a mill at Duffin's Creek, near the present line of the Grand Trunk Railway, but it did not long continue in operation. James

Demorest built a sawmill on lot 12 on the 6th concession, which was of immense benefit to that portion of the township. A Mr. Sicilly had also a sawmill and gristmill on lot 15 on the 5th concession, which he subsequently sold to Mr. Howell, a Cork man, who erected a distillery and built a store, and with his sons carried on a considerable business. Crawford's, Palmer's and other mills were soon afterwards built on both branches of the Creek.

The closest settlement eastward was rear of the 5th concession (now Kinsale), where were located the Messrs. Mackie, John Clerke and Isaac Campbell. Beyond this there was no open road. Captain Macaulay, having considerable wild lands in that quarter, gave 50 acres to have the side line between 10 and 11 in the 4th and 5th concessions; and 6 and 7 in the 6th and 7th concessions, and south part of the 8th concession opened. Notwithstanding the want of roads, the lands in all this neighbourhood were all soon bought up and settled. Most of the settlers after 1834 were immigrants, and were composed pretty evenly of English, Irish and Scotch. It was at this period that Samuel and Joseph Jones with their large families settled on the 7th concession, where they have left their descendants in the enjoyment of comfortable homes. Messrs. Waddell, Hickingbottom, Gordon and James I. Davidson settled on their homesteads about the same time.

John Miller first settled in Pickering in 1832. John brought out from Scotland some stock to his uncle George Miller, of Markham, at this date. The father, old Mr. William Miller, shortly afterwards followed, locating on the old homestead, lot 25 in the 7th concession. The Millers afterwards engaged in the importation of thoroughbred stock, for which they have long obtained such a deservedly high reputation.

The township meeting for 1835 was held at Thompson's tavern on the 5th concession, at which place the township meetings continued to be held for many subsequent years. Here is another specimen by-law, passed in 1835 :—

"Voted that any dog found two miles from his master shall be shot."

In 1836 John Clerke appears as Township Clerk. The commissioners appointed were John Haight, Isaac Campbell and Joseph Wilson. The names of Linton, Logan, Bentley, Agnew, O'Connor, Heaney, Carpenter, Michell, Sullivan, Gibson, Burns, Brennan, Stickney, McKittrick, Gilchrist appear for the first time in the list this year. The commissioners met several times during the year and gave judgment in a good many cases, and appear to have been especially severe in fining parties for road obstructions and non-performance of statute labour.

In 1837 it was resolved that the township, on every concession, be divided into four divisions, and that every division appoint its own overseers. This does not appear to have worked well, for at the next meeting of the commissioners it is " resolved that it have no effect."

Mr. Ebenezer Birrell was elected one of the Town Commissioners in 1839, and Mr. James Sharrard, Town Clerk.

The name of Peter Matthews, which hitherto appeared year after year very prominently for several years in the list of township officers, disappears this year. He was the unfortunate Peter Matthews who was hanged with Captain Lount for the part taken by them in the rebellion of '37.

The names of Gregg, O'Leary, Valentine, Anson, and other well known Pickering families of the present day appear in '39, '40 and '41. Joseph Wilson was appointed clerk in 1840 ; and in '41 the township had a librarian, Mr. Thompson, the tavern keeper, to take charge of the books (viz., Journals of the House of Assembly) presented by the then sitting member, Mr. Small, to the township.

The first district councillors were elected in 1842. They were Alexander Campbell and W. H. Michell.

In 1846 Mr. Hector Beaton, who with his brother settled on 100 cres in Pickering in 1836, was first appointed collector. In 1849 Ir. Beaton was appointed to the three offices of assessor, collector nd clerk. For more than thirty years subsequently he held the ffice of clerk and treasurer, and discharged the duties with the tmost satisfaction. A more upright and faithful officer no munipality ever had, as the universal testimony of the whole people f Pickering bears witness. Mr. Beaton's son now fills the office of ownship clerk, and is a worthy successor of his honoured father.

Mr. Truman White came into Pickering in 1845 from the djoining township of Markham, where he was born twenty years efore. He built the sawmill and gristmill at Whitevale (previously known as Majorville), and established a large business. He also erected extensive woollen mills, which were subsequently urned down, and again rebuilt. He filled the office of reeve of the ownship for several years with much advantage to the municipality, and was elected warden of the county. Mr. White took a eading part in municipal and political affairs for many years, and has always been a strong Liberal. He was the candidate of the Reform party of South Ontario in opposition to Hon. T. N. Gibbs n 1873, and was only defeated by a very narrow majority in the hard battle which he then fought.

James McCreight, of Cherrywood, a county of Dublin Irishman, who settled in the township in 1834; Squire Green, of Greenwood; Joseph Monkhouse, of Altona; the Hoovers, of Green River; the Mackies, Parkers and Palmers, are amongst the old representative families. Dr. Tucker settled in Pickering nearly forty years ago, and was during a residence of nearly thirty years a very prominent man n the township. He was a defeated candidate in the memorable election contest of 1867 between Hon. George Brown, for the Commons, and Doctor McGill for the Provincial Legislature, as the candidates on the Reform side, and T. N. Gibbs and Doctor Tucker on the Conservative side, when Messrs. Gibbs and McGill were elected.

The services of Squire Green (after whom Greenwood village was named) and Squire Birrell were somewhat in demand in those days, as magistrates, and rough customers they sometimes had to deal with. The "court" was generally held in Sterling's Hotel in a sitting-room off the bar-room. In the fall and spring fairs were held in the village—the fall fairs usually attracting large crowds of both sexes. Jumping and running, putting the stone, lifting heavy weights, and other athletic amusements and feats of strength and skill formed part of the programme—the admiration of the ladies present upon those occasions being no little incentive to the competitors. At one of those fairs, thirty odd years ago, a quiet, modest young man, a farmer's son from the front, proved himself the best jumper on the ground. His rival, Mick R——, a big, burly fellow and a noted bully, who claimed the championship of the fair, felt so mortified at his defeat that, after some words of insult, he hit the young farmer a sudden cowardly blow on the temple and knocked him senseless. Burly Mick was arrested and brought before Squires Green and Birrell. He was abusive and insolent; threatened to choke the constable, and clean out the "court." He mocked the magistrates, and his language and manner became so violent and insulting as to be any longer unbearable. There was only one constable, a weak, elderly man, and Mike considered himself beyond all magisterial restraint, especially as a large part of the crowd present belonged to the "Order," of which he was one of the "brethren." "I can't stand this any longer; can you?" asks Squire Green of his brother magistrate. The latter said something about the power of the magistrates to summon assistance, and even to call out the *posse comitatus*. "*Posse comitatus* be d——d," exclaimed the irate Squire Green, "I can lick the scoundrel myself in less than two minutes. Adjourn the court. I declare this court adjourned for five minutes until I lick the fellow!" And adjourned the court was. And when it re-opened very shortly afterwards, the discomfited bully held a handkerchief to his face, on which latter were signs of a black eye and bloody nose, and there was no meeker or quieter individual in court during the remainder of the proceedings.

CHAPTER XXV.

REACH, in the second tier of townships from the lake, was surveyed in 1809 by Mr. Wilmot. Contents, 62,237 acres:
assessed value, $2,489,480. Up to 1st January, 1856, Reach and
Scugog were united. On the latter date, under a by-law passed at
the June session of the County Council, Scugog Island became an
independent municipality. The soil through the centre of the
township of Reach is rather light; the land to the north-east and
north-west is of excellent quality. Reuben Crandell, who has left
numerous descendants, is said to have been the first white settler,
and his son Benjamin, lately deceased, always claimed to be the
first white child born in the township.

The municipality formerly included Port Perry (as well as
Scugog), which with the growth of population became a separate
corporation. Reach contains a number of thriving villages with
splendid names, including Prince Albert, Manchester, Epsom,
Utica, Saintfield, Greenbank. The municipality sends a reeve and
two deputy-reeves to the County Council. Mr. Thomas Paxton (late
Sheriff of the county) was the earliest representative to the County
Council after the county had been set off. The names of McKercher,
Hurd, Covey, Croxall, Truax, Crowther, Stoutenberger, Christie,

Crowther are those given amongst the earliest of the other early settlers.

Property in Scugog has increased immensely in value since the building of the bridge connecting the Island with the mainland after Scugog had become a separate municipality. It contains some fine improved farms and handsome residences. The assessed value in 1886 was $350,854. The Island contains 11,016 acres. The county valuators place land in Scugog at $38 per acre in equalizing the assessment rolls for county purposes. The population of the Island is about 400. There is an Indian reserve of about 800 acres, with a remnant of about fifty Mississaguas thereon.

The Island was surveyed in 1816 and '17 when it formed a portion of both Reach and Cartwright. Shortly afterwards one Purdy erected a milldam across the Scugog River, causing the latter to overflow its banks and converting Scugog into an island. Charles Nesbitt, an Irishman from the County Monaghan, was the first settler; he went to live on the island in 1842.

Brock, although not laid out or surveyed until 1817, is one of the oldest settled of the northern townships. It was named after the celebrated general, the conqueror of Queenston Heights. The first settlers entered the township by way of Yonge Street and Newmarket, and those later by Uxbridge when the road was opened from Duffin's Creek to the latter place. According to the last revised assessment roll, the township contains 66,181 acres; number of acres cleared, 40,000; value of real property, $2,779,602; population about 5,000. A large portion of the township consists of excellent land—a heavy clay loam; but there is considerable broken and marshy land along the Beaver River. Old Philip St. John, an Irishman from the County Limerick, the genial "King of Brock," as he delighted to be called, settled in the township in 1821 and reared a large family. Several of his descendants have long been prominent men in the township. James Vrooman, the kind-hearted old "colonel," and after whom the village of Vroomanton was named, was a still earlier settler. Mr. James Reekie was a still older settler, and the record of himself and family is one of the best of the independent yeomanry of Brock. Mr. Reekie was a native of Dundee, Scotland, where he was born in 1797. He left home when only sixteen years of age, and followed a seafaring life for two or three years, being engaged in the King's service. He came to Brock on the 10th of October, 1818. The first night he slept under a tree, making his bed at the foot of a remarkably large pine, on lot 3 in the 4th concession. And here he settled and made his future home until his death on the 4th December, 1877, in his eighty-first year. He lived for several years a lonely bachelor's life, and was often for weeks together without seeing the face of a white man or woman. In 1824 he married Mary Hume, by whom he had nine sons and three daughters—all of whom survive him. The sons are all thorough Reformers, and before their father's death it was his pride to have them accompany him to poll their votes for the Reform candidate. Mr. Reekie was for many years a Justice of the Peace for the Home District, and afterwards for the county of Ontario. The hospitality of the Reekies—and the children in this respect keep up the good reputation of the parents—was well noted; and in the early days of settlement the new-comers to the township and the passing traveller could well appreciate its value. Reuben Way came into Brock in 1826 from the Bay of Quinté, and was the first settler to venture north of the Reekie settlement. Mr. Way settled on lot 13 in the 1st concession of Brock. He was one of the old District councillors. He was also a staunch Reformer, and, like James Reekie, a total abstainer. The ancestors of the Shire family, James Ruddy, George Smith, John O'Leary, the Keenans, and the families of Spieran, King, Ewart, Fordiff, Campbell, Amey, Bagshaw, Brethour, Bolster, Brabazon, Hart, McPhaden, Cowan, Ruttle, Monroe were all settlers of the following twenty years. Mr. Malcolm Gillespie came later, and has since his entry into the township occupied a very prominent position in municipal and political matters; he has been repeatedly reeve, and was also elected to the honour of warden of the county. John Hall Thompson was long a prominent figure in Brock; he was elected warden of the county as often as five times, and also represented the North Riding in the Dominion Parliament. Much of the township of Brock was settled before Whitby was known farther back than the 3rd concession.

The construction of the Nipissing Railway, towards which the township gave a bonus of $50,000 has greatly added to the value of land, and the people have learned to value and appreciate the advantage of railway communication. Had their railway education been of earlier date, it would have been an important matter for the county, and more especially the county town. Undoubtedly had Brock and the townships north been as favourably disposed thirty years ago to the aiding of railways, and understood then as well as they do now the benefits of railway connection, the grand county scheme of a railway line through the length of the county from Lake Ontario to Georgian Bay would have succeeded. Brock is noted as a very Tory township, and has been the scene of many hard political struggles. The majority for the Conservative candidate is generally piled up to between two and three hundred, counterbalancing the majority of about the same figures usually given in the Liberal township of Uxbridge in the Reform interest. Sunderland, Vroomanton, Vallentyne, Wick and Cannington (the latter now incorporated as a separate municipality) are the most important villages in the township.

The township of Scott was surveyed as early as 1807, by Mr. S. S. Wilmot, but settlement did not begin until a quarter of a century later. Contents, 49,219 acres; population, 2,400; present assessed value, $1,525,789. Evans Jones, a hardy Welshman, was the first known settler. He entered the township in 1830. From that date to 1834 the principal settlers were Andrew Turner, Hugh Mustard, Peter Leask, William Stewart, Thomas

Hood, the Weldons, the Phillipses, Vernons, Pirts, James Gallo-way, George Smith (who afterwards kept a tavern in Whitby), David Urquhart, Thomas Thompson, William Sinclair, George Smith (who was for many years reeve, and in 1875 warden of the county), Robert Rowland (for several years deputy reeve), William Nelson (formerly reeve and now township clerk), who all came in after the rebellion of 1837. A considerable portion of the land is very good soil, part inclined to be light, and interspersed with swamp. Scott has the character of a splendid wheat township. Of late years the township has progressed rapidly, roads have been opened up and improved, and bridges built where necessary, and such good husbandmen are the men of Scott that the county valuators extol the township as being the best cultivated and possessing the best fences of any township in the county.

CHAPTER XXVI.

THORAH, which lies immediately north of Brock, contains 44,320 acres. Valuation, nearly $700,000. The township was surveyed, part in 1820 by J. E. White, and part in 1827 by D. Gibson. White, the surveyor, settled on the south shore of Lake Simcoe, a little north of Beaverton, in 1822. In the same year Ensign Turner, a retired half-pay officer, settled in the south-west corner, near Georgina, where his descendants are still living. James White and Elizabeth Turner, son and daughter of the respective gentlemen named, were the first white children born in the infant settlement. In 1824, under the leadership of Donald Cameron, commonly called "Squire Cameron," a few immigrants arrived from Glengarry. Amongst these were the ancestors of the families of the Campbells, McRaes, McDonalds and Camerons, who so largely preponderate in the population of the township of the present day, and who have all made successful and become prosperous settlers.

Between 1824 and 1828, several British half-pay officers and pensioners, veterans who fought under Moore and Wellington, amongst them the names of Ross, Neil, Murray and O'Donnell, took up grants of land bestowed upon them for military services. Lieutenant Cameron settled upon a splendid 500-acre block on the smiling shore of Lake Simcoe, which he soon largely improved, and where he resided during the remainder of his life. It is the farm now owned by Messrs. Grant and Hodgkinson. A Lieutenant Osborne settled near Mr. Turner's, and a Captain Gibbs on the 1st concession near Squire Cameron's.

Donald Calder, with the McMillans and Fadgens and other natives of the Isle of Islay, Scotland, afterwards arrived from North Carolina, in the United States, where they had been sojourning, and became welcome and valuable additions to the township. Calder was the first to erect a grist and sawmill. And primitive as they were in appearance and construction, they soon proved a great boon to the settlement. Many of the earlier settlers had to carry their bushels of flour upon their backs from the Holland Landing, a distance of forty miles! The first bridge was at this time thrown across the Beaver River, near where the present structure stands. It was built by the voluntary efforts of the sparse settlers themselves, without any outside help. Through the exertions of Squire Cameron, a road was "blazed" from Beaverton to Oshawa. Neither place had then much of an existence as a town or village, and were not known by their present names. The roads through the township were blazed lines with the underbrush cut, and fallen logs chopped, so as to allow of the passage of an ox-sled.

The year 1830 brought a large influx of immigrants from Ross, Sutherland and Argyll, Scotland. Amongst them were John Bruce, John Gunn, James Gordon, Neil Murray, Alexander Fraser, Duncan McLellan, and several others, all of whom (with the exception of the two first named), having served their day and generation, have gone to rest.

George Proctor came in 1833, and settled in the village. He was eminently successful as a merchant and miller; his was the second store opened in the place. The first was by Kenneth Cameron in 1830, when the place was called Milton.

Mr. Charles Robinson, to whom reference is made elsewhere, for many years reeve of the township, also elected warden of the county, an upright magistrate and estimable citizen, settled in Thorah in 1833. He died a few years ago, having lived some fifty years in Thorah. Mr. Robinson has left numerous descendants. A son of his is Mr. C. Blackett Robinson, the well known publisher of *The Presbyterian*, and another, Mr. John G. Robinson, barrister-at-law, both worthy scions of a good stock. Mr. George Bruce, of Beaverton, for several years reeve of the township, and who was also elected warden of the county, married a daughter of Mr. Robinson.

In the year 1833 the Ellises also came to Thorah, and so did John McKay, for many years township clerk. Up to 1835 there was no post office nearer than Georgina, a distance of eighteen miles. The late Col. Cameron, of the 79th Highlanders, settled on a lovely spot along the lake shore, in this latter year. His influence with the Government got a post office at the place, which was then designated Beaverton. The first postmaster was Mr. Ellis, who afterwards erected a carding, spinning and dyeing establishment, still continued by his son. The progress of the township was slow until the establishment of the Home District Council. Hard toil, distant markets, bad roads, low prices and small returns had all to be encountered by the struggling settlers.

On the establishment of the old Home District Council, Colonel Cameron was the first representative of Thorah. Aided by Mr. Peter Perry, from the front, he succeeded in getting several grants of money for the improvement of roads. This timely assistance gave an impetus to much-needed improvements in the way of road-making. The County Council afterwards helped, and the Township Council made liberal grants from year to year in the same direction, until Thorah is now supplied with roads and bridges second to those of no other municipality in the county.

The granting of a bonus of $50,000 to secure the extension of the Midland Railway from Lindsay to Beaverton was a good investment for the township, and from that time forward the progress of both village and township was most marked.

Mr. George Proctor, sen., represented the township municipality in '48, '49 and '50.

In '52 Mr. Robinson succeeded Colonel Cameron, and took the active part already related in establishing the new county, and in making Whitby the County Town.

Thorah, since its first settlement, has been strongly Presbyterian. The first Presbyterian Church, a well-built stone edifice, was built in 1843; it is built upon a 100-acre grant from the Crown. Rev. David Watson was the first minister, and occupied the manse for over a quarter of a century. The reverend gentleman has since seen a splendid new church erected through his exertions at a cost of $14,000. The Canada Presbyterian congregation have since erected a handsome and expensive brick church, costing over $11,000. And the Roman Catholics have built a neat frame church on lot 11 in the 4th concession, also upon another 100-acre Crown grant. The Church of England and Methodist bodies have also put up handsome brick churches in the village.

Beaverton was originally called Milton. It is now incorporated into a separate municipality with its own municipal council. The village is very pleasantly situated on both banks of the Beaver River, which winds its way through beautiful groves of second-growth cedar, and enters Lake Simcoe at this point. A large grist-mill with the latest roller process improvements replaces the old log mill of 1829, put up by Mr. Proctor. There are also steam sawmills, a planing factory, and other manufactures have been added.

In 1834 the total taxes payable by Thorah to the Home District amounted to £34 currency. This year (1887) the valuation of the Township is $642,480, and of the village of Beaverton, $240,000.

CHAPTER XXVII.

THE township of Mara was first, in part, surveyed in 1821 by J. G. Chewitt. The survey was completed in 1836 by Robert Ross. Up to the rebellion of '37 there was but a very scant settlement, and that along the lake shore, in Mara. The character of the soil at that time had a good deal of the appearance of a cedar swamp. As clearings were made the character of the soil turned out to be excellent, and Mara now proves to be one of the best farming townships in the county.

As early as 1823, Patrick Corrigan, an Irishman, took up his abode in the wilds of Mara. He was followed by Arthur Kelly in 1827. Kelly died at the age of 106. He was a great admirer of Mr. Thomas Paxton, for whom he regularly polled his vote. In the contest between Cockburn and Madill, he could not understand why his favourite was not in the field. And when brought to the poll to vote for the Reform candidate, he wished to give an open vote, saying: "I votes for Paxton." After these came the Camerons, the families of McDonagh, McDermott, Doyle, O'Boyle, Flinn,

Harahy, Duffy, McNulty, Mahony, O'Connor, McGrath, O'Leary, O'Brien, McLennan, etc., showing a large Irish and Catholic settlement in the township, which character it still retains. The Highland Scotch Catholics are also numerous. Mr. Philip McRae, for several years reeve of the municipality, is of the latter extraction, and was born on the farm which he owns at Point Mara. He was also elected to the warden's chair by the County Council, and was an unsuccessful candidate for Parliamentary honours. Mr. Alexander Kennedy, a Glengarry Catholic, represented the township in the County Council, having defeated Mr. Hewitt, the old representative who took the place of Mr. Michael McDonagh. Mr. Kennedy built the mills at Atherley, and afterwards removed to Orillia, where he died some years since.

Mr. J. P. Foley, also a former reeve, came to Mara about 1860, and built up the village of Brechin. He has proved himself a most enterprising and worthy resident, and has been a great acquisition to the locality. The Midland Railway runs through the township and has stations at Brechin, Uptergrove and Atherley, all secured for a bonus of $10,000 given by the municipality. The railway has added much to the value of land in Mara. The adverse vote of Thomas McDermott, who represented the township in the County Council in 1854, prevented the railway enterprise of that date from receiving such county assistance as would have secured to the whole county the benefits of direct railway communication between the north and the south, and ever afterwards he was nicknamed "the Basswood Reeve." This was not one of the brothers, James and Thomas McDermott, both of whom afterwards creditably filled the position alternately as reeve of the township. Mara contains 61,050 acres; population, about 2,500 and increasing. The valuation in 1886 was $946,507.

Mara and Rama were united for municipal purposes up to 1869. On the first of January of that year, a by-law previously passed by the County Council came into force, erecting Rama into an independent municipality.

Rama, the most northerly township of the county of Ontario, contains 82,124 acres. The first survey was made in 1834 by William Keating, and embraced about one-third of the township, on the west side along the shore of the beautiful Lake Couchiching. The second survey was made by William Unwin, in 1855, on the south-east boundary, where the Monck Road is located, and the final survey, in which the remainder of the township was laid out, was made a few years later by Mr. Dennis.

In 1835 quite a number of British officers, availing themselves of the appropriations made by the Imperial Government, took up lands along the lake. All the lots in Keating's survey (with the exception of a few Clergy Reserve lots), were located. Captain McPherson settled in 1835. He was the father of Mr. James McPherson, who, for almost half a century, has been the foremost man in Rama. In 1836 Captains Garnett, Coppinger, Yarnold, Rouke and Pass settled. A few years later Yarnold, Rouke and Fry got into difficulties with the old Bank of Upper Canada, and the Bank at that time being all-powerful with the Government, got the Indian Department to purchase their lands—some 2,500 acres altogether. The officers cleared out, and the Mississagua Indians, then at Orillia, were located in Rama. A number of small houses were built for them by the Indian Department on a rising ground overlooking Lake Couchiching—a most picturesque spot, and since known as the Indian Village of Rama. Captain Pass died on his holding. His son was afterwards killed by the falling of a tree, and the rest of the family soon afterwards left the place. Captain McPherson removed to Orillia in 1845. Only Captain Garnett was then left and Mr. James McPherson, already mentioned, who had married a daughter of Captain Garnett. The latter died in 1861, so that Mr. McPherson is the only representative of the settlement of British officers now surviving. Mr. McPherson was for a long time the remotest white settler in the county. He has added largely to his possessions, engaged extensively in quarrying and in the lake navigation, in which trade he still owns a steamboat, and has done much in developing the resources of the township. He has served many years as reeve, was elected warden of the county, is an active magistrate, and is a gentleman highly respected and esteemed for his many excellent qualities.

For a long time white people did not care much about settling close to the Indian village. The land got into the hands of speculators on that account, and thus settlement on the old survey was for a time much retarded.

The building of the Longford Mills and the location of Mr. John Thomson, towards 1870, gave a fresh impetus to the settlement that helped on the township very much. His early death, some six years ago, was a great loss, both public and private, and was very much regretted. He was a fine liberal-minded, open-handed and large-hearted man, who secured to himself the good will and esteem of the whole community. His sons have since his death carried on the business with much success, and have proved themselves worthy of the good name and noble character of their lamented father.

Of the settlement of the town and township of Uxbridge, already noticed in the earlier events of Mr. Gould's life, some further particulars may be here added.

The township of Uxbridge was surveyed in 1804-1805 by S. S. Wilmot. It contains 51,712 acres, a large portion of which is light and sandy soil. The county valuators place the valuation at $1,128,013, or an average of $21.81 per acre. The most important villages are Goodwood, Atha, Siloam and Rothes. The settlement of the south-west corner of the township commenced about 1806 by settlers from the State of New York. The principal families were the Mordens, Kesters, Browns, and those of Wideman, Forsyth, McWain, Townsend and French, a number of the descendants of whom are still to be found in the township. Thomas Hilborn, the leader amongst the Quakers from Pennsylvania, first settled on the farm owned and occupied by Abraham Bagshaw. Amongst the names of other early settlers, not already mentioned, those of the families of William Ferguson, on the hill—lots 33 and 34, 5th concession; John Johnston, lot 35; the Boyds, lot 28; the Burdocks, lot 30; the Wagges, Blackburns; George Hutchinson, lot 31; and of Peter Thompson, who built the first house on the west half of lot 25 in the 5th concession should not be omitted. Mr. Ira Chapman, a son of one of the old pioneers, and now himself past man's allotted threescore years and ten, was born upon the farm originally settled by his father. He formerly filled the office of reeve of the township with much credit to himself and his constituents. The wife of Mr. Isaac J. Gould, M.PP., is a daughter of Mr. Chapman. Other members of the Chapman family settled in Pickering. The Kennedys, lot 29 in the 6th; the Munros, lot 28 in the 7th; old Mr. Shell, who died at the age of ninety, lot 22 in the 4th; Thomas Pearson, lot 33 in the 6th; J. B. Feasby, for several years reeve of the township; Alexander Reid, lot 16 in the 8th concession; the Allcock family, of lot 30 in the 4th; the Sherrard family, of lots 15, 16 and 17 in the 6th, were amongst the old settlers, who were and are represented by prominent men in the township. Amongst other prominent men who have taken, and some of whom still take, an active part in business and local affairs, and by whose enterprise the progress of Uxbridge has been advanced, the names of Thomas Bolster, William Hamilton, Dr. Nation, A. T. Button, George Wheler, ex-M.P., A. D. Weeks, Brown, Finch, Williams, Dr. Black, Henry, Captain Robert Spears, Thomas Johnston, Rev. Mr. Cockburn (son-in-law of Mr. Gould), William Smith (ex-warden of the county) and his father, who came from Paisley and settled in Uxbridge in 1841; Hiram Crosby (another son-in-law of Mr. Gould), I. G. Crosby, R. P. Harman, the present reeve; Dr. Bascom, the present worthy mayor, and son of the gentleman who built the first tannery; James Watt, Mr. F. Keller, of the *Journal* newspaper, who was born in the adjoining township of Markham, stand prominently forward, and numbers of others, the enumeration of whose names might be extended to a bulky volume.

The village of Uxbridge was incorporated in 1872. In 1886 it obtained the dignity of a town. The assessed value in 1886 was $580,000. Uxbridge possesses important manufactures, and is now lighted by electricity, the power being supplied by Mr. Isaac Gould, M.PP. It is the first town in the county that has secured electric light, Oshawa coming next.

CHAPTER XXVIII.

THE County Town of Whitby was incorporated in 1855 by special Act of Parliament. The limits of the corporation comprise the large area of 4,240 acres. The population has fluctuated a good deal in the years that have since passed; but although the character of the buildings has vastly improved, the numbers of the people have scarcely, if at all, perceptibly increased. According to the last year's census, taken under the direction of the Board of School Trustees, the figures are under 3,000.

Up to the time of its incorporation the town (then the village) remained an integral part of the township municipality. Since then it has had its mayor and corporation—the municipality being divided into three wards, each electing three members. The mayor is elected by the general vote of the electors, and so are the reeve and deputy reeve sent to represent the town in the County Council; so that the body corporate is composed of twelve members. The history of the early settlement up to the period of incorporation belongs altogether to that of the township.

After the arrival of Peter Perry, in 1836, it was called Perry's Corners, and retained the appellation for some years. Mr. Perry infused new life into the little village, and from his time it began to grow into a place of some note and importance. Houses, and blocks of houses, were built, and town and corner lots became more and more valuable, as population increased and new buildings accumulated.   The harbour was improved; so were the roads northward leading into it; warehouses were built at the wharf, and its natural advantages and shipping facilities established Whitby as a first-class grain market and shipping port.   The erection of the county buildings, and emerging from a mere village into the dignity of a County Town, with its resident county officials, courthouse and gaol, made Whitby an important centre.   The period of inflation caused by the building of the Grand Trunk Railway had arrived.   The fever of speculation in town and village lots was at its height.   And Whitby with its hopeful future; its many great natural advantages; its noble harbour; its splendid, well-settled back country tributary to its market, and all its newly added glories of a County Town became at once a point of attraction for the business man seeking to establish himself in a rising locality, and for the speculator at which to carry on his operations.   In Whitby, as at many other places at that time, the latter swarmed. Almost every owner of desirable building sites within the corporation became a speculator himself or was tempted to sell to speculators.   Blocks of land were bought on speculation and measured off and sold in town lots, at prices that would have gone far to purchase improved farms.   Merchants and tradesmen came in, in the meantime, and established themselves in business, and the mania of speculation was at its height when the collapse came in 1857.   Of the merchants and tradesmen who had settled down numbers were caught in the meshes of the speculators and remained crippled in their resources for years afterwards.   The speculators themselves, working as some of them did upon imaginary values and paper capital, came to grief.   It was easy to buy (at the speculator's price) by making a first payment and giving a mortgage at a high rate of interest for the balance. The result was that most of the town property was under heavy mortgage in one shape or another; that enterprise was checked, and that the men of enterprise who were not wholly ruined were so crippled in their resources as to be brought to a stand still with a mountain of debt to face, hindering them and hampering them at every turn in all their future operations.

During the next ten years the growth of Whitby was slow and gradual, but some private houses of superior pretensions were put up—notably the residences of John Ham Perry, James Wallace, Sheriff Reynolds, and a score of others; not one of which now remain in the possession of the original owners or of their families. Mr. Reynolds's residence, "Trafalgar Castle," as he was proud to call it, has received large additions since it became the Ontario Ladies' College, for which latter purpose it is now admirably adapted. It is one of the best and most flourishing institutions of the kind in the Province, or perhaps in the Dominion. Some good stores and brick buildings have replaced the old frame structures of thirty odd years ago; the streets and sidewalks are in a better condition; some imposing church edifices, with "spires pointing the way to heaven" have been built; there are very good school buildings, including Collegiate Institute and Model School; there is a railway track through the town, and a railway station near Dundas Street, and railway shops (without mechanics or workmen), there is a fine town hall and a market in a central locality, and there is a new elevator at the wharf, and there are of course the county buildings, and altogether Whitby presents an improved appearance. But Whitby, although better dressed, has not grown. And it is far from being the stirring place of business of which there was once so much promise. The people of the County Town have tried to do their share. They have heavily taxed themselves in order to secure the benefits of railway connection and improve their business prospects. But success has not attended their efforts. They were not in time. When they moved it was too late. Their pushing neighbours to the east and to the west had

already stretched out their lines of railway into the territory properly tributary to the County Town, and cut off the trade of the
north. Whitby had done much, and made many sacrifices to
secure this trade. Before the era of railways, the representatives
of the town voted steadily in the County Council for all appropriations for the improvement of the roads in the north leading to the
town. It was good policy; for though it increased the county rate
of the front taxpayers, it brought the grist to the town mill. And
in those days it was no unusual sight to see a string of farmers'
teams more than a mile in length extending from "The Corners"
to the warehouses at the bay, bringing the produce of the farms of
the north to the Whitby market. Of course farmers and farmers'
wives then dealt with the town storekeepers and bought all their
chief supplies from Whitby merchants. But this did not last long.
The outside railways carried off the trade of the north in other
directions, and the people of Whitby lost all the advantage of the
expenditure on roads which they found they had only helped to
make for the benefit of northern farmers.

All subsequent efforts to retrieve the loss of that trade by securing direct railway communication between the northern and southern
part of the county were unavailing. The influences of the Toronto
and Nipissing Railway on the one side and of the Port Hope and
Lindsay Railway on the other were too strong for the Whitby promoters of a direct county line, and the result was, as stated elsewhere in these pages, the present inadequate railway connection,
without any advantages of workshops, etc., or of a competing line
which Whitby gave its $80,000 to secure.

Adverse circumstances have hitherto told against Whitby and
Whitby men in the past. It is to be hoped that the Whitby men
of to-day will profit by the lesson of the past, and will be more fortunate in their efforts to secure for the County Town of the county
of Ontario that position which its favourable location and undoubted
natural advantages should command.

Several unsuccessful efforts were made to establish manufactures in the town. Bonuses have been given and the burdens of the rate-payers added to for the purpose. But the result has not been satisfactory. It is very doubtful whether anything in the shape of permanent, solvent industries can be obtained by such means.

Very few of the prominent first residents of Whitby now survive. Ezra Annes, his eldest son, Henry; James Rowe, John Welsh, John Sprowle, John Watson, Dr. Ham and his eldest son, John; Chester Draper, Henry Hopkins and his son, George; Hugh J. Macdonell, Daniel Cameron, Jas. H. Gerrie, J. O. Dornan, Henry Hannam, Benjamin Yarnold and his son, Robert; Alexander McPherson, for long years postmaster, William Jeffrey, J. R. Armstrong, Jacob Bryan, Levi Fairbanks, for many years Division Court Clerk, Sheriff Reynolds, Henry Betts, Daniel Betts, Joshua Richardson, Alexander Ross, Revd. J. T. Byrne and his son, James; Samuel Cochrane and his son, S. H., at his death County Attorney; Colonel Wallace, and his brother, George; John Hamer, Hutton Starr, T. N. Scripture and a long roll of the men who early took an active part in the doings of the county town have all passed over to the majority. Others who figured conspicuously in town affairs and as business men, such as Robert E. Perry, Francis Keller, Thomas Myers, Joel Bigelow, Christopher McDermott, J. M. Lowes, James Hodgson, Carleton Lynde, H. Post, Wm. Thew, Wm. McCabe, Thomas H. McMillan, Thomas Kirkland, W. H. Higgins, John M. Lowes, Joseph Dickey, W. W. Caldwell, Francis Clarke, N. W. Brown, ex-M.PP., John Bengough and his clever sons, James Hamilton and others moved away to other localities, where some have grown exceedingly prosperous, and most of them have bettered their condition in life. There were a good many others who settled in Whitby for a while, and after making more or less of a flourish, "pulled up stakes" and sought "green fields and pastures new," but with whose names it is unnecessary to encumber this record. Of the old stock there are very few remaining. They would be included in the names of J. H. Perry, Wm. Laing, Dr. Gunn, Thos. Dow, G. Y. Smith, Wm. Blair, Major Harper, J. Hamer Greenwood, James Campbell, Judge Burnham, Judge Dartnell, John Spurrell, J. K. Gordon, R. H. Lawder, W. H. Billings, Thomas Huston the town clerk, and perhaps half a dozen others of less prominence.

The "new-comers" who have settled down in the interval and made Whitby their permanent home have been mostly of the better class of people who take up their residence in country towns. Among them are some enterprising and public-spirited business men (such as Mr. Charles King, owner of the tannery), whose good business qualities and intelligence give a town a reputation.

Whitby has always preserved a high reputation for the hospitable and social character of its inhabitants.

The valuation in 1886, for county purposes, was $786,550.

CHAPTER XXIX.

OSHAWA was formerly known as Skae's Corners, after Mr.
Edward Skae had opened a store there. Before that time
several other names, after those of the old settlers, were given the
locality. But it has retained the old Indian appellation of Oshawa.
The Indian meaning of the word signifies Salmon Creek. The
names of the pioneer settlers have been already given in the
chapter on the settlement of the township of Whitby. All have
long since gone to "that bourne whence no traveller returns."
The descendants of quite a few of the first settlers are, however, to
be found; some of them occupying prominent positions, and most
of them enjoying a competence and living in houses and with
surroundings that would have astonished their forefathers and
have bewildered the Indians who raided poor Benjamin Wilson's
little hut and carried off his year's provisions.

Mr. Thomas Conant is a worthy Canadian representative of his
ancestors, who with the Burks and Trulls of Darlington settled on
Barber's Creek in 1794. The Farewell brothers who "paddled their
own canoe" up the Creek from Oshawa harbour have numerous
representatives. Abraham Farewell, ex-M.PP., the head of the
family, still enjoys robust health and there are nephews engaged in
all the learned professions as well as on the farm. In this

connection it may be mentioned that the mother of Nelson Pickell, of Oshawa, was claimed to be the first white woman born in the old township of Whitby. Mr. Thomas Dow, manager of the Western Bank at Whitby, opened the first mail bag that came to the Oshawa post office, when a young clerk in Mr. Skae's store.

Very different is the Oshawa of to-day with its large manufacturing industries and splendid buildings to that of the time when Joseph Gorham built the first mill in South Oshawa. The old families of what might be called the second period, the Skaes, the Warrens, the Arklands and the Gibbses have scarcely a representative left in the town. Col. Grierson married a daughter of Mr. J. B. Warren, and his children are the only direct representatives of the Warrens of Oshawa. Mr. Wm. Warren of the tannery is a nephew, and a son of old Mr. Wm. Warren, of Whitby. Oshawa had the honour of giving the two county members to the Dominion Parliament at the same time in the persons of the brothers, Hon. T. N. Gibbs and W. H. Gibbs, the former a Cabinet Minister. Neither is there a representative of Col. Fairbanks, once so prominent and deservedly popular, in the town. Oshawa also gave two other prominent gentlemen as representatives for South Ontario—Dr. McGill in the Legislative Assembly of Ontario, and Mr. F. W. Glen (who defeated Hon. T. N. Gibbs) in the Dominion Parliament. Mr. Glen for more than twenty years carried on the celebrated Hall Works, established by his father-in-law, Mr. Joseph Hall. The extensive iron manufactures of all kinds in which he engaged and the large employment given by him largely built up the town and made the name of Oshawa known far and wide. So did the celebrated agricultural implement manufactures of A. S. Whiting & Co., still carried on by Mr. Hamlin. The malleable works so profitably carried on by the Messrs. Cowan; the Stove Foundry, managed by Mr. Larke; the works of the Masson Manufacturing Company; those of Messrs. Coulthard & Scott; the Single Works, and other branches carried on more or less extensively still keep up the reputation of Oshawa as an important manufacturing centre.

Oshawa was the first village incorporated in the county. It is now a town, divided into four wards, and comprises an area of 2,400 acres. With its mayor, reeve, two deputy reeves, and three councillors from each ward, it has a bulky corporate body of sixteen members. The population is estimated at nearly 5,000. The valuation of the county valuators in 1886, for equalization purposes, was $1,060,550.

In 1852 the total population was 1,106; the value of real property, £4,296, and of personal property, £1,368 currency.

Port Perry was incorporated as a village on the 1st January, 1872; the by-law for the purpose had been passed at the previous June session of the County Council. From an insignificant hamlet on the "banks of the melancholy Scugog," it has become a populous business centre, with well built stores and handsome public and private buildings.

Peter Perry was the first who put up a small store at the place about forty years ago, and from him Port Perry received its name. The late Chester Draper, of Whitby, was employed by Mr. Perry as clerk, and placed in charge of the store. Sawmills were subsequently erected at the head of the lake. The first sawmill was put up by Samuel Hill. A large lumber business was carried on, for several years by the Messrs. Paxton and W. S. Sexton. The building of the railway from Whitby to Port Perry gave the latter place its first good start. Being the terminus, until the extension to Lindsay, was a further help. With the construction of the road, and Port Perry the terminus, town lots went up to a high figure, and the owners of real estate in the village made quite a harvest. In a few years the place grew up to its present proportions, with a population of 2,000, with fine churches, schools, town hall, factories banks, two newspapers, and all the evidences and surroundings o extended trade and industry. Port Perry is a large grain market and good shipping point for timber and lumber brought up the lake and river, and re-shipped by railway to Whitby and the front. The village has suffered from two or three disastrous fires, but has speedily recovered from their effects, through the enterprise of its business men, and a still better class of buildings has taken the place of those destroyed.

Port Perry has an area of over 500 acres, and is extending. The valuation (for county purposes) in 1886 was $591,000. Mr. Joseph Bigelow was the first reeve and representative of the village in the County Council. The foundation and history of Port Perry must always remain inseparably connected with the names of Perry, Paxton, Bigelow and Sexton.

Cannington was the next village of the county that obtained incorporation as a separate municipality. It was separated from the township of Brock for municipal purposes in 1878. It is a thriving village, beautifully situated on the Beaver River. It possesses good manufacturing facilities, and is an important station of the old Toronto and Nipissing, now forming part of the Midland Railway system in connection with the Grand Trunk.

' The population, 1,100; valuation of real property, $320,000.

CHAPTER XXX.

THE county of Ontario, under the Act 14 and 15 Victoria, cap. v. (1851), consisted of the townships of Whitby, Pickering, Uxbridge, Reach, Brock, Georgina, Scott, Thorah, and Mara and Rama—the two latter one municipality, and the Island of Scugog which formed part of the townships of Reach and Cartwright, and was united to Reach. The county thus composed formed one of the United Counties of York, Ontario and Peel.

In this union it was held by the representatives of Ontario that their county was not getting fair play, and that in the equalization of the assessment rolls the value of the Ontario municipalities was raised, while the value of those of York were lowered for assessment purposes. Hence the agitation for separation by Ontario.

The first Provisional Council was composed as follows :—

TOWNSHIPS.	REEVES.	DEPUTY REEVES.
Whitby	James Rowe	James Dryden.
Pickering	W. H. Michell	Peter Taylor.
Reach and Scugog	Thomas Paxton	A. W. Ewers.

TOWNSHIPS.	REEVES.	DEPUTY REEVES.
Brock	Robert Sproule	A. Carmichael.
Uxbridge	Joseph Gould	
Scott	James Galloway	
Georgina	James Bouchier	
Thorah	Chas. Robinson	
Mara and Rama	James McPherson	
Oshawa Village	T. N. Gibbs	

Mr. Bouchier, of Georgina, was appointed to preside as chairman until the provisional warden was elected. The first meeting under the proclamation took place on Monday, 3rd May, 1852, and was held in a frame schoolhouse near St. John's Church at the Bay. Mr. Joseph Gould, of Uxbridge, was elected first provisional warden of the new county, and Mr. William Powson, of Manchester, in Reach, county clerk. The seat for the united townships of Mara and Rama was claimed by Mr. Michael McDonagh, who contended that Mr. McPherson had resigned, and that he (Mr. McDonagh) had been elected. Both gentlemen produced certificates of election from the township clerk. Mr. McPherson, however, took his seat and voted during the proceedings, under protest from the adverse claimant. A resolution in favour of appropriating the necessary amount for the erection of the county buildings was the principal business before the meeting. As the existence of the new county hinged upon this appropriation being then made, a special interest attaches to the proceedings which took place. Mr. Gould moved " That the council do now proceed to appropriate at once the amount necessary to erect the county buildings, the same to be raised in sums so as to cover a term of twenty years."

He said that the time had now arrived for a separation from the old county. The accumulating county business, which is now literally choking up every department of our county affairs, in this huge county, has long cried for a division of the county of York, and especially now when other counties, of not half its extent or population, were cheerfully availing themselves of those district divisions which of necessity forced themselves on the Government, and were successfully working out their own local concerns, un-trammelled by an overwhelming centralizing influence, such as we had to contend with in the city of Toronto. The time had arrived, the general voice of the people now demanded a separation, and he had always, and was always ready to bow to that voice, especially when he heartily concurred in the justice of the demand. The mainspring of every action is self-interest, and he trusted that no man present was so insensible to the interests of his constituents as to refuse to secure them now by the immediate erection of our county buildings and a speedy separation. What could we avail by delay? Could we stave off the net work of taxation that is now being prepared to be cast over us by the city of Toronto. The county of York is not only erecting a court house, which the adverse interests to this section have needlessly hurried on the council in anticipation of the present event, but they con-template further improvements and heavy expenditures, to avoid which is our solemn duty to our constituents. Why did they hurry in this matter? The great and expensive improvements that have been made in the past years render the county buildings sufficiently convenient for many years to come, and after our separation, more than sufficient; but York and Peel wish to get a bite out of us first, and the sooner we separate the sooner will we get rid of these debts of their contracting. (Cheers.) Any opposition here now will be but adding additional power to the efforts of York and Peel to take from us to the utmost farthing. We cannot stave off separation indefinitely. It will ultimately come; and what claim can we have hereafter, by arbitration or otherwise, on the county of York for refunding our equitable share of these contemplated assessments if we delay the hour? Can we ask them to refund a share of the tax that we have voluntarily submitted to? Certainly not with any shadow of justice on our side. Let us proceed then at once and place ourselves out of danger, and not remain at the further mercy of York and Peel. (Cheers.)

Mr. Michell moved, seconded by Mr. Gibbs, " That no appropriation be made until the question be referred to a direct vote of
the ratepayers of the county." He said that the people ought to
give an expression of sentiment on the question. Should his
township be in favour of the appropriation he would not oppose it.
Mr. Gould holds up the bugbear of taxation, but the old county
never taxed us improperly, and he had no proof that they ever
would. He considered the expense of building our county buildings would be £10,000, and the cost of transferring registration of
titles, £3,000; but notwithstanding this, if he could see how we
were to be benefited by a separation, he would not oppose it.
The people did not want it. Petitions had been circulated, but
how were they signed? Again, is this a proper time to involve
the county in heavy expenditure, when every kind of produce is so
low, and the people impoverished? Other counties, it is said,
less populous and wealthy, have erected their buildings; but they
are not satisfied—they complain of expense and neglected roads.
When he was in favour of division, it was when we had not the
handling of our own money; and when we heard a gentleman in
Toronto say that he hoped to see the grass grow in the streets of
Whitby, then he told Mr. Perry he would go for a division. Circumstances, however, have changed since then, and the same
necessity does not exist; besides, the Government, acting on
fictitious petitions, have taken the matter out of the people's hands,
and he wished it restored to the people. Not till then would he
yield a compliance. The cry for division was but an *ignis fatuus*,
and the people would rise upon those that led them into the snare.

Mr. Gibbs thought the amendment was the best under existing
circumstances, and such as he expected Mr. Gould himself would
introduce, from the expressions he had often heard him make.
But that gentleman has changed his mind. He dreads a tax to be
levied by the old county; but how can he show that we will be
relieved from it? It was well ascertained at the last meeting of

the council in Toronto that a tax would not be levied on York and Peel without Ontario partaking of it, and it was resolved to refund any amount raised from Ontario for improvements in the old county when separation should take place, and he would therefore be in favour of letting the taxpayers decide the question. Why this haste? What has changed Mr. Gould's mind? He thought, surely, that the extension of the Division Court Act had lessened the necessity of separation. He found that the expenses of the new county would be about $2,000 per annum, and the people are now complaining of taxes. True, we could not enjoy municipal government without taxation, but the taxes for gaols and court houses were not necessary for the good of the people—at least, he would give the people the opportunity of saying whether they were so or not, and then he would yield to their decision.

Mr. Ewers would oppose the amendment of Mr. Michell, because that gentleman had not brought a single argument in favour of delay. Mr. Gibbs says the Legislature will settle the amount to be refunded by the old county, thus showing, even in his opinion, a separation is not far distant; and if not far distant, why not at once, and before we are thoroughly fleeced by the old county? Should the question of choosing the site for the county buildings be left to the people, where should we not want them? What would Mr. Gibbs have us do, if not do as Oshawa once did: asked the Government to shut up the road leading to Whitby harbour? (Hear, hear.) If the site had been chosen in a certain neighbourhood, Mr. Gibbs would not refuse £10,000, or £20,000 if need be, for the public buildings. (Cheers.) He would therefore vote for the resolution.

Mr. Galloway opposed the resolution, because the petitions for division were signed by names of persons who, he would not say were unborn, but to his knowledge the names of suckling babies were attached to them.

Mr. Paxton said that in his belief the whole people were in

favour of the appropriation, and this being so, was it not their luty, according to their oath, to consult their interests—not the interests of this or that neighbourhood individually, but the whole county? We have contended for a division for six years, and had we such obstructionists as Messrs. Gibbs and Michell, we might have to contend many years. The selfishness of Mr. Michell led him to favour a division when the back townships were unequally assessed, and when they had to pay as much tax for an acre of swamp as the front had to pay for an acre worth forty dollars; but now that the assessment is equalized, and the front has to bear an equal proportion with the rear in the cost, he turns about and opposes it. (Cheers.)

Mr. Gibbs, in answer to Mr. Gould, said that as he had been confined by illness, he could not learn whether the courthouse in Toronto had been sold or not, and went on to show the expense of carrying on the county business, which he estimated yearly at £2,000.

Mr. Michell denied that the equalization of taxation was the cause of his opposition now, and enquired the cause of Mr. Gould's change of position.

Mr. Gould said he opposed a division formerly, on the ground that Mr. Michell supported it—the unequal burdens on the back townships by an arbitrary assessment law; and he supported it now on the grounds that Mr. Michell opposes the appropriation—because the burden is now equal. If Mr. Michell be such a stickler for appeals to the people in everything that the people expect him to act on, why not ask for an appeal to the people before he voted for the assessment in Toronto for the new buildings? (Cheers.)

Mr. Taylor was astonished at the factious opposition of Mr. Michell. He had nominated him, on the ground of his promise not to oppose the appropriation, but he has wonderfully changed. For himself, he had always been the same under every circumstance, and would now vote for the appropriation, not only because

he believed it to be just and sound policy, but because he believed
the majority of his constituents thought likewise.

Mr. Dryden said that seven-eighths of the criminal cases of the
counties belonged to Toronto, and therefore if but one-third of the
expense were borne by us, the amount would be but trifling compared to the estimates of Mr. Gibbs.   That gentleman must be
fond of exaggerations.   Mr. Dryden spoke at considerable length,
and believed Mr. Gibbs' opposition to the appropriation arose more
from disappointment than anything else, for that gentleman knew
well that should an assessment be levied in one year for erecting
the buildings, it would not exceed a penny in the pound.

Mr. Michell rose to defend his constituency from the foul
aspersions that had been cast upon it by Mr. Gould and others.
He denied that he was influenced by selfish motives, either when
he opposed or advocated a division.   He had circulated petitions
in Pickering, but with all his influence could not get ten signers.

. Mr. Gould asked the reeves and deputies to canvass the consistency of Mr. Michell.   He tells us at one time, when he was in
favour of division, that four-fifths of Pickering were for division,
and again that he could not get ten signers to the petitions for that
object with all his influence.   His arguments can no more hang
together than the consistency of his various movements, and he
regretted exceedingly the humiliating position that that gentleman
had placed himself in before a new county.   Mr. Gould continued
speaking at great length, going fully into the different improvements of the old county buildings, for which we have been taxed
different times ; the object of the old county in pushing forward
the present tax ; and strongly urging the Council to make this
glorious effort to advance the interests of this section of the county
by voting the appropriation.   He sat down amidst great cheering.
The question was then put, and the resolution to appropriate
carried by the vote of the warden.

The Council then adjourned, to meet again after the adjourn-nent of the United Counties' Council at Toronto (provided that the day be not Sunday, and if so, then the Monday following), in the Free Church at Whitby Village. Mr. Hannam's residence, corner of Brock and Mary Streets, was the old Free Church ; it was free to all denominations, and was largely used for public meetings.

On the same evening the Provisional Council embarked for Toronto on board the *Admiral*, to take their seats in the United Counties' Council.

When the Provisional Council met again on Monday, 10th May, there was no quorum, the members opposed to separation, numbering one-half the body, all absenting themselves from the meeting, by preconcerted arrangement as was charged, in order to prevent the transaction of business; and so block further proceedings.

Thus was the county of Ontario organized on the 3rd of May, 1852. The passage of a resolution to raise the necessary funds for the erection of the county buildings was their first important act. For six years previously the friends of the new county had struggled hard to give it existence. The difficulties in the way were numerous and formidable, and had to be encountered at every step. There was a strong city influence of the bankers, merchants, and others of Toronto opposed to separation from the county of York, which, with the local jealousies and divisions then raging, principally on account of the location of the county town at Whitby, might well have deterred from the task men less courageous and determined than those who entered the early struggle for county independence. The record gives the yeas and nays on the vote as follows : YEAS—Messrs. Rowe, Paxton, Gould, Robinson, Dryden, Taylor, Ewers—7. NAYS—Messrs. Michell, Gibbs, Sproule, Galloway, Bouchier, McPherson, Carmichael—7.

The double vote of Mr. Gould carried the day. Had he failed his friends, or hesitated to exercise his right to give the casting vote, as provisional warden, in favour of the appropriation at that supreme moment, the separate existence of the county of Ontario might have been indefinitely postponed, and Whitby's chances of being the future county town hopelessly jeopardized. The construction of the Northern Railway in 1853, touching Lake Simcoe, and giving the northern townships a new front, would have lost Thorah and Mara and Rama, and probably Brock.

Nor was the struggle yet ended. A protest had been entered against what had been done, and a document drawn up and signed by six of the protesters, withdrawing from further attendance on the meetings of the Provisional Council. The ostensible reason put forward for this course was, that they wanted the whole question submitted to a vote of the ratepayers. This could, however, be only a pretence, for the ratepayers had been consulted at the previous municipal elections, and had already instructed their representatives how to vote. Nevertheless, the Council, as constituted, had pronounced in favour of the by-law, which was immediately published, to raise six thousand pounds for the purpose of defraying the expenses of the erection of the county buildings.

The next meeting of the Provisional Council was held on Tuesday, 1st June, "in the brick schoolhouse," Whitby. Nine members were present on this occasion, viz.:—Messrs. Carmichael, Dryden, Ewers, Gould, McDonagh, Paxton, Robinson, Rowe, and Taylor.

Mr. McDonagh had established his claim to the seat for Mara and Rama to the satisfaction of the Provisional Council. He made a speech in favour of the new county, stating that he had swam his horse across an arm of Lake Simcoe, in order to be present to do justice. He was well received, and entertained by the people of the town and the friends of the new county. Mr. Carmichael explained his position with regard to signing the protest, recanted, said, " he had come to perform his duty under the law," and approved of the course which the Provisional Council were pursuing.

At this meeting William Paxton, jun., was appointed county treasurer. The motion was moved by Mr. McDonagh, seconded by Mr. Ewers. The following resolution was also passed; it is here given to settle a question of fact :—

Moved by Mr. McDonagh, seconded by Mr. Ewers : "That the provisional warden be instructed to receive as good and sufficient securities the following persons, viz. : James Dryden, Esq., William Paxton, sen., Thomas Paxton, Esq., and Mr. George Paxton, to the amount of £3,000, for the faithful performance of the duties of Provisional Treasurer of the County of Ontario."—Carried.

A resolution was also passed requesting the Government to appoint immediately a Registrar and County Judge.

The by-law to raise the £6,000 for building purposes was again passed at this meeting, the legality of the previous action of the members of the Council, who did not constitute a full quorum, being doubtless regarded as open to question.

While the war of separation raged at this time, meetings were held in the various municipalities, at which resolutions were passed for and against, and in approval or disapproval of the action of their representatives at the County Council. Uxbridge especially passed resolutions heartily approving of the course of Mr. Joseph Gould. In Pickering, Peter Taylor's course was condemned at a public meeting, while that of W. H. Michell was approved. The township was at the time divided into wards. The ratepayers of Mr. Taylor's Ward (No. 1) subsequently held a meeting, voting confidence in him and denouncing Mr. Michell.

At the next meeting, which was held in the Free Church on Thursday, 24th June, the report of a committee appointed to draft an address to the Government recommending parties for appointment to the several county offices, was presented. The recommendations made were—for Sheriff, Ezra Annes ; for Registrar, John Ham Perry ; for County Judge, Zaccheus Burnham ; and for Clerk of the Peace, Chester Draper. The report was amended by substituting the name of Charles Robinson, of Thorah, for that of Ezra

Annes, and was so adopted. An unsuccessful attempt was made, through the interference of the Court of Chancery, to stop further proceedings in the new county. The courts were also appealed to to quash the by-law for raising funds for erecting the county buildings, and to quash a second by-law passed by the Provisional Council for raising £887, to meet contingent expenses. In the latter the opposition were successful, the by-law being quashed on technical grounds. Peter Taylor's seat was attacked, on the ground that he was ineligible, inasmuch as he was treasurer of the township of Pickering, for which he sat as deputy reeve in the Provisional Council. Mr. McDonagh's claim to the seat for Mara and Rama was disallowed in Toronto, and Mr. McPherson retained by the United Counties' Council as the representative of the northern townships. The proceedings against the new county came to nothing. The representatives of York and Peel in the United Counties' Council, taking advantage of the differences between the Ontario representatives, manipulated the assessment rolls to their own advantage. In equalizing they took no less than $200,000 off their own municipalities, and placed the amount upon the new county then struggling into life. Reach was increased £62,000, Whitby, £56,000, Uxbridge, £13,000, Brock, £20,000, and so on. Nor did Oshawa escape; its value was also largely increased. Mr. Gibbs took fire at this treatment, and joined with the friends of the new county in resisting the injustice.

The site for the county buildings was another bone of contention. Some half-dozen were laid before the building committee—one of five acres, north of Dundas Street, belonging to the Perry estate, being first selected. This was not agreeable to the residents at the Bay, and, as a compromise, the site upon which the county buildings now stand—two acres of the Worden estate—was accepted.

When the Provisional Council met on the 7th of June, the by-law to raise £6,000 for county buildings was finally passed, and the site agreed upon approved. The contract was let to Mr. James Wallace. After this there was a breathing spell. It was, however, but of short duration. It was discovered that Oshawa, as a municipality, was not rated highly enough on the aggregate assessment of the county, upon which the rate was to be levied for paying the debentures and interest, issued for the £6,000, and this it was believed would prove fatal to the legality of the by-law. Oshawa was rated at £61,666 instead of £92,500, the correct amount. The representatives of Oshawa in fact, who had hitherto fought against paying anything for erecting county buildings at Whitby, now complained of the lightness of their taxes for that purpose ! They had previously been taking advantage of the error of under-valuation, and paying less county taxes than their just proportion in the United Counties' Council. They now sought to take advantage of their own wrong with the view of quashing the by-law ! Mr. G. H. Grierson got the credit of making the discovery of this legal point. The courts were again resorted to ; but. the attempt to quash the by-law utterly failed, the lame arguments. of the relators in the case being scouted by the court.

CHAPTER XXXI.

First meeting of Provisional Council, 1853—Members present—Proceedings—Mr. Gibbs elected warden—Displaced—Captain Rowe elected—A retrospect—Claimants for the County Town—A better understanding—Action of Georgina—Secedes—Mr. Hartman's conduct—Unjustifiable legislation—Remonstrance of Mr. Gould—Progress of the County buildings—Laying the Corner stone—An account of the grand doings upon that occasion—Testimony in favour of Mr. Gould's noble course—A letter from him placed with the deposits under the Corner stone.

AT the first meeting of the Council for 1853, which was held 10th February, there were present:—From Whitby—James Rowe, reeve; James Burns, deputy; Pickering—John Lumsden, reeve; Peter Taylor, deputy; Reach—James French, reeve; P. A. Hurd, deputy; Brock—George Brabazon, reeve; N. Bolster, deputy; Uxbridge—Joseph Gould, reeve; Scott—James Galloway, reeve; Georgina—John Boyd, reeve; Thorah—Donald Cameron, reeve; Mara and Rama—James S. Garnett, reeve; Oshawa—T. N. Gibbs, reeve.

Mr. Gibbs was elected provisional warden, the vote being taken by ballot. Some members of the Council took umbrage at remarks made by Mr. Gibbs on taking his seat. He was understood to say that his election to the wardenship showed that his course in the past, in opposing the setting off of the new county, had been right, and had been approved of. This was by no means the case with some of the northern men, who voted for Mr. Gibbs because of his personal fitness, and they resolved to let him see it by displacing him, or rather, as was expressed at the time, to test the opinion of the Council on the subject. Mr. Gibbs thereupon tendered his resignation. James Rowe, Reeve of Whitby, was then elected to the vacant chair by the casting vote of the township of Whitby, as having the largest number of names on the assessment roll, The vote stood six to six. Bolster, Brabazon, Gould, Lumsden, Taylor and Rowe, voted yea; Burns, Boyd, Cameron, Gibbs, Galloway and Hurd, voted nay. Garnett had disclaimed the seat for Mara and Rama, and French, of Reach, was inveigled off "to dine with a friend," and kept out of the way until after the vote was taken.

Looking back now, at this distance of time, at the proceedings in connection with the organization of the new county, one is amazed at the bitterness of feeling displayed, and the tenacity of purpose with which every inch of ground was fought by both sides. The press teemed with letters full of charges and counter-charges, impeaching the motives and actions of individual members; broad-sheets filled with earnest appeals, and full of forebodings of future ruin, protests and earnest appeals to the rate-payers against separation, were scattered broadcast throughout the country, and public meetings and demonstrations of all kinds were continuously held to keep up the excitement. The prize of the county town was, however, the great stumbling block to union and independence, for even those who opposed separation could not fail to see how Ontario was being fleeced, session after session, by the majority, in the union with York and Peel. To be the county town was a prize worth fighting for, and perhaps no representative is to be blamed for doing his best to secure it for his own locality. The claimants, with Whitby, were Brooklin, Manchester, Uxbridge and Oshawa. With the publication of the proclamation appointing Whitby, all but Oshawa succumbed. The latter fought it out as long as there was a hope or a chance, led on by Messrs. Gibbs, Farewell and Grierson. James Rowe's election to the wardenship, under the circumstances, was a bitter pill to have to swallow. But, after all, it appears to have had the wholesome effect of bringing about a better understanding. At the very next meeting we find Mr. Gibbs voting with the majority, side by side with Mr. Gould and Mr. Taylor, against a resolution of the representative of Georgina, " That no further action be taken in the construction of the county buildings, but that it would be conducive to the interests of the townships to remain in connection with the county of York." Oshawa appears to have at last accepted the inevitable.

The work of the county buildings was allowed to go on without further interruption, and all active opposition had subsided, at the session of the Provisional Council held in March, '53. Georgina was unrepresented at this session, having applied to the Legislature for a special Act to be reunited to York. Mr. Hartman's presence in Parliament secured the desired legislation from Mr. Hincks, against the remonstrance of the county of Ontario. Georgina was lopped off and annexed to York, and Mr. Hartman's seat was thereby made more secure.

Mr. Gould exerted himself to the utmost to prevent the departure of the wayward child, Georgina. He soundly berated Mr. Hartman for his conduct—an angry correspondence between them being the only result. He protested against action being taken by the Government—writing friendly letters of remonstrance to Mr. Hincks on the subject. In a letter under date of the 11th of March, 1855, addressed to Hon. Francis Hincks, Inspector-General, he says :—

As provisional warden and as a county man, I protest most solemnly, against Georgina being detached ; I protest against the bill now before the House, and for the reasons already explained to you, and of which I again beg to remind you—that the whole of the county, except Georgina, are opposed to it. And finally, I beg of you to use your influence as a minister to prevent the passage of the bill.

He concludes by telling Mr. Hincks that he has written Messrs. Wright and Hartman on the subject.

But all remonstrances were to no purpose ; the deed was done, and a most shameful piece of work it was.

A glance at the map will show that Georgina properly belonged to Ontario, and that attaching it to York was a piece of legislation that could only have been permitted by a Government desirous of serving a friend.

The county buildings progressed rapidly in the hands of Mr. Wallace the contractor. On Thursday, the 30th June, the corner stone was laid with imposing Masonic ceremonies. The day was a red-letter day in the annals of the county, and the event is thus recorded in the *Reporter* of the week following, in which the "heroic fortitude of Joseph Gould" is conspicuously referred to :—

According to the intimation in our last we now proceed to record the event of the laying of the corner stone of the Court House of the county of Ontario. It is not needed of us to enter into a recapitulation of the almost overwhelming struggles of our public men in the attainment of the great and important object of which the laying of the chief corner stone on the 30th June, 1853, was the triumphant consummation, nor of the heroic fortitude of Joseph Gould, of the noble township of Uxbridge, who, amidst the whirlwind of rage and disappointment of the enemies of this county, and every species of abuse that malice could invent, with the firm and unwavering spirit of a man who can be relied on in an emergency, braved the storm, and by his casting vote on the 1st of June, 1852, according to the provisions of the municipal law founded this county. He witnessed on the 30th ult. the laying of the corner stone of the county buildings, for which he laboured so incessantly, and the benefits of which to this section of country we hope he will live many years to enjoy. At no distant day we trust that both he and his co-labourers in this work will witness the whole length of this county spanned by the iron rail, and its fertile townships the thoroughfare of the commercial traffic between two great lakes.

Pursuant to the request of the provisional warden, James Rowe, Esq., and the contractor, James Wallace, Esq., the fraternity of Freemasons began to assemble at an early hour on Thursday, 30th ult. The day was beautiful, and the town of Whitby presented a gay appearance as every avenue leading to it poured in its line of carriages filled with happy faces. Along the east front of the Court House, an area was enclosed, and strong and substantial raised seats at either end erected. In the centre was a raised dais covered with carpet, appropriated to the officers of the Grand Lodge of Freemasons of the Province of Canada, the provisional warden of the county, the provisional council, the members for the county, the bar, the clergy and distinguished strangers. The arch that spanned the opening to the area was surmounted by a large crown, formed of evergreens and roses, and under which was suspended, in letters formed in evergreens the initials of our glorious Sovereign V.R., the whole surmounted by the Union Jack, and from various other points flags were suspended. At about three o'clock the area began to fill up, and at the time of the ceremony the seats presented an interesting appearance, filled as they were with the youth and beauty of the county. The Brooklin brass band being engaged for the occasion, arrived at an early hour, preceding the brethren of Mount Zion Lodge, Borelia; shortly after which the lodge at Bowmanville arrived, and about two o'clock p.m. the steamer was announced with the officers of the Grand Lodge and brethren from the different lodges in Toronto, accompanied by the city band. The Right Worshipful Grand Master, Sir Allan Napier McNab, was announced to officiate on the occasion but being suddenly attacked with illness, and the Deputy Grand Master, Mr. Ridout, being absent on Railroad business at Quebec, the duties devolved on Bro. Richardson, Grand Secretary. The carriages conveying the grand officers and brethren from the landing having arrived at the lodge rooms of the Composite Lodge, the Provincial Grand Lodge was opened in due and ancient form, after which the brethren, being properly marshalled, proceeded in open lodge to the Court House building. There were represented the—

Cadets of Temperance.
Sons of Temperance.
Bar.
Clergy.

Magistrates.

The Members for Ontario.

Freemasons.

Brethren in proper masonic clothing (*i.e.*, black suit, with the exception of the vest, which is white, white neck-cloth and gloves), and such Aprons and Ornaments as they were entitled to wear :

Two Tylers with Drawn Swords.

Music.

Brethren Members of Various Lodges, Two and Two.

A Cornucopia with Corn, carried by a Master.

Two Ewers with Wine and Oil, carried by Masters.

Grand Steward.   Grand Steward.

Grand Pursuivant.

Grand Organist.

Assistant Grand Director of Ceremonies.

Grand Director of Ceremonies.

Grand Superintendent of Works (Architect of the Building)

With the Plans and Inscription Plate.

Past Grand Sword Bearers.

Past Grand Deacons.

Past Grand Secretaries.

Grand Secretary with Book of Constitution on a Cushion.

Grand Registrar, with his Bag.

Grand Treasurer, with Phial containing Coins, etc.

Past Grand Wardens.

Visitors of Distinction.

The Corinthian Light carried by a Master.

The Column of the Junior Grand Warden carried by a Master Mason.

The Junior Grand Warden with the Plumb and Rule.

Banner of The Grand Lodge.

The Doric Light carried by a Master.

The Column of the Senior Grand Warden, carried by a Master Mason.

The Senior Grand Warden with the Level.

The Junior Grand Deacon.

Grand Steward—The Grand Chaplain with Bible on a

Cushion—Grand Steward.

The Deputy Grand Master, with the Square.

The Ionic Light, carried by a Past Master.

A Past Grand Warden, with the Mallet.

Grand Sword Bearer.

The Grand Master—Senior Grand Deacon.

Two Grand Stewards.

Grand Tyler.

Having arrived at the Buildings, and the acting Deputy Grand Master, Bro. Richardson, having taken his stand on the platform assigned to him, pursuant to ancient custom addressed the great assembly from all parts of the county in these words :—

Men, women and children, here assembled to-day to behold this ceremony, know all you, that we be lawful Masons, true to the laws of our country, and established of old with peace and honour, in most countries, to do good to our brethren, to build great buildings, and to fear God, who is the Great Architect of all things. We have among us secrets which may not be revealed, and which no man has discovered, but these secrets are lawful and honourable to know by Masons, who only have the keeping of them to the end of time. Unless our craft were good and our calling honourable, we should not have lasted so many centuries, nor should we have had so many illustrious brothers in our Order, ready to promote our laws and further our interests. To-day we are assembled in the presence of you, to lay the Foundation Stone of Buildings for the public use of this new county, and promote harmony and brotherly love, till the world itself shall end. So mote it be.

A prayer was then offered up by the Grand Chaplain, Rev. Bro. Mayerhoffer, when amidst a strain of music from the band, the Acting Grand Master descended, accompanied by his officers, and approached the north-east corner. The stone being previously raised, the Acting Grand Master placed the deposits underneath. (The deposits were:—Minutes of Provisional Council, Toronto papers of Thursday, June 30th, Scobie's Almanac, Ontario *Reporter* and Oshawa *Freeman*, a List of the Executive Government, Members of both branches of the Legislature, of the Judiciary, and other functionaries of the Province, last number of *Canadian Journal*, various silver and copper moneys of the realm,

copy of a letter of Joseph Gould, Esq., concerning the new
ınty.)

The following inscription is engrossed on parchment, and also
ıced in the bottle, which was carefully embedded in pulverized
ırcoal in the cavity :—

This

The Chief Corner Stone

Of the Court House and Public Offices

Of the County of Ontario,

was laid on

Thursday, the Thirtieth day of June,

in the year of our Lord one thousand eight hundred and fifty-three.

In the seventeenth year of the Reign

of

Her Most Gracious Majesty Queen Victoria,

The Right Honourable the Earl of Elgin and Kincardine, K.T.,

being

Governor-General of British North America,

by

The Grand Lodge

of

Free and Accepted Masons of Canada West.

On the invitation and in the presence

Of the Municipal Council and the Inhabitants

of the said County.

ɔ Provisional Municipal Council :—James Rowe, Esq., Warden ; Thomas
N. Gibbs, Reeve of Oshawa ; James Burns, Deputy-Reeve of Whitby ;
John M. Lumsden, Reeve of Pickering ; Peter Taylor, Deputy-Reeve
of Pickering ; Thos. Paxton, Reeve of Reach and Scugog ; Abel W.
Ewers, Deputy-Reeve of Reach and Scugog ; Nathaniel Bolster,
Deputy-Reeve of Brock ; George Brabazon, Reeve of Brock ; James
Galloway, Reeve of Scott ; Donald Cameron, Reeve of Thorah ;
Joseph Gould, Reeve of Uxbridge, Michael McDonagh, Reeve of
Mara and Rama ; William Powson, Clerk ; William Paxton, Treasurer.

Cumberland and Storm, Architects.

James Wallace, Contractor.

The mortar being spread, the stone was then slowly lowered to
permanent resting place amidst the solemn and magnificent

strains of the National Anthem by both bands. The plumb, square and level were then each respectively handed by the Chief Architect to the Acting Grand Master, who after applying them pronounced the stone " well formed, true and trusty."   Three immense cheers were then given for the Queen, and three for the county of Ontario.   The silver vessels containing the corn, wine and oil were then presented by the Grand Wardens, and were each successively poured on the stone by the Acting Grand Master, saying :—" May the all-bounteous Author of Nature bless the inhabitants of this place with all the necessaries, conveniences and comforts of life ; assist in the erection and completion of this building, protect the workmen against every accident, and long preserve the structure from decay ; and grant to us all, in needed supply, the corn of *nourishment*, the wine of *refreshment*, and the oil of *joy!*"

"Amen !   So mote it be !   Amen !"

The stone was then struck three times with the *mallet*, and the ceremony was concluded amidst immense cheering from the vast multitude.   The procession was then re-formed, and proceeding through the principal streets of Whitby, returned to the lodge room at Scripture's, and the Masonic Lodge was closed.

Amos Wright, Esq., member for this county, made some encouraging remarks touching our railroad prospects from his place on the platform, and was followed by the Rev. J. T. Byrne.

There was a grand dinner after the ceremony, at which everybody was toasted and everybody's prosperity drank, as well as the future prosperity of the new county.   The presence of Mr. Gibbs and others who had taken part in opposing the setting off of the county shows that all were now working amicably together.

CHAPTER XXXII.

THE appointment of County officers caused the next commotion. For the offices there was the usual scramble on such occasions, id more than the usual excitement in the struggle to secure them. he applicants were many and clamorous, each believing his own erits and his personal and party claims to be the best. Judge urnham had been already appointed Associate Judge of the United unties of York, Peel and Ontario, in 1852, on the petition of the rovisional Council, and had been previously Judge of the Division ourt. Mr. J. H. Perry received the appointment of Registrar in ctober, 1853. He was appointed under a special provision in the atute respecting the junior counties of Ontario, Peel, Elgin and ambton. The "scrimmage" went on over the other offices, id especially for the shrievalty was the contest hot and warm. r. Ezra Annes was a prominent applicant; Mr. John Campbell id pretensions to it, as well as to the Registry Office; Mr. Charles obinson was the nominee of the Provisional Council; Mr. S. B. airbanks had been recommended by the member for the county Ir. Wright), and also by Mr. Hartman. Mr. Wright was brought book for the latter recommendation, and was forced to withdraw at a public meeting, which also petitioned the Government ;ainst the bestowal of the appointment on Mr. Fairbanks. Finally legates were appointed and a convention held in Reach, where ie merits of the respective candidates were discussed. The voting was in favour of Mr. Charles Robinson for Sheriff. There were ten candidates for the office of Clerk of the Peace, the contest finally settling down between Mr. Chester Draper and Mr. William Powson, the latter carrying the day. Mr. Peter Taylor, of Pickering, was recommended for the office of Registrar, the convention being evidently in the dark as to the appointment of Mr. Perry having been already made. There was afterwards a lull on the surface, although, beneath it, applicants for office and their friends were working like beavers to secure them during the remainder of 1853.

On the 1st of January, 1854, the following proclamation was issued dissolving the union of counties, and erecting Ontario into a separate and independent county of the Province :—

PROCLAMATION.

Province of Canada. } William Rowan.

VICTORIA, by the Grace of God, of the United Kingdom of Great Britain and Ireland, Queen, Defender of the Faith, etc., etc., etc.

To all to whom these presents shall come—Greeting :

John Ross, Attorney Genl. } WHEREAS, by an Act of the Parliament of Our Province of Canada, passed in the twelfth year of Our Reign, Chaptered Seventy-eight, and intituled, "An Act for Abolishing the Territorial Divisions of Upper Canada into Districts, and for providing for Temporary Unions of Counties for Judicial and other purposes, and for the future dissolution of such Unions as the increase of wealth and population may require," certain provisions are made for the dissolution from time to time of the different Unions of Counties by the Separation of the Several Junior Counties as respects all matters both Judicial and Municipal, and for all other purposes whatsoever, and which provisions are by the said Act made applicable to the dissolution of such Unions in General. And whereas, by another Act of Parliament of Our said Province, passed in the Session thereof held in the fourteenth and fifteenth years of Our Reign, intituled, "An Act to make certain Alterations in the Territorial Divisions of Upper Canada," it is amongst other things in effect enacted, that so soon as the Court House and Gaol in any one of the Counties of Elgin, Waterloo, Ontario, Brant, Grey, Lambton, or Welland, shall have been erected and

ompleted at the County Town of such County according to the provisions
f the fifteenth section of the said first mentioned Act, and the other pro-
isions of the said fifteenth section shall have been complied with by any
ne of such counties, and so soon as certain appointments mentioned in the
eventeenth section of the said first recited Act shall have been thereafter
made in any one of the said counties, it shall and may be lawful for the
Governor of Our said Province, in Council, to issue a Proclamation dissolving the union between any one of such counties and the county or counties
to which it may be united.   And whereas, a Court House and Gaol for the
said County of Ontario, one of the United Counties of York, Ontario and
Peel, in our said Province, have been erected and completed at Whitby, the
County Town of the said county, according to the provisions of the said
fifteenth section of the said first mentioned Act and the other provisions of
the said fifteenth section have been complied with by the said county, and
the appointments mentioned in the said seventeenth section of the said Act
have been made :   And whereas the Provisional Municipal Council of the
said county have, thereupon, by their petition to Our Administrator of the
Government of Our said Province in Council, Prayed that a Proclamation
might be issued by Our said Administrator of the Government in Council,
disuniting the said County of Ontario from the said Union :   And whereas
it hath by Our said Administrator of the Government in Council been,
thereupon, thought expedient that such Proclamation shall be accordingly
issued, to bear teste on and to declare such separation upon, from and after
the thirtieth day of this present month of December: Now, therefore,
know ye, that We, taking the premises in Our Royal Consideration and fully
approving of the Resolution so come to by Our said Administrator of the
Government in Council in that behalf have thought fit to issue this, Our
Royal Proclamation for dissolving the said Union.   And we do accordingly,
in pursuance of the provisions of the said Acts of Parliament, hereby declare
that upon, from and after the said Thirtieth day of December instant,
the said Union of the said United Counties of York, Peel and Ontario, shall
be and the same is hereby absolutely dissolved, and that from thenceforth
the said County of Ontario shall be disunited from the said Counties of
York and Peel, and have a separate and independent organization of its own
as to all matters Judicial and Municipal, as well as for all other purposes
whatsoever.   And we do further declare, that the Provisional Municipal
Council of the said County of Ontario shall, upon the day aforesaid, lapse
and be absolutely dissolved, and that from thenceforth none of the Courts

nor Officers of the said Union shall as such have any jurisdiction or authority whatever in or over the said County of Ontario; anything in their respective commissions, or in any Act of Parliament, either of the Province of Canada or late Province of Upper Canada, to the contrary thereof in anywise notwithstanding.

And we do further, in pursuance of the said first mentioned Act of Parliament, hereby further declare, that the said remaining Counties of York and Peel shall, upon, from and after the said Thirtieth day of December instant, constitute and form a Union of Counties under the said Acts, by and under the name and style of the United Counties of York and Peel, and shall continue so to form such last mentioned Union until the same shall be in like manner dissolved in due form of law. And know ye, that we have commanded and ordained, and by these presents do command and ordain that all Magistrates and other Officers holding commissions from us, or by our authority or otherwise howsoever of, in or for the said United Counties of York, Ontario and Peel, except only such of Our Justices of the Peace for the said United Counties as shall be now resident in the County of Ontario, shall, in Our name, or otherwise according to law, continue to exercise the duties of their respective offices in and for the said United Counties of York and Peel as if they had been appointed in and for such last mentioned Union, until our Royal Pleasure shall be further made known therein, or the authority of such officers in that behalf shall be otherwise determined according to law. Of all and singular which premises all Judges, Justices, Sheriffs, Magistrates, Constables and Officers of the said United Counties of York, Ontario and Peel, and all Our loving subjects of the said Counties, as well as of all others whom it doth or may in anywise concern, are hereby required to take notice and to govern themselves accordingly.

IN TESTIMONY WHEREOF, we have caused these Our letters to be made Patent, and the Great Seal of Our said Province of Canada to be hereunto affixed. Witness Our Trusty and Well beloved William Rowan, Esq., C.B., Administrator of the Government of our said Province, and Lieutenant-General Commanding Our Forces therein, etc., etc., etc., at Quebec, in our said Province, this Thirtieth day of December, in the Year of Our Lord One Thousand Eight Hundred and Fifty-three, and in the Seventeenth Year of Our Reign.

By Command,

P. J. O. CHAUVEAU, *Secretary.*

Simultaneously with the issue of the proclamation of December, 1858, the official *Gazette* contained the following appointments: Z. Burnham, Esq., to be Judge of the County and Surrogate Courts of the county of Ontario; Nelson Gilbert Reynolds, Esq., to be Sheriff, and Bernard Frey Ball, Esq., barrister-at-law, to be Clerk of the Peace.

At the same time Joseph Clark, Joseph R. Thompson, Wm. McMullen and Robert W. Clarke, M.D., were appointed County Coroners.

The following commission of the peace also issued—J. B. Warren, W. Bagshaw, M. Cowan, M. McDonagh, A. Bagshaw, W. Allison, A. Campbell, E. McMillan, J. H. Thompson, A. Hurd, J. Campbell, C. Robinson, Wm. Dunbar, J. Dryden, J. Lomax, J. Reekie, P. Whitney, R. Campbell, G. Bostwick, L. Mackey, S. Mason, E. Birrell, W. F. Moore, A. Spears, F. Green, W. Don, J. Hunter, W. H. Gibbs, J. Foote, A. Fullerton, G. W. Post, H. Major, T. P. White, J. Clerke, W. H. Michell, P. Taylor, J. Vail, J. Churchill, I. B. Carpenter, J. Nichol, J. Burns, J. Campbell, C. Campbell, A. Farewell, E. Annes, J. H. Perry, C. H. Lynde, J. S. M. Wilcox, R. J. Gunn, J. Hepburn, J. Harnden, jun., J. Radcliffe, G. Brabazon, C. Gibbs, M. Cowan, jun., R. Way, M. Gillespie, T. Paxton, W. Powson, R. Wells, J. Burnham, R. Lund, G. Currie, J. K. Vernon, L. Card, J. McPherson, J. S. Garnett, G. Smith, G. Proctor, K. Cameron, W. McCaskill, D. Cameron, J. Gould, R. Spears, J. Wideman, W. Randall.

On the 21st Mr. J. V. Ham was appointed Clerk of the County Court and Registrar of the Surrogate Court for the county.

Mr. Reynolds, the new sheriff, was a stranger residing in Belleville. He had no claim whatever to the office, and was appointed through the influence of Hon. John Ross. As might be expected, the setting aside of the claims of county men and giving the office to an outsider was not received with satisfaction.

CHAPTER XXXIII.

THE first meeting of the new County Council, now an independent county *de jure* and *de facto*, was held on Monday, 23rd January, 1854, at the new courthouse in Whitby. The following gentlemen were the Reeves and Deputy-Reeves of the several municipalities:—Brock, John Hall Thompson and John Hart; Mara and Rama, Thomas McDermott; Pickering, John M. Lumsden and Peter Taylor; Reach and Scugog, Thomas Paxton and Robert Wells; Scott, Jas. K. Vernon; Thorah, Neil McDougall; Uxbridge, Wm. Hamilton; Whitby, John Ham Perry and Abraham Farewell; Oshawa, T. N. Gibbs. Mr. Gibbs was elected Warden. Mr. H. J. Macdonell was at the same time appointed County Clerk.

Mr. John Shier, P.L.S., was appointed County Engineer.

On the death of Mr. Ball, in 1856, Mr. Macdonell received the appointment of Clerk of the Peace, and filled the office up to his death, in 1877, when it fell to Mr. J. E. Farewell as County Attorney. Previous to that Mr. W. H. Tremayne was appointed County Attorney, in 1858; and after him Mr. S. H. Cochrane, in

1863, on whose death, in 1872, Mr. Farewell was appointed. Judge Dartnell's appointment as Junior County Judge took place in 1873. Mr. Shier was appointed County Clerk on the death of Mr. Macdonell, and Mr. Farewell on the death of Mr. Shier. Mr. Wm. Laing was appointed County Treasurer on the death of Mr. Peter Taylor, who succeeded Mr. Paxton in the office. Mr. Jas. B. Laing, the present incumbent, was promoted from assistant treasurer to his father's position in 1882.

The new courthouse was opened on Tuesday, 4th April—the first sessions of the peace being on that and the following day by his Honor, Judge Burnham : Mr. Donald McKay, of Pickering, was foreman of the first grand jury. His Honor, in the course of an elaborate and able charge, referred to the difficulties that had to be encountered in securing separation from York, and the encouraging prospect before the new county.

Mr. Gibbs appears to have made a very successful Warden during his year of office. A very practical address delivered by him, on the state of the county finances and general business, is reported in full in the proceedings of the following June session,. and a complimentary resolution is also passed him for his services. Mr. Gibbs made advances of money at the time for carrying on the county's business, and generally identified himself with the county's interest and future prosperity, now that the question of the county town was settled beyond recall. At the meeting of the council, 22nd January, 1855, he was re-elected Warden. And at the June session following we find the following resolution passed at the close of the proceedings :—

"Mr. McDougall, seconded by Mr. Hewitt, moves—That the members of this Council cannot separate without first expressing their warmest and sincere thanks to the Warden for the able and impartial manner in which he has always acted in presiding over this Council ; and it is the sincere wish of every member of this Council that this county will have the benefit of his valuable and indefatigable labours as Warden for many years to come."

The first Court of Assize for the county was opened by Mr. Justice Burns on Monday, 10th April, 1854. There was only one criminal charge (a case of larceny) and three records for trial. The late Judge Morrison attended as Solicitor-General; Carelton Lynde was foreman of the Grand Jury.

In their presentment, Sheriff Reynolds is praised for his efficiency, and it is added—"Our Sheriff, though a stranger, merits the approbation of all for the foresight and judgment displayed in the arrangements made for conducting the assizes ; and although we may feel disposed to condemn the principle involved in the Government appointment, we have no reason to find fault with the man." The appointment of an outsider as sheriff, contrary to the voice of the people of the county, as expressed at public meeting, was naturally distasteful, and especially so to the resident applicants for the shrievalty Mr. Sheriff Reynolds's conduct, however, although "a stranger" was not long in securing for him the good opinion of the community The other officials of the court, and especially the high constable, Mr Keller, get a favourable word. The ladies are not omitted ; they were invited to reserved seats in court ; a dinner was given a' Scripture's hotel, and there was general complaisance and rejoicing all around. Thenceforward the county pursued " the even tenor o its way." Railroads and Road and Bridge appropriations were the important questions up for discussion at several meetings.

The project of a railway from Whitby to Georgian Bay had been agitated long before the separation of the county. With the inau guration of the new county the special agitation of the question commenced. Now, said the men in advance of the slow growth o public opinion respecting railways, in that day, that we have th county question settled, the next thing to be secured to the pro gressive welfare of the county is a railroad from Port Whitby to Georgian Bay ; and if we put our shoulders to the wheel with a will this great achievement can also be accomplished. A preliminar, meeting was held on the 13th November, 1852, in Whitby, at which

James Rowe presided, and John Ham Perry acted as secretary. A committee to forward the project was appointed, consisting of Dr. Gunn, Messrs. James Wallace, J. H. Perry, E. Annes, Hugh Fraser, Lewis Houck, R. H. Lawder, James Rowe and L. H. Schofield. A public meeting was next got up, the requisition calling it being signed by the leading men of the town and townships.

The meeting was largely attended, James Rowe occupied the chair, and H. J. Macdonell acted as secretary. We are told that "the wealth and intelligence of the township"—then including the town of Whitby and East Whitby—"were well represented."

The following resolutions passed :—

Moved by Mr. Wm. Laing, and seconded by Mr. T. Dow :

Resolved,—"That this meeting views with pleasure and satisfaction the probability of shortly having through this beautiful Province a through system of railroads, which in addition to their being the great civilizers and benefactors of mankind, are well calculated to draw out the industry and enterprise of a people and unfold the riches and treasures of a county."

Moved by Mr. Ezra Annes, and seconded by Mr. Jas. Hodgson :

Resolved,—"That the position of the western part of Upper Canada is such, situated between and bounded by Lakes Ontario, Erie and Huron, it naturally can, with prudent and judicious arrangements command the great carrying trade of the far west to the Atlantic cities, and *vice versa.*"

Moved by Mr. John H. Perry, and seconded by Dr. Foote :

Resolved,—"That the tract of country from Port Whitby, on Lake Ontario, to Sturgeon Bay, on Lake Huron, offers many and important advantages for the construction of a railroad, over all other projected routes between those lakes—viz., while, for instance, the Toronto, Simcoe and Huron Railroad, which stands next in favourableness of route to this proposed line, will lessen the distance between Mackinaw on the west, and New York and Boston on the east, about 810 miles, the Port Whitby and Huron Road by narrows

Lake Simcoe, will again decrease the distance some forty miles below the Toronto and Huron route—a sufficient consideration to be able always to compete successfully with rival lines, and, in addition to having natural harbours at both terminuses, no excavating, embankment or bridging of account will be required, and will open up an extent of country which for fertility of soil, healthiness of climate and natural advantages is not surpassed in Canada."

Moved by Mr. Wallace, and seconded by Mr. Hopkins:

Resolved,—"That immediate steps be taken to obtain, at the adjourned session of Parliament, a charter to incorporate a company with a capital of £———, to construct a line of railroad from Port Whitby to Sturgeon Bay, or some other suitable point on Lake Huron."

Moved by Mr. R. H. Lawder, and seconded by Mr. McPherson:

Resolved,—"That a committee of thirteen be appointed, to consist of Dr. Alliston, James Wallace, J. H. Perry, Wm. Laing, James Rowe, John Welsh, Dr. R. J. Gunn, E. Annes, Wm. Gordon, James Hodgson, and John Shier, whose duty it shall be to carry out the above resolution, and perform and transact all other business and matters requisite for the speedy prosecution of this important work."

Moved by Z. Burnham, Esq., and seconded by Mr. Annes:

Resolved,—"That the co-operation of Amos Wright, Esq., and Joseph Hartman, Esq., M.PP.'s for the third and fourth ridings of York, is respectfully requested to aid and assist the above committee to obtain a charter for the proposed road, and carry out the views of this meeting."

Moved by Dr. Gunn, and seconded by Mr. Wallace:

Resolved,—"That a subscription be now entered into for the purpose of meeting the expenses of obtaining a charter and other disbursements necessarily arising out of the foregoing resolutions, to be collected by the aforesaid committee and paid over to the treasurer by them appointed, whose duty it shall be to pay out such money on the order of the chairman of the said committee, counter-signed by their secretary."

A subscription was then entered into and upwards of one hundred pounds subscribed by parties attending the meeting, for the purpose of paying preliminary expenses, etc.

Meetings were held in town and county during the next few months at a lively rate, at all of which the propriety of constructing the railway was fully discussed and approved of. Mr. A. J. Robinson and Mr. John Shier made preliminary surveys of portions of the route and estimates of cost—the latter being set down at £4,000 per mile.

In April, 1853, the first railway charter was granted. It was to incorporate " The Port Whitby and Lake Huron Railway Company."

The corporators named in the charter are Joseph Gould, Peter Taylor, Henry Daniels, James Rowe, Wm. Laing, Ezra Annes, James Wallace, John Shier and R. J. Gunn. Capital £250,000 divided into 25,000 shares of £10 each. At the first meeting of the provisional directors, held 15th May following, Ezra Annes was elected President; W. Laing, Vice-President; John H. Perry, Secretary and Treasurer ; and John Shier, Engineer.

Meetings were immediately held and surveys pushed forward, and the directors appear to have gone to work with vigour to bring the merits of the undertaking prominently before the public. A preliminary survey as far as Manchester was made, and the route found quite favourable. The hopefulness of the project is spoken of as follows : " In fact there are no engineering difficulties to contend with on the whole line. The whole country, from the southern terminus to the Georgian Bay, cannot be excelled in the Province in its natural advantages for the easy and cheap construction of a railway to connect the two great lakes, Ontario and Huron. Our peculiar position in relation to Lakes Scugog and Simcoe also is such that no line of road of the same length in the Western Province can command the trade of the same extent of country as the proposed northern line from this point. Take Port Whitby as the starting-point—for twenty-four miles north the country is rich and flourishing, laps the head of Lake Scugog, which will be a feeder to the road, drawing the trade and traffic from the north-east (of a distance from sixty to one hundred miles) in this direction. Another section of twenty-two miles will bring us to Simcoe, there to compete for the trade bordering on that lake. And a third section of thirty miles, also running through a portion of country unsurpassed for its fertility of soil, and we are at the Georgian Bay, in direct communication with the far west, and the rich and valuable mines of Lake Superior. The road once built, it would be the shortest, cheapest and no doubt the favourite route of travel from the Atlantic cities to the west and *vice versa*, and, irrespective of its local advantages from the through trade and travel alone, it would become the leading and favourite road of the Province."

The agitation went on and meetings continued to be held, one of the results being that even at that early day the ratepayers of the township of Mariposa agreed to take £20,000 stock, provided the road ran through that township. They had offers of a road then from Peterborough across the county, but they looked to Whitby as their natural outlet. In November, 1853, the Company had an offer from Sykes & Co. to build the road from lake to lake —an offer so entirely favourable as should have recommended its instant acceptance.

The offer was as follows :—

"I am directed by Messrs. J. Sykes & Co. to say that they will build the Port Whitby and Lake Huron Railway in first-class manner, and furnish the required rolling stock and make arrangements for the stock to be taken up in England on the following conditions :

"1st. That municipal aid to the extent of £3,000 sterling per mile be loaned to constitute a first charge upon the road.

"2nd. That sufficient stock be taken within the district to

purchase right of way, office (your own) expenses, including Engineer, Solicitor, Secretary, and if any such is appointed, the salary of a paid Director (during the construction of the road), and any other incidental expenses connected with your own acts.

"The road shall be equal to any road in the Province and they will guarantee to build it within reasonable time, paying interest upon the bonds during construction, and at a reasonable price, and will be prepared to go over the road and give tender as soon as you have the municipalities pledged to the undertaking.

"Your obedient servant,

"W. C. EVANS."

The acceptance of this offer would have placed the county in an excellent position. If the road earned enough to pay interest on £3,000 a mile, it would not cost the county a shilling. While the road was in progress of construction the interest would be paid by the contractors, and to secure principal and interest a first mortgage would be given on the line. A large county meeting was held at Epsom on the 15th December, at which resolutions were passed approving of the liberality of the offer of Sykes & Co., and pledging those present, individually and collectively, to adopt the best means in their power to procure the desired loan upon the credit of the county.

The municipal elections in the following January mainly turned upon the railroad question. The two parties, Railway and Anti-Railway, were very evenly balanced in the Council. At the first meeting of the County Council, in January, 1854, Mr. J. H. Perry brought up the question. He moved for leave to introduce a by-law to loan the credit of the county to the amount of £———, for the purpose of constructing a railway from Port Whitby to Lake Huron. A discussion ensued. Mr. Perry stated that he only desired to pass the by-law through a first reading and print it for the information of the people. Mr. Thompson, of Brock, moved in

amendment that it was inexpedient to print such a by-law.
Messrs. Lumsden and Taylor, from Pickering, opposed the introduction of the Bill altogether, having been pledged to do so by
their township. Mr. Hamilton, of Uxbridge, opposed the first
move being made, because he thought "a good farmer should
prevent the first seed of a poisonous weed from getting into his
field." To which Mr. Wells replied that "the Reeve of Uxbridge
stated what was not good farming in fact, for land could not become
rich without becoming manured, and he would not withhold manure
for fear of its containing a poisonous weed." Such are specimens
of the arguments then used.

Mr. A. Farewell warmly espoused the railway cause from the
start, and sacrificed his popularity in his own section to what he
rightly regarded as the interest of the county as a whole. What,
he said, it was proposed to do was to take the initiatory steps,
by laying information before the county as to the amount to be
guaranteed, the nature of the security required, the terms of
disbursement as the works proceed, and other matters which it was
desirable the people of the county should know.

He wished to show the county that the proposition of Sykes &
Co. would secure the road, and cost the county nothing. The
question on amendment being put, the yeas and nays stood as
follows: Hamilton, Hart, Lumsden, McDermott, Taylor and
Thompson—six for; Farewell, McDougall, Paxton, Perry, Vernon
and Wells—six against and in favour of submitting the by-law.
The Warden, Mr. Gibbs, voted with the yeas, for the amendment,
which he declared carried. This first check to the enterprise was
disastrous in its consequences; it not only prevented the Company
from taking steps which would enable them to avail themselves of
the favourable offer of Sykes & Co., but by putting back the project
gave Port Hope and the railway promoters to the east and west the
wished-for opportunity of striking in vigorously and cutting off the
trade which properly belonged to, and naturally would flow through

the length of the county to the county town and port of Whitby. Subsequently Hon. George Brown made an offer on behalf of a railway contracting firm, to construct the road from point to point at £4,500 per mile, but that, too, fell through. Surveys had been made, and especially an exhaustive survey, costing hundreds of pounds, by Mr. Shanly. The County Council was appealed to again and again, in vain, no substantial encouragement could be obtained from the county, as a corporation. Railways were then new to Canada; their advantages were not understood; many honestly believed that a railway would not benefit the county, while the representatives from the east and west opposed it because they conceived the centre of the county and the county town would only be benefited, and that to the detriment of their own localities. Hence their active hostility from the very inception of the scheme. The agitation for the next few years is one of constant meetings, discussions, amended charters, and, worst of all, local squabbles and personal differences between the promoters themselves.

The town of Whitby had courageously come forward and voted for a by-law taking £75,000 stock; the directors had worried and worked themselves sick, and spent no small amount of money out of their own purses in placing the feasibility of the scheme and all the facts before the public, but still little headway had been made.

Once more, at a special session of the County Council on 10th November, 1857, convened for that purpose, the railway question was brought forward. After a lengthy discussion, a by-law was passed authorizing the Warden to subscribe for four thousand shares, or £100,000, in the capital stock of company. The representatives of Pickering, Oshawa, Brock, Uxbridge and Scott voted against the measure; while it was sustained by the representatives of Mara and Rama, Thorah, Reach, Scugog, Whitby and Town of Whitby. The by-law was submitted to a vote of the ratepayers, to be taken on 16th December following. The result of the vote in the different localities was the rejection of the by-law. The defeat of the by-law in the county was overwhelming. Still the promoters lost neither courage nor confidence in the cherished enterprise. Still the railway continued to be the question of questions in the county. It entered into all municipal contests, and many of the best representatives were defeated at the polls because of their railway sympathies—because they were able to see farther ahead as to the benefits to be derived from railways than were the bulk of their neighbours. The great depression of '57 and '58 by which the county was overtaken, and which paralyzed so many other enterprises, kept the railway question in the background for some time. The great mistake of the county municipalities, in rejecting a proposition which would give them a railway from lake to lake— making the county of Ontario the grand highway for the trade of the west and north—was seized upon by the rival communities to the east and west to extend their railway operations. Lines running across the county were projected and charters obtained; the Midland extended, and the Toronto and Nipissing built, Uxbridge and Brock giving bonuses of $50,000 each to the latter, and the township of Thorah $50,000 to the Midland, and a large portion of the trade of the county was thus diverted from its natural channel. In these adverse circumstances, it was seen that the larger and more comprehensive scheme of a railway from Whitby to Georgian Bay could not be immediately accomplished; but that if any portion of the trade of the county were to be retained, and in fact the county itself saved from being dismembered, prompt action was necessary—something had to be done by the central portion of the county to secure railway connection with the front.

The history of the railway campaigns and the adventures of those engaged in them at this time would fill pages. John Ham Perry, James Rowe, Sheriff Reynolds, Chester Draper and others in the front, backed up by Thomas Paxton, Joseph Bigelow, W. S. Sexton, J. B. Campbell, James Dryden, and that tried and staunch friend of the county for so many years, Charles Robinson, in the north, never wearied in their exertions, and worked night and day in promoting the cause they had undertaken; nor were their purses made any heavier by the very considerable personal expenses to which they were subjected. Mr. Gould did all he could in favour of the county line, and paid a large share of the expenses of the preliminary survey. That failing, he took up the cause of the promoters of the Nipissing line. He took stock to the amount of $10,000, and secured all the benefits possible to be obtained for Uxbridge by railway connection with Toronto.

The Nipissing line to Uxbridge was formally opened on the 14th of September, 1871. The following account of the celebration of the occasion is taken from the Uxbridge *Journal* of the ensuing week :—

FORMAL OPENING OF THE TORONTO AND NIPISSING RAILROAD.

On Thursday last, the 14th inst., the Narrow Gauge Railway, known as the Toronto and Nipissing road, was formally opened with considerable *éclat*. According to previous announcement, the excursion train arrived at this station at one o'clock, with about four hundred visitors on board, comprising a number of specially invited distinguished guests—members of the Ontario Cabinet, city aldermen, the Railway Board of Management and others. These were met by the leading men of our village, and, headed by the band of the 10th Royals, which had accompanied the party from Toronto, were escorted to the drill-shed, where a handsome repast awaited them. Along the line of railway the various stations were tastefully festooned with evergreens and appropriate mottoes. The Uxbridge station was elaborately decorated with an arch of evergreens and the motto on the building, "Onward to Fort Garry." Five other arches were erected in the village, displaying with appropriate devices the following mottoes: "Space Conquered;" "Labor Omnia Vincit;" "The Old Times have Vanished;" "Who'd have Thought It;" and "Welcome to Uxbridge." Our merchants and others seemed to vie with each other in aiding to the beautifying of the place. Union Jacks and St. George's crosses floated from almost every building, while streamers crossed the streets from house to house. The printing-office was decorated with evergreens, interspersed with which were the following mottoes: "Cead Mille Failthe," and "Broad Gauge Principles but Narrow Gauge Railways for us."

Arrived at the drill-shed, the party were not long in introducing themselves to the excellent substantials which had been provided —a keen relish for which we have no doubt had been engendered by the morning's ride—and to which ample justice was done.

The cloth having been removed, the chairman, Mr. John Shedden, stated that he had received letters from many of the most prominent citizens of Canada, all of whom expressed their wishes for the success of the Toronto and Nipissing Railway, and their regret at not being able to be present at the banquet. He then proposed "The Queen," which was duly honoured by the company.

Song—"God Save the Queen."

The next toast from the chair was "The Governor-General," which was received with all the honours, after which followed "The Lieutenant-Governor of Ontario."

The chairman then gave the toast of "The Dominion Government," and in doing so he said that he was sorry there was not a fuller representation of that Cabinet, but he was glad to see that it was worthily represented in the person of the Hon. J. C. Aikins.

Mr. Aikins responded, saying that he knew how gratified every member of the Government would have been to be present on the occasion, but they could not neglect public affairs to attend the present meeting, however much they might feel interested in it. He thoroughly believed in the narrow gauge railways, and considered that the country needed them very much. The Government had now a railway scheme of their own in progress—he alluded to the Pacific Railway—so that all parts of the country would be accessible to each other, and the people of the North-

West brought into direct communication with us. Twenty years ago it might be said that there were not ten miles of railway in Canada, and now there were over three thousand miles. Great as the progress of the country had been in times past, he believed that it would be still greater in the future; and that it might be so, every encouragement should be given to emigration by the Dominion Government, in order that the waste places of the land might be brought under cultivation. He was much pleased with what he had seen in connection with the Nipissing line, and it had his best wishes for its prosperity.

The chairman, in a few prefatory remarks, gave the toast of "The Ontario Government and Legislature."

Hon. M. C. Cameron, who was warmly received, stated that no matter what might be the political feelings of those comprising the meeting, he was sure that all of them would agree that enterprises such as that the establishment of which they had now assembled to commemorate the members of the Government had always cordially supported. The progress of the country had been very great for the past few years, and though he did not claim for the Government that to them the credit for this progress was altogether due, yet he would say that in a great measure this prosperity was due to the efforts they had made to promote the advancement of the people. They had established facilities for more general education amongst the people, and had in every manner taken advantage of all the means which presented themselves to aid in developing the country. He could say sincerely on behalf of his colleagues that each of them was desirous of assisting to the utmost the progress of the Province, and when the people felt convinced that others more competent than the members of the present Administration to administer the affairs of the country would be found they would cheerfully retire and give place to their successors. He thanked the company for the reception of the toast, and resumed his seat amid loud cheers.

Messrs. Paxton M.PP., and Coyne, M.PP., also responded on behalf of the Legislature.

Mr. George Laidlaw, who was greeted with loud cheers, then proposed " Success to the Toronto and Nipissing Railway." He alluded to the difficulties which had to be overcome before the railway could be built, but these had all been conquered by energy and perseverance, and from the appearance of things, everything in connection with the road was run in good working order, and its promoters felt every confidence in it, that its career would fully anticipate their earnest anticipations.

Mr. Shedden responded to the toast, and said so far everything in connection with the railway had worked satisfactorily, notwithstanding the numerous difficulties that had to be met and overcome before the line could be built. He felt much pleasure in congratulating the shareholders and all interested in any way in the success of the Nipissing road that things were now so far advanced that there was no question that the enterprise would prove all that was anticipated by its friends.

Mr. Wm. Gooderham, jun., also responded to the toast to the same effect as the preceding speaker, stating that no one could help feeling thoroughly satisfied with the manner in which the railway had been pushed forward to its present state of completion.

Mr. T. C. Chisholm, being called for, also made a few remarks. He said that the great thing the company had to depend upon was the Government and the municipalities, who he thought should liberally support the Nipissing road. The road would soon be in thorough working order to Coboconk, and then it would speak for itself. In the meantime the line was in a very satisfactory condition, and he trusted that all the anticipations of the shareholders would be realized fully.

Mr. Joseph Gould, Uxbridge, in responding to the toast, also urged upon the Government the great desirability for assistance on their part and that of the municipalities to the narrow gauge railroads, for the benefits which these roads conferred upon the country were unquestioned. The Government would fail in its duty if it did not do all in its power to forward enterprises such as these.

The toast of "The Bar and Bench of Ontario" was next proposed and responded to by Judge Hagarty, who made a brief but eloquent reply. After expressing his cordial approval of the narrow gauge lines of railway, and the pleasure he felt at being present at the ceremony of the formal opening of the Nipissing line to Uxbridge, he referred to the magnificence of the country which these railroads tended to open up and improve. In one of the novels of the great and good Walter Scott, whose centenary had lately been celebrated in all portions of the civilized world, one of that worthy's heroes was represented as coming in sight of the beautiful city of Edinburg, nestled under the crags, and with the picturesque waters of the Forth in the distance, and overpowered by natural emotion, asking himself where was the coward who would not dare to fight for such a land. He (the speaker) had some time ago stood on the heights of Queenston, by Brock's monument, and never had he seen a fairer view of a more beautiful landscape. He had also witnessed the magnificent scenery on the St. Lawrence, and the same thought as that given expression to by Scott's hero came into his mind— " Where is the coward who would not dare to fight for such a land ? " (Applause.) We had a great destiny before us, and it depended upon ourselves to improve the opportunities which were placed before us to make Canada one of the foremost nations of the earth. Let us work so that when our eyes close in death our children might have as good a heritage as could be bestowed upon them—a smiling and prosperous land, over which the Union Jack would wave to gladden their sight. Pounds, shillings and pence were not the only considerations to be thought of ; and he hoped that by mere mercenary motives none would be led to forget the glorious heritage handed down to them, and seek to sever their connection with Great Britain, for wherever its flag had gone Christian liberty and all the

blessings of civilization had followed.   The chains had fallen off
slaves wherever the meteor flag of England had appeared, and in
its place came progress and improvement.   May our children and
grandchildren live under the protecting folds of the Union Jack—
God bless it !

Judge Duggan also responded in a few well-timed remarks.

Hon. Mr. McDougall then proposed "The Commercial and
Banking Interests of Canada."   He referred in pleasing terms to
the position in which the people of Uxbridge and surrounding
country now found themselves in regard to the railway which had
just been built.   It was only a few years since he and his friend
near him (Hon. M. C. Cameron) had contested the representation
of North Ontario, and each had defeated the other on two different
occasions, and he could bear witness to the great improvements
visible in that section since he canvassed there.   In regard to the
constitution under which we were now happily living, he might say,
as one who had a share in the framing of the new system, that it
was intended by its framers that the local Governments should be
more municipal in their nature than political—that the heat of
party spirit and strife should not be carried into these assemblies,
but that all local questions should be discussed in a free but unpre-
judiced manner, leaving more strictly political warfare to be contested in the Dominion Parliament.   If the people think they would
be better off in having party politics in their Local Houses, all well
and good.   Speaking individually as a taxpayer and a citizen, he
would say that, looking back to the legislation of the past four years,
there was nothing in it with which he could find fault [applause];
and in particular could he say that he cordially agreed with the
railway policy of the cabinet.   He referred to the fact that he had
suggested the appointment of Mr. Sandfield Macdonald to his
present office, and concluded a very pleasing address by referring to
the banking and commercial interests of the country.

Mr. Wm. Gooderham, sen., Mr. R. W. Elliot, Mr. A. R.

IcMaster, and Mr. J. D. Merrick responded. The last-named entleman stated that, however much some persons might feel gainst the Grand Trunk Railway, that institution had dealt with he narrow gauge railways in a most liberal spirit, and without the earty co-operation of the directors of that road the new lines of ailway would not be in so prosperous a condition as they were at he present time. He therefore had much pleasure in proposing he toast of " The Railway Interests of Canada," coupling with it he Grand Trunk Railway.

Mr. Aquila Walsh, in responding, drew attention to the fact hat the money invested in the Grand Trunk Railway was a good nvestment to the Government, and that that road had proved of ncalculable benefit to the people of Canada. For the railway with :hich he was connected—the Intercolonial—he could say that verything was progressing satisfactorily in its building, and that efore long it would be completed and the people would then :itness the cheapest and best railway in Canada. The whole tructures connected with the line were to be of wood, in order that t might be built with the greatest economy, and that it might also :c successful as a commercial undertaking. Steel rails and iron :cdges were to be used altogether in the construction of the rail-:ay, so that in every respect it would be, when completed, the best oad in the Dominion. The Parliament of the country had acted iberally towards railways, and there would be nothing lost by them n continuing the policy they had hitherto adopted.

Mr. Chester Draper also responded. He said that the word ' Canada " now composed a large territory, extending from the .tlantic to the Pacific—far different from what Canada literally was few years ago—and to develop and settle this vast region enter-·rises like the present they were now engaged in celebrating were ceded in every direction before our resources could be thoroughly eveloped.

Mr. Bellingham, of Montreal, being called upon by the chairman, also replied to the toast. He said that he had come to this province on the present occasion to witness the working of the narrow gauge railways, and he could say that he had been much gratified with what he had witnessed. They had experimented with wooden railways in Quebec, but after repeated trials they had not been found to work well, and he could not therefore recommend them to the people of Ontario. The Government of Quebec had dealt liberally with railway enterprises, having made a grant of 10,000 acres in aid of a new line in that province. He had been forty-six years in Canada, and he had lived to see it become a great and prosperous country, with every indication of continued advancement.

Mr. Sweetnam said he had a toast to propose which he was sure would be heartily received. He referred to those whom he might term for the present "Our American Cousins," who had greatly benefited this country, and had shown extraordinary enterprise in opening and extending railways.

Col. Shaw thanked the company for the kind manner in which the toast had been drunk. He alluded to the time when, not more than forty years ago, but a small railway was in operation in his native country, and now the land was intersected in every direction by railways—from the north and east to the far south and west. After a few further remarks, eloquently expressed, the speaker concluded by expressing his earnest hope that Canada and the United States might ever remain in peaceful relations to each other, and that both countries might go on conquering and to conquer in the highways of peace.

"The Corporation of Toronto" was next proposed, the names of Aldermen Harman and Dickey being coupled with it. The former gentleman regretted the absence of the mayor, who had missed the opportunity of making a reply to the toast proposed in such a handsome manner. He (the speaker) referred to the vast strides Toronto is now making, the value of its real property eight years

go being $20,000,000, while now it was $30,000,000. Recognizing
ully this fact, who could estimate what further progress would be
made in the next decade ? He heartily congratulated the Nipissing
Company on the success which attended their efforts, and it would
always be with a feeling of gratification that his name as the then
Mayor of Toronto was signed to the debentures issued by the corporation in behalf of the Nipissing Railway.

Alderman Dickey could but say that he felt highly gratified
at the completion of the railway to Uxbridge. Even the most rabid
opponent of the road was now convinced of its value to the country.

Captain Taylor made a few remarks in reference to his personal
labours when the railway was being inaugurated.

Mr. Gould proposed the health of the father of the narrow gauge
railways in Canada—Mr. George Laidlaw.

The toast was drunk with great enthusiasm ; and in response
Mr. Laidlaw said it was the proudest moment of his life, but he
would say that, without the aid of many of those whom he saw
about him, all his efforts would have been futile. To the Hon.
I. C. Cameron, who had so warmly assisted in getting the Bill
of Incorporation through the House of Assembly, and through the
vote of whose Premier the measure was at length passed ; to the
merchants of Toronto—to such firms as John Macdonald & Co.,
McMaster Bros., Gordon, McKay & Co., and others, the thanks of
the community through which the Nipissing Railway passed were
largely due ; also to the members of the Toronto Corporation and
the rural municipalities who had pushed the enterprise forward by
liberal grants of money. These formed the bridge which had carried the railway over safely. On account of the present late hour
he would not detain the company, but would again thank them
most sincerely for their kind reception of the toast.

The next toast was that of the Toronto, Grey and Bruce Railway, which was responded to by Hon. Mr. McMurrich in a few
well-chosen remarks.

Mr. J. G. Worts gave "The Municipalities Along the Line o
the Railway." Responded to by Hon. David Reesor.

One or two other volunteer toasts followed, and the meeting
broke up.

The visitors then repaired to the cars in waiting at the station
and thus ended the ceremonies in connection with the first three-
feet six-inch gauge railway in the Dominion.

CHAPTER XXXIV.

HAVING, after fifteen years' agitation, failed to secure the greater
scheme of a railway to the Georgian Bay, a railway from
Whitby to Port Perry, as the first link in the chain, was determined
upon, a charter was obtained, and the following directors appointed
in March, 1868:—A. Farewell, Thos. Paxton, M.PP., Joseph
Bigelow, Charles Marsh, W. S. Sexton, Edward Major, Dr. Foote,
Dr. Gunn, James Holden, Chester Draper, Sheriff Reynolds. Mr.
Bigelow was elected president, and subsequently Mr. Draper, and
after him Mr. Dryden. Of the capital, $250,000, the charter pro-
vided that $100,000 should be *bona fide* subscribed and ten per cent.
paid thereon, before the company could go into operation, and that
the original subscribers or their assigns should never be released
from their liability until the whole of the stock was paid up—a
stringent provision contained in no other charter in the history of
Canadian railway legislation. After considerable difficulty the
necessary amount was obtained, ten per cent. paid in, and the
company organized. Three gentlemen, Messrs. Sexton, Paxton
and Bigelow, of Port Perry, subscribed $10,000 each, and subscrip-
tions were obtained of from $5,000 and $3,000 downwards in
Whitby. The corporation of the town of Whitby gave a bonus of

$50,000, and afterwards subscribed $10,000 stock; Whitby township, $15,000; from the township of Reach, $30,000; and Scugog Island, $2,500.   Tenders were asked for and a favourable contract entered into with Messrs. Starratt and Kesteven.   But dissensions immediately afterwards sprang up at the board; it was also found that the contractors were not men of means, and they were got rid of.   Mr. J. H. Dumble stepped in, after a time, and the contract was awarded to him at $290,000 and $40,000 stock, the latter a fruitful source of much trouble afterwards.   The first sod was turned on Wednesday, 6th October, 1869, by His Royal Highness Prince Arthur, with great ceremony, when the following proceedings took place, the occasion being made a grand holiday in Whitby. The proceedings are thus chronicled :—

VISIT OF H. R. H. PRINCE ARTHUR.

The Prince and party arrived at the Grand Trunk Station precisely at twenty minutes past ten o'clock.   The special train numbered five cars and one baggage-waggon.   The engine was tastefully decorated, as was also the station and the surrounding buildings.   Thousands awaited the arrival of the Prince's party, and hailed the coming in of the train with loud acclamations.   The party at once alighted, and presentations were made by the Mayor of the members of the Town Council and others, to both the Governor-General and the Prince.   The party alighted on the south side of the station, arches being extended across the track, and a platform; the passage-way over being handsomely carpeted.

Immediately on arrival the party entered carriages which were in readiness awaiting at the G. T. R. station, and proceeded at a brisk pace through the town.   The carriages of the members of the Corporation and Warden headed the procession; next came that of His Excellency the Governor-General, accompanied by Mr. Turville, his private secretary, Mr. Gerrie the Mayor, and Mrs. Howland. The Prince's carriage, with Lady Young, Col. Elphinston and the

Sheriff; and after these Lieutenant-Governor Howland, Sir John A. Macdonald, Hon. John Sandfield Macdonald and Miss Macdonald, Mr. Potter, of the Grand Trunk Railway, Mr. Brydges, Mr. King, of the Bank of Montreal, Mr. Justice Morrison, Judge Duggan, Mayor Harman, of Toronto, Mr. White, of Hamilton, Mr. John A. Donaldson, Emigration Agent, and others.

Along the line of procession crowds awaited and cheered the Prince. No fewer than about one hundred carriages and many equestrians waited at the station, and accompanied the procession from thence to the town. The town-bells rang out, cannon belched forth, the bands played martial airs, and the Prince's party received a right loyal and hearty greeting from the loyal people of the Town of Whitby. Everywhere arches and decorations were visible; flags, banners and streamers fluttered in the breeze; and Whitby presented one of such holiday appearances as—

> When Royal Mary, blythe of mood,
> Kept holiday in Holyrood.

On the arrival at the grounds, where the ceremony of breaking the first sod was to take place, the Prince and party were greeted with loud acclamations from between five and six thousand of Her Majesty's assembled lieges, one of the most interesting features of the reception being the greeting, the National Anthem, which was sung by the school children of the town, who were marshalled under their respective teachers on a roomy platform specially arranged for their occupation on the occasion. Platforms were also erected for the Prince and party, the town and county councils, and invited guests:

As we have just said, there were between five and six thousand persons present, and they did not include about 130 officers and men of the 34th Battalion, under Colonel Fairbanks, who mustered on the occasion and received the Prince as a guard of honour, and assisted materially throughout in preserving the best of good order.

The Mayor, after a short space of time, during which invited guests (and some who were not), obtained the Prince's and Governor-General's platform, delivered the following address :—

"*To His Excellency the Right Hon. Sir John Young, Baronet, K.C.B., Governor-General of Canada, etc., etc.:*

"May it please Your Excellency—

"The Mayor and Corporation, on behalf of the Town of Whitby, most cordially embrace this opportunity of tendering to Your Excellency a hearty welcome to this section of Canada. It is with no ordinary feelings of loyalty and attachment to the Crown and Constitution of our country that we approach Your Excellency as the representative of Her Most Gracious Majesty.

"We feel a just pride in acknowledging the wisdom and consideration of Her Majesty's Government in selecting as Governor-General of the Dominion of Canada one whose distinguished abilities have done so much for other portions of the British Empire. We confidently trust that your administration of the Government will secure lasting prosperity and happiness to the people of this Dominion, and additional glory to the British Empire, as well as increased honour to Your Excellency.

"We sincerely hope that Lady Young and yourself may derive much pleasure from your journey through the Province, and our earnest desire and prayer is that Heaven's best blessings may attend you both.

"JAMES H. GERRIE, *Mayor*."

To which His Excellency replied :—

"*To the Mayor and Corporation of the Town of Whitby:*

"Mr. Mayor and Gentlemen—

"I appreciate at their proper value the warm feelings of loyalty to the Crown and attachment to the Constitution happily existing in Canada, which prompt you to approach me, as the representative of the Royal Authority, with a hearty welcome to the prettily situated and thriving Town of Whitby.

"I am aided in the discharge of my duties by able statesmen, the choice of the people, and possessing the confidence of Parliament. I trust that by their sage counsels my administration of affairs may be guided to good purpose, so as to merit approbation and promote the moral and material welfare of the country. Lady Young and I have derived much pleasure from our journey through the Province of Ontario, and unite in warmly thanking you for the earnestness with which you implore that blessings may attend us.

"JOHN YOUNG."

The Mayor next proceeded to that portion of the platform occupied by His Royal Highness, and read the following address to the Prince :—

"*To His Royal Highness Prince Arthur William Patrick, K.G.:*

"May it please Your Highness—

"We, the Mayor and Corporation of the Town of Whitby, beg most respectfully to approach Your Royal Highness on the occasion of your visit to this portion of Canada.

"We hail the presence in our Dominion of a scion of the illustrious House of Brunswick as a fresh token of the kind and queenly consideration of our dearly beloved Sovereign, and beg your Royal Highness to accept the assurance of our veneration for and devoted attachment to the person of our gracious Queen, whose benign sway has been fraught with untold blessings, not only to the great empire over which she reigns but to the remotest corner of the world.

"We sincerely trust that the stay of Your Royal Highness in Canada may prove as agreeable to yourself as it is gratifying to us.

"JAMES H. GERRIE, *Mayor.*"

To which His Royal Highness replied in an audible and pleasing voice :—

"*To the Mayor and Corporation of Whitby:*

" Gentlemen—

" My visit to this town, associated as it is with an undertaking which I trust will increase the prosperity of this county, cannot be otherwise than most agreeable to my feelings.

" For your welcome to myself, I feel, I assure you, sincere gratitude, but it is still more satisfactory to me to witness your affectionate attachment and loyalty to the Queen, who has the welfare of her people sincerely at heart. " ARTHUR."

The Warden was next presented to His Excellency, and read the Address of the County Council :—

"*To the Right Honourable Sir John Young, K.C.B., etc., etc., etc., Governor-General of Canada :*

" May it please Your Excellency—

" We, the Warden and Councillors of the Corporation of the County of Ontario, bid Your Excellency a hearty welcome to the confines of this flourishing county, and hope that at some future day Your Excellency will be able to pay a more lengthened visit to a portion of the Province second to none in material prosperity and enterprise.

" Such undertakings as have this day been happily inaugurated are at once the sign and cause of progress, and indicate that the self-reliance and energy which distinguishes the country we are proud to call our Mother-land are not wanting in her sons under other skies and circumstances.

" We take this opportunity of expressing to Your Excellency our gratification that, in nominating you to your high office, the choice of our gracious Sovereign has fallen upon one whose ripe statesmanship, large experience and enlightened views will aid in securing concord in the councils and stability in the institutions of our Dominion.

"We desire to assure Your Excellency, on behalf of the inhabitants of this portion of the Province, of our unwavering loyalty to our Sovereign, and devoted attachment to the institutions we have inherited from the land of our forefathers.

"Whatever shape our alliance with that country may hereafter take, we crave no other lot than to continue to form a part of the great Empire upon which the sun never sets ; to share her glories, and, if possible, contribute to her renown.

"We would ask Your Excellency to convey to Lady Young our expression of respect towards her, and we venture to hope that her Ladyship may retain pleasing recollections of this your first visit to the County of Ontario.

"JOSHUA WRIGHT, *Warden.*

"County Council Chambers,
    "Whitby, October, 1869."

The Governor-General replied :—

"*To the Warden and Councillors of the Corporation of the County of Ontario :*

"Mr. Warden and Gentlemen—

"I thank you very cordially for the words of hearty welcome with which you greet my arrival amongst you, and I have pleasure in assuring you of my entire reliance on your loyalty to the Queen, and your attachment to those British institutions which have been so happily established in Canada.

"The purpose for which we are assembled here to-day is one of great importance. No works are of greater general utility than those which facilitate and extend the means of communication. They give a stimulus to industry by adding value to its products. Without such aids civilization cannot advance ; with them, the prosperity of the country and the comforts of daily life are materially enhanced.

"I am glad, therefore, to have the opportunity of being present on this interesting occasion, and Lady Young. joins me in wishing you all possible success, not merely in your present, but in your future undertakings.   "JOHN YOUNG."

The Warden next approached the Prince, to whom he was presented by the Mayor, and delivered the following address :—

"*To His Royal Highness Prince Arthur William Patrick, K.G.:*

"May it please Your Royal Highness—

"We, the Warden and Councillors of the Corporation of the County of Ontario, beg to express our appreciation of the high honour conferred upon us, in being permitted for a second time to receive a visit from a scion of your Royal House.

"We are again enabled to avail ourselves of the opportunity of expressing, on behalf of ourselves and the inhabitants of this populous and prosperous county, our devoted loyalty to our Most Gracious Sovereign, your royal mother, our deep sense of the blessings we enjoy under her wise and beneficent rule, our undying attachment to the form of constitutional government established in our land, and our earnest desire that our new Dominion, in increased territory, wealth and power, may ever form a part of a great confederate British Empire, bound together by the ties of patriotism, mutual interest and mutual support.   "JOSHUA WRIGHT, *Warden.*

"County Council Chambers,
    "Whitby, October, 1869."

To which the Prince replied :—

"*To the Warden and Councillors of the Corporation of the County of Ontario:*

"Gentlemen—

"I thank you for your address, and heartily appreciate the

sentiments of loyal devotion to your Sovereign, and attachment to the institutions of her Empire, which you have just expressed.

"I regret that my present visit, like the one of my brother, the Prince of Wales, does, unfortunately, not admit of a long stay amongst you; but I am glad that, notwithstanding the shortness of the time, my visit here is associated with a work of public utility, which I trust may prove a source of increasing prosperity to this neighbourhood.   "ARTHUR."

The addresses were all well read by the Mayor and Warden, and were replied to in audible and distinct tones by His Excellency and His Royal Highness, and with what appeared to be much earnestness. The proceedings were listened to throughout with great attention.

His Royal Highness next descended from the platform, accompanied by the Governor-General, Mr. Bigelow, President of the Whitby and Port Perry Railway, and Mr. Dumble, the contractor, and went through the ceremony of "turning the first sod."

A handsome silver spade, and a bird's-eye maple wheelbarrow, specially prepared for the occasion (and now in possession of the author), were brought into requisition, and the Prince, with much ease and deliberation, performed the ceremony of "turning the first sod" of the Whitby and Port Perry Railway amidst ringing shouts of applause.

The auspicious proceedings with which the turning of the first sod was inaugurated did not help the road along.

The work proceeded more or less satisfactorily, under Mr. Dumble, with a board of directors representing antagonistic personal interests over which individual members never ceased squabbling. Mr. Dumble sold out to Mr. English, from Toronto, who carried on the work a stage further, and quarrelled in turn with the directors, who were ultimately left to finish the road themselves, and with a number of lawsuits on their hands. They succeeded admirably in "running the whole thing into the ground," to use an expressive phrase; in hopelessly involving the Company and placing the members of the board, who had made themselves personally liable for obligations in carrying on the work, and in defending and maintaining lawsuits, in a position to be overwhelmed with loss of their private property. It was at this crisis that Mr. James Holden came to the front. And, certainly, if men had ever reason to be thankful for a timely rescue, they were the directors of the Whitby and Port Perry Railway at that time. Mr. Holden had already shown his public spirit by subscribing and paying up $3,000 stock; and, although an active member of the board, became utterly disgusted with the mismanagement and selfishness of some of his co-directors. He succeeded, however, as has been remarked, at the critical moment, when absolute ruin stared all concerned in the face, in enlisting as his copartners in the scheme for buying out the bankrupt concern Messrs. Austin, Fulton and Michie, of Toronto, the result being the speedy completion and equipment of the line to Port Perry. Matters soon changed for the better under the new *régime*. The line was freed from debt, the involved directors relieved from the pecuniary embarrassments which encompassed them, caused by their connection with the undertaking, and the whistle of the locomotive was shortly heard along the line, with trains running regularly, conveying freight and passengers. Whitby took a fresh start on the road to prosperity. Property was enhanced in value, and Port Perry was built up, from an insignificant village at the head of Lake Scugog, to the dimensions of an important town, where quarter-acre lots became as valuable as one hundred acre farms had been a few years before in the same neighbourhood.

CHAPTER XXXV.

VARIOUS efforts continued to be made for the extension of the
line northward, and the construction of the branch to Uxbridge
and several plans, all embracing promised bonuses from the municipalities immediately interested, devised, but they came to nothing.
At length Mr. Holden, allowing other propositions for extension to
remain in abeyance for the time, bent all his energies on carrying
the line to Lindsay. He expected that connection with the Victoria
Railway at that point would secure to the Whitby line a large proportion of the traffic coming over the former ; or, in other words,
that the Whitby line must be the main outlet for the volume of
traffic coming over the Victoria road ; that that connection once
secured, every mile built of the Victoria would in reality be an extension of the Whitby line northward ; and further, that the Whitby line
would be in a position to compete successfully with the Midland for
the trade to the front. The town of Whitby at once came forward
and backed him up with a further bonus of $20,000 ; Port Perry
followed suit for a like amount ; the co-operation of the leading
men of Lindsay, Ops and Mariposa was secured, and a bonus of
$85,000 was obtained by grouping these municipalities, and also,
subsequently, Government aid to the extent of $2,000 per mile. In
the summer of '76 the contract was let. In the hands of Messrs.
Gibson and Dixon, the contractors, the work was vigorously prose-

cuted, and on the 31st July following the line to Lindsay was formally opened. After a long struggle of a quarter of a century, railway communication between the port of Whitby and the far North was at last secured, although not in the direction originally contemplated, through the centre of the county.

Not long afterwards the road became amalgamated with the Midland; the Midland became part of the Grand Trunk system; and the municipalities that gave the bonuses lost the benefits of a competing line, for which they gave their money. The Ontario Central Railway, projected by the late Mr. Chester Draper, connecting Whitby Harbour with Nottawasaga Bay, and the charter of which was allowed to lapse at his death; the projected Toronto and Ottawa Railway, to aid which Reach, Port Perry, Pickering and Scugog, grouped, passed a by-law granting a bonus of $90,000, next occupied the public mind for a while. The scheme resulted in the Ontario and Quebec line, now forming part of the C. P. R. system, and which runs across the county. The Toronto and Nipissing narrow gauge was converted into a broad gauge line, and now also forms part of the Midland system of the Grand Trunk. A connecting link from the Manilla Junction, by Wick, unites the old Nipissing and Whitby lines in the present system. The Whitby, Port Perry and Lindsay, north; the Toronto and Nipissing, through Uxbridge and Brock; the Midland, through Thorah and Mara; and the Northern, crossing at the Narrows, and running through a portion of Mara and Rama to Gravenhurst; and the C. P. R., already mentioned, form the railway lines and railway connections within the county.

CHAPTER XXXVI.*

VISIT OF H. R. H. THE PRINCE OF WALES.

THE visit of the Prince of Wales to the county, in 1860, was a memorable event. His Royal Highness was presented with addresses by the County Council and Town Council, and was received with great demonstrations of loyalty and enthusiasm. We give the proceedings, as a matter of historical record, from the *Chronicle* of that day.

EXTRACTS of a special session of the County Council, held September 4 and 5, to consider the propriety of giving a grant towards receiving the Prince of Wales at Whitby on the 7th September, 1860, as reported in the Whitby *Chronicle* of September 8, 1860 :—

TUESDAY, September 4, 1860.

A special session of the County Council was held, on call of the Warden, at the Courthouse, on Tuesday. It was five o'clock p.m. before the Warden took his seat. The roll having been called over the following reeves and deputies answered to their names :—Messrs. Brown, Bartlett, Rowe, Smith, White (Pickering), White (Whitby), Wright. Absent, Messrs. Pirt, Sangster and Wixson.

The Warden said that in calling the Council together specially

---

* This chapter is taken out of its proper chronological order so as to avoid making a break in the complete railway narrative of the County.

it was necessary for him to state that he did so in consequence of the visit of His Royal Highness the Prince of Wales—the heir apparent to the great empire of which we formed a part —to this country. A visit, he said, from such a person was unprecedented in the history of Canada, and he had no doubt of the good it would produce. To have the future ruler of the realm, to which we were so nearly allied, amongst us, and carry back with him a personal knowledge of our unbounded resources and unparalleled progress, would be productive of the best results in the future. He believed that every one must admire the virtues of Her Majesty our Queen, who was deserving of all the respect and esteem that her loyal subjects could show towards a good and virtuous sovereign. And when Her Majesty had graciously accepted our invitation—although not honouring us with her own royal presence—by sending the Heir Apparent to the Throne, and when the Prince had placed himself at our disposal it was due to our Sovereign and to ourselves that we should express our deep sense of the unexampled honour conferred upon us. Under these circumstances, he (the Warden) had no hesitancy in calling the Council together, that the county of Ontario, with every other part of the Province through which His Royal Highness passed, might take the opportunity to give expression to those sentiments of welcome which, he felt quite sure, were entertained by every rate-payer of the county. The Warden further stated that he had deferred calling the Council together until so late a period because no requisition had been placed in his hands, but that having received a resolution, passed at a public meeting most respectably attended from all parts of the county, he felt that he could no longer hesitate ; and he believed there was still sufficient time to take the necessary steps for giving expression to the deep sense of loyal esteem which they all felt.

Mr. Hewett did not know whether all gentlemen in the Council were in the same position as himself; but he did not exactly comprehend the nature of the business that it was necessary for the Council to transact in this matter. He quite agreed in the propriety of the remarks of the Warden as to giving the Prince a becoming reception, and of doing everything in a proper sense. Such a circumstance as the heir of the British Crown visiting this country never having taken place before, the honour was deserving every effort. But he was not exactly aware of the way in which the Council was called upon to operate. Everything was crude at present, but he had no doubt, when they understood things, the Council would do their duty. He asked Captain Rowe to explain what had taken place already in relation to the reception of the Prince at Whitby.

Mr. Campbell was not prepared to do anything until he saw his way clearly.

Captain Rowe explained very briefly and explicitly what all our readers know already; that the town had invited the Prince to stop at Whitby, and had appropriated $300 for the presenting of an address; that a requisition to the Sheriff to call a public meeting of the ratepayers of the county had been got up; the meeting called, and an address adopted, which the Sheriff had been appointed to present on behalf of the county, and which the Prince had also agreed to receive at Whitby; and that it was expected the County Council would grant a sum equal to the small amount voted by the town towards the reception; that the Prince was expected here some time on Friday—about mid-day.

Mr. Ratcliffe believed in the necessity of doing something, but he believed the Warden was the chief elected magistrate of the county, and the proper person to present the address on behalf of the county; that, as the matter had been taken out of the Warden's hands, he (Mr. R.) did not think it would be proper to have anything more to do with it, and would therefore go for no appropriation.

Mr. White felt a good deal embarrassed at the awkward position in which the Council was placed, and scarcely knew what to do; he expected the Warden, in his address, would have told them precisely what action was necessary.

Mr. Smith said he considered that the Warden stated expressly the purport of the meeting in his address. He, however, found fault with the way in which matters stood; considered that the Warden was the proper person to present the address, and stated that, unless some arrangement was come to, he was not disposed to vote for an appropriation.

Mr. Wright saw no reason why an address could not be presented on behalf of the Warden and Corporation.

After some further observations, a resolution, moved by Mr. Hewett and seconded by Mr. Smith, was carried, appointing a committee of five, consisting of Messrs. Ratcliffe, Smith, White (Pickering), Campbell and the mover, to confer with the Sheriff and the Executive Committee, to get explanations, and to report to the Council that evening.

The Warden then left the chair until eight o'clock. In the evening the Council resumed, and the special committee reported an interview with the Sheriff and the Executive Committee of the Town and County for the Prince's reception. The report gave a *résumé* of certain facts, and recommended that no appropriation be granted, inasmuch as an address would be then too late to be presented, and that the Council had no power to make the appropriation for presenting an address on behalf of the Warden and Corporation of the county. The report was adopted.

Council adjourned until ten o'clock next day.

WEDNESDAY, September 5.

The Council did not meet until after eleven o'clock. There were present Messrs. Rowe, Robinson, Smith, Bartlett, Brown, Hewett, Wright, White (Pickering), White (Whitby), Hart, McGregor and Gamble—twelve.

A resolution, moved by Mr. Wright and seconded by Mr. Smith, to reconsider the report adopted the previous evening, on the ground that the report was adopted through error, inasmuch as it was stated therein that an address would be too late, and such now appearing to be not the case, was carried without dissent.

The report was amended in committee, and, on motion of Mr. Wright, the Warden and Messrs. Hewett, White (Pickering), Smith, and the mover, appointed to draft an address.

Messrs. White (Pickering) and Gamble opposed and voted against the amendment.

The Warden left the chair at two o'clock, and the Council resumed at three o'clock, when an address was reported, and the Warden, with Messrs. Hart and Robinson, appointed a special committee to wait on His Excellency the Governor-General's Secretary, at Belleville, the next day, to ascertain whether the address would be received.

On motion of Mr. Robinson, seconded by Mr. Smith, a sum of $300 was appropriated towards the reception, and the Warden and the County Engineer appointed to see to the expenditure. The Warden was appointed to present the address, accompanied by the Council.

Friday last, the 7th September, will long be remembered as a great and important day in the annals of the good town of Whitby. On that day Albert Edward, Prince of Wales, the heir to the British throne, honoured Whitby with his illustrious presence, and received the addresses, congratulations and warm and enthusiastic plaudits of Her Majesty's lieges of the county of Ontario. From an early hour in the morning a continual stream of teams, buggies and vehicles of every description, filled with men and women, dressed in their best holiday attire, kept pouring in from the country. Every avenue approaching the town, from the north, east and west, was thronged with equestrians and pedestrians making their way to see and welcome the Prince; and on the south the harbour contributed its share to the spectacle, no less than eight steamboats freighted with passengers having steamed in to witness the embarkation. Alongside the wharf, with the Prince's steamer, the *Kingston*, were the *Zimmerman*, the *Maple Leaf*, and the propeller *J. L. Tucker;* outside the harbour five other steamers were in sight, decorated with flags from stem to stern. The town presented a most gay and lively appearance; flags streamed from every house-top and from all the public buildings. Not a particle of the town was there which did not exhibit decorations of some kind; people everywhere vied with each other in the variety and costliness of the display. The Mayor and Sheriff had received telegrams an-nouncing the time of arrival of the Prince as between the hours of twelve and two o'clock, and before the latter hour fully twelve thousand persons had assembled at the railway station and at the wharf, and on the route between these two points. At the north side of the station a lofty pavilion, thirty-six feet by twenty-four, richly decorated, was erected. Over the pavilion were the letters "A. E." entwined of evergreens, and in large, bold letters the words "God Save the Queen." A rich carpet of crimson cloth covered the space inside the pavilion, and from thence to the Prince's car extended a novel and tasteful carpet, ornamented with maple leaves, the handiwork of the ladies of Whitby. The railway station was covered with flags, ensigns, Union Jacks, St. George's crosses, and streamers of every kind, and one immense royal ensign floating from a flagstaff on the most easterly point of the station. The sight from every point was a grand one, and well worthy to meet the view of a Royal Prince. The multitude was immense— on every side nothing but a living ocean of human beings. Upwards of three thousand persons were provided with seats immediately in front of the pavilion, for which the small charge of twenty cents each was made. In waiting on the pavilion to receive the Prince were H. J. Macdonell, Esq., Mayor of Whitby, attended by the Town Clerk, Mr. Huston, and the following members of the Town Council:—James Rowe, J. H. Perry, William Lang, R. J. Gunn,

M.D., C. Draper, C. Lynde, N. W. Brown, James Cameron, Ira Vail, N. G. Reynolds, Esq., Sheriff of the County, attended by his Secretary, Mr. C. Nourse; John Hall Thompson, Esq., Warden of the County, and the following members of the County Council:— Mr. White, Deputy-Reeve of Whitby; John Ratcliffe and William Bartlett, Reeve and Deputy-Reeve of East Whitby; T. P. White and Josiah Wixson, jún., Reeve and Deputy-Reeve of Pickering; Joshua Wright and H. McGregor, Reeve and Deputy-Reeve of Reach; J. Gamble, Reeve of Scugog; W. Smith, Reeve of Uxbridge; Charles Robinson, Reeve of Thorah; D. G. Hewett, Reeve of Mara and Rama; and John Hart, Deputy-Reeve of Brock; the members of the Oshawa Corporation, consisting of J. Hislop, Esq., Reeve; James Carmichael, G. H. Gilchrist and J. Dickey; Z. Burnham, Esq., County Judge; W. H. Tremayne, Esq., County Attorney; J. Shier, Esq., County Engineer; Wm. Paxton, County Treasurer; Hon. O. Mowat, the member for South Ontario; and J. Gould, Esq., member for North Ontario; Lieut.-Col. McPherson, First Battalion Ontario Militia; J. B. Warren, Esq., Manager of the Ontario Bank at Oshawa; N. G. Ham, Esq., Barrister; James Dryden, Esq., G. Wallace, Esq., A. Farewell, Esq., Philip St. John, Esq. (King of Brock), David Spalding, Esq., Rev. J. Pentland, Rev. Eugene O'Keefe, Rev. Mr. Warner, Rev. J. T. Byrne, Rev. Mr. Wickson, Rev. Mr. Taylor, Rev. Mr. Law, and the following members of the press:—W. H. Higgins, of the Whitby *Chronicle*; E. Oliver and James Holden, of the Prince Albert papers; W. H. Orr, of the *Vindicator*. The Whitby Highland Rifle Company, commanded by Captain Wallace, and the Oshawa Fire Brigade (Chief McElroy) were drawn up in front of the pavilion.

Precisely at twenty-five minutes to four o'clock the train containing the Prince of Wales and suite came in sight, and the arrival was greeted by the firing of cannon and the most vociferous cheering from the multitude. Immediately afterwards the Prince and royal party alighted, and were conducted by the Mayor, Sheriff and Warden to the pavilion, where the Prince was again loudly cheered.

The County address was presented by the Sheriff first as follows:

"To His Royal Highness Albert Edward, Prince of Wales:

"May it please Your Royal Highness—

"We, the inhabitants of the county of Ontario, in the Province of Canada, beg to approach Your Royal Highness to express our heartfelt gratitude for the opportunity afforded us at this time of greeting Your Royal Highness with a hearty welcome, and of expressing our unswerving loyalty and devoted attachment to the throne and person of our Most Gracious Sovereign the Queen, to whom we also hereby express our deep sense of obligation for her gracious condescension in readily acceding to the invitation from our representatives in Parliament to visit in person, or by representation on the part of some member of the Royal Family, this very important part of her empire.

"The auspicious visit of Your Royal Highness we regard as an event of great national importance to this country, and one which we feel confident will have the happiest effect in deepening and perpetuating that devoted allegiance and attachment felt by us to be due not more on account of the manifold blessings we enjoy under that benign government, than for the eminent virtues which adorn your illustrious mother, and by which, we hope Your Royal Highness, to whom we proudly look as the future Sovereign of these realms, will ever in like manner be distinguished.

"We earnestly hope that the visit of Your Royal Highness will not only be agreeable to you as it is gratifying to us, but will increase the interest already so long and warmly manifested on the part of the Queen and Government of Great Britain towards this important appendage of the British Empire.

"We beg further to express our ardent desire, and hope that when Your Royal Highness may leave us for your native shores, you may enjoy unbroken health and comfort, and by a gracious Providence be safely restored to the bosom of your illustrious family."

To which H. R. H. replied :—

"*Gentlemen*—

"I thank you sincerely for the address which you have presented to me.

"In the Queen's name I acknowledge the expressions of your loyalty to her crown and person, and for myself I am grateful to you for the welcome to your neighbourhood."

The Warden followed with the address of the County Council, which read :—

"*To His Royal Highness Albert Edward, Prince of Wales, Duke of Cornwall, etc., etc.:*

"May it please Your Royal Highness—

"We, the Warden and Council of the Corporation of Ontario, in Council assembled, beg respectfully to congratulate Your Royal Highness upon your safe arrival in this county, and at the same time we desire to convey to Your Royal Highness the assurance of our respect for and our attachment to our beloved Queen.

"That many advantages will arise from Your Royal Highness's visit to this country, we have every reason to hope ; and trust that it may afford pleasure to Your Royal Highness, and a more intimate knowledge of the resources of Canada than could otherwise be acquired.

"We heartily welcome Your Royal Highness to the loyal county of Ontario, and desire respectfully to convey through Your Royal Highness the high esteem in which we hold the many virtues of your Royal mother, our Queen ; that she may be long preserved a pattern to other rulers is our earnest prayer."

The reply to the address of the Warden and County Council was precisely the same as that given to the Sheriff.

The Mayor next proceeded to read the town address, which ran :—

"*To His Royal Highness Albert Edward, Prince of Wales, etc., etc.:*

"May it Please Your Royal Highness—

"We, the Mayor, Corporation and Citizens of the town of Whitby, in the county of Ontario, most humbly beg leave to approach Your Royal Highness, to express the great pride which we, in common with others of our fellow-subjects in the Province, feel at the presence of Your Royal Highness in this extensive and, we may proudly add, important portion of Her Most Gracious Majesty's Dominion.

"We offer to Your Royal Highness a most loyal and heartfelt welcome, and we trust that the evidence of civilization and advancement which have greeted Your Royal Highness's progress thus far have not induced Your Royal Highness to deem the pioneers of the land, or their descendants, wanting in the energy and intelligence characteristic of the race from which they sprung, or undeserving of the incomparable honour which Your Royal Highness now confers upon them.

"We pray Your Royal Highness to be pleased to convey to our Sovereign our fervent feelings of loyalty and attachment to Her Majesty's crown and person, and our grateful appreciation of the inestimable blessings of freedom and prosperity which, in common with all Her Majesty's subjects, we enjoy under the benign rule of our good and gracious Queen."

To which the Prince replied :—

"*Gentlemen*—

"I thank you sincerely for the address you have presented me in the Queen's name.

"I acknowledge the expressions of your loyalty to Her Majesty's crown and person; and for myself, I am grateful to you for this welcome to your town."

The Prince handed the several addresses as received to the

Duke of Newcastle, who stood at his left hand, the Governor-General being at his right.

Three cheers were next proposed by the Sheriff for the Queen, three for the Prince Consort, and three for the Prince of Wales.

Three splendid bands, brought from Bowmanville, Oshawa and Prince Albert, and which had kept the crowd in good humour while waiting all the morning, struck up "God Save the Queen," the cannons commenced blazing away, and the Prince, amidst all rejoicing, accompanied by the Governor-General, descended and entered the handsome carriage of John Ham Perry, Esq., which had been placed at the Mayor's disposal, and in a few minutes the Royal party reached the wharf. The Oshawa Fire Company and the Highland Rifle Volunteer Company followed at a long distance behind, the carriages having been driven at so rapid a rate that it was impossible for those on foot to keep up with them. An immense crowd lined the streets, and accompanied the carriages to the wharf. Ample accommodation had been provided for the Prince's suite by the Executive Committee, and the grand sight as a whole was not excelled at any similar demonstration in the Province. The streets along the route were somewhat dusty, and this, together with the desire to reach Toronto before nightfall, hastened the procession of the Royal *cortège*.

At fifteen minutes past four o'clock His Royal Highness reached the wharf, and at once went on board the steamer *Kingston*, which in a few seconds steamed out of the harbour for Toronto, the immense crowd vociferously cheering until the steamer got far outside the pier. The sight along the wharf, which is more than half a mile in length, running out into the lake, beggars all description. It was one living mass of men, women and children, carriages and horses, huddled together so compactly that with every surge of the ocean of heads one wondered how hundreds escaped being precipitated into the water which bounded each side. However, no acci-

dent happened.   Everything went off smoothly and pleasantly and
"merry as a marriage bell."   The good order maintained by the
marshals of the procession was admirable.

The Mayor and Sheriff, both of whom followed in the Prince's
retinue to the wharf, accompanied the Royal party to Toronto.
The steamboats and the train, which was sent off from the Grand
Trunk station on the departure of the Prince, were loaded with
passengers, all anxious to witness the disembarkation at Toronto,
but only those, we believe, who were fortunate enough to get on
board the cars were in time for the purpose.   Altogether the visit
of His Royal Highness to Whitby was under the most favourable
auspices.   The weather was delightful, the arrangements complete
and satisfactory, and the people joyously pleased and enthusiastic
to behold their Prince ; and in the latter respect we are very happy
to state that so well were all the arrangements carried out, we have
not heard of a single disappointment—all were gratified with the
sight of the future heir of the British Empire.

The only thing to give the people of Whitby any cause of regret
in connection with the Prince's visit is that time did not permit His
Royal Highness to visit their handsome and well-decorated town.
The town proper, as almost every one knows, is fully a mile and a
half from the railway station and harbour, so that it was impossible
for His Royal Highness or those in his train to see the preparations
made there to receive them, in case it were possible to prolong his
stay by driving through the town.   At the railway station and at
the wharf, however, we venture to say that enough was to be seen
to demonstrate satisfactorily the loyalty, enthusiasm and hospitality
with which the people of Whitby and the county of Ontario desired
to welcome their Prince.   We have already mentioned part of the
display at the railway station.   In addition to this, there was
erected north of the station, on the junction of the street approaching from the base line, a very handsome and well-decorated arch,
with the words "Welcome, One and All," over the arch, in the

centre, between the letters "A. E.," wreathed in evergreens and surmounted by shields bearing the Prince of Wales's plumes.

Next to the display at the station was a splendid arch erected on the approach from Brock Street to the harbour. This was a superb structure, built in the Gothic style, with extended wings, surmounted by flags, banners and streamers of every variety and colour, representing the signals used by the Royal Navy. Over each wing were suspended shields emblazoned with the Royal arms and the Prince's plume, and painted in gorgeous colours. This arch appeared almost a permanent structure, being strongly built of lumber, and covered in the most tasteful manner with evergreens. Immediately west of the arch a point jutted out into the water beside the warehouse of Messrs. James Rowe & Co., through whose kindness seats were erected for the accommodation of about six hundred children, trained and schooled to sing the "National Anthem" during the approach and embarkation of the Prince. Over the large warehouses of this company there were some very appropriate devices, of a small ship at one side, and a huge sheaf of wheat and agricultural productions at the other, and extended between them the words, "Agriculture and Commerce." From the roofs of the buildings and high above floated from the elevators innumerable flags of every kind, presenting a gay and very animated appearance. Large ensigns, Union Jacks, and other coloured flags were unfurled over the residences of Messrs. Rowe, Watson and Warren, and from, with scarcely an exception, every house and building at the bay, most of which were also decorated with evergreens, and contained handsome mottoes and devices. But it was up the town the gayest of the gay appearances was presented. Brock Street, from Pollard's hotel to the Market, was one continued arch of evergreens. Almost every merchant's store had its arch or its grove of evergreens opposite, as had likewise the several hotels; and flags in profusion floated from every housetop. The most extensive arch, however, was that put up at the "Corners,"

which was extended in the shape of a crown over the entire area
from Black's hotel to Laing's store, and thence again to the other
side of Dundas Street to Bain's and the corner opposite on Brock
Street.   This arch was quite a splendid affair, and was very much
admired.   It was richly and profusely decorated with flags; and
from its centre were run up on flagstaffs ensigns and Union Jacks,
which waved gaily in the breeze.   From Crocker's hotel to Hamilton & Roberts' store another handsome arch spanned the street,
heavily decorated, and surmounted by a large sheaf of wheat, from
the centre of which flags were run up.   Extended across Brock
Street, from the *Chronicle* office to Zwickey's harness-shop, was a
very beautifully designed arch, or rather a succession of arches,
for the broad sidewalk at each side was covered by arches, and
two arches spanned the street itself.   From the centre an immense
flagstaff, between fifty and sixty feet in height, arose, from which
a large Union Jack fluttered, and the arch was also decked out
with gay colours of various designs.   From two large poles at
each side of the street immense pumpkins were suspended, and
from the centre pole a sheaf of wheat; and these poles and the
other portions of the arch were again decorated with corn, fruit
and vegetables, and garlands of flowers.   This was intended for
the agricultural arch.   At the residence of Mr. J. H. Perry a
tasteful arch was erected over the gate entrance.   It was surmounted by a handsome shield, bearing the plume of the Prince
of Wales, and decorated with small flags.   Handsome flags, large
and small, also swayed from Mr. Perry's residence, and the fence
surrounding his pleasure-grounds was also overspread with gay
St. George's crosses.   Splendid flags were unfurled from the towers
and roof of the Sheriff's new mansion, and from his present residence, which was very tastefully decorated.   The residences of the
Mayor and other prominent citizens presented a similarly gay
appearance, and in fact—without entering into the tedium of enu-
merating each separately—there was scarcely in the whole town,

from the county buildings downwards (and if we except our own precious market building), a house on a prominent point from which similar demonstrations of joy and welcome were not extended. On Brock Street, at the entrance to Mr. Francis Clarke's cottage, a pretty arch was placed, which we had nearly omitted to notice; and across the street, at the base-line south of the railway bridge, an arch partly constructed was left unfinished, through, we are grieved to state, an accident happening to one of the workmen—a young man named Wallis—whose arm was broken by the fall. This is the only accident of any kind which we are called upon to report.

In the evening a bonfire was lit in the town, and the rejoicings kept up until a late hour. As our space will not permit our supplying a more extended statement, we have only to add that all the arrangements were as complete as it was possible they could be, taking everything into account; that the several committees, and their chairmen and secretaries, deserve the people's thanks for carrying out their wishes as they have done; and in particular, Messrs. James Rowe & Co. have earned for themselves all praise for the immense exertions made by them at the harbour in making everything appear to such advantage.

CHAPTER XXXVII.

THE county of Ontario now possesses very good gravel roads throughout its extent. Through the townships in the front the roads may be said to be of an excellent character, and in the north they are fast improving. The Township Councils are quite liberal in their appropriations to this end. In the early years of settlement the want of good roads, or in fact of any roads, good or bad, was one of the greatest discouragements the settler had to encounter. In the course of time bridle-paths through the dense forests gave way to blazed lines and corduroy clearings cut through the woods. Constant yearly expenditures of money and labour, with the increase of population and settlement, brought about the desirable state of things in the way of good and permanent highways, which, thanks also to the excellent provisions of the Municipal Act, we now find in existence in every direction. The Government laid out the main or Centre Road through the centre of the county, from Port Whitby to the Narrows Bridge. There was also then laid out a leading road—the old Brock Road—to the west through Pickering, north, and the road from Oshawa, known as

Simcoe Street. At the time of the sale of the roads and harbours in Upper Canada by the Government, in 1852, the Whitby, Lake Scugog, Simcoe and Huron Road Company became the purchasers of the Centre Road and Whitby Harbour. The Company spent $30,000 in improving the road as far as Manchester, making it one of the best travelled roads in the Province. They also spent $15,000 on the harbour. Simcoe Street and the Nonquon roads leading to Oshawa and harbour, and the western roads were improved by private companies, and by grants from time to time from the County and Township Councils. In 1860, after much discussion over a general scheme for improving the main county roads to the north, and when the railway scheme had been allowed to rest for a time, a by-law was passed by the County Council appropriating $20,000 for the purpose. Of this amount there was given to Simcoe Street $2,000; the Centre Road, north of Manchester, $8,000; and to the Brock, or Western Road, $5,000. Scugog Bridge, the Narrows Bridge, the Talbot Bridge, the bridge across the Black River, between Scott and Georgina, and smaller bridges and pieces of road in various localities, and especially in Mara and Rama, had previously, and during this and following years, had considerable sums voted for improvements. The bridges specially named have, since the setting off of the county and being assumed as county works, been a source of considerable annual expense, and have annually drawn largely upon the county revenue to keep them in repair.

Each of the three harbours has a history of its own. Whitby, originally called Windsor Harbour, and still marked as such upon old maps, was improved by the Government in 1843 and 1844; piers were built, a good deal of dredging done, and a considerable sum of money expended. As early as 1833 Mr. John Welsh had built a storehouse and tramway for shipping wheat and flour, which was done in scows, being taken out through the mud a long way beyond the present breakwater. Mr. Welsh had also opened a general store, and did a large business for years afterwards. He was a native of Clones, County Monaghan, Ireland, and few men in his day were better liked or more respected in any locality. He died in 1860. The Windsor warehouse (since pulled down) was built in 1842, Messrs. Perry, Cochrane, Campbell, Nicholl and Mitchell forming a company, known as the Windsor Warehouse Company, for the purpose. Mr. John Watson, another Irishman, a native of the County Dublin, retained the various positions of Manager, Director, Secretary and Treasurer of the Company for seven years. He had been with Mr. Welsh for two years previously. Mr. James Rowe, better known afterwards as "Captain Rowe," another warm-hearted Irishman, from the Queen's County, had in the interval, in partnership with Mr. James Cotton, obtained the contract for dredging the harbour, with other Government works. After the building of the piers, Messrs. Watson, Welsh and Rowe entered into partnership, purchased two lots of the Goreham property on the beach, and built the present warehouses, where business was afterwards carried on for so many years and with so much success by them under the name of James Rowe & Co. In 1852 the Whitby, Lake Scugog, Simcoe and Huron Road Company, already mentioned, was formed by the three partners, who purchased the road and the harbour from the Government. The Company spent large sums in improving the road and harbour, and paid some $54,000 to the Government. Like other companies who had purchased works of the kind from the Government, which became depreciated in value after the construction of the Grand Trunk Railway, the company fell into arrear, and were dispossessed, their property seized under a writ of extent, and the road and harbour re-sold under the Sandfield Macdonald Government, in 1863. Messrs. Joseph Gould and Chester Draper became the purchasers. After two years these gentlemen severed the joint connection, Mr. Draper taking the harbour and Mr. Gould the road. The road was surrendered in the summer of 1876 to the county under the statute.

Mr. Draper died in December of the same year, and the property of the harbour afterwards passed into the hands of its present owners. A special Act was obtained to enable the town to purchase the harbour property, which could have been obtained on most advantageous terms. The ratepayers were consulted, and the offer voted down. This was another opportunity lost. Whitby would have been immensely benefited by the ownership of its harbour. Its possession would not only have netted the town a large certain annual revenue, but it would have enabled the Corporation to make terms with the railway companies, which could not fail to have enured to the lasting benefit of the people of Whitby. As in many other matters, the ratepayers were led away by foolish talk. They were talked and argued out of their right senses by noisy individuals in refusing the ownership and control of their own harbour, and in rejecting a source of revenue that would have very much lightened the burden of taxation, and perhaps secured the cancellation of the entire railway debt.

Large sums of public and private funds have been expended in improving the harbours of Pickering and Oshawa. Both are also in the hands of private companies. A canal route through the county from Georgian Bay to Lake Ontario is another project to which public attention has been for a long time directed. In view of the importance of its advantages, the County Council, at the June session of 1863, made an appropriation of $600 for the purpose of ascertaining by a survey the practicability of a route through the county. The survey was entrusted to Mr. T. C. Keefer, C. E., who made the following report :—

" *To Silas B. Fairbanks, Esq., Oshawa, Chairman of the Standing Committee on Roads and Bridges, County Council of the county of Ontario:*

" Sir,—I have the honour to report that, in compliance with your instructions, I have examined the country between the townships of

Whitby and Thorah, in the county of Ontario, as well as the valleys of the Scugog, Sturgeon and Balsam Lakes, and the Talbot Portage Route, in order to determine the practicability of constructing a canal between Lake Simcoe and Lake Ontario by the route of Lake Scugog.

"The practicability of connecting Lake Simcoe and Lake Huron is assumed ; and I have no reason to doubt that this may be done, either by the natural route of the Severn River, or by the Nottawa-saga—so that if Lake Simcoe can be connected with Lake Ontario, via Scugog, a route for a Georgian Bay Canal may be had, which will be as direct as any other, and at the same time be in communication with the inland waters or the Trent navigation.

"The renewed importance which has been given to a Georgian Bay Canal, since the diversion of a western trade from the Mississippi to the Great Lakes, has induced your county authorities to undertake this examination, in order to bring forward the merits of the Scugog route, in competition with the only one hitherto agitated, that by the valleys of the Holland and Humber Rivers west of Toronto.

"Before proceeding to give the result of my examination, I will refer to the question of a canal between Lakes Huron and Ontario generally, in order to show that the two routes above mentioned are the only direct ones which offer any inducements for consideration.

"The object sought by the Georgian Bay Canal, in contradistinction to the Welland route, via Lake Erie, on the one hand, and the Ottawa route, via Lake Nipissing, on the other, is to afford a navigation which will avoid the *detour* and extra insurance of Lakes Erie and St. Clair—the Detroit and St. Clair Rivers, and especially the shoals known as the 'St. Clair Flats'; and at the same time give a route not only to Montreal, but from Chicago to New York, via Oswego, which the Ottawa route could not do. The height and breadth of the dividing ridges between Huron and

Ontario make it impracticable to use the waters of the former as a feeder, and thus obtain the minimum lockage, as is the case between Erie and Ontario on the route of the Welland Canal. A higher intermediate level must therefore be resorted to ; but there is a shortening of the route between Chicago and Oswego of two hundred and fifty miles, to be set off against the increased lockage required on the Georgian Bay route.

" The range within which a canal route between Huron and Ontario can be sought for is limited to the valley of Lake Simcoe, which is common to every route ; and, as already mentioned, this lake may be entered from Lake Huron, either from the mouth of the Nottawasaga or Severn Rivers ; but the range by which communication between Lake Simcoe and Lake Ontario is possible is much wider, extending from the Humber Valley, west of Toronto, to the mouth of the Trent, in the Bay of Quinté.

" As the extreme eastern outlet, although the natural one, embraces a length of navigation of over two hundred miles between Huron and Ontario, in addition to the maximum lockage, it cannot come into competition with either of the other routes in point of distance ; and the question then arises whether the difficulties in overcoming the natural barriers between Simcoe and Ontario, on any direct route, would force a resort to the circuitous one of the inland waters.

" To this it may be said that there is evidently a limit within which the route of the Georgian Bay Canal may be lengthened, because, with the inevitable excess of lockage, a direct route is the only one which could, on commercial grounds alone, be advocated in competition with the enlargement of the Welland Canal—a canal which has the advantage not only of the minimum lockage and cost, but also of accommodating the trade of Lake Erie, as well as that of Huron, Michigan and Superior.

" In a military point of view there would be an advantage in favour of a Georgian Bay route (besides the local benefits conferred) over any enlargement of the Welland, or of a second canal on that route; and if the St. Clair Flats may be regarded as a permanent obstacle to navigation, the commercial superiority of such a route for the trade of Huron, Michigan and Superior would be very decided. As a mere military work, the extreme eastern route already mentioned, by the Trent and Bay of Quinté, might be preferred; but if commercial considerations prevail the question of route will be limited to the townships of York and Whitby. In these comparisons the question of cost is omitted : the surveys which have been made not having been carried far enough to give the data for arriving at the probable cost upon any of the routes, although enough is known to show that any direct navigation between the Georgian Bay and Ontario must be a costly undertaking in proportion to its length.

"The old surveyed route, via the Trent and Bay of Quinté, would evade the formidable ridges south of Lake Simcoe, but, from the extent of shoal water and rock which would be encountered upon the route, the cost for a deep water navigation, such as is now demanded by the exigencies of through commerce, would probably be as great a total (though not so great per mile) as upon the shorter routes.

" With these preliminary remarks, I will now describe the natural obstacles to direct navigation between Lakes Simcoe and Ontario, to follow which it is necessary to bear in mind that Lake Huron is 340 and Lake Simcoe 475 feet above the level of Ontario.

"The peninsula of Eastern Canada, from the banks of the Niagara River, the natural outlet for the waters of the Upper Lakes, rises gradually from an elevation of about 360 feet. Ontario, at the Great Western Railway near the Suspension Bridge, to 550 feet, on the line of the Hamilton and Port Dover Railway, and 750 feet on that of the Great Western, between Hamilton and the Grand River, where the high land, sweeping round to the north-east, an elevation of over 1,000 feet above Ontario, is encountered at the summit of the Grand Trunk Railway in Esquesing, between Toronto and Guelph. Here the elevated plateau bears off nearly due north, running into Lake Huron above Collingwood, with a precipitous escarpment on the eastern face—a fall of between 300 and 400 feet taking place rapidly in that direction. From the face of this escarpment a lower ridge (at about the general level of 700 feet above Ontario) sets out from a point about midway between the head of Lakes Huron and Ontario, having its summit north of Toronto, at a point half way between Ontario and Simcoe, but approaching the former as it proceeds eastward until it reaches the township of Whitby, where the summit, which had set out at Caledon, the third township back from Lake Ontario, enters the north-east corner of Whitby, a township fronting on that lake. Before reaching this point, however, the ridge attains its highest elevation (about 900 feet) in Uxbridge, from whence a broad 'spin' strikes out to the north-east, the angle between the main line and spur being occupied by Lake Scugog. This spur, separating Scugog valley from that of Lake Simcoe, extends at a very uniform elevation (with one remarkable break) up to Balsam Lake, where it falls off. The main line of the ridge between Scugog and Ontario has a summit of about 800 feet above Ontario, but here the ridge attains its narrowest dimensions, being 'drawn up,' as it were, the breadth on the top being from 200 to 300 yards. At a level one hundred feet below the summit, the breadth through is less than half a mile. The spur between Scugog and Simcoe valleys has a tolerably uniform summit of 750 feet above Ontario, but it has great breadth, the high ground approaching near to Lakes Simcoe and Scugog. The spur is nearly cut through, on a direct line between Beaverton on Lake Simcoe, and Port Perry on Lake Scugog, by the valleys of the Beaver and Nonquon streams, on which route a narrow ridge, giving a summit of about 650 feet above Ontario, is found, which extends only half a mile, after which this is reduced to 630 and under.

"Scugog Lake stands about 575 feet above Lake Ontario; so

that the highest ground between it and Simcoe would be about 75 feet above the level of the former, while the extreme summit of the ridge between it and Ontario would be 212 feet above Scugog Lake on the lowest, but 234 feet on the shortest route. The hilly country between Scugog and Simcoe; the difficulty of following the timbered and swampy valleys, and the circuit required by reason of so many road allowances being closed, make repeated levelling necessary to ensure exactness. I think, however the above figures will not be seriously altered by a more careful survey. The first question which presents itself in projecting a canal between Simcoe and Ontario, via Scugog, is a supply of water.

" Scugog Lake could not be depended upon for this purpose, and a supply either independent of it or auxiliary to it must be sought. This can only be obtained from that portion of the Trent waters which lie above the Scugog level.

" If Lake Scugog be made the feeder an auxiliary supply must be thrown into it; and this can only be done either by bringing Sturgeon Lake to the same level with Scugog (abolishing the dam at Lindsay), and sending a portion of the waters which pass Bobcaygeon dam at Port Perry; or by bringing down a feeder from Cameron Lake and throwing it into the Scugog, *above the dam* at Lindsay.

" To effect this it is probable it would be found advisable to lower Scugog Lake, say one-third, and raise Sturgeon Lake two-thirds of the difference between them. But in order to make Scugog a feeder, it would be desirable in view of the summit to be overcome between it and Simcoe and Ontario, to raise rather than lower its level, as every foot which could be put upon it would seriously diminish the cost of the summit cuttings.

" It is impossible without a careful survey to express any opinion as to the effect of raising Scugog Lake above its present level any definite number of feet. If it be raised at all, or even maintained upon its present level, it would be necessary—as there is no probability that Sturgeon Lake could in that case be brought to the same level with it—to resort to the more expensive plan of bringing down a feeder from Cameron's Lake. There would be the disadvantage that as Cameron's Lake is over fifteen feet higher than Scugog Lake, the whole benefit which could be derived from such an expensive feeder would not be obtained unless Scugog Lake could be raised ten feet more—a proposition, I take it, which could not be entertained.

"In view of the formidable character of the cutting between Scugog and Ontario, and the great length of the summit one between Scugog and Simcoe it would very much diminish the difficulty and cost of these, which are the keys to the undertaking, if a feeder at least as much higher than Scugog as the depth of the proposed navigation could be procured, by which these cuttings could be reduced in length and depth, and through drainage in both directions be secured. Moreover it would be desirable that the schemes should be carried out without affecting the physical features of the country to the extent which would be done by serious alterations in the level of Sturgeon and Scugog Lakes.

"The plan which therefore appears to me the most feasible would be, to make Balsam Lake or Gull River the feeder, the waters of which could be had at an elevation of nearly 600 feet above Ontario, and to throw a sufficient quantity of these into Talbot River, and conduct them by a feeder towards Cannington, in Brock, near which it would strike the line of the proposed navigation. With a feeder at a level, say, 13 feet above Scugog, the length of the cutting between Scugog and Simcoe would be still a long one, say nine miles, averaging 25 feet, with the exception of the half mile of summit, where the cutting would reach 70 feet. If Gull River can be tapped above the level of Balsam Lake, the height of the ridge or spur before described, between the east branch of the Beaver Creek and the head water of Talbot River, is such that it should carry a feeder on a higher level than Balsam Lake, and thus attain a greater command of the ridge between Simcoe and Scugog. Of course every foot added to the height of feeder would add two to the lockage of the route, but, within certain limits, this would be preferable to long, deep cuttings in the bottoms of valleys which have high banks, or in swamps.

"With respect to the supply of water which could be afforded from Gull River, or Balsam Lake, I am of opinion that it could be materially increased by impounding the flood waters in the lakes which are the sources of this stream, nor do I doubt that a survey would show a further supply could be added by diverting the waters from the sources of such streams as the Muskoka, Madawaska, Petawawa, or Burnt River, or some of these. I have generally found that the chains of lakes which occupy the 'height of land' are divided often by low and narrow barriers, and that water may be turned from the higher into the lower without serious difficulty.

"If the feeder be maintained on a level above the Scugog Lake, the canal need not enter this lake at all (except by locks for the purpose of branch navigation), unless the lake were raised to the level of the canal by a dam at its outlet, which would not probably be entertained. Instead of this the Nonquon Valley might be dammed across at the junction of the north and south branches on the 13th line of Reach, and the canal be continued in the South Branch Valley as far as the 10th concession, when it could be taken out to the shore of Scugog Lake, and thence by the valley of Cedar Creek to the Pine Ridges.

"No steps were taken to ascertain the character of the summit cutting between Scugog and Simcoe, in the Nonquon and Beaver Creek Valleys and intervening ridges, but as I believe no rock has been discovered in Brock or Reach, it may be assumed to be earth excavation. As to the more lofty elevation southward of Scugog, it would be difficult to surmise what would be found at the bottom of an excavation of 200 feet and over, in its deepest portion, and several miles in extent. As shown on the top the ridge is a hard clay, overlaid in some places with sand. It may be that the core of the ridge is rock, which material is found near the Ontario level at Port Hope and Toronto, and again at Lindsay, on the Scugog River.

"In a cutting of such depth, and in a district devoid of stone, rock would be the most desirable material to encounter, as it would be a guarantee against slides, and give the minimum quantity to be removed; while, if of a useful quality, its value to the work would be considerable.

"If the Severn route were adopted, between Lake Simcoe and Lake Huron, the Georgian Bay Canal route, via Scugog, would be between five and ten miles shorter than the one via Humber and Holland Rivers; but if the Nottawasaga route be taken between Simcoe and Huron there would be about the same difference the other way.

"If the Severn route be found preferable, it would not be necessary to enter Lake Simcoe at all; and this may then prove the better course. It would be better for the canal if it had a continuous towing-path (like the Welland) from Huron to Ontario, as both these lakes are well adapted for sailing craft. Since the feeder will leave the Talbot River valley, it may be found practicable to continue upon it as the main line of the canal, and descend from thence to Lake Couchiching or Severn Bridge; or the canal may be kept above the lake level from the shore near Beaverton to the same points, and thus avoid the cost of a harbour, dredging, towage, etc., which are involved by entering the lake.

"The total lockage on this route would be very heavy, amounting to 840 feet, or about 500 feet greater than that upon the Welland Canal. The lockage upon the Holland and Humber Rivers route, with Lake Simcoe as the feeder, would be 230 feet less than this, as that lake is 100 feet lower than Scugog, and 115 feet lower than the proposed summit or feeder level of a canal through the county of Ontario; but the obstacles are so great to any route with a feeder so low as Lake Simcoe that I am of opinion the extra lockage would be preferred to attempting the long, deep cutting between the Holland and Humber Rivers. I have shown a section of ridge compared with the one south of Lake Scugog, by which the difference in the two undertakings will be shown at a glance."

CHAPTER XXXVIII.

Educational interests—Growth of education in the County—A retrospect of the past—
Statistics—Public Schools—Separate Schools—High Schools of the county—County
Model School—Ontario Ladies' College—Demill College—Pickering College—Founda-
tion of the High Schools—Brief sketches—Indian School, etc.

IN treating of the portion of the historical sketch having reference to education in the county of Ontario, there is little to be
said in a general way in reference to the rise and growth of our
present system of education that might not with equal justice be
affirmed of almost every other county in the Province. The beginning was entirely insignificant, but the issue has been, except to
eye-witnesses, amazing beyond credibility. The oak has indeed
sprung from the acorn, and its boughs cover all the land. Inasmuch, however, as there is, perhaps with increasing years,
increasing danger that our young people, judging from the smiling
scenes of prosperity, both material and educational, that greet them
on all hands, may imagine that the present state of things has
been continual, or may through sheer inability to believe, regard
the tales of the hardships in the pursuit of knowledge that fell to
the lot of our pioneers as the dreams of distempered imaginations
worthy to be reckoned with the adventures of Sinbad or the
exploits of Munchausen, it may be well to put upon record some
authentic facts of these olden times, as described by the few
ancients that still connect us with the primeval forest, and to
revive those memories which are fast becoming lost in the
multiplied experiences and ever-shifting panorama of these modern
days. There are people still living whose memory can carry them

to the time when there was not a schoolhouse in the county of Ontario. There are many who can recollect when schoolhouses were few and far between, when the machinery of education was of the rudest description, and when the highest ambition of parents was that their children might be able to read and write. There are hundreds who can remember when the literary attainments of the teacher were gauged by his own appraisal of them, when an itinerant system of boarding supplemented his scanty wages, when " healths five fathoms deep " and mighty potations were thought no discredit to him, nor were supposed to obscure his mental vision nor mar his usefulness ; when a prime requisite for success in his work was not so much the ability to impart knowledge as to inflict innumerable punishments of the most fantastic complexion for the most trifling offences, and to subdue backwoods lawlessness to some system of transatlantic civilization. In these primitive times the schoolhouse was constructed of logs frequently unhewn, and it contained but a single room. The furniture was of the rudest description, consisting chiefly of long pieces of deal supported by pins inserted in the wall used for desks, in front of which extended huge pieces of square timber supported by legs of uneven length, whose unaccommodating unparity afforded more opportunities to the pupils of determining the centre of gravity than practising the art of caligraphy. Utterly blank were the walls, except indeed where some adventurous youth had carved his name, or with bold design had traced in carbon the well known visage of " the master." Maps, charts and all the other triumphs of Caxton's art that now adorn the walls of the humblest schoolhouse in the land were then unknown, and we doubt not many middle-aged men and women can recall their first impressions when they beheld unrolled before their admiring gaze a map of this stately planet, which they heard for the first time had been bowling around the sun for thousands of years. Like many dwelling-houses of the time, the schoolhouse was heated by means of an immense fire-place, upon whose ample hearth blazed tremendous logs cut from the adjacent woods—a system that served the double purpose of heating and ventilation. Of fresh air, indeed, there was no lack, for after a few years' occupation this building disclosed many holes and crevices through which wind or rain found an easy entrance, and through which the youngsters, tired with their unaccustomed toil, might espy the progress of the world without. Tradition tells us that the first stove in any schoolhouse in the county was made from an old potash-kettle, two accidental holes—one in the bottom and the other in the side—suggesting to some ingenious patron of learning the stoking-hole and the flue. Turned bottom up and furnished with a chimney, what need to state that it became the admiration of all the country-side. Rude and destitute conveniences as these first schoolhouses were, they nevertheless cost the early settlers much patient labour and no little self-sacrifice. Often the burden of completing them fell upon two or three public-spirited men of the section, and often too, extreme difficulty was experienced in raising sufficient means wherewith to pay the teacher.

These striking memorials of backwoods times are fast disappearing, and giving place to elegant and commodious structures which dot the landscape in every direction, and which are no less the pride than the ornament of the whole country. May they all soon disappear, and may not antiquarian zeal nor blighting parsimony prevent them being replaced by schoolhouses more in accord with the progress of education and the necessities of the times! Time and space will not permit us to go into any detail as to the various steps by which the means of education, from its rude and unpromising beginning have attained to their present happy condition; it must suffice to mention results.

According to the report of the Minister of Education, laid before the House at the last session of the Legislature (1887), the school population of the county numbered 12,291; the total number of pupils attending the Public Schools was 10,417—5,598 boys and

4,819 girls. The total receipts for Public School purposes were $80,475.90; of which amount $59,843.28 were raised by municipal school grants and assessments. There were 146 Public School teachers employed who received salaries aggregating $52,451.13. These figures do not include the towns of Whitby and Oshawa.

The school population of Oshawa was 1,634; total number attending the Public Schools, 975—490 boys and 485 girls. Total receipts for Public School purposes, $6,725.44; and the amount paid for teachers' salaries, $4,749.16.

The number of pupils attending the Public Schools of Whitby was 677—372 boys and 305 girls. Total receipts, $5,993.35; and the amount paid for teachers' salaries, $4,540.

There is only one Roman Catholic Separate School in the county, at Mara; the total amount received for which is $590.20, and the amount paid to teacher, $396.

Mr. J. P. Foley, J.P., of Brechin, already mentioned in these pages for his munificence in connection with the township of Mara, has largely aided in the erection of the school building.

There is also a Roman Catholic Separate School at Oshawa, and one at Whitby. The total receipts of the former are $637.70; amount paid to teacher, $400. The total receipts of the Whitby Separate School are $649.03; amount paid to teacher, $475.

There are four High Schools in the county—Oshawa, Port Perry, Uxbridge, and Whitby Collegiate Institute.

The total receipts for Oshawa High School were $3,328; amount paid for teachers' salaries, $2,766.

Port Perry, receipts, $3,848.49; amount paid for teachers' salaries, $2,868.

Uxbridge High School, total receipts, $3,332.27; amount paid for teachers' salaries, $3,115.

Mr. Gould built the first Grammar School in Uxbridge about 1856; it was a frame building, and was erected at his own expense.

Whitby Collegiate Institute, total receipts, $5,495.48; amount paid for teachers' salaries, $4,943.

The number of pupils in attendance were—

Oshawa High School	164
Port Perry High School	114
Uxbridge "	101
Whitby Collegiate Institute	161
Total	540

This is stated to be the largest number of High School pupils of any county in the Province.

There are also two first-class Model Schools, one at Whitby and one at Port Perry. Last year the number of student-teachers on the Whitby roll was 26—14 males and 12 females. All the males and eleven females passed the final examination. Port Perry School makes an equally good exhibit.

The Indian School at Rama is favourably reported on by the County Inspector, Mr. James McBrien. The building is very comfortable, and has ample accommodation, and the equipment is good. At his last visit (1886) there were but twenty-two pupils present; but there were twice that number of school age. Fair progress was being made in reading, writing, spelling and geography.

Through the exertions of this efficient County Inspector much interest is now taken in planting trees on the school grounds. As many as 2,252 had been planted out on last Arbour Day (1886), averaging about twenty trees for every school section in the county, and the work was still progressing.

Some of the best schoolhouses in the county are to be found in Whitby, Oshawa, Port Perry and Uxbridge, and in Pickering.

Prior to the year 1871 the inspection of the Public Schools was conducted chiefly by resident clergymen, appointed to the duty of examining schools by the County Councils, and not a little of the progress of education, not only in this county but throughout the Province, is due to the untiring energy of many of these men.

Among many men of note in this county, whose personal efforts in early times contributed much to the advancement of the schools, was the Rev. Dr. Thornton.

In the year 1871 many important changes took place. All the Public Schools were made free, trustees were compelled to provide adequate school accommodation, and the County Inspector, Mr. McBrien, was appointed. The County Board of Examiners was constituted, and several other changes in school matters took place which are common to all counties.

The facilities for higher education in the county are of the most satisfactory character. There are, as stated above, four High Schools, called County High Schools, and two Model Schools for the training of both sexes for various grades of Public School Teachers' Certificates, and for preparing candidates for the Universities and for entering the learned professions generally. These schools are conveniently situated, and are all exercising a very great influence in their respective communities, and contributing very largely to the growth of knowledge and culture throughout the county.

Whitby School was established 1846
Uxbridge   "   "   1856
Oshawa   "   "   1865
Port Perry "   "   1868

Formerly there was a High School in the village of Cannington and one in Beaverton, but both were closed for lack of funds. The schools are supported equally by the Government, Legislative and the County grants being made in aid of them, according to a system depending partly upon the average attendances of the pupils and partly upon their proficiency in the subjects of a curriculum uniform for the Province, the number of teachers employed, and the equipment and buildings.   •

In addition to these High Schools there are also private institutions: (1) The Ontario Ladies' College at Whitby, (2) the Demill Ladies' College at Oshawa, and (3) the Quaker School at Pickering (now closed, but expected to be again re-opened).

A mere list of these places for higher education is sufficient to indicate the immense progress that has been made.

The Whitby High School (now the Collegiate Institute) has a standing of over forty years, and was long known as the Senior County Grammar School. It was founded in 1846 by the liberality and public spirit of Peter Perry, Samuel Cochrane (the veteran of 1812) and Ezra Annes, to whom the county of Ontario in general, and the town of Whitby in particular, must ever owe the deepest gratitude.

The school was opened with Mr. James Hodgson, late Inspector of Public Schools of South York, as head master.

The successors of Mr. Hodgson in office were William McCabe, LL.B., Thomas Kirkland, M.A., S. Arthur Marling, M.A., George H. Robinson, M.A., and the present head master, L. E. Embree, M.A. Under the direction of these well-known masters the school has attained to a more than Provincial fame; its pupils are being drawn from all parts of the Dominion, and its alumni found in every quarter of the globe. The old school was built two stories high, only one flat of which, however, was occupied or even finished; but the rapid success of the school soon laid under requisition both flats, and for some years the new improvement sufficed. But in 1872 the pressure for more accommodation became so great that the Board of Trustees determined to erect a structure commensurate with the prospects of the school and adapted to the modern ideas of education. The present beautiful and commodious structure was erected in 1873, and now stands amongst the most elegant and commodious schoolhouses in the Province.

The Port Perry High School was opened in 1868. Notwithstanding the disadvantages of an unsuitable building and a want of necessary apparatus, it sent forth many scholars, who have shown by their subsequent success that their training was thorough and substantial.

In 1873 the Board of Trustees determined to erect school buildings in some degree corresponding to the enterprise and prosperity of the village, and, as the result of this determination, we have the present handsome and commodious High and Public Schoolhouse.

The schools of Oshawa and Uxbridge have been equally successful, and both towns have shown commendable liberality in providing educational facilities for the rising generation.

In this connection the long services of Dr. Bascom and Rev. Mr. Cockburn in the cause of education deserve especial mention. For more than a quarter of a century the worthy Doctor has acted in the capacity of Secretary of the Uxbridge Board. Rev. Mr. Cockburn has for a period of fourteen years filled the office of chairman, and was also a member of the Board of Examiners of the county for several years.

CHAPTER XXXIX.

Farming—Stock-breeding—Position of the Farmers—First County Agricultural Society—
Officers—North Ontario County Society—Prizes in '53 and '86—Volunteer Companies
—Formation of 34th Battalion—County Wardens—Parliamentary Representatives—
The County Press.

IN improved methods of agriculture, as well as in stock-breeding, the farmers of the county of Ontario stand foremost in the Province. The farms are generally well tilled and well stocked, and most farmers of the county have, now, comfortable dwellings, good horses and modern farm implements; large roomy barns; fine orchards and gardens, and every farm convenience, as well as the means of comfort and enjoyment. The front townships have often been described as the "Garden of Canada," and at the present day many of the townships north are little, if any, behind them. Years of persevering toil and praiseworthy self-denial have brought about this improved state of things for the successors of the early settlers, who, bare and ill-provided, entered the bush, and through struggles and hardships, of which their descendants know little, conquered such smiling homes from the Canadian forest. The Agricultural Societies have done their share towards the great progress that has been made, and the Farmers' Clubs are now helping them on in the grand work.

Mr. Gould, as has already been gleaned from these pages, early in life took a deep interest in farming, and that interest was continued up to his death. At one time he worked between six and seven hundred acres. He was always advising his farming friends to work the land better and graze more stock.

The first County Agricultural Society was formed in February,

1853. The officers were :—Ebenezer Birrell, president; John Ritson, 1st vice-president; Samuel Widdefield, 2nd vice-president; John Ham Perry, secretary; John Corbett, treasurer. Directors— Joseph Pierson, John Clerke, John Shier, J. C. Stirling, A. Farewell, Adam Spears and William Boynton. Before that time there were township societies, which held small fairs, sometimes united in order to make a better show. Those of Whitby and Pickering were held at Oshawa, Duffin's Creek, Greenwood and Whitby alternately. Cattle fairs were also held at Ashburn, Columbus and Greenwood.

In 1855 the North Riding set up as a separate County Agricultural Society. Both societies have since grown and flourished. The amount awarded in prizes at the first county show, held in Whitby, in September, 1853, was £56 ($224). This was for the whole county. The amounts awarded in prizes by the South Ontario County Agricultural Society for several years past, average $2,500 per annum. And at a fair held at Port Perry in the north last year sums amounting to over $5,000 were given in prizes. These are indications of the progress which agriculture has made in the county of Ontario.

The 34th Battalion, now commanded by Col. M. O'Donovan, is the County regiment of volunteers, with headquarters at Whitby.

In 1858, under Baron de Rotenburg, the then Adjutant-General of Canada, the first company of volunteers was raised by Captain James Wallace. During the *Trent* affair companies were formed in Oshawa, Greenwood, Uxbridge, Beaverton, Brooklin, Cannington, Port Perry, Columbus and Whitby, which were incorporated into the 34th. The battalion was commanded by Col. Fairbanks up to the time of his death, and afterwards by Col. Wallace, and for a short time by Col. Warren, of Oshawa. On Col. Wallace's leaving Canada, the command fell to Col. O'Donovan.

Officers and men have been always prompt to the call of duty, and both the County Council and the local municipalities of the companies have always given substantial recognition of their services.

COUNTY WARDENS.

The following are the names of the gentlemen who have filled the Warden's chair, and the year of their election :—

1853......Joseph Gould.		1870......W. S. Sexton.
1854.... { T. N. Gibbs. / James Rowe.		1871......Geo. Wheler.
		1872......W. H. Gibbs.
1855......T. N. Gibbs.		1873......James O. Guy.
1856......J. H. Thompson.		1874......Philip McRae.
1857......J. H. Thompson.		1875..... Geo. Smith.
1858......D. G. Hewett.		1876......John Miller.
1859......Chas. Robinson.		1877......Yeoman Gibson.
1860......J. H. Thompson.		1878......Malcom Gillespie.
1861......T. P. White.		1879......James Graham.
1862......Wm. Smith.		1880......James McPherson.
1863......John Ratcliff.		1881......Geo. F. Bruce.
1864......J. H. Thompson.		1882......Peter Christie.
1865......J. H. Thompson.		1883......Isaac J. Gould.
1866......Calvin Campbell.		1884......J. L. Smith.
1867......J. H. Perry.		1885......Henry Gordon.
1868......J. B. Bickell.		1886......Chas. Gould.
1869......Josh. Wright.		1887......Joseph Monkhouse.

REPRESENTATIVES IN PARLIAMENT.

The county of Ontario was represented in the Canadian Parliament from the setting off of the county up to the confederation of the Provinces as follows :—

NORTH ONTARIO....1854 to 1861............Joseph Gould.
    "   "   ....1861 to 1863............Hon. Sir M. C. Cameron.
    "   "   ....1863 to 1864............Hon. Wm. McDougall.
    "   "   ....1864 to 1867............Hon. Sir M. C. Cameron.
SOUTH ONTARIO....1854 to 1857............Jno. M. Lumsden.
    "   "   ....1857 to 1866............Hon. O. Mowat.
    "   "   ....1866 to 1867............Hon. T. N. Gibbs.

Since Confederation the members have been, for the House of Commons :—

NORTH ONTARIO..1867 to 1872......Jno. Hall Thompson.
  "   "   1872 to 1874......W. H. Gibbs.
  "   "   1874 to 1876......Adam Gordon.
  "   "   1876 to 1878......W. H. Gibbs.
  "   "   1878 to 1882......Geo. Wheler.
  "   "   1882 to 1887......A. P. Cockburn.
  "   "   1887 to ———......F. Madill, the sitting member.

SOUTH ONTARIO..1867 to 1874......Hon. T. N. Gibbs.
  "   "   1874 to 1876......Hon. Malcolm Cameron.
  "   "   1876 to 1878......Hon. T. N. Gibbs.
  "   "   1878 to 1887......F. W. Glen.
  '   "   From 1887........William Smith, the sitting member.

For the Provincial Legislature :—

NORTH ONTARIO..1867 to 1879......Thomas Paxton.
  "   "   1879 to 1883......Frank Madill.
  "   "   From 1883........Isaac J. Gould, the sitting member.

SOUTH ONTARIO..1867 to 1871......Dr. McGill.
  "   "   1871 to 1875......Ab. Farewell.
  "   "   1875 to 1879......N. W. Brown.
  "   "   1879 to ———......John Dryden, the sitting member.

Of newspapers the county of Ontario would certainly appear to have its fair share. There are no fewer than fourteen now published within the county.

The *Tribune* and the *Friendly Moralist* were the earliest ventures. They were brought out in Oshawa in 1848 and 1849. They were followed by the *Freeman* and *Reformer*, in 1850—small sheets which had only a short existence. The *Whitby Freeman* first appeared in 1850, and was replaced by the *Whitby Reporter* for a few months, published by J. S. Sprowle. It then became the *Ontario Reporter*, a sheet of somewhat respectable dimensions, published by

Messrs. Perry and Dornan, and was afterwards published up to 1857 by J. O. Dornan alone. The Whitby *Commonwealth* was started in the town in 1855. The publication of the Whitby *Chronicle* was commenced in 1856, and was continued to its twenty-eighth year by W. H. Higgins. A semi-weekly edition of the *Chronicle* was also published, together with the weekly, from March, 1859, to September, 1860, and dropped after eighteen months' trial. In 1883 the office was purchased by Messrs. J. S. Robertson and Brothers, who after an experience of two years, sold out to the present proprietors, Messrs. Henderson and Graham. Mr. John Stanton, who entered the *Chronicle* office in the early part of the year 1857, is still foreman, having been over thirty years in the same office. The *Commonwealth* and *Reporter* were followed by the *Ontario Times*, the *Watchman*, the *Press*—all of which, after short intervals, disappeared, leaving the field to the *Chronicle*. The *Gazette* next took the place of the *Chronicle's* old rivals. It has gone through a great and varied number of changes of editors and proprietors, and has been in the hands of the present publisher, Mr. Newton, between two and three years. The *Vindicator* has been continuously published at Oshawa since 1854. It was established by Messrs. Luke & Orr. After Mr. Orr's retirement, a quarter of a century ago, the firm became Luke & Larke. Mr. Luke and Mr. Larke both retired from the printing business, and sold out to the present publisher, Mr. Carswell. The *Reformer* was first published in 1870 by Mr. W. R. Climie; and was continued, upon his retirement, by Messrs. Luke and Larke, who afterwards sold out to Mr. Mundy, the present proprietor. The *Oshawa Journal* was started in Oshawa in 1861 by W. H. Higgins, but was given up, the *Chronicle* requiring his undivided attention. The publication of a paper called the *North Star* was attempted in Brooklin in 1855; but there were only a few numbers printed. Some ten years ago Mr. James Cuttle gave Brooklin a printing office, and he publishes a small sheet called the *Times*. The *Pickering News* was established by W. H. Higgins in 1882, and in 1883 the office was sold to the present proprietor, Mr. Ackerman.

In North Ontario the first newspaper attempt was made in 1855 by William Hillam, who published the *Packet* for a couple of years. In 1857 Mr. James Holden commenced the publication of the *Observer* at Prince Albert. Shortly afterwards Mr. Oliver, who had been Mr. Holden's editor, published the *Review* at the same place, but the latter journal only lasted a short time. Messrs. Baird & Parsons afterwards purchased the *Observer*, and removed the plant to Port Perry, where the *Observer* still flourishes. Several attempts were made to publish a newspaper at Uxbridge previous to the establishment of the *Journal* and *Guardian*, but they were all unsuccessful. Mr. Mundy kept the *Advocate* going for a while, but it had to succumb for want of support, and the *Standard* was afterwards established by him at Port Perry, with better appreciation. A third paper, the *Times*, has now been placed at Uxbridge. It has been brought out as a party organ, and will have to be kept up as such, or by some other means than those which the legitimate business of the place affords. Indeed one printing office and one paper, instead of three, would be all-sufficient to meet the requirements of a town of the size of Uxbridge, and afford a printer a chance of making a decent living. Cannington has had a newspaper for fifteen or sixteen years. The *Gleaner* was first published by Mr. Currie. Beaverton has now its *Express*, and Sunderland has, or had for a short time, its newspaper and printing press. While the usefulness and benefits of the newspaper press are undeniable, it is very questionable whether the multiplication of so many little sheets within such narrow limits can be altogether beneficial, or indeed serve any good purpose.

CHAPTER XL.

MR. GOULD had been long urged by his political friends to allow
himself to be brought forward as a candidate for a seat in
Parliament. When Ontario was erected into a new county, comprising two constituencies, he was regarded on all sides as "the
coming man" for the representation of the North Riding. On the
defeat of the Hincks-Morin Government, in June, 1854, and the
dissolution and general election which quickly followed, Mr. Gould
was at once brought prominently into the field to contest the North
Riding in the Reform interest—being selected as the standard-
bearer at the party convention.

The nomination took place at Vroomanton, in the township of
Brock, on Monday, July 27, the new sheriff of the county, Mr.
N. G. Reynolds, being the returning officer. The following were
the gentlemen nominated, and the "show of hands" for each,
which it was then the practice to take at nominations :—

Allan Macdonald, Toronto, moved by Col. Cameron, and seconded
by John Campbell, of Thorah—show of hands—5.

John Hall Thompson, Brock, moved by Henry Gorman, seconded
by Wm. Cowan—show of hands—7.

Archibald George McLean, of Toronto, was also moved by Col.
Cameron, and seconded by Lachlan Davidson, and his show of
hands was 5.

Abraham Farewell, of Harmony, was moved by Robert Wells,

and seconded by Aaron Ross, of Reach, and declined the nomination.

T. N. Gibbs, of Oshawa, moved by George Brabazon, Brock, seconded by Donald Cameron, Beaverton—show of hands—3.

Ogle R. Gowan, Toronto, moved by Thomas Bolster, and seconded by Joseph Johnson, of Uxbridge—show of hands—(about) 100.

Joseph Gould, of Uxbridge, moved by George Currie, of Prince Albert, seconded by Joseph Bigelow, of Port Perry—show of hands—between 80 and 90.

John Ham Perry, of Whitby, and Nathaniel Bolster, of Brock, were also nominated, but declined, and no show of hands was called for them.

The show of hands was declared in favour of Mr. Gowan. A poll was demanded on behalf of Messrs. Gould, Gibbs, Thompson, McLean and Macdonald.

The nomination being held in the centre of the Tory stronghold of Brock was not expected to result otherwise than in favour of the Tory candidate, Mr. Gowan. The latter declared upon the hustings that he had his choice of seven constituencies open to him, but that his preferences were given to North Ontario. He desired to be the first representative of the new constituency. Mr. Gowan was a leading Orangeman, and as there was a large Orange vote in the North Riding—the brethren swarming in Brock—he felt very confident of capturing the new constituency. He raised the cry of "loyalty," and taunted the Reformers with being "annexationists" and "rebels," and these were the main grounds on which he appealed to the electors for their suffrages. The real questions at issue—the settlement of the Seignorial Tenure and Clergy Reserves —he evaded.

In the speeches made by the other candidates and their movers and seconders the railway question largely entered.

Mr. Gould made a telling speech upon this occasion. After

refuting some charges that had been brought against him, and which were circulated through anonymous fly-sheets distributed at the meeting, as to the sale of the county debentures, he turned the tables on Mr. Gowan by "showing up" the Tories who had signed the annexation manifesto; referring to their treatment of Lord Elgin, the Queen's representative, whom they pelted with rotten eggs, and to the benefits of Responsible Government, which had been secured by those who had been branded as "rebels." He was able to refer to his own record and services as a County man, and convinced the electors present that they were listening to a friend who had their interests at heart.

The polling days were fixed for the 31st July and 1st of August, and all parties went to work with a will. Meanwhile Mr. Gould issued the following address:—

To the Independent Electors of the North Riding of the County of Ontario:

GENTLEMEN,—Having been solicited by a convention of the Reformers of this Riding, and also by the principal Reformers of the townships of Scott and Brock (those townships not being represented at the convention), to allow myself to be put in nomination at the coming election, I now beg most respectfully to announce that I shall, in accordance with the wishes of my friends thus expressed, offer myself as a candidate for your suffrages to place me as your representative in Parliament.

Gentlemen, I do not think it necessary for me to enter into any lengthened explanation of my political views; I am not a stranger among you, having lived among you all my life, and having been most prominently engaged in every political contest for the last twenty years, and having voted for a professed Reformer at every election during that time. And also having been a member of our District and County Council for the last twelve years in succession, ample opportunity has been afforded for you to form an opinion upon my character and stability as a politician.

Gentlemen, in coming before you as a candidate for your suffrages, I do not think it necessary to make any great swelling promises of what I shall do or what I shall not do if elected; suffice it to say that I will not support any ministry who will not introduce a measure for the secularization of the Clergy Reserves and the abolition of the Rectories.

It may not be out of place for me to hint at a few of the measures which would meet with my hearty support, and which I would wish to see brought before the House, were I a member, viz: A union of all the Provinces with a local legislature for each, and a general assembly for the whole; an elective legislative council; reciprocity, in the fullest sense of the word; abolition of seignorial tenure; abolition of separate and sectional schools; a fixed day for Parliamentary elections; a set time for the meeting of Parliament, and a thorough investigation into the reported stock-jobbing, railroad, Point Levis, and Bowes and Hincks jobbing of the Ministry, with the hope that for the credit of Reformers this may turn out not a tithe so bad as reported.

Gentlemen, to all local questions affecting the interests of the Riding I shall pay most particular attention; a resident among you, with all the interest I have in the world staked on the prosperity of this county, it is quite clear that whatever is your interest is my interest, and all our interests are mutual; and therefore in the distribution of the public revenues for the improvement of the country, I shall endeavour to see that this Riding gets a fair share in proportion to her necessities and the amount to be distributed. Hoping to see you in your several localities before the day of polling, where we may exchange views, and come to an understanding with reference to the great questions before the country, I have the honour most respectfully to be, gentlemen,

Your obedient servant,

JOSEPH GOULD.

Uxbridge, July 10, 1854.

Mr. Gould was elected by exactly one hundred majority over Mr. Gowan, the other candidates being far away behind. The vote stood as follows :—

	GOULD.	GOWAN.	GIBBS.	MACDONALD.
Mara and Rama	15	1	5	39
Thorah	24	5	10	55
Uxbridge	124	62	..	..
Brock	58	113	98	9
Reach	200	125	34	1
Scott	30	45	3	..
Total	451	351	150	104

The hollow defeat of Mr. Gibbs in this election was Mr. Gould's complete triumph as a County man. They had taken different sides in county matters, Mr. Gould's course was approved, while that of Mr. Gibbs was condemned. The defeat of Mr. Gowan was a great triumph for Reform principles. He was an astute politician; had already sat in Parliament; was an Orange leader, and had all the Orange support of the Riding at his back. Mr. Macdonald, who was a Scotch Catholic, had detached from Mr. Gould the votes of the Catholic Liberals of the Riding, and this, it was expected, would make the seat certain for the Tory candidate. But the intriguers had reckoned without their host. Mr. Gould worked hard; his past election experience stood him in good service; he held meetings and organized, and triumphed over all opposition, and all the influences brought to bear against him inside and outside the county.

The Whitby *Reporter*, speaking of the result, in the next issue of that paper after the contest, said :—

"The North Riding has redeemed the character of the county of Ontario in the triumphant return of Joseph Gould, Esq., a well-tried and independent Reformer.

"In the election of Mr. Gould for the North Riding of Ontario, we have every reason to feel the same confidence in his integrity as a supporter of the pure principles of Reform that we did in his advocacy of county interests. His firmness in the Provisional Council, when surrounded by the persuasions and intimidations of a selfish clique, and when the least wavering would have been fatal to the many advantages now enjoyed by the people of this county, gives a guarantee for his conduct in the House when surrounded by more powerful influences."

Of Mr. Gowan, the same paper said :—

" It will be seen that Mr. Gowan made an unhappy choice in the seven ridings that invited him."

And of Mr. Gibbs :—

" Poor Gibbs ! He went out to ask the people of the north for their sweet voices, and they gave him their boot-taps ;"—was what was said.

The Oshawa *Freeman* was scarcely any more consoling in what it had to say of Mr. Gibbs's defeat. " It is surprising," says the editor of that sheet, " that Gowan should run so much better than Gibbs in a riding where it had been supposed Mr. Gibbs was one of the most popular men."

The writer had forgotten that the undivided Orange vote went for the Orange leader.

Mr. Gibbs fared badly with both parties. He was abused in the *Patriot* as having been the cause of the Conservative defeat. And on the day of declaration of the result of the poll, Mr. Gowan was unsparing in his denunciations and his charges against the gentleman from Oshawa. He charged Mr. Gibbs with writing a letter to Mr. Thompson, a Reformer, offering to resign in his favour as " they held similar views on the questions of the day," while he, at the same time, wrote him (Mr. Gowan) another letter asking him to retire, as they were both in the same interest !

CHAPTER XLI.

ALL the reforms advocated by Mr. Gould have long since been conceded. He saw the Seignorial Tenure question settled; the Clergy Reserves secularized, and the Rectories abolished, and had the privilege of recording his vote in Parliament in favour of the settlement of these important measures. He also gave his support to the bill abolishing the old detested system of Crown-appointed Legislative Councillors, and witnessed the election of men who were the free choice of the people to the Upper Chamber. What a gratifying change this must have been to the man whose first introduction to the same chamber was as a closely-guarded prisoner, and an alleged "rebel" at that! And what feelings must there have been awakened in his breast on meeting within the walls of Parliament the arch-rebel, William Lyon Mackenzie, on whose head a reward of $4,000 had been placed, now also a representative of the people! What memories must have crowded on both men since they met at Montgomery's on the memorable 6th of December, 1837! and since that night at Stouffville, just before · the "rising," when Mr. Gould objected to a resort to arms, and was taunted as a "coward" because of his pacific views!

While still an ardent admirer of Mackenzie, and entertaining for him the kindliest personal feelings, Mr. Gould did not take sides with him on entering Parliament. Mr. Gould wished to see the reform measures to which he stood pledged passed by the Hincks-Morin Government, and 'was one of the nineteen reformers who gave their vote to sustain the Government for that purpose. Mr. Mackenzie and Mr. George Brown, too, voted with the Tories in order to defeat the Government. They preferred the settlement of the Seignorial Tenure and Clergy Reserves and other burning questions by a Tory Government, with Tories such as Sir Allan MacNab at its head. Mr. Gould desired the settlement of those questions by a professed Reform Government, and asserted his own independence, although reproached by Mr. Mackenzie with inconsistency. Indeed the inconsistency appeared to be the other way. And Mr. Gould, retorting on Mackenzie, did not fail to tell him so.

The little episode in the House is referred to by Mr. Gould in the following manner :—

" He [Mackenzie] reproached me with inconsistency in supporting Hincks and Morin with about nineteen Reformers to secularize the Clergy Reserves and to abolish the Seignorial Tenure in Lower Canada and get reciprocity and an elective Legislative Council, after he, Brown, and the Tories, all of Upper Canada, had carried a vote of want of confidence while those measures were pending, and had got a pledge from Sir Allan MacNab and his friends that they would carry them through if we supported them. For this Mackenzie gave me a tongue-thrashing in the House. I told him that he had always been an impractical man whose hand was against every man, right or wrong, that would oppose him, and I should not be afraid to warrant that if he should have the forming of his own Administration, and select such men as were capable of carrying on a government, he would find a majority against him in less than a month's time."

Mr. John M. Lumsden was returned for the South Riding of Ontario at the same general election. He was of Conservative

antecedents, but professed Reform principles during the canvass
and on the hustings, and declared himself a secularizationist to the
fullest extent. Mr. Abraham Farewell was his opponent. The vote
stood :—

	LUMSDEN.	FAREWELL.
Oshawa............................	61	22
Pickering	271	137
Whitby	215	323
Total....................	547	482

Majority for Lumsden—65.

Parliament met, in the ancient capital of Quebec, on 5th Sep-
tember, 1854. The Government was beaten on the Address, and
Mr. Hincks was forced to resign. Sir Allan MacNab was sent for
by the Governor-General, Lord Elgin, to form a Cabinet, which
resulted in the formation of a Coalition Government. The Lower
Canada section of the Hincks-Morin Ministry—Messrs. Morin,
Taché, Chabot, Drummond, Chauveau and Dunbar Ross retained
their places. Sir Allan MacNab, Wm. Cayley, Jno. A. Macdonald,
Henry Smith, Robert Spence and John Ross composed the Upper
Canada section of the Cabinet. Messrs. Ross and Spence were given
portfolios as representing the Reformers of the Upper Province.

Some fault was found with Mr. Gould for voting with the Hincks-
Morin Government. What else could he do, and be consistent?
The Government had promised to secularize the Clergy Reserves
and pass the other reform measures advocated by Reformers. It is
therefore difficult to see how Mr. Gould's conduct could be open to
censure for the course taken by him. Other well-tried Reformers,
older in Parliamentary experience than Mr. Gould, voted at the
same side. It was simply a question of who were best deserving of
Reform support—the Reformers in power, pledged to Reform
measures, or the Tories who would take their places if Hincks were
turned out. Mr. Gould and others believed it best to trust the men
of their own party. Mr. Mackenzie and Mr. Brown thought other-

wise, and voted with the Tories. The inconsistency in this case, on the face of the record, was certainly not chargeable to the side espoused by Mr. Gould. His constituents appeared to be of this opinion, for we find that at a meeting of the Reformers of North Ontario, held at Uxbridge on the 30th of September, the following resolutions were passed :—

"Moved by James K. Vernon, Esq., of the township of Scott, and seconded by William Smith, Esq., of Uxbridge, and

"*Resolved:* That the course pursued by Joseph Gould, Esq., in Provincial Parliament meets with our approbation, and that it is the wish of this meeting that he will use his influence to secure those measures that the country has so unequivocally expressed a wish to obtain, and that he will 'give his support to any Ministry that will bring forward and support those measures."

"Moved by Joseph Bigelow, Esq., of the township of Reach, and seconded by Jonathan Moredan, Esq., of Uxbridge : That we exceedingly regret the factious opposition against the late Ministry by certain Reform members, thereby placing in jeopardy those measures that the country most requires.

"RICHARD LUND, *Chairman.*
"ROBERT SPEARS, *Secretary.*"

The strength of the Coalition Government was proved by the vote on the Address in reply to the speech from the Throne. It was carried by a vote of 70 to 33. Mr. Gould voted with the majority, and for the same reasons that he had supported Hincks. The Coalition stood pledged to carry out the Reform measures of their predecessors. In the Address the word "adjustment" appeared instead of "secularization," as applied to the Clergy Reserves. Mr. Hartman moved an amendment to substitute the latter word for the former. Mr. Gould was blamed by some of his friends for voting against this amendment. But he was after the substantial measure itself, and it was a matter of perfect indifference to him the mere form of words in which it was promised. In this he had the

approval of his constituents, who had expressed themselves as dis-
countenancing factiousness, and what was no better than a mere
piece of clap-trap. Mr. Gould, as was his habit, took a common-
sense view of matters, and acted straightforwardly and above-board.

The Clergy Reserves Bill was introduced according to promise
by the Ministry, and on the 25th of October carried to a second
reading. Mr. J. W. Gamble, member for West York, moved an
amendment to the effect that the secularization of the Clergy
Reserves would be a violation of the public faith. The amendment
was defeated by a vote of 93 to 12.

Mr. Lumsden, the member for the South Riding, of whose sound-
ness upon the Clergy Reserves question there was some doubt,
voted with Mr. Gould on this occasion, at the side of the majority,
and gave mortal offence to his Tory friends in Whitby and Pickering
by so doing.

Mr. Gould took part in the debate, and was active in opposing an
amendment of Mr. Dorion, of Montreal, proposing to merge the
funds remaining, after providing for the stipends of the present
incumbents, into the consolidated revenue. Mr. Gould contended
that the municipalities of Upper Canada alone were entitled to share
in this fund, and that it would on every ground be most unfair to
the people of the Upper Province to permit the municipalities of
Lower Canada to participate in it. He wanted a good plan of
secularization, come from what quarter it might, and he, together
with the eighteen other Reformers from the western Province who
voted for the Bill, accepted the measure of the Coalition Government as the best settlement that could be obtained of the vexed
question. He was actuated by similar motives when, joining with
the same prominent Reformers, he voted in favour of the Seignorial
Tenure and Elective Legislative Council Bills of the Government.
The latter bill was rejected by the Legislative Council. Mr. Gould
pursued a course that was at once reasonable and patriotic, and
the prudence and sound policy that dictated his votes have since

been abundantly justified. The settlement of the Seignorial Tenure and Clergy Reserves, which in their tendencies and results so deeply affected the political, civil and religious interests of the country, was an event of the highest importance. The questions had been fruitful of years of fierce agitation, and had greatly retarded the progress of the country. With their settlement a season of peace and quiet had been secured, and the material and social interests of the country advanced in an important degree. The words of the Governor-General, Sir Edmund Head, in proroguing Parliament in June, 1855, may well be recalled as the best vindication—if any were necessary—of the vote of Mr. Gould. Said the Governor :—

"An Act assented to by my predecessor has finally settled the long-pending dispute of the Clergy Reserves, and it has done so in such a manner as to vindicate liberal principles, whilst it treats the rights of individuals with just and considerate regard. The same may, I trust, be said of another important law—the Act for the abolition of the Seignorial Tenure. Great changes cannot be made without some hardship, but Canada will appear in history as the only country in the world in which the feudal system has expired without violence and revolution."

CHAPTER XLII.

AFTER the settlement of the Clergy Reserves and Seignorial
Tenure, the subject of Representation by Population began to
be discussed. Mr. Gould was amongst the prominent Reformers
who early favoured the principle and continued the battle until the
fight was won by Confederation. In his address to the electors of
North Ontario, issued 10th July, 1854, and in his enumeration of the
reforms which he would like to see take place, he says : " I should
wish to see brought before the House, were I member—*A union
of all the Provinces with a local legislature for each and a general
assembly for the whole.*" Just the remedy that was adopted after
thirteen years of political agitation. Mr. Gould saw, in advance of
most of his contemporaries, the true remedy for the existing system,
under which it was complained that Upper Canada was bearing so
much larger a proportion of the public burdens than Lower Canada.
He was one of the earliest Canadian politicians who placed himself
on record on the subject, and he lived to see the principle, which he
first mooted in 1854, carried out into the great and comprehensive
measure resulting in the Dominion of Canada—Canadian Confederation.

At the next session of Parliament, which opened on the 15th

February, 1856, and which under the alternating system was held in Toronto, the subject of a permanent seat of Government came up for discussion.

Mr. Gould was not opposed to the principle of a permanent seat of Government; but the subject was brought up in the House in such a way, by amendments and amendments to amendments, that the abstract principle was lost sight of. The aim of each of the movers was to secure a vote in favour of the location in Montreal, Quebec, Kingston, Ottawa, etc. It was well understood that Upper Canada would never submit to have the seat of Government in Lower Canada, so long as representation was not based upon population. The union of the two Provinces at the time was indeed regarded as a doubtful experiment, and it was under these circumstances that we find Mr. Gould declaring, in a speech on the question, in favour of the alternate system. What he said was—"Unless there was to be a permanent union, it would not be expedient to change the present system of alternating Parliaments in the respective Provinces." He voted against the motion placing the seat of Government at Quebec, and against the appropriation for new buildings.

During this session Mr. Gould introduced the bill incorporating the Whitby and Lake Huron Railway Company. He also moved for a return of all the timber berths assigned to individuals on the waters flowing into Lakes Huron and Superior, and for copies of the contract entered into by the Government for the sale of the Whitby Harbour, and relative to the Narrows Bridge and the public roads of the county of Ontario.

The Ministerial changes during the session excited much more than the ordinary interest caused by such occasions. Sir Allan MacNab, Hon. John Ross and Mr. Drummond were driven out of the Cabinet, their places being taken by Col. (afterwards Sir E. P.) Taché and M. (afterwards Sir George) Cartier, Mr. John A. (now Sir John) Macdonald taking Sir Allan MacNab's place as Attorney-

General West, and Mr. Vankoughnet as President of the Council in the new coalition. Mr. Gould was no friend of coalitions. After the fall of the Hincks-Morin Reform Government, he voted with their coalition successors for the sake of carrying the Seignorial Tenure and Clergy Reserves Bills, to which they stood pledged. Farther than that, neither his sympathies nor support extended. He was one of the fifty-four members who voted for Mr. Dorion's non-confidence motion against the coalition and new arrangement.

It was during this session that the petition against Mr. Gould's right to the seat was disposed of. A petty contract had been taken in his name for carrying the mails some few miles on a mail route. Mr. Gould permitted the use of his name in order to secure to the people of the locality the convenience. He had no personal interest in the matter. But Sir John Macdonald sought to punish him because he opposed the Coalition. The petition prayed that the seat be declared vacant, and a select committee of the House was appointed to investigate the frivolous allegation. The report of the committee, which was presented by Sir Allan MacNab, found that there was no disqualification; that the Post Office Act imposed disqualification upon certain contractors, but not on contractors for carrying the mails. The seat was declared not vacated. This was Mr. Gould's first "constitutional" victory over Sir John.

The session was a memorable one in many ways, but especially by the unexpectedly spirited action of the Legislative Council, which, by a vote of twelve to nine, defeated the action of the Assembly in refusing to vote the appropriation of £50,000 in the Supply Bill for erecting Parliament buildings at Quebec. Thus was the seat of government question staved off for another session.

Under the Elective Legislative Council Act, passed the previous session of Parliament, the Electoral Division of Queen's included the North Riding of Ontario, the West Riding of Durham and the county of Victoria. On the 19th of August, 1854, a meeting was held at Manchester for the purpose of selecting a candidate in the Reform interest to represent the division. The calling of the meeting originated with Mr. Gould, who was desirous of securing unanimity amongst Reformers, and uniting the party upon one man. The meeting was very largely attended, and there was a good deal of speech-making. The names submitted to the meeting were John Simpson (afterwards Senator), of Bowmanville, and Thomas Paxton, of Port Perry (afterwards M.PP., and late Sheriff of the county of Ontario). The appearance of the latter gentleman as a candidate was a surprise to Mr. Gould, who had already committed himself to Mr. Simpson's interest, and upon whom he wished all the Reformers of the division to unite. He addressed the meeting at some length with this object. The meeting resulted in the appointment of a committee for each candidate, who were to try to come to some arrangement. The committee met in the evening, but were unable to come to any definite understanding; they had agreed to leave it to three members of the Assembly to decide which would be the best candidate to put in nomination in the Reform interest. The names of Messrs. Mackenzie and Hartman were agreed to by both parties. Mr. Paxton's friends insisted upon Mr. J. S. Smith being the third name; and this being rejected by Mr. Simpson's friends, both parties separated without being able to arrive at a settlement. At the nomination held afterwards both gentlemen were nominated in the Reform interest, and Mr. H. J. Ruttan, of Cobourg, in the Conservative interest. Through the interference of mutual friends, and especially by the good management of Mr. Gould, Mr. Paxton was induced to retire in favour of Mr. Simpson, who was elected by a large majority over Mr. Ruttan.

CHAPTER XLIII.

AT the next session of Parliament, which opened at Toronto, on 26th February, 1857, the Seat of Government question was one of the first mooted. After a four-days and nights' discussion, a Government resolution, moved by Attorney-General (Sir John) Macdonald, referring the location to Her Majesty the Queen was carried. The vote stood 63 to 53. Mr. Gould voted with the minority.

Mr. Gould introduced and carried through a bill to confirm certain by-laws of the late Home District Council establishing certain roads in the county of Ontario. He voted steadily with the Opposition during the session, and spoke vigorously against the Grand Trunk Aid Bill and other Government measures, which he believed to be dictated by corrupt motives, or which he feared would have an injurious effect upon the interests of the Province. He made a strong and successful fight for the amended charter of the Whitby and Lake Huron Railway, which had been applied for this session, and which was strenuously opposed by members in the interest of the Port Hope, Lindsay and Beaverton Railway Company.

A dissolution of Parliament and an appeal to the electors followed the reconstruction of the Macdonald-Cartier Ministry in

November, 1857. The Reformers of the North Riding held a convention, and again nominated Mr. Gould. The nomination took place on the 21st, and the polling on the 28th December. Mr. Gould issued an address in which he placed himself on record on the questions then forced to the front in Canadian politics. He declared himself in favour of immediate representation based on population, without reference to a dividing line between Upper and Lower Canada; retrenchment in every department of the Government; annexation of the Hudson Bay territory; no grant of public money for Separate Schools or sectarian purposes; no appropriation of the public moneys without the consent of Parliament, and finally, he declared his hostility to the newly formed Coalition Government. The nomination was held at the old place, Vroomanton, in Brock. The candidates nominated were Mr. Gould and his old opponent, Mr. Ogle R. Gowan. A few of the recognized political speechmakers upon such occasions were also nominated, so as to give them a chance to exercise their calling. They harangued the meeting until dark, when the show of hands was taken, and was largely in favour of Mr. Gowan—this point being, as has been heretofore mentioned, the centre of his Orange stronghold.

Mr. Gould commenced his address by explaining that he had supported the Hincks-Morin Administration, because they had pledged themselves to settle the Clergy Reserves question and to give their aid to the settlement of the other reforms then demanded. He also, he said, voted with the MacNab Coalition Government for the same reason, and because if the Clergy Reserves were not then secularized, the measure was likely to be deferred for long years. He disapproved of the commutation clause, but accepted the measure as it was, on the principle that half a loaf was better than no bread. He was in favour of representation by population, irrespective of a dividing line, because it was the only means of protecting Upper Canada, so long as the union continued in its present shape. He was opposed to Separate schools and to all kinds of sectarian legislation, because he was honestly convinced that they worked injuriously to the whole people. He was in favour of the youth of all sects and creeds receiving instruction together, without in any way interfering with their religious views or feelings. He was opposed to all ecclesiastical corporations, whether Protestant or Catholic, and to the giving them power to hold property. He was opposed to the incorporation of religious establishments, such as convents, just as he was opposed to the incorporation of Orange-men. He did not believe in ladies being confined in nunneries, and thought on the contrary that woman had a higher, holier and more useful sphere as a wife and mother than being buried in such institutions.

Here Mr. Gowan interjected that he "had a great respect and admiration for the good work done by the ladies of those convents." "Oh, you have!" replied Mr. Gould; "and yet your Orange supporters speak of them as disrepectfully as they would of common houses of ill-fame. I am different from that." At this point there were expressions of dissent and a good deal of confusion. Mr. Gould resumed his speech, blaming the Government for not settling the question of the Seat of Government and referring to the railway project then before the county. He concluded by replying to the charges of "rebel" and "atheist" that had been hurled against him in this contest. He defended the part which he took in the rising of 1837; and as to his being an atheist, there could be no foundation for the charge. He professed himself a very humble follower of the Lord Jesus Christ. He was brought up a Quaker, and he believed in the tenets held by that body of Christians, and in the efficacy of the blood of the Saviour for the redemption of all mankind.

Mr. Gould was re-elected by a majority of 210.

During this election contest, the name of "Moderates" was taken by the Government supporters, out of deference to those Reformers who joined hands with the Conservatives in supporting the Coalition. It was, however, dropped after the next campaign, and

the good old names of Tory and Conservative resumed.   It was
after the defeat of the Hincks-Morin Administration that the term
Clear Grit was first generally applied to the Reform followers of
Mr. George Brown, in contradistinction to those who called them-
selves "Baldwin" Reformers, or Reformers who supported the
Coalition, or the "Moderate Party," as they were designated by
the *Leader* newspaper of that day.   The "Grit" was the Canadian
Radical in contradistinction to the Canadian *Reformer*.

CHAPTER XLIV.

MR. GOULD'S speech on the hustings at Vroomanton in reference to ecclesiastical corporations and convents, and especially
the latter, was for a time much misrepresented in order to serve
party ends.   He was held up to Roman Catholics as a calumniator of
their religious institutions ; and to give force to the charge, he was
accused as using for himself, and as his own opinion, the language
towards convents which he simply attributed to Orangemen as the
sentiments which they held towards those institutions.   The repetition of the charge had the effect of detaching the Roman Catholic
vote in the riding from Mr. Gould at the next election, as well as to
cast unjust odium upon him for bigoted opinions which he never
held.   Mutual explanations were subsequently made by Mr. Gould
and the reporter of the proceedings at the nomination (who was
none other than the author), in which Mr. Gould was completely
exonerated, and which were entirely satisfactory to the Catholic
people.   And this was made known in a letter written by the
Catholic priest of Brock, Rev. Father Brayere ; but not till after
the election of 1861, in which Mr. Gould was defeated.

The South Riding followed the example of the North Riding in sending a thorough Reform representative to Parliament at the general election of 1867. The gentleman elected has since left his impress upon Canadian politics and has largely influenced the legislation of the country.

Mr. Oliver Mowat, then a barrister at the head of the Chancery bar, and now Attorney-General, and the distinguished statesman and popular Premier of Ontario, won his first seat in Parliament at the general election of 1857. He was elected for the South Riding of Ontario—defeating Hon. J. C. Morrison (the recently deceased and lamented judge, and then a member of the Coalition Cabinet) by a large majority. It was during this election contest that the term "Christian Politician" was first, and has been since applied by way of derision to Mr. Mowat by his opponents. In his address to the electors, Mr. Mowat made use of the following words :—

"But I may say generally that, if elected, my desire is to perform my duty in Parliament in the spirit and with the views which become a Christian politician."

Mr. Mowat may well look back with pride to this his first utterance on entering political life. Some of his opponents, who then sneered and scoffed and called it " political cant," have long since been numbered amongst his most ardent supporters. He has, through many trials, proved himself true to the performance of duty " in the spirit and with the views which become a Christian politician." And the whole of his blameless private and useful public life has served to convince the people of Canada that it is possible to be a true Christian gentleman and at the same time a politician faithful to public duty. The death of Addison, the celebrated Secretary of State for England—but far more celebrated by the excellence of his writings and the purity of his life—was pointed to with admiration as showing how a Christian could die. Mr. Mowat's life can be instanced as showing how a Christian statesman ought to live, and no nobler epitaph could be placed upon the monument which Canada is certain to raise to his memory, than the words "CHRISTIAN POLITICIAN"—exemplified in his life and labours.

Mr. Gould invariably voted with Mr. Mowat, from the time the latter entered Parliament, in favour of Liberal principles. And, at the close of his life, he had the great gratification (which he declared he prized much more than all his own successes in political life), of seeing his old constituency of North Ontario transfer the confidence they once placed in himself to his son Isaac, and elect him as their representative to support his father's old friend, Mr. Mowat, in the Legislature of the Province. He lived to see the stigma of bigotry and intolerance wiped out from his name, and the Catholic electors of North Ontario amongst the strongest supporters of his son.

Mr. James Dryden, who was Reeve of the township of Whitby at the time of Mr. Mowat's first candidature, was also one of his most ardent supporters. And now his son, Mr. John Dryden, the sitting member in the Provincial Legislature for Mr. Mowat's old constituency of South Ontario, follows in his honoured father's footsteps in supporting the Premier of Ontario. To have succeeded, through all the political and party changes which thirty years have brought about in retaining the confidence of influential County families, from father to son, in this way, is perhaps the highest testimony that could be adduced to the Provincial Premier's popularity.

On his third appeal to the electors of North Ontario, in July, 1861, Mr. Gould was defeated by a majority of ninety-nine, his opponent being the late Chief Justice Sir Matthew Cameron, then one of the foremost men at the bar, and popularly known as "Mat" Cameron. There was a very heavy vote polled, the figures being Cameron, 1,102; Gould, 1,003. Mr. Gould made a gallant struggle. But there was a most influential and well-organized combination against him, and his friends were overborne by the united forces of "Orange and Green." The Orangemen embraced the opportunity to "pay him off" for his votes against their incorporation bill, and in favour of Mr. Foley's resolution to prevent the appointment of

Orange Crown prosecutors; and the Catholics desired to avenge the insult which it was erroneously believed had been offered to their religion by Mr. Gould.

In the subsequent political contests in the Riding Mr. Gould did not wish to have his own name submitted as a candidate. But he helped with all his might to fight the battles all the same, and supported with all the weight of his influence the standard-bearer of the Liberal Party. Nor were his exertions confined to North or South Ontario. He took a prominent part in the Legislative Council elections, both of King's and Queen's divisions, and aided largely in bringing about the victories gained in those divisions by the successful Reform candidates. As president of the Reform Association of North Ontario, which office he held for the quarter of a century preceding his decease, he did much in maintaining party organization. His great services in this position were repeatedly recognized by complimentary resolutions and addresses.

Mr. Gould's efforts were not confined to political and municipal affairs. Education, the town schools, the agricultural societies, and all commercial enterprises connected with his own immediate locality, as well as the county at large, received every encouragement and assistance at his hands. His usefulness was widespread, and was felt everywhere both in public and in private.

Although Mr. Gould was sometimes regarded as a hard man at a bargain, and as being over-sharp in his business dealings, he had in private life performed innumerable acts of kindness of which the world knew nothing. Instances are related by Mr. Joseph Dickey, Inspector of Division Courts, and who for many years transacted Mr. Gould's confidential business, which place his character in a most favourable light in this respect. More than one farmer in the county, we are assured, owes the possession of his farm to-day to Mr. Gould's timely help. Towards his brothers and their families he has all his life acted a fraternal and kindly part; and indeed in every other respect, and in every relation of life, he has acted the part of a good citizen.

CHAPTER XLV.

ONE of Mr. Gould's lucky speculations was the purchase of the
Hamilton property in 1856. It comprised about 300 acres—
the east half of lot 31 in the 6th concession and the whole of lot.
32—less perhaps twenty acres sold for village lots. The purchase
money was $19,000, and was considered at the time an exorbitant
price. But the man of shrewdness and foresight saw much farther
ahead of him than did his neighbours. Inside of two years of the
purchase, he sold the mill-site to Mr. Edward Wheler, of Stouffville,
for $11,000; and in one day a sale of town lots made by him
produced over $10,000. The total sales of lots fell short of thirty
acres. So that, making allowance for the twenty acres already
sold, he had 250 acres left, free and clear, and the whole of the
purchase money paid, and $2,000 over, from this bold and lucky
venture.

At his death, on the 29th June, 1886, Mr. Gould left surviving
him his widow, then aged seventy. The following are the children
of the marriage :—

1. Isaac James Gould, of Gouldville, born 13th November, 1839;
M.PP. for North Ontario; head of the firm of Isaac J. Gould &
Bros., bankers, etc., Uxbridge. First elected to Parliament, 1883;
was also Warden of the county of Ontario, and for several years
Reeve of the municipality of Uxbridge. Married, 23rd September,

1862, Rebecca Chapman, daughter of Ira Chapman, Esq., of Ux-bridge. Has issue two sons and five daughters living. The eldest son, Joseph Walter, born 27th May, 1863, engaged in business with his father and uncles.

2. Joseph E. Gould, born 2nd July, 1841; engaged largely in lumbering operations and as sawmill owner. Married in 1864 Elizabeth Sterling, daughter of ex-Alderman Sterling, of Toronto. Has issue four daughters and one son.

3. Charles Gould, born 15th April, 1843; of the firm of Gould Bros., mill owners, etc. Has been for several years Reeve of the municipality, and was elected Warden of the county of Ontario in 1886. Married, first, Miss Vernon, daughter of Silas Vernon; secondly, Miss Annie Smith, of Scott, by whom he has issue.

4. Rachel Gould, born 27th February, 1845. (Died young.)

5 and 6. Twins—Mary and Sarah. Mary married H. A. Crosby, Esq., of Uxbridge, and Sarah is the wife of Thomas Watt, Esq., of Brantford; both have large families.

7. Elizabeth, wife of Rev. Edward Cockburn, M.A., Presbyterian minister, of Uxbridge. Has issue.

8. Jonathan Gould, born 20th May, 1852; farmer; Deputy-Reeve of the township of Markham. Married Miss Plank, daughter of Bartholomew Plank, Esq., and has issue.

9. Ruth Alma, born 27th October, 1854—the date of the battle of Alma, from whence the second name. Married Mr. Thomas Dale, farmer, etc., and has no issue.

10. Harvey James Gould, born 1st May, 1857; of the firm of Gould Bros. Married Martha, daughter of the late George Sharpe, Esq., and has issue.

11. Annie, born 3rd October, 1860; died young.

By his will, dated 15th June, 1886, after bestowing some small legacies upon members of his brothers' families, the bulk of his estate is vested in his executors for the purpose of carrying into effect the trusts therein mentioned. Amongst other bequests there is one for the purpose of building a Mechanics' Institute (now being erected), at a cost of $4,500, for the benefit of the town of Uxbridge. This building is to be put up according to plans prepared and approved of by him previous to his death.

Another bequest to the town of Uxbridge is a sum of $2,500, which is devised by him to the Mayor and Corporation. This sum is to be invested by the Mayor and Council, and is to be kept invested by their successors in office, and the interest to be applied annually for the relief of the poor of the town. He is moved to making this bequest, he says, "as I feel satisfied that a large number of families have suffered, on account of the use of intoxicating liquors obtained at the Mansion House hotel, of which I am the owner." And he directs that, in appropriating the proceeds to the destitute persons residing in the town, the cases of those so rendered poor and destitute through the evils of intemperance have especial consideration. The fund is to be known as "The Gould Relief Fund."

Mr. Gould was a firm upholder of temperance principles, although his infirmities late in life prevented him from being a total abstainer, as he was obliged to use liquors in small quantities medicinally.

In his contributions for religious purposes he set a good example to others. He always gave liberally for church building purposes, and he gave to all without any exception. He felt this to be a public duty, and gave large help towards the erection of every church edifice in the town, Roman Catholic as well as Protestant.

Mr. Gould's interest in the cause of education has been already referred to, but scarcely with that adequacy and fulness which his well-directed labours deserve. He was one of the first and most earnest advocates of free schools; and this, notwithstanding his already large school assessment was trebled by his action. He also took strong grounds in favour of compulsory education. He never forgot the want of educational facilities of his boyhood, and was most zealous in insisting that every child was entitled to free education at the public schools. But, whilst taking this position, and whilst an ardent admirer of our School system, he had a great contempt for what he called "cramming" and the "higher branches." He deplored the valuable time wasted by persons in getting what was considered an advanced education, that was not likely to be of any practical use to them in after life. He did not believe that it was necessary for a man, in order to be a good farmer, that he should spend years in acquiring a smattering of Greek and Latin. He was a great stickler for devoting more attention to the teaching of practical book-keeping in the Public Schools, and worked strenuously to this end on the School Board, of which he was chairman for more than twenty years. In fact, so strongly did he feel on this point, and so much reason did he see for finding fault with the slurring system in vogue, that he had in contemplation the endowing of a Chair in the Uxbridge School, so as to make the teaching of book-keeping a specialty. The changes which he desired to see take place in respect to the subjects of book-keeping and elocution were afterwards introduced, and the money which might have gone to found a Chair was devoted to the Mechanics' Institute. For his own children Mr. Gould did his best in this direction; and the efficient discharge of the duties of the public positions which his sons have been called upon to fill proves that they have not neglected their opportunities.

In the disposition of his property amongst his children Mr. Gould exercised the same prudence and foresight so characteristic of him in business matters. He became, to a certain extent, his own executor, and did not permit his children to wait in anxious longing for his death in order to become entitled to their shares. Some years back, after the youngest had become of age, he made a general distribution between them of a large sum. To the boys he gave absolutely $20,000 apiece, and on each of his daughters he settled a sum of $10,000. With each child he kept a regular debit and credit account, and the portion which each took under the will was regulated in this way: those who had overdrawn during his lifetime, or for whose pecuniary help he had to give more largely, had the amount charged against the shares to which they became entitled under the will. The total of his fortune thus distributed amounted to over a quarter of a million, or perhaps nearly $300,000.

The firm of Gould Bros. are extensively engaged in milling operations. The mill property acquired is still owned by the sons, Isaac J. Gould owning the old sawmill power, and also the old gristmill power, and Charles and H. J. Gould owning the North mill and also the Wheler mill. New oatmeal mills of enlarged capacity, and with all modern improvements, have been recently erected by the firm; and, although the manufacture exceeds one hundred barrels per day, it all finds a ready home-market.

Besides banking, milling and farming on a large scale, the firm of Gould Bros. are also largely engaged in general mercantile business in the town. Mr. Isaac J. Gould has, at his own cost, just introduced the electric light, by which the town of Uxbridge is now nightly illuminated. Mr. Gould did not live to see this, the latest and one of the most marvellous inventions of civilization, extended to the town, which he may be said to have founded; but he lived long enough to see his sons worthily fill his place as business men of the highest standing in the community, and following in his footsteps, in engaging in and encouraging every enterprise calculated to advance their, and their father's, native town of Uxbridge.

For several years Mr. Gould was a great sufferer from asthma, which had the effect of checking his activity in public matters, inasmuch as it prevented his going out at night and speaking at public meetings.

Shortly before his death he underwent an operation for cancer in the nose, which did not seem to cause him much pain or suffering, and which was performed most satisfactorily.

From the time that he had passed his seventy-seventh year, his bodily weakness increased ; he felt more acutely Death's nearer approach, and he frequently told members of his family that he knew the end was near ; that he was prepared ; that he lived in hope and would die in hope, and that he waited for death in joy and peace.   He repeated those beautiful lines of Watt often, and, as he said, with " comforting effect " :—

> This life's a dream, an empty show :
> But the bright world to which I go
> Hath joys substantial and sincere ;
> When shall I wake and find me there ?
>
> O glorious hour ! O blest abode !
> I shall be near and like my God !
> And flesh and sin no more control
> The sacred pleasure of the soul.

He had lived eight years beyond man's allotted threescore and ten.   He saw nearly all the men with whom he had fought side by side, or who had led the hosts of the enemy, pass away.   He was one of the last, as he was one of the first, of the pioneers of his own township and of the county.   He saw his sons and daughters all grown up and married, and settled in life ; and in their children the aged grandfather saw his own youth renewed and his race perpetuated.   He loved to play and frolic with his grandchildren. And the great delight of young and old was the annual family gathering.   It was the custom to have a grand family gathering once a year at the family residence in Uxbridge.   This took place on the 1st of January—the anniversary of the marriage of the father and mother, when—

> The gay grandsire, skilled in gestic lore,
> Had frisk'd beneath the burden of threescore.

As the sons and daughters grew up and married, and the " olive branches " increased with each of them, these anniversary gatherings grew into larger and larger proportions, until at that immediately preceding his death they numbered some sixty-odd, young and old. He was very fond of reading the Psalms, and upon these occasions would repeat the verse : " Thy wife shall be as a fruitful vine by the side of thine house ; thy children like olive branches round about thy table."

At his home and in the social circle he was of a pleasant good-humoured manner, and even up to his latest days could enter into all youthful frolics and amusements with a zest and a relish that was most enjoyable and made him as welcome a guest as he was himself the most hospitable of hosts. He never declined a political encounter, and his vast stores of political and general information made him always a formidable opponent. Indeed he was a man—

> Exceeding wise, fair spoken and persuading.

The task which we have undertaken in sketching the life and labours of Joseph Gould is nearly completed. Ours has been the office of the literary workman. We have felt it to be more our duty to record facts and events than to attempt to judge and criticise. Our aim has been to supply an impartial narrative. In doing this, we have endeavoured to assume neither the position of champion nor defender. We chose no hero to glorify. Our subject was—we were going to say—an ordinary man. But that would have been a mistake. Joseph Gould was no ordinary man. In his life he has left an example worthy of imitation. His perseverance, industry, self-reliance and determination, as man and boy, to conquer a place amongst his fellows are evidenced everywhere in these pages ; accident did not favour him. He had to fight his way from the first. And he did so manfully — sometimes against untoward circumstances. He set out with good intentions—and he kept them. He carried out his own plan in life—and stuck to it patiently, honestly and conscientiously. He never failed to be punctual in meeting his engagements. He tells us of the straits to which he put himself rather than break his pledged word. And his life tells us how all this served him, and of the worth and value of punctuality in business matters. Were there none of those interesting reminiscences and descriptions of pioneer settlement; were there none of the important details and events in political and municipal life with which in his time he became so closely connected, and which have passed into the history of the country, the life of Joseph Gould of Uxbridge, was not a barren one. He not only created a large fortune; but he literally and actually made a name and founded a family. The good that he has done will live after him. An humble stone marks his grave. His remains lie interred in the peaceful Quaker Hill burial ground beside those of his sturdy father and beautiful Quaker mother, Rachel Lee :—

So may he rest, his faults lie gently on him.

FUNERAL NOTICE.

The following notice of the death and funeral of Mr. Gould appeared in the *Uxbridge Journal* of the 2nd July, 1886 :—

Mr. Joseph Gould, ex-M.P., died at his residence, Uxbridge, on Tuesday, the 29th ult., in his seventy-eighth year. Dissolution took place about half-an-hour before midnight, and was rather unexpected. Up to the last he possessed full consciousness, and spoke within a few minutes of his death. He passed away so quietly and peacefully that it was thought he was sleeping; but it was the sleep that knows no waking. He gave his orders and transacted business up to the last. Only the previous Saturday did he take to his bed, and the day before his death he gave directions and did some business. He himself had a premonition that the end was approaching, for he said to members of his family, on lying down, that he was going to take his final rest—that he was sure he would not rise alive again from that bed of sickness. He had been for years a martyr to asthma, and latterly, as the burden of years grew upon him, his health had become more and more enfeebled. The appearance of the germs of cancer in the face a short time ago, for which he underwent an operation, and which were removed without apparently much pain or suffering, must have helped still further to enfeeble his once vigorous frame. Withal, he carried the weight of his nearly fourscore years so jauntily, and had baffled disease so long, that his friends had hopes that his life would have been prolonged a few years further at least; none of them certainly anticipated the end being so near. But as there is nothing more certain than death, neither is there anything more uncertain than the time of dying.

> Life's latest hour is nimble in approach,
> And like a post, comes on in swift career.

Joseph Gould was born at Uxbridge, 29th December, 1808, and was exactly seventy-seven years and six months old at the time of his decease. He was the son of Jonathan Gold—a member of the Society of Friends—one of those excellent Pennsylvanian Quakers who emigrated to Canada in the first years of the present century, and settled at Uxbridge. Their location was called and is still known as Quaker Hill. It is delightfully situated on a rising ground within a mile and a half of the present prosperous town of Uxbridge. The old homestead, which the father and grandfather helped to clear and reclaim from the primeval forest, still belongs to the family. Mr. Gould underwent all the trials and hardships incident to the life of the early Canadian settler in the " bush," and whilst doing so, by his persevering industry and courageous self-denial, laid the foundation of the large fortune afterwards acquired by him during an honourable, well-spent life. He was a hard worker all his life, and a shrewd, intelligent business man. With the growth of settlement, he saw the face of the country changing from the unbroken forest to cultivated fields and thriving towns and villages, the seats of busy trade and commerce. He did his share as a worker in bringing about the change for the better, and profited by it by his enterprise and sagacity. He built sawmills, and grist-mills, and woollen mills, laid out town plots, and built on them, and encouraged others in building, and was mainly instrumental in securing to the town the benefits of railway communication. To him more than any other man the Uxbridge of to-day owes its existence. And with what feelings of pride must he have contem-plated its growth, from the few log houses of his infancy—from the little old sawmill put up by Dr. Beswick in the first decade of this century—to the ranges of spacious brick stores, the fine mansions, the town hall, large mills and manufacturing establishments, rail-ways, telegraphs and telephones of to-day !

It was not alone in the building up and material prosperity of his native Uxbridge that the deceased Joseph Gould took an active part ; he took an interest in, and helped on, every movement and good work calculated to promote its moral and educational advance-ment ; and one of his last acts was to give a free site and money to build a fine Mechanics' Institute and Free Library. He was also eminently a County man. His efforts contributed largely to the early setting off of the county of Ontario from York and Peel. And his efforts on behalf of County independence did not go unrecognized, for at the first meeting of the Provisional Council, held 3rd May, 1852, he was elected warden. He always took a leading part in county matters. He did his best to obtain a charter and promote the construction of a county railway—a line running through the entire length of the county, from Georgian Bay to Lake Ontario, with a branch to Uxbridge. His efforts in that direction proving fruitless, he joined in with Mr. George Laidlaw and the promoters of the Nipissing Company, and secured to the people of his own locality the benefits of that line—which now forms part of the Mid-land division of the Grand Trunk.

From his earliest youth Mr. Gould was an active politician.

His mind was early imbued with the principles of freedom and liberty of conscience inherited from his Quaker parentage. He may be said to have been born a Canadian Liberal. Throughout his long life he was a consistent, unflinching Reformer. And he was a man who stood up boldly for his principles. When the political grievances of the country led to Mackenzie's unsuccessful rising in 1837, Joseph Gould was no shirker. He took sides with the " patriots," who, failing in their efforts to obtain peaceable reforms, felt themselves justified in resorting to revolution—a course for which they had before them plenty of British precedents. And he suffered the penalty of his patriotism. He was arrested, and incarcerated from the 13th of December, 1837, to October, 1838, when he was pardoned on giving security to keep the peace and be of good behaviour for three years. The man who was stigmatized as a " rebel of '37," and who never felt abashed or ashamed of the taunt, was, like his leader and many of his compatriots, afterwards elected to every office in the gift of the people for which he was induced to offer himself as a candidate. Previous to the insurrection he represented his municipality under the Township Commissioners' Act. Afterwards he was elected to the District Council from 1842 to 1854 ; he was elected first reeve of Uxbridge when the county of Ontario was separated from York and Peel, and subsequently, as has been already stated, first warden of the new county. He was also the first member of Parliament elected for North Ontario, in 1854, and was elected for a second term in 1857-8. His defeat on the next appeal to the people, by the present Chief Justice Cameron, was owing to local combinations, an account of which would be here out of place. Continuously since then, he was year after year elected president of the North Ontario Reform Association, and held the position of honorary president at the time of his death. No man was more trusted by his party or had more influence in his own section. He lived to see his political character fully vindicated, and his eldest son, the present popular member for

North Ontario, in the Local Legislature, take his place in the councils of his country.

. . . .

Joseph Gould was a man of sterling principle and high honour and integrity, and was as well respected as he was widely known. No man will be more missed in this community in which he had so long lived. But whilst his family and friends mourn their loss, they have the consolation that he died full of years and honours, a true and humble Christian, leaving an untarnished reputation and good example behind him in the lesson of his well-spent life. He leaves a fortune of upwards of quarter of a million dollars, to be divided amongst his children, according to the terms of his will.

THE FUNERAL.

The *Globe*, giving an account of the funeral, which took place on Friday, the 2nd inst., has the following :—

The remains of the late Joseph Gould, of Uxbridge, were interred at the Friends' burial ground, Quaker Hill. The funeral cortège was perhaps the largest ever witnessed in that section of the country. It extended in almost a continuous line from the family residence to the place of burial, a distance of nearly two miles. Besides the large concourse of people on foot there were some 150 carriages in the procession. From early morning people from a distance poured into the town in large numbers, and the railway trains brought in their quotas from every direction. The citizens of Uxbridge turned out *en masse*, the Mayor having issued his proclamation requesting the closing of all places of business during the afternoon. The Board of Trade passed a resolution to the same effect, and tendering their condolence to the family. The Mayor and members of the Town Council headed the procession, the firemen turned out in their uniform, and although the funeral cortège had been announced to move at two o'clock it was close upon four before it started, in consequence of the crowds which kept thronging forward in order to have a last look at the well-known features of him whom they had come to honour. The pall-bearers were Hector Grant, of Thorah, the veteran Reformer, who had fought so many gallant battles side by side with Mr. Gould; A. T. Button, Hugh Miller, John Leys, T. C. Forman, and W. H. Higgins. Amongst others present from a distance were A. P. Cockburn, M.P.; J. D. Edgar, M.P. ; John Dryden, M.PP. ; Sheriff Paxton; George Wheler, ex-M.P.; Messrs. George and James Watt, of Brantford ; reeves and representatives of most of the municipalities of North and South Ontario, and from several of the municipalities of adjoining counties. The gathering of the old " stand-by " Reformers was immense, and many leading Conservatives were also present to pay the last tribute of respect to the remains of the old Reformer to whom they had so long stood opposed as a leading man of his party. Rev. Mr. Dorland, minister of the Society of Friends, preached the funeral sermon, and the casket containing the body was placed in the grave with the simple funeral services of that religious body.

NOTE.

During his trip to the great American Centennial, in 1876, Mr. Gould took occasion to visit Germantown, the home of his ancestors. He employed the oldest cabman he could get to drive him round, and look up the old places. One of the first spots visited was the little churchyard where sleep the remains of his great grandfather, Michael Gold, the first Irish exile of his name who " sang the bold anthems of Erin-go-bragh " by the banks of the Susquehanna. He had no difficulty in tracing out the homestead of his grandfather, Joseph Gold, and the house where his father, Jonathan, the future Canadian immigrant, was born. He appeared to know all the landmarks as well as if he had been born and reared on the spot, he says, so vivid was the picture impressed upon his retentive memory by the oft-repeated description of the locality which he had listened to from the lips of his father and mother. The cabman was an Irishman named Corcoran, who had known the place for upwards of fifty-five years, and he was, as he acknowledged, "nonplushed entirely" at the facility with which Mr. Gould was able to trace out the different locations in the neighbourhood. Of the Gold family the cabman had heard many stories. He had heard all about "Michael Killbuck," the deer-slayer, and he had heard of two sons of Joseph (the grandfather), by his first wife, who had joined the patriotic army of Washington and who had, according to his story, performed prodigies of valour on the field of battle. "England," said this Irish-American Jehu (who, like many of his congeners, was a bit of a wag), "England, an' English goold, begorries, won many battles; but it was Goold, afther all, an' the Irish Goold at that, that wallopped 'em at Germantown." Mr. Gould went over the old battle-ground with his talkative cabman, who was full of anecdotes of the scene. The only Gold he could trace up was Charles Gold, who was absent at the time, and whom Mr. Gould consequently did not see. The cabman described "Charley" as "a strapping big fellow." "He has been to the war," said he, "an' did a citizen-soldier's share in puttin' down sesesh an' slavery. He can knock down more men and drink more whiskey than any man in the State; an' he is a thrump every time." Mr. Gould, after this, did not take much further trouble to hunt up his relative, the "Thrump," and left the Centennial without making his personal acquaintance. Of the great exhibition, he speaks with his usual intelligent observation, and with that admiration which was felt by all who saw the grandeur and magnificence of the display.